KYN KRONICLES BOOK 3

SHADOW'S MOON

JAMI GRAY

Cover Art: Deranged Doctor Design, www.derangeddoctordesign.com
Publisher: Celtic Moon Press Revised edition, 2018
ISBN: 978-1-948884-20-4 (ebook) ISBN: 978-1-948884-21-1 (print)

First edition, May 2014, Black Opal Books ISBN: 978-1-626941-29-8 (ebook)
ISBN: 978-1-626941-30-4 (print)

SIGN UP FOR FREE READS FROM JAMI!

Join Jami's newsletter to be the first to hear about new releases, free books, special prices and other nifty events.

Sign up at: https://www.subscribepage.com/jami-gray-books

WHAT READERS SAY...

About Arcane Transporter:
"Taking a refreshing approach to fantasy magic, this fast-paced, economical thriller is told from a highly likable perspective." —
Red Adept Editing

About PSY-IV Teams:
"This story is an emotional roller coaster, from betrayal, anger, fear, love..." —InD'tale Magazine

About the Kyn Kronicles:
"...a fantastic paranormal action novel is quite possibly the best book I've read this year. I could not put it down, and had to exercise serious self-control to keep from staying up all night to finish it." —The Romance Reviews

About Fate's Vultures:
"...if you like your characters with a bit more bite, with secrets, with hidden agendas, and all those sorts of things, and your worlds are a far more deadlier place, then this is for you." —
Archaeolibrarian

ALSO BY JAMI GRAY

ARCANE WONDERLAND

Last Call

Bitter Spirits

Rune & Tonic

ARCANE TRANSPORTER

Ignition Point (*Prequel Novella*)

Grave Cargo

Risky Goods

Lethal Contents

Collision Course

Blind Spot

Terminal Drift

THE KYN KRONICLES

Shadow's Edge

Shadow's Soul

Shadow's Moon

Shadow's Curse

Shadow's Dream

Shadow's Fall

Tangled in Shadows (*Short Story Collection*)

FATE'S VULTURES

Lying in Ruins

Beg for Mercy

Caught in the Aftermath

Fear the Reaper

PSY-IV TEAMS

Hunted by the Past

Touched by Fate

Marked by Obsession

Fractured by Deceit

Linked by Deception

BOX SETS

PSY-IV Teams Box Set I (Books 1-3)

The Collapse: Fate's Vultures (Books 1-4)

The Kyn Kronicles Box Set (Books 1-6)

Arcane Transporter Box Set I (Books 1-3)

Arcane Transporter Box Set II (Books 4-6)

To my mom - who taught me to be strong.

To my Knight - who showed me how to bend without breaking.

To my sons, affectionately known as the Prankster Duo - who uncovered the fluffy inside the steel.

*To the other Evil 7 - who dared me to do a love story—
CHALLENGE ACCEPTED!*

ACKNOWLEDGMENTS

No matter how many times I read, "Writing is a solitary thing," I have to shake my head. Granted, I may sit down and wander the rain-slicked streets with my characters, but there are so many who help ensure the final story is told in all its glory.

This is for them—my editors, who care enough to argue over things that would drive most people insane, my readers, who give endless encouragement, even when they don't realize it, my critique partners, who have no problem taking the other road (you know the one with all the burnt out street lights), and my family, who never once laughed when I said, "I'm going to be a writer."

CHAPTER 1

"How many deaths will it take?" The distorted voice circled through the well-appointed home office, creating a pervasive menace that curled around the warm woods and plush leather, leaving behind an unsettling chill. "A real alpha protects the pack. Who are you protecting, Vidis?"

Warrick Vidis, the Northwest Kyn's most powerful shifter and alpha of the Motoki Pack, leaned forward and jabbed the disconnect button on the phone, silencing the taunting voicemail. He quashed the impulse to throw the phone across the room. It would do nothing to alleviate the anger and frustration roiling in his stomach. Instead, he sat back, his movements ruthlessly controlled.

Across the desk his pack's Second, Ryuu Kern, watched with a frown. "I don't recognize the voice."

"Neither do I," Warrick answered. "I'm assuming they're using a voice modifier."

"It's a threat." Ryuu tapped his fingers on the arm of his chair. "Even you can't deny it this time."

"It's a challenge," Warrick corrected. "Someone wants to let the humans know we're here." Restless, he rose to his feet and strode around the large desk to the huge bank of windows.

Oregon's trademark rain misted the winter-bare branches of the surrounding forest. His home, unlike his office at Taliesin Security, was an oasis of privacy. Something both he and his inner wolf craved, especially now, when someone was threatening their territory.

"Revealing our existence to the masses isn't a smart move," Ryuu muttered.

Warrick's lips tightened at the comment. No, there was no possible scenario where the humans would welcome his kind with open arms. His kept his back to Ryuu as he said, "I think Neil Eilers is tied in somehow."

"Eilers is a maverick, Vidis. He chose to remain outside of the pack."

Warrick tilted his head in acknowledgement, never turning from his view. "Yet he said nearly the same thing, word for word, when he threatened me."

Ryuu snorted. "He's a barely controlled pup. He challenges you and he might as well dig his own grave."

Under his skin, Warrick's wolf agreed, his low, barely suppressed growl rumbling in his chest. "If he was truly working alone, perhaps."

"You think someone's using the mavericks to create problems for the pack?" Ryuu wasn't really asking as he could follow a trail as well as his alpha.

Warrick watched a doe step delicately between the trees lining the edge of the forest. She caught scent of his territory markers, her head jerking before she froze, leaving only her tail to twitch. As the deer bounded back into the foliage, he answered, "I think someone is using any tool they can find to damage us."

"Including the two Bitten wolves Xander had to kill in the last couple of weeks?"

Warrick was glad his back was to Ryuu, in case some reaction escaped at the mention of her name. Xander Cade. His lover and now reluctant mate. The one woman guaranteed to drive him and his wolf insane. Ever since their return from Arizona a few weeks ago, he found it harder than ever to sit back and let her continue her job as the pack's Tracker. The position kept her front and center on the firing line, something the man respected, but his wolf had a hell of a time accepting.

"Highly probable." Warrick pushed his personal issues aside to focus on the immediate threat. "The full moon's already passed, yet both of them managed a partial shift when confronted." It was an anomaly that triggered all his warning bells.

"The Bitten aren't supposed to be capable of holding a partial shift." Puzzled disbelief sharpened Ryuu's words. "Hell, for that matter, I've never heard of one shifting when it wasn't a full moon."

"Neither have I," Warrick confirmed.

"To mess with a wolf's ability to shift would require some serious magic." There was an underlying thread of worry in Ryuu's voice.

Warrick turned to face his Second, one of the few men he trusted, and shared his growing suspicion. "Or some serious science."

"You think the humans are behind this?"

"I don't think we should discount them." Warrick knew for a fact that humans had managed to alter the very nature of some Kyn. "We need to find out where the threat is coming from, and to do that we need Neil Eilers alive."

Ryuu stood, his face grim. "I'll call Xander."

Ignoring his wolf's internal howl of protest for putting Xander in danger yet again, Warrick nodded, his movement stiff. "As soon as you have a starting point, call me."

Something perilously close to sympathy flashed across Ryuu's face. "I'll watch over her." He didn't wait for Warrick's answer, but slipped out of the office.

Xander Cade crept through the shadows of the wooden pavilion perched next to the tranquil, lotus-strewn lake. She followed the erratic path of her prey, one Neil Eilers, a dangerously enraged shifter, whose scent wound under the swaying willows. Drawing in a deep breath, she automatically catalogued the smells—wet earth, with a jarring hint of fish, and the spicy bite of moisture-laden fir and pine from the structure next to her. Quivering under it all, like a shy rabbit, was something not quite right.

Between the wispy clouds and the dancing branches, the light of the half-moon played along her skin, calling to the wolf crouched within. She tilted her head back, taking a moment to bask in the ethereal call. The faint tang of copper teased her nose, the familiar scent of spilt blood made her stomach clench, even as her wolf struggled to rise.

Not yet, she soothed the wild half of her soul. *Work now, play later.*

Dropping her head, she scanned her night-shrouded surroundings. Portland's Classical Chinese Gardens were quiet. Much like her natural wolf counterparts, she could detect the smallest nuances in the various shades of gray. A helpful skill as she slipped among the heavy greenery.

Light didn't stick around long during Northwest

winters, which meant the popular tourist attraction closed at five. A small blessing. In a couple more months, spring would take center stage, bringing in meandering crowds, which would've made tracking the rogue shifter a nightmare, not to mention offering him an all-he-could-eat-buffet.

The longer it took to track Neil down, the more her hope of stopping him before he killed again whimpered into oblivion. She followed his subtle scent trail, gliding deeper into the forty-thousand-square-foot garden.

Her footsteps were light, nearly silent, as she crept over a small bridge leading into the darkened interior of stone and trees that made up the northwest corner of the Gardens. Bamboo posts connected by thick ropes herded visitors on set paths. Xander ignored them. Skirting small pools of water, she scaled the rocky outcroppings. Working her way around, she stopped just outside three small caverns created by the craggy structures. The muted thunder of falling water from inside help mask her movements.

Large, flat stepping-stones lay in a shallow pool, offering a dry path to the grotto. Her booted foot slid off the first one and water beaded over the cuff of her leather pants with a soft splash. She reached out to steady herself, her fingers brushing against the stone etched with Chinese characters. Yet the crisp combination of moisture from the merrily tumbling mini-waterfall and the dense greenery couldn't drown out the bitter scent scraping across her senses.

She was close.

Crouching, she traced a visible smudge on one of the stones, the residue transferring to her fingertips, leaving a dark smear behind. She brought it to her nose, inhaling the pungent odor and matched it the sharp stench of shifter blood. Blood that belonged to her prey. Her quarry must be injured.

Perched on the stone, she sank her hand into the icy water, letting it wash away the stain. She straightened, shaking the moisture from her skin, and eyed the three adjoining niches in front of her.

Enie, menie, minie, moe.

Deep shadows wrapped around the left one, making it the perfect place to hide a kill. Anticipation hummed under her skin, setting the fur of her inner wolf on end. Carefully, she made her way closer, until she stood on the last stepping-stone.

She was fairly certain her prey wasn't waiting to pounce, but in case the dead decided to rise, or Neil was indulging in more than his lust for blood, she tapped into her intrinsic magic. Small pinpricks ran from her wrists to the tips of her fingers as her bones elongated. Fur sprouted on the back of her hands, covering the pale skin. In moments, her hands had shifted into a weird mix of human and wolf. The partial shift left her with instant weapons—thick, sharp claws.

She slipped inside the carved entrance, grateful for her small stature when she discovered the shadows gave the mistaken impression it was deeper than it was. Two steps in, her biker boots skidded against the slick ground, sending her into ankle deep water. She scrambled for purchase as a gasp of surprise escaped before she could call it back. Uttering a soft curse, she gave up trying to stay dry.

Her vision adjusted to the murky interior and snagged on the crumpled form sprawled against the back wall. There was no imminent threat. Neil had struck and left.

Sighing, she released her partial shift. Under the sleeves

of her brown biker jacket, her wrists and hands returned to normal. Xander shook away the resulting tingle then tapped the earpiece nestled in her right ear. "Ryuu. You copy?"

There was a brief crackle of static, then a growling, "Yeah. What's up?"

"Found a body in the Gardens." She turned it over. The surrounding water made a soft sucking sound as it released its victim. With a careful touch, she pushed damp hair off the ghostly pale face.

"Tell me it's not the ex-girlfriend." Faint street noises leached around his demand.

"Nope. It's a male." She leaned down and inhaled. The water diluted the coppery stench of blood, leaving behind the familiar odor of raw meat. Crouched within, her wolf perked up. "Human."

A low string of curses danced in her ear. "Damn it!" Then a sigh. "Wounds?"

She dug into the inside pocket of her jacket, pulled out a small penlight, then played it over the victim. One side of the male's skull sported a very large dent. The semi-dried blood added a macabre touch to the frozen features. "Heavy bruising, no claw or teeth marks. Looks like Neil bashed the poor guy's head against the rocks."

"So he hasn't shifted yet. I guess we should be grateful for small miracles."

"Maybe," she muttered, pity moving through her. The victim had been no more than a boy, maybe mid-twenties. Once upon a time, he'd been attractive. Now, death and fury left him a broken version of who he'd been in life. "From the amount of damage, I'd say Neil was furious."

"How much you want to bet our vic was flirting with the ex?"

"That's a sucker's bet." From her position, she ran her penlight over the confined space. Dark crimson marks splattered the far wall. "Considering he stashed the body where it wasn't likely to be found easily, I'd say Neil stalked him first. The chase would've appealed to his wolf, but the beating was all man."

"Since he didn't dine out, you think the human side is still in control?" Ryuu asked.

"Maybe." She clicked off the light and stood up. The last two wolves she hunted hadn't been completely Feral, a condition where the human intellect was devoured by the wolf within. But they had been oh so close, enough to pull an unexpected partial shift. Here, it looked as if the one they chased managed to stay human. That small realization didn't quiet her internal alarms. Maybe he just hadn't been pissed enough. Yet. She squashed the nightmarish flash of claws, screams, and blood before it could grab hold. "If he catches up with the girl and she challenges him, his wolf will rise."

Ryuu sighed. "Sara is human."

Xander grimaced. "What the hell is the allure of dating a human? They're way too fragile."

Ryuu's snort sounded in her ear. "Variety is the spice of life, Xander."

"Whatever." She paused. "Do we know if Neil was Born or Bitten?"

"Bastard's another Bitten."

"Lovely." The Bitten had two forms—human or, under a full moon, completely wolf. If he, or she, followed the rules. Lately, it seemed the rules were on an extended vacation. "It's a waning moon, so if we're lucky, he'll be stuck playing hunter in human skin. Keep your eyes peeled."

"Do you know how many people are out tonight?" His voice came out perilously close to a whine.

She began making her way out of the cavern. "It's Saturday night, Ryuu. Most people aren't running around chasing psychotic furballs."

"Instead, they're all trying to get laid," he groused.

His obvious disgruntlement curled her lips into a small grin. "Jealous?"

"Please," he scoffed. "Even if I was, I've had plenty of offers tonight."

She didn't doubt it. Ryuu's mixed heritage left him with the alluring combination of almond eyes, dark hair and gold tinted skin from his Asian mother, while blessing him with the whipcord physique and height of his Anglo father. Add in his inherent confidence of being the Motoki Pack's Second, and he was catnip for women.

"The night's still young, so there's a chance to take one of your pretties up on her offer," she teased, quickly retracing her steps through the dark garden. "Maybe it'll mellow you out." She made her way to the back fence where the trees stretched over the garden's walls. "Where are you?"

"Third Avenue. Over by Hobo's."

"Where they do the tunnel tours?" She stopped beneath the spreading branches of a tree guarding the stone wall. She made the easy leap to the top of the six-foot wall. Leaning around the overhanging branches of a tree, she checked to see that no one was coming down the sidewalk on the other side.

"Yeah," Ryuu confirmed. "Sara's neighbor said she and her friends were hitting some of the bars around here."

When the sidewalk remained empty, Xander dropped lightly on the other side. The heavy shadows from the dense trees camouflaged her sudden appearance from anyone watching. She brushed loose leaves from her shoulders and strode out to the sidewalk. "Are you working your way north or south?"

"North," came the answer. "Forget Drucilla's."

Xander's lips twitched. Drucilla's boasted a raunchy drag-queen show. One in which Ryuu played a prominent role in the week before. She came to the end of the street and made a left on to Third Avenue. "Afraid you'll be asked to do an encore?" she murmured as she passed an older couple. The male gave her a short nod, his companion tucked lovingly under his arm as they hustled by. Xander ignored the tiny pang at the image they created.

Ryuu's low growl distracted her. "A purple wig, Xander? I looked like a damn Anime character."

"Not my fault your team can't hold onto their football." Lights from the various clubs and restaurants chased away the cloying darkness. Small clusters of young people wove down the sidewalks, their energy turning the night bright and sparkly. "Besides, I warned you not to bet against me."

"Whatever," he answered. "I'm coming up on the Boiler Club."

"I'll check out 88 Ivories across the street. If you spot either of them, holler." She twisted and narrowly missed being trampled by an obviously inebriated male in jeans and a Storm-Trooper T-shirt proclaiming, *I had friends on that Death Star.* Her quick move caused him to stumble.

"Whoa, man—sorry," he slurred, lurching to the side.

"Watch it," she snarled, before turning back to her hunt.

"Hey!" Unexpectedly, the drunk managed to snag the back of her jacket. "Don't rush off, baby," he leered. "Why doncha come with me and my friends? We can show ya a good time."

Pivoting on her heel, she grabbed his wrist. She might be small, but one advantage to being a shifter was that even if you looked like you couldn't lift a feather, you could bench press a small car and barely break a sweat.

"A good time?" She slowly increased the pressure on his wrist, feeling his bones creak under her grip.

"Hey, man! That fuckin' hurts!" he yelped, twisting in an attempt to get away.

"Dan, you okay?"

The question came from behind her. She turned, dragging the inebriated Dan along while ignoring his protests. Recognizing pack mentality of the three approaching males, her wolf prowled close to the surface, changing her voice to a growl. "This belong to you?"

They drew up short, uncertain of who, or what, they faced. She knew what they saw. A small blonde woman with short, spiky, purple-tipped hair, wearing a battered brown motorcycle jacket over a fitted fluorescent green T-shirt. Soft leather pants met heavily soled biker boots, complete with silver chains. Add in the intricate tattoo trailing over the right side of her face and you had Hell's-Angel-meets-Goth-fairy-princess come to life.

"Let him go." The taller blond male took an aggressive step forward. A wanna-be alpha.

"Gladly." With a little shove, she pushed the drunken idiot into his friend.

The blond stumbled back as his friend tumbled into him. "You don't have to be such a bitch." He passed his friend off and closed in on Xander.

"I haven't even come close to being a bitch," she said as he loomed over her, as if his height gave him some sort of advantage. She rocked back on her heels, keeping her body loose. There really wasn't time to teach these kids a lesson but, seriously, they needed to learn some manners.

"You think you're some kind of bad ass with that stupid tattoo?" he sneered, his fists clenching at his side.

Keeping a pleasant smile on her face, she decided to let her wolf come out and play, changing her eyes to a burning amber. "Oh, it's a lot more than that. Haven't you heard? Dangerous things come in small packages."

He paled.

"C'mon, Matt," one of his friends called. "Let it go. She's not worth it."

"Yeah, Matt," she taunted softly, "let it go."

Fear flashed over Matt's face as he stumbled back. She took a step forward, to chase, when the beep of her earpiece pulled her up short. She hit the button to talk, but kept her gaze on Matt and his friends. "Yeah?"

"Boiler Room is clear." Ryuu's voice filled her ear. "I'm heading over to 88 Ivories. Where are you?"

"Just visiting with the local nightlife." The little pack of college boys scurried away, but Matt kept shooting her looks as they retreated. She flashed more teeth and he hurried after his friends down the sidewalk, disappearing into the crowd.

"Well, when you can tear yourself away, perhaps you'd like to see if our little monster found his way to the club?" Ryuu drawled.

"They started it. I just finished it." She turned around to resume her hunt. Inside, her wolf chuffed with satisfaction at making the boys run. "I'm almost there."

She threaded her way through the milling crowds and stepped through a brick entryway to an open patio. Small clusters of people dotted the area while music pulsed into the night air. Scents wove around her—alcohol, sweat, perfumes, soaps, fabrics—a maelstrom of odors. Years of practice had her picking through them until she found the distinctive musk of shifter. *Bingo.* Somewhere inside was her prey.

Stopping outside the door where repetitive bass beats rattled the walls, she tapped her earpiece. "Ryuu?"

A brief spurt of static cleared, replaced by a faint echo of the beat and a gruff, "What?"

"I'm on the Ivories's patio."

"You waiting for an engraved invitation?"

"Aren't you a funny one?" she quipped. "Wanted to make sure you wouldn't miss the party."

"I'll be there in a minute. See if you can spot him."

She stepped through the double doors. There were no screams of horror, no flying debris or body parts. Just wooden tables and chairs surrounding the dance floor. Most were filled with one, sometimes two bodies to a chair.

The miasma of fried food, alcohol, and perspiring bodies hit her like a battering ram. There was no using her nose in this mess. She shook her head and made her way deeper inside.

The dance floor was packed. At the far end sat the bar's infamous, dueling, black baby grand pianos. Tonight no one tickled the ivory keys. Instead, the DJ was lost in the rhythmic beats of the pounding music, spinning his vinyl. The club's lighting leaned heavily on a strobe effect, which guaranteed a rousing headache by the time the night was over. The snaps of brightness stung her eyes, but she did her best to ignore it as she tried to make out individual faces.

Needing an aerial view of the packed room, she found a lone empty chair sitting against the wall. Climbing up, she stood on tiptoe, stretching to see over the sea of bobbing heads. Between bursts of light, a disturbance in the rhythmic mass caught her attention. Two burly bouncers were making tracks from the bar to the back of the club. Patrons stumbled out of their way, leaving a visible path. The bouncers pushed through with identical grim expressions. The strobe lights flashed off the taller one's bald head, while his buzz-cut partner pointed toward something ahead.

Following the gesture, Xander found Neil arguing with a pretty, honey-brown-haired young woman. She tapped her earpiece. "Ryuu?"

"Yeah?"

"How long before you get here?"

"I'm almost there." There was a pause. "You found him."

"Oh, yeah. And it's going to get ugly. Quick." Xander watched the woman jerk away from the tall, lanky, dishwater blond, shaking her head. "I think I've found Sara, too."

Xander jumped off her chair just as Neil reached out to snag the girl, fury evident in his bared teeth and curled hands.

"We're out of time," she told Ryuu, pushing her way through the dense crowd.

"Be careful." Ryuu's warning was lost as she hit a broad shouldered form in front of her. The answering bump knocked her hard enough she lost her earpiece. Screw it. Done being polite, she gave him a shove, sending him into the arms of his buddy as she continued toward the impending showdown at the back of the club.

Through the sea of gyrating bodies, she caught glimpses of the confrontation. Sara was verbally ripping Neil a new one, while the club's security duo drew closer to the arguing couple. Sara's tirade wasn't the reaction Neil expected. Under the strobe lights, his face contorted into something not altogether human.

Dread morphed into grim acceptance as Xander continued to shove her way through the crowd. The distance between her and the impending epic disaster might as well have been miles instead of feet. "Damn it. Damn it," she muttered.

So much for keeping the existence of monsters on the down low from humans. Neil was going to shift and she was too far away to stop it. If she didn't stop him before he tore his way through the surrounding club goers, the good people of Portland were going to have irrefutable proof that the Kyn, all those creatures they had relegated to scary campfire stories, were shockingly, violently real.

The song switched, the music's driving beat ramping up faster and louder. In response, the crowd surged and she lost sight of her targets. Forcing her way through, she ignored the litany of complaints and shouts. She made it a couple more feet when the first terror filled scream cut through the heavy music and her withering hope like a blade.

Another scream, this one deep, agonized, male, accompanied the perfumed tang of freshly spilt blood in the air. Before the cry faded, the sea of bodies turned into a herd of panicked prey. A chorus of screams drowned out the music. As panic set in, some of the club's patrons fell under the press of the fleeing crowds.

As hard as it was for Xander to ignore the cries and pleas from those being trampled and crushed, she fought her way forward. It took her precious minutes to break through the battering throng and stumble free. She wiped away the blood from a shallow cut that something—

probably the sharp edge of a purse—had opened along her temple.

Greeting her was a scene that would have done any horror flick proud. Neil was crouched near the back wall, sporting a bastardized version of the Born's half form. Instead of the graceful meld of wolf and human, he was a monstrous mix of beast and twisted human features. Thin lips curled back from a hairless muzzle, revealing elongated canines nestled among other sharp, pointy teeth. Tufted ears rose above lank blond hair—hair that merged into patches of heavier fur more at home on a wolf's pelt.

His chest and shoulders had expanded with inhuman muscle, tearing his T-shirt along the seams and leaving it hanging in tatters from the intact collar. The mishmash of human and wolf was downright disturbing, almost as disturbing as the surrounding carnage.

Blood smeared the back wall with the abandon of a child's finger-painting. Baldy twitched on the floor, his severed right arm lying a few feet away in its own puddle of gore. His partner was curled into a fetal position, in a futile effort to keep his pale gray intestines from spilling onto the floor. Sara cowered against the wall, as far from the wreckage as she could get. Her arms, scored with deep claw marks, were wrapped around her head as she tried to make herself smaller, attempting to disappear.

Not everyone in the club portrayed the intelligence to get the hell away from the monster. While the majority of the crowd kept trying to make the exits, a foolish few remained behind, either too stubborn, or too dense, to understand the danger they were in. A couple of very buff males were trying to keep Neil's attention away from Sara and the two downed bouncers.

They succeeded. Unfortunately, they were woefully

unprepared to face the nightmare in front of them. Improvised weapons of broken bottles didn't do much to dissuade the shifter. Lethal nails, tipping what once were human fingers, glinted under the sporadic lighting, leaving more red ruin and agonized screams behind.

Xander shoved past the last ring of shocked onlookers and stalked forward, drawing the monster's attention. His nails scraped against the floor as he pivoted to face her. His amber gaze, awash in a demonic red glow, was filled with single-minded murderous purpose as he focused on her. His threatening growl flashed deadly fangs and raised every hair on her body. She stilled, but didn't look away from the feral intelligence staring back at her.

Around her, the human on-lookers scrambled back, finally realizing what stood before them was something they had no chance of defeating. The music cut off, leaving behind the low moans of the injured and dying. Sara's piteous mewls of terror and the discordant sounds of fleeing masses played like a ghostly chorus while the tension between her and Neil stretched, creating a small well of eerie quiet.

"Come get me," she taunted.

It was never smart to bait the insane, but she had one chance to stop this before it got any worse. Just one.

She'd probably get hurt.

Okay, scratch that. She was definitely going to get hurt.

Small price to pay for getting some answers as to what the hell was turning wolves into psychotic furry monsters. Hopefully she could bring Neil in alive. The last two wolves didn't give her a choice, and she was tired of dragging broken bodies back to her alpha.

Neil darted forward, forcing her back as he swiped out.

She jerked, sucking in her stomach, but not in time to

miss the burn of his nails against her skin. Dammit, the one area her open jacket didn't manage to cover. Even as she spun out of reach, the warning kiss of heat filtered through her thin T-shirt to the skin beneath.

Pivoting to follow her, he turned, keeping her trapped between the back wall, the torn bodies, and him.

She held her position, trapping his maddened gaze with her own and let her wolf join the fight.

Neil paused, his nose twitching, taking in her altered scent. Realization of who he faced hit, causing his muscles to tense even as a cunning intelligence emerged under the insane fury, twisting his features.

With no time to shift into full warrior form, Xander kept her transformation localized until her fingers mirrored the same deadly talons as her opponent.

His rumbled snarls echoed through the club as he closed the distance between them, one stiff step at a time.

Curling her lip, she met him halfway. Their bodies hit and her heavy leather jacket shredded under his claws. His fetid breath fanned her face as the warped wolf snarled and snapped, trying to find an opening. She managed to rip her claws across his ribs, causing him to grunt, as she momentarily forced him to retreat. Undeterred, he rushed back in.

All of Xander's training took a back seat to instinct as she faced the maddened creature. Her focus narrowed to the whirlwind of fangs and claws as they grappled for dominance.

Skin, hers and his, tore under the merciless attacks. Menacing growls and painful yips punctuated the sound of snapping teeth. She blocked his repeated attempts to tear out her throat by slashing her nails over his distorted muzzle, forcing him to pull back. Her jacket sported a collection of ragged tears, and her T-shirt offered a poor layer of protection between his lethal swipes and her skin.

Fresh blood decorated the floor at their feet. She used her smaller stature to go in low, trying to hamstring him. He twisted and spun away. Changing direction, she sprang up, curled her nails into lethal hooks, and dug them into his muscled back. With a wrench, she dragged them down his spine, leaving scarlet slashes behind.

His pain-filled yelp quickly turned into a low threatening growl as the iron rich scent of blood flooded the air. With unexpected speed, he grabbed her arm, yanked her over his back, and flung her to the floor. Her spine met the concrete, slamming the breath from her chest, and slowing her reactions.

She struggled to sit up, barely getting her arms in front of her to hold Neil off. Time slowed. Razor sharp teeth snapped inches from her face. Inch by precious inch, she forced him back, her arms trembling under his weight.

He was so close, there was no way to miss the moment when his bloodlust rose, sweeping away what little remained of the man and leaving behind a homicidal-crazy wolf. As he turned Feral, her option of bringing him in alive took a flying leap.

Done with the kid gloves, she let the pressing weight of her attacker drive her back and down. Distracted by the potential meal, he didn't notice as she curled her legs and tucked her feet against his stomach. Keeping one claw-tipped hand wrapped around his neck, she shoved with her feet. Neil went airborne. The force of his flight left her holding a chunk of bloody meat that once was part of his throat.

Before the gravely injured monster could hit the ground, another shape sprang out of the shadows and sailed over Xander, crashing into the rogue and sending him sprawling across the blood-slicked floor. Xander rolled to her hands and knees to find Ryuu crouched over the downed shifter. A series of low, dangerously serious noises trickled from Ryuu's throat.

"A little late to the party, aren't you, Ryuu?" Xander asked, carefully getting to her feet. Her movements pulled her torn skin, causing her to grimace. Needing a minute to regain her breath, she examined the tattered remains of her leather jacket. "Damn it, I loved this jacket."

Walking over to the two men, she released the magic holding her partial shift. She shook out the pins and needles of her hands as she brushed past Ryuu, who didn't take his eyes off Neil. Kneeling beside her injured prey, her fingers drifted over the wound in Neil's throat.

"Why isn't this healing?" she murmured. When Neil tried to snap at her, she whacked his distorted muzzle. "Settle down."

Unless silver was involved shifters were notoriously fast healers.

Blood continued to pool from the wound, a dark puddle that sucked the club's muted light into its abyss. Murmurs grew around them, but no one dared to come forward. Yet.

She was about to lose her only lead. If Neil took his human form, maybe he could heal enough to keep breathing. She grabbed his snout and forced him to meet her gaze. "Change, damn you!"

Savage madness stared back.

She shot Ryuu a look. "You need to take over."

The slender Asian man knelt next to her and pushed her hand away. He grasped the warped face in his hands.

Xander scooted back to give him room while the warm brush of magic rose. Movement on the edge of her vision had her looking up in time to spot some brave soul making her way over to one of the bleeding men who faced Neil with a broken bottle.

Pale and shaken, the young woman met Xander's gaze briefly before dropping her eyes. "I'm a second year med student," she said as her glance flicked back up.

Xander gave her a short nod and the med student scrambled to the wounded man. Xander felt the energy gathering around Ryuu. Her wolf pressed against her skin, wanting to get closer to the familiar warmth of the pack. She fought her instinctive reaction to the magic Ryuu was drawing on to heal Neil. As the Motoki Pack's Second, the amount of power he used would normally force an injured shifter to change, allowing them to heal. Yet, the form under Ryuu's hands quivered, but didn't transform.

"Ryuu?" Alarm rose. This didn't make sense.

"Not now, Xander," he gritted through his teeth. The magical energy deepened, like electrical currents before a lightning strike.

Neil's misshapen hands began to churn, his nails scraping against the rough floor. A great shudder wracked his grotesque body.

Ryuu let go and sat back on his heels, his face grim. The frantic scrapes and magical energy stopped, leaving an odd, uneasy silence in their wake. He met Xander's gaze and shook his head.

She turned to watch Neil's eyes dull as death crept in. His twisted body dissolved into a battered young man with longish, dishwater-blond hair and a torn throat. His chest rose once more, then stilled.

CHAPTER 2

Confusion and frustration created a nauseous mix in Xander's stomach as she knelt beside Ryuu, Neil's lifeless body sprawled in front of them. She ignored the twinges of discomfort as her wounds continued to heal. She was breathing, the boy in front of her wasn't, so there really was no room for complaints. "What the hell is going on?"

Ryuu's forehead furrowed as he met her gaze. "Don't know, but we're in deep shit."

"You think?" She took in the carnage around them. The majority of humanity remained unaware of the Kyn's existence. That little golden nugget of knowledge belonged to a few select humans working in the highest levels of government, military, and science. However, tonight's lovely demonstration threatened to rip that thin veil of secrecy into wisps of wishful thinking.

Ryuu stood, dug out his cell phone and moved a few steps away.

Rising to her feet, she moved toward the now still bouncers, careful to step around the spreading blood. "Are you calling in Division?"

Division, also known as the Preternatural Crimes Division, was a deeply cloaked, specialized FBI unit created to help the Kyn handle supernatural crimes.

"No," he answered. "Vidis."

Xander turned around and shot him a narrow-eyed glare. "Don't you think we might want Division here when the cops start trying to haul us away in handcuffs?"

"I'd be happy to call Division, if you'd like to call our alpha," Ryuu offered.

There was no stopping her low growl of frustration.

"That's what I thought." His too-knowing gaze pinned her. "You need to get over it, Xander."

She snarled and snapped her teeth at him, but he just curled his lip. "It's between me and our alpha," she gritted out before crouching down to check Buzz-cut's pulse. There wasn't one.

A not-too-subtle snort sounded. "Yeah, well aim for the next full moon, will you?" Male amusement was evident in Ryuu's dry voice.

She went to the other fallen man and found the same frustrating results. "Full moon?"

Ryuu raised a finger, holding off on answering her.

She stood and moved to Sara. Even with the din of moans and cries from the injured, she heard the familiar cadence of Warrick's voice when he answered after the first ring.

She tried not to listen to the short conversation, concentrating on checking Sara's injuries. Patiently, she coaxed the girl into letting Xander examine her torn skin. The poor girl was nearly catatonic—not unusual or, sadly, unexpected. It wasn't every night your ex turned into a raving monster right before your eyes.

Prowling the downtown streets of Portland wasn't the best place for a frustrated werewolf, but Ryuu's earlier call didn't leave Warrick a choice. *Damn Neil Eilers!*

Neil had gone and lost his damn mind and now they had to track down the idiot and his ex-girlfriend before things got ugly. The smartest move the maverick could take, would be to tuck tail and run. Unfortunately, it appeared Neil was determined to court trouble and not to play it smart

Warrick should've seen it coming. During their last conversation, Neil told Warrick to go fuck himself. The idiot then followed that little jewel up with the asinine declaration that a true alpha wouldn't cower from the humans in the shadows, but take his rightful place at the top of the food chain.

Top of the food chain? Warrick snorted at the immaturity. The ass had a human girlfriend. The boy was going to find it a little hard to be top dog if he was too busy trying to stick his dick in someone he considered food.

Under normal circumstances, Warrick would let Ryuu and Sebastian, his Third, bring the damn fool in to find out what a challenge really entailed. But, based on Ryuu's last update, these were far from normal circumstances.

In fact, things were heading rapidly downhill, if the dead human stashed in the Gardens was any indication. The only way they could hope to contain this whole mess was if Ryuu and Xander could get Neil under wraps and away from the humans.

A small chirp from the earpiece tucked inside his ear, pulled him up short. "Vidis," he answered.

"It's Ryuu. We got him."

Warrick glided out of the current of humanity drifting along the sidewalk and stopped by the darkened windows of a closed storefront. Sebastian took up a position in front of him, blocking his view of the passing crowds. "Where?"

"88 Ivories, but we have problems."

"Problems?" Warrick's gut clenched at the faint moans of pain drifting through the phone. "What a surprise."

"Neil went after the girl, like we thought," Ryuu ignored his boss's obvious sarcasm. "He caught her at the club."

"How bad?"

"Two dead, maybe more. The crowd panicked and the girl is almost catatonic," Ryuu paused. "He shifted into a warped version of the warrior form."

Everything in Warrick stilled as a low level of dread formed. Reaching for the control necessary to every alpha, he kept his voice level even as his wolf surged against the prison of human skin, wanting to race to his mate's side. "Xander?"

"Still standing," Ryuu answered. "She's with the girl now."

Relief had him closing his eyes and taking a deep breath. "We'll be there in five minutes."

"Cops will be here in ten," Ryuu said. "You shouldn't be inside when they arrive."

Warrick ignored the warning. "I'm calling Division. Then I'm coming in." He hung up, cutting Ryuu's protest off mid-word. "Let's go," he snapped at Sebastian and started toward the club.

The thought of Xander facing down a deranged killer set his wolf, already upset about sending her out in the first place, prowling and clawing under his skin. Even the constant sidelong glances from Sebastian, pacing alongside, couldn't quiet the sub-vocal growls rumbling in his chest.

Since returning from Arizona, Warrick's patience was paper-thin. The smallest things tended to set his wolf off. Between the anonymous threats to his pack, this delusional pup, and Xander, he was hanging on to the perilous edge of his legendary control by his fingertips.

He needed to see Xander for himself. Images of her broken and bleeding in Arizona still haunted him. To save her, he tied her soul to his. Those ties did nothing to diminish his need to keep her safe. Neither he nor his wolf would be in any shape to deal with tonight's challenges until he put his hands on his mate.

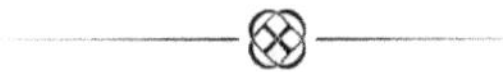

The claw marks on Sara's arms would scar, but she would heal—physically. Mentally might be a different story. She shook so hard Xander was afraid the girl would shatter into hundreds of pieces. Using strips of her tattered T-shirt, Xander began binding the more severe wounds. When she was finished, she noticed the traumatized girl had slipped into unconsciousness, even as her body continued to tremble.

Xander found a relatively clean spot on the hard floor and sat, settling Sara's head in her lap. She brushed a gentle hand through the girl's hair. Maybe her touch would give Sara an anchor and help still the constant tremors. She felt Ryuu come to stand next her. "Maybe we can get a healer to help blur her memories?" she murmured.

"Maybe," Ryuu answered quietly. He took a seat next to her, his back to the wall, facing the decimated club. The faint, distant whine of sirens drifted to them.

"How soon before he gets here?"

"Five minutes."

"That's fast."

"He was already on his way."

She shot him a dark look.

Ryuu didn't look away. "I called him when you found the body in the Gardens."

Tension sang through Xander and, in her lap, Sara whimpered. Xander forced her body to relax and made soothing noises, lulling Sara back into oblivion. In a soft voice, she asked, "Division?"

He shrugged. "Vidis is calling them en route."

She sighed. *The police, Division, and my alpha, oh my!* It was going to be a long night. "So," she kept her tone low. "What's the deal with the next full moon?"

A small smile played on Ryuu's lips. "I've got money down you two will only last until the next hunt."

"Seriously?" The pack was betting on her and Warrick? She wasn't sure if she should be amused or terrified.

Ryuu's tone turned sly. "I know how stubborn you can be. If any female was going to make him work for it, it would be you."

She choked off a bitter laugh and let her head thump against the wall behind her. "Wish he'd realize it." She managed not to clench her hands in Sara's hair, keeping her touch gentle.

Ryuu's amusement disappeared and the lethal intelligence that made him the pack's Second shone bright. "Whatever happened in Arizona changed both of you. Now it's impacting the pack. It needs to be fixed."

Resentment flared but she beat it down. She knew damn good and well what affected their alpha also affected the pack. Until recently, her position as Tracker not only kept her out of their pack's power structure, but allowed any member, high or low, to approach her about anything, without the press of hierarchy. It was like being the pack's advisor. The solitary role fit Xander like a glove.

Of course, being a Tracker also led her into interesting situations, such as waking up after fighting off a soul-sucking demon only to discover she was now the alpha's bonded mate. Something most women would be thrilled about. However, sitting in a blood-soaked club in downtown Portland wasn't exactly the best place to delve into her personal relationship, even if Ryuu was a friend.

Time to change the subject. "You said he was Bitten."

She caught Ryuu's flash of frustration. "Fine. Yes, that's what I was told," he answered. "Neil Eilers, twenty-three, college drop-out, bitten two years ago while traveling with friends in Europe. Was staying in some run-down apartment out in Holbrook." He recited the information, his arms resting against up-raised knees.

"Two years with no previous outbursts?" She was mindful to keep her touch light as she stroked the hair of the girl in her lap.

Ryuu nodded.

The more information she uncovered, the less sense it made. "So explain to me how a Bitten had a half-form, screwed up though it was."

Shifters constituted one fourth of the Kyn population in the Northwest and fell into two groups—Bitten and Born. The Bitten were human victims of vicious attacks by deranged shifters and the basis for the humans' werewolf stories.

"I can't," Ryuu's frustration came through loud and clear. "He shouldn't have been able to come even close to that. Only the Born can achieve half-forms."

Born shifters weren't tied to the moon's call and could take any of their three forms—wolf; human; and warrior form, a combination of the two—at any time, depending on the strength of their bloodlines. Most Born, like Xander, had a few drops of other Kyn blood, such as Fey or Magi. Yet, there were a rare few, like their alpha, who could claim pure Lycan bloodlines for generations.

"This is getting old." She sighed and studied Neil. Gods, it was such a waste. To survive a werewolf attack and make some sort of life for two years, only to end up here. She forced out the next question. "Does he have any family?"

"No." Resignation echoed in Ryuu's answer. "From what I could dig up, he's been roaming up and down the west coast since his change. Never stayed in any one place for long. He managed to stick it out here for the last seven months."

"Long enough to hook up with Sara," Xander murmured.

Even unconscious, Sara jerked at the sound of her name. Xander made shushing noises, never ceasing her gentle petting.

Pity moved over Ryuu's face. "At least she's alive."

"Yeah…"

At the edge of the decimated floor, the second year med student was still working on one of the would-be heroes, occasionally flicking a wary glance in their direction. Probably worried they'd sprout fur and claws any second.

The sirens drew closer. They only had a handful of minutes before the police made it through the maze of downtown streets. Less than that before Warrick showed. "Do you have someone picking up the body from the Gardens?"

Ryuu gave a short nod.

"He's the third wolf I've had to put down in two weeks," she said.

Ryuu blinked but said nothing.

She chewed on her lower lip. Three wolves in two weeks meant something else was happening, something threatening Warrick. Generally, as Tracker, she only had to worry about the occasional Feral wolf, but this—no, this was something very different. Different was dangerous. "Before Warrick gets here, you have to tell me who's been looking to challenge him."

"You can't play assassin," Ryuu admonished gently.

She let her wolf rise, adding a bite to her voice. "I have no problems with taking out those who threaten my alpha or my pack."

When Sara trembled violently under her hand, she forced her wolf back down.

He shook his head. "That's not what I meant and you know it. Whether you accept his mate claim or not, you can't fight his battles for him." His attention sharpened. "He'd never forgive you."

She locked gazes with Ryuu, tension stringing tight between them. "I'm not going out and killing every person who's threatened him, but I need a place to start."

"Then you better start by looking in a mirror." Ryuu's words cut deep. "For the last few weeks, the only person who's dared to challenge Vidis's decisions is you."

She flinched at the underlying anger vibrating in Ryuu's voice, then sucked in a short breath as her jerky movement pulled her still-healing skin.

Moving with the inhuman speed inherent to all shifters, Ryuu spun to crouch over her, careful not to touch her or the girl in her lap, but invading her personal space. "What is so wrong with him that you refuse to accept his claim?"

His question was a punch to her gut, because denying Warrick was the last thing she wanted to do. And that was the problem.

Ryuu didn't back off. "The fact you won't fully accept the bonding is setting the entire pack on edge. No one would dare step up to challenge him. Do you know why, Xander?"

She held still, letting her friend rip her apart, one word at a time.

His eyes glittered with a wild edge as his voice lowered. "Because he'd kill them without breaking a sweat. You have him so wound up that his control is paper thin." He lowered his head until mere inches separated them and hissed, "You and I both know what that means. You may be angry with him, but you have no right to fracture our pack. So figure it the fuck out and fix it."

CHAPTER 3

Warrick, with Sebastian on his heels, pushed his way through the clusters of people huddled together in front of the club, 88 Ivories. He knew it would be smarter to wait until the authorities arrived, but the urgent need to see Xander pushed all rational thought aside. He stepped inside the bar. Strobe lights painted the walls and floor, the sporadic illumination revealing scattered humans trying to help those on the ground, and shock on the faces of the few club-goers who were trying to figure out what the hell had happened. Sobs and moans echoed eerily in the large interior.

Sebastian grabbed his shoulder and pointed to the back of the club. "Over there."

Bodies, some moving, some not, sprawled across the floor where Ryuu crouched over something or someone. Warrick's pulse began to pound and he searched the surrounding devastation for the familiar purple-tipped blonde hair. Not finding it, he focused on his Second. Something in Ryuu's posture made Warrick rapidly cut the distance between them as his keen hearing finally processed Ryuu's words.

"You may be angry with him, but you have no right to fracture our pack. So figure it the fuck out and fix it." The harsh recrimination in Ryuu's voice had Warrick's lips lifting in an instinctive snarl. There was only one person he could be talking to, and if his Second knew what was good for him, he'd better change his tone.

When Ryuu abruptly rose to his feet with fluid grace and stepped back, Warrick caught a glimpse of a pale-faced Xander sitting on the floor. Anger and fear churned as he caught sight of her shredded T-shirt and beloved leather jacket. Deep scratches marred her body, some still seeping blood, as she cradled a girl in her lap. The mutinous line of her lips was highlighted by two red flags of temper dusting her sharp cheekbones.

This close to her, the bond they reluctantly shared flared into brilliant life. His wolf lunged, needing to go to his mate's side. Warrick barely managed to hold him back as Xander set the girl aside started to get to her feet. The whip of Ryuu's accusation had laid its mark across her heart. Unprepared for the raw wave of her turbulent emotions sweeping down the bond, his fragile control snapped. His wolf shoved him aside and raced to face the threat to his mate.

Xander curled her trembling hand into a fist and fought back her wolf's need to release the cauldron of frustration and confusion caused by her friend. Ryuu's accusation was like a stinging slap. Instead of striking out with her teeth and claws, she focused on calming her wolf as she gently lifted Sara off her lap and repositioned her on the floor. She barely got the wildness inside her to settle, when a low challenging growl raised the hair on the back of her neck.

Xander was on her feet before it ended, her pulse speeding. She recognized that sound. It was an enraged wolf, defending his mate against a perceived threat. She and Ryuu had been so caught up they somehow missed Warrick's arrival. Obviously, he caught some of their conversation. To say he wasn't happy was a massive understatement. She wasn't going to be physically fast enough to stop the impending bloodshed. Ryuu's words may have hurt, but there was some truth behind them.

There was only one chance to pull Warrick up short.

As she raced across the club's floor toward the furious man bearing down on Ryuu, she grabbed their psychic connection. After spending the last three weeks keeping it locked down, she now ripped it wide open. *"Warrick!"*

The shock of her unexpected psychic call pulled him up just long enough for her to reach him. She stepped between the two men, keeping her back to Ryuu. Placing her hands on Warrick's chest, she leaned in, letting him feel the heat and weight of her body, giving him and his wolf something else to concentrate on.

His hands automatically wrapped around her hips, pulling her closer.

She lost her breath as he tugged her tight against him. Heated skin and steely strength wrapped around her. Struggling past the overwhelming desire to burrow closer to his familiar cinnamon and clove scent, she stretched her five-foot-three-inch frame and nipped his chin.

Under her hands, Warrick's chest vibrated with another low growl.

She let her claws slip out enough to prick through his T-shirt and leave a lasting impression on his skin.

He lowered his head and she refused to flinch under his amber gaze. Warrick's wolf had swallowed the man.

She raised one hand to cup his jaw, feeling the tension under her palm. "Warrick, stop."

He could be so ordinary with his sun-streaked brown hair, brown eyes, and average build. Nothing that stood out, until his mask slipped. Then the predator wrapped in human skin could make you crawl.

Heeding her instincts, she kept her end of their connection wide open, sharing her chaotic emotions regarding their relationship, the bond, and her shame at the sting of truth in Ryuu's accusation. "He didn't harm me."

She ignored the tension emanating from Ryuu, standing so still behind her, more worried about the wolf in front of her. "I'm okay," she whispered, not flinching from the wild fury flickering in Warrick's eyes.

A flare of lethal protectiveness touched her, leaving a lump in her throat. His lips peeled back from his teeth in a purely canine expression and another growl vibrated through him.

She dropped her head against his chest and curled her fingers into his shoulders, knowing he needed the anchor of her touch to sooth the wildness inside. A warm hand wrapped around the base of her neck, holding her close.

She could feel his wolf's driving need to protect and under it, his human intellect battling to regain control. In that moment, the truth of Ryuu's words became shatteringly real. Her indecision was driving the normally disciplined Warrick to the edge. She needed to make a decision on their bonding, before what was between them destroyed everything and everyone in its path. Little by little, he gently closed down his end of their connection, pushing her away.

His quiet rejection hurt.

Warrick buried his nose in her neck, his warm breath sending a cascade of chills down her spine. She closed her eyes and arched her neck, giving him access, letting him drag her scent into his lungs. If she hadn't been touching him, she would have missed the slight shudder as his wolf slowly retreated and let the man ascend.

A few tense moments passed before he straightened and began to pull back.

She reluctantly stepped away, catching sight of Sebastian standing off to Ryuu's side. Where Ryuu was the embodiment of a deadly Katana sword—slender and lethally edged. Sebastian was the opposite. Broad shoulder, thick chested, he was more of a two-handed broadsword—brutal and efficient.

Right now, he was glaring at her. She met his gaze, holding it until he finally turned away. Obviously, Ryuu wasn't the only one upset with her. She sighed and slowly followed in Warrick's wake as he made his way over to Neil.

He crouched down to study the bloodied body. "Any ideas on what we're dealing with?" His voice was rough, the wolf still hovering close.

"No," Ryuu answered.

Xander made her way over to Sara. Even though her eyes were still closed, small keening noises came from the girl. Xander reached for a semblance of calm and kept her movements slow and gentle, all the while angling her body between the traumatized girl and the wolves.

Warrick tracked her movements as he continued to crouch over Neil's body.

"The ex-girlfriend," Xander said, catching his questioning look. She sat on the floor and pulled Sara's head into her lap.

"How bad is she?"

"In shock and needing stitches."

His intense perusal drifted over her, leaving her more exposed than her shredded jacket and T-shirt warranted. She didn't bother to fight the bloom of heat along her skin. When those brown eyes finally met hers, they were smoldering. "Those are claw marks."

"Yep." Her flippant answer had Warrick's nostrils flaring. He turned his glare on Ryuu.

Undaunted, Ryuu shrugged. "She doesn't wait around for help, Vidis."

Her friend's answer sparked her temper. Even knowing how protective male wolves were, she did not intend to let them get away with trying to wrap her in bubble wrap.

She was about to blast them both, but from the other side of Neil, the sound of Sebastian's disbelieving snort cut in. "The Bitten don't change unless it's a full moon."

Gritting her teeth at his condescending tone, she gave him a poisonous smile. "Well, this one did." She didn't bother to mask her disdain. Sebastian's outdated attitudes always managed to push her buttons.

Offended male fury flashed in Sebastian's eyes, but Warrick's voice cut off his response. "We're dealing with something more complex than a rash of Feral shifters."

"What did Division say?" Maybe in reaching out, they could glean some information on what the hell was going on. Find out if this was part of a larger pattern.

"Until tonight, this was pack business," Warrick stated, his attention on the body in front of him. "As far as Division is concerned, this is simply a rogue wolf attack gone wrong."

Damn stubborn male! She wanted to hit him, but instead she continued her gentle strokes through Sara's hair. The tremors wracking the girl had slowed. Calling on years of patience cultivated from dealing with arrogant, smug, male wolves, she kept her tone level. "And is it?"

Instead of answering her, he said, "I got an interesting phone call earlier tonight."

She stared at him. "Interesting how?"

His gaze flicked to the girl in her lap before going back to the torn body in front of him. "My loyalties were questioned." All emotion leeched from his voice, leaving it flat. He raised his head and met her gaze.

A faint echo of the taunting words drifted through their bond, then Warrick's resulting protective rage snuffed them out. Before she could respond, he tightened his end of their connection further, shutting her out completely.

Her jaw tightened. "That's not nice."

He said nothing.

She fought the urge to slam her end of the bond closed out of spite. The only thing holding her back was a niggling worry that it would trigger his wolf to rise again. Ryuu's earlier accusation still resounded in her heart. No matter how upset she was with him, he was still her alpha and she should try not to snap his control in front of others.

"Why sacrifice Neil?" Ryuu's question broke their staring contest. She and Warrick turned to him. He simply watched them. "What does taking out a Bitten who lives outside of the pack accomplish?"

She shrugged. "Since he's not pack, perhaps they thought he'd be harder to track?"

"He's easier prey," Sebastian added. "Yet, it still gets your attention."

"Not just ours." She nodded to the milling humans stumbling around near the club's entrance.

Warrick ran a hand through his hair as he studied the remains. "If you're both right, it shows knowledge of how our pack works."

Dread settled like a stone in her stomach. Someone had an ax to grind with Warrick. The psychic peek of those venomous taunts directed at him was very personal. Normally, it wouldn't give her pause. Her alpha was more than able to take care of himself, but something about this made her and her wolf uneasy. The urge to protect this stubborn male dug in with vicious claws. "Do you think it's Tomás Chavez?"

He rose to his feet and shook his head. "No, Chavez hasn't had enough time to set something like this in motion."

Three weeks ago, Warrick stood aside while another killed the Southwest alpha's psychopathic mate. Not only had she tried to kill Xander, but she had trapped her dead son's soul into a horrific bondage. Three weeks. Not nearly enough time for Chavez to forget Warrick's involvement.

"He'll come hunting us." Her voice was soft, but her certainty rock solid. No wolf, no alpha, would forgive the death of a mate. Even if their mate deserved it.

"I know." Warrick moved to stand beside her. "But this isn't his doing." He turned back to Ryuu and Sebastian. His leg brushed her shoulder, sending a streak of heat through her that chased away the icy trepidation.

"Then which enemy are we facing?" Ryuu's question was drowned out by the shrill song of sirens. Tires screeched outside the club.

Xander set Sara aside once again and rose to her feet.

The thump of car doors slamming sounded, soon followed by raised voices, trying to corral the agitated crowd outside.

Warrick's lips thinned and his frustration seeped through their connection. The loss of this lone wolf had hurt him, just as it was supposed to.

An echo of the hateful taunt whispered across her mind. *'How many deaths will it take?'*

"The phone call says it's personal." She kept her voice low and even as she moved closer. No need for his wolf to think she was challenging him.

Those who knew Warrick understood the line between his human mind and his wolf was thinner than most. Which meant you had to deal with the animal as much as the man. She could challenge the wolf in private, and had done so numerous times, but in front of the pack he was first and foremost her alpha.

Standing next to him, she couldn't miss his low growl or the way tension left him stiff. She fought her wolf and kept her hackles down. Sebastian and Ryuu kept their gazes lowered. No one moved, holding still and giving Warrick's wolf a few precious moments.

Slanting a look at him from under her lashes to judge his control, she continued. "Someone wants your job. Who've you pissed off lately?"

Suddenly, he crowded her. The weight of the power that made him alpha pressed against her, demanding submission. "Just you."

She let her wolf out just enough to stand against him. It was dangerous, so dangerous to do this dance with him publicly, but it was necessary. The main reason she was fighting their bond so hard was because Warrick was the most dominant male in the Northwest. And she had no intention of turning into his submissive bitch.

She wanted to be a partner, not a doormat. She fought tooth and nail for her independence. There was no way she would toss it all away because he decided she was his. Even if Warrick was a wickedly intelligent hunter who knew all about patience and prey.

"Besides me?" she hissed.

Even as she stood her ground, a tiny part of her wanted to tuck tail and bare her throat in the face of his fury. But the woman knew if she gave in, whatever slim chance they had of this relationship working would be snuffed out. So, she locked her knees, clenched her fists, gritted her teeth, and met that burning stare without blinking.

Grim amusement lit his dark eyes. "No one else important."

"Vidis." Ryuu's voice snapped the tension. "Incoming."

Warrick shifted his attention from her to the club's entrance, and inserted his body between her and the approaching humans.

She let out a shaky breath and prayed Warrick wouldn't lose it. "Non-threatening," she muttered the reminder and stepped around him. Too many witnesses meant they had to stick around and help. At least until Division joined the party.

His eyes narrowed as she stood at his left. She raised her hands above her head and arched an eyebrow at him. His lips quirked as he copied her movements. Sebastian and Ryuu followed suit. She sighed and watched the cops pour into the club.

CHAPTER 4

Outside 88 Ivories an hour and a half later, Xander sat on the brick edge of a planter, wearing a scratchy blanket like a kid's superhero cape. The ambulance carrying Sara to the nearest hospital was long gone. A plethora of emergency response vehicles were clustered on the street and visible through the wrought iron fence. Circling around the edges like vultures were various local news agencies.

The rattle of metal wheels on concrete heralded the arrival of the last body bag. It was the third such delivery to the coroner's van. Probably Neil. She watched the grim procession and sighed. "Wonder how they're going to explain this one."

The man standing silently beside her answered, "You'd be amazed at how much the witnesses' stories will vary. It won't be as hard as you think to spin it."

Xander pulled her legs up to the ledge and readjusted the blanket until she could rest her chin on her upraised knees. "Sounds like you've done this before."

His teeth flashed white in his mahogany skin as he leaned against the brick wall. "A few times. You'd be surprised at how easily the human mind tries to find the simplest explanation for the unexplainable." At her bland look, he chuckled. "Okay, maybe you wouldn't."

"So what do you think the story will be this time?" She rubbed her chin across her knees.

Her wolf was pacing under her skin, making it hard to sit still. She may be outside but she was still trapped, unable to leave until Warrick made it back outside or Division's sector chief let her go.

Her babysitter, Special Agent in Charge Reynolds, turned his attention to the few determined reporters still trying to breach the scene. "Enraged boyfriend confronts ex-girlfriend in local club with deadly results." He pushed away from the side of the building to take a seat on the low brick planter next to her. "The reporters will relegate the various stories to alcohol consumption, some will even imply heavy drug use, and Joe Q. Public will swallow every word."

"And the videos that are going to pop up all over social media? Is Division going to prove all those conspiracy theorists true by impeding the American public's right to the truth?"

Reynolds pushed his hands into the pockets of his dark slacks, his shoulders shrugging under his matching suit jacket. "Videos can be doctored, and the best way to dampen public curiosity is to ignore it. Eventually someone will step up and claim it was all a hoax, people will debate the truth, then when the next inebriated reality TV star decides to see if their convertible Porsche can double as a yacht, this will all be forgotten."

"Maybe," Xander said. "But if I were you, I'd make sure your waders are ready."

"Waders?"

"To slog through all the bullshit Division is going to have to start shoveling when the public catches a clue."

"Trust me, Ms. Cade," Reynolds drawled, utterly unoffended. "The Kyn have a few more years before they have to face the music. Humans don't want to believe they're living next door to werewolves, demons, witches, wizards, or faeries."

His dismissive tone raised her hackles. With animalistic grace, she rolled to her feet and crowded him, her wolf rising to the forefront. His burnished skin noticeably paled as he jerked back, but stuck between the planter and her, he had no where to go.

"I've watched as humans have been forced to face unpleasant truths that mar their perceived reality. It isn't pretty. So excuse me if I'm a little worried about whether 'me and mine' are going to be hunted down and mounted on some wall as a hunter's latest trophy, while your government scrambles to cover its ass." The spark of fear skittering across his face pleased her wolf but drew her up short.

She took a quick step back, shaking her head. Scaring humans wasn't something she did. That was more Warrick's style. Which meant that this flash of rage wasn't hers, but his. *Stupid psychic bond.*

"Damn it," she muttered. She pushed her wolf back and reined in the need to stalk closer until Reynolds broke and ran. "I'm sorry. That was uncalled for."

The SAC studied her carefully. "It's been a long night."

She gave a graceless snort. "You have no idea."

The sound of her name had her spinning around to find Warrick walking toward her, while a tall, lean man in a suit kept stride next to him. Behind them, Sebastian and Ryuu emerged from the club, stopping near the door. Ryuu gave

Sebastian a short nod then Sebastian disappeared into the night. Probably off to ensure the situation in the Gardens was being dealt with. Ryuu leaned against the doorjamb of the club's entrance, watching his alpha's back.

Warrick and the suit stopped in front of her and Reynolds.

The suit held out his hand. "Victor Osborn, Sector Chief."

She gave it a brief shake. "Xander Cade, Taliesin Security." She took in Osborn's white-streaked brown hair and razor-sharp gaze. "Did Williams finally retire?"

A brief smile cracked the serious lines of Osborn's face. "Yep, a couple months back. He finally sold his place and headed down south for sunnier weather. Said he wanted an actual chance to enjoy his retirement before the Grim Reaper came to collect his due."

"Good for him." Xander genuinely liked Robert Williams, the previous sector chief. For a human, he had been uniquely adept at traversing the relationship maze between Kyn and humans.

"Chief Osborn has a couple of questions for you," Warrick said, the underlying tension in his voice drawing Xander's attention.

"Okay."

It amazed her how the human was seemingly oblivious to the lurking predator standing beside him. Warrick's normally brown eyes held flickers of amber, and his skin was stretched thin. His wolf was too close and she didn't know why. And unless he unlocked his end of the bond, she'd have to wait until they were alone to find out what had happened while she'd been outside chatting with Reynolds. Which had about as much chance happening as the humans dismissing tonight's events.

"What's your position with Taliesin Security?" Osborn asked.

"Personal Security." Her answers were going to be short until she could figure out what he was fishing for.

"And that involves?"

"Protecting individuals from outside threats and pursuing investigative leads on missing persons."

"So you're a private investigator?" he clarified.

She nodded.

"Ms. Cade, before tonight had you ever met Neil Eilers?"

"No."

"How did you know he would be here tonight?"

"I didn't. I stumbled across his trail while following tips from various sources." Some of those sources were now buried deep in pack territory.

Osborn canted his head. "Was one of those sources Sara Anders?"

She gave him a brief nod. "The ex-girlfriend's family was concerned Mr. Eilers wouldn't leave Sara alone. I knew she was out tonight with friends, so I thought I'd track her down and see if she could give me some more information on Mr. Eilers or his whereabouts."

Osborn pulled a small notebook out of his pocket and consulted it. "I have your statement of what happened inside." He looked up, the friendly agent from earlier now replaced by a grim, ruthless investigator. "Were you aware that our office has responded to four separate incidents of wild wolf attacks in the last two months?"

She shook her head as her hands clenched the blanket tighter. *Four victims?* Add in tonight's body count and they were up to seven, possibly eight or nine if the two guys the med was working on didn't make it. This wasn't good. It was as if someone wanted to force the Kyn into the spotlight in the bloodiest way possible.

"How long has your pack been having control issues?"

It took every ounce of discipline to hide her flinch as the underlying accusation in Osborn's question scraped against her skin. Instead of answering, she slid toward Warrick, placing her body between her alpha and the foolish human who unknowingly challenged him. With her back to Warrick, she rocked on her heels until her spine pressed against his chest. It was like sticking a finger in a dam, hoping to hold back the flood. If Warrick snapped, Osborn would get a very up close and personal answer to his question.

"Do you have proof of this said loss of control, Chief Osborn?" a new male voice asked.

Osborn spun on his heel to face the newcomer, eyes narrowing. "I have four dead bodies, not counting tonight's little fiasco."

"Can you link them definitively to actual pack members?"

Osborn's expression soured as if he had sucked on a lemon. "Let me guess, you're a lawyer?"

The young blond nodded, his pleasant expression never changing at the obvious distaste in the chief's voice. "Ethan Cade, lawyer for Warrick Vidis and the Motoki Pack."

Osborn slanted a look at Xander. "Brother?"

She gave him a wicked grin. "And a damn good lawyer."

Ethan walked over to stand with Warrick and Xander. "Your four dead bodies—do you have proof that they were attacked by actual Motoki Pack members?"

Instead of responding with the expected anger Xander's brother could generate, Osborn backed down. He paced a few feet away then came back and stopped to study the little group in front of him. "I spoke with the previous chief when the second victim turned up. He told me that in all the years he had served, he'd never had a problem with the Motoki Pack. They were, in his opinion, a well-disciplined, highly respected pack in the Kyn community." He paused. "If that's true, then what's going on?"

Ethan turned to Warrick, raising an eyebrow. Warrick's nod was slow in coming. Behind those actions, a wordless conversation was being held. Warrick, as the Northwest alpha, could speak telepathically to any of his wolves through their pack ties.

Tied as she was to him, she could feel the flare of power as they talked. Too damn bad she couldn't actually hear what the hell they were saying.

She fought back the wave of resentment as the silent conversation continued. If Warrick kept shutting her out, there would be no way of finding some sort of middle ground for them. Which meant that whatever was between them would be over before it could even begin. She stiffened and went to step away from him, only to find herself anchored by his hands at her waist.

Conversation complete, Ethan turned back to Osborn. "Eilers was a maverick."

Osborn folded his arms across his chest. "My understanding is that mavericks are wolves who exist outside of the pack, so they have no place within the pack structure."

"Mavericks—" Warrick's chest vibrated against her back as he spoke up, "—are lone wolves who choose not to be part of the pack. They prefer to roam and never settle too long in one place."

"Are they subject to the same rules as pack members?" Osborn pressed.

This time it was Xander's turn to answer. "No. The rules are more rigid for them."

"How so?"

The flex of Warrick's fingers on her waist warned her to pick her words carefully. "They're required to make their presence known to the local alpha once they enter the territory. They're allowed entry only if they agree to the alpha's terms."

"And those terms are?" Osborn wasn't a sector chief for nothing.

"No killing, no hunting, no exposing themselves to the humans, and they're restricted to a specific time limit for staying in a territory." Ethan's answer was smooth.

"What happens if they decide not to follow those rules?"

"Or kill someone," muttered Reynolds, so low he probably didn't expect to be heard. Unfortunately, for him, shifter hearing was phenomenal.

"They're brought in front of a Tribunal," Warrick said.

Osborn quirked an eyebrow. "Was that what you were going to do with Eilers?"

"If he hadn't tried to rip my throat out, yeah," Xander said.

Phantom pleas from another time and place echoed in her mind. Her jaw firmed and she shifted her weight from one foot to the other. Now wasn't the time to revisit the past. It was just exhaustion, not guilt, she reassured herself. She understood better than most the necessity of taking down those who lost control and given into the beast that roamed under their skins. The damage and destruction they could leave in their wake reverberated for years.

The fickle bond she shared with the stubborn male behind her loosened. The feel of heavy fur and warm comfort surrounded her spirit. His unexpected gift brought a lump to her throat. *Damn him!* Warrick's hold on her waist changed from restrictive to protective.

Osborn put his hands on his hips, watching them carefully. Silence stretched before he said, "Are you telling me Eilers was the one behind these attacks?"

"Yes," Ethan answered.

If Osborn or Reynolds had been a shifter, they would have smelled the deception in his answer, but since all they had to go on was body language, they believed him.

CHAPTER 5

"I don't know if I can do it," Xander said softly. She stood next to Ryuu in a dark parking lot, blocks away from 88 Ivories, leaning against her modified Ducati motorcycle, watching her brother nod at something Warrick said.

"Do what?" Ryuu followed her lead, keeping his voice low.

The itchy blanket had been exchanged for her brother's sweatshirt, procured from the back of his sedan. Avoiding Ryuu's too-knowing gaze, she focused on meticulously folding the long sleeves back. "Accept the mating bond." The words emerged like shards of glass, ripping her throat raw.

Instead of the expected chastisement, Ryuu's tone was thoughtful. "Do you know the main difference between a mated couple versus a bonded one?"

She shook her head.

"Someone once told me a mated couple connects at the heart level, and a bonded couple connects at a soul level."

Her restless movements stilled as she thought it over. "There's a difference?"

He gave a short nod. "A mated wolf loves their mate, so much so they'll protect and shelter that mate until they die."

There was a lump in her throat and the press of tears stung her eyes. Her parents were mated and watching them over the years left her yearning for the same kind of happiness. But what she shared with Warrick was something altogether different—had been even before this stupid bond snapped into place.

Oblivious to her turmoil, Ryuu kept going, "They can even develop the ability to track their mates through their bond, and I've heard some can even share feelings."

Her stomach churned. Sharing wasn't something her alpha did well. In fact, she tended to be the one offering her heart, not him. Over the last year, her relationship with Warrick had been far from easy. Before Arizona, she spent much of their time together trying to chip through his protective walls with little success. It was exhausting and discouraging.

"Bonded couples are connected beyond that," Ryuu continued. "Probably because both human and wolf aspects are generally in harmony. They don't survive the passing of each other and share a connection that strengthens and deepens until there are no barriers between either person or their wolves."

Which was a beautiful concept. In theory. Reality could be far crueler. Say Warrick chose to never let her in, what then? At the dark thought, fear sank its teeth into her heart. Even scarier, what if the more dominant personality trampled the other until all that was left was a weak reflection? Was she strong enough to hold her own against someone as dominant as Warrick? And if so, for how long? Gods above and below knew the man's picture was right next to the words Stubborn Ass in the dictionary.

She loved him, had loved him when she allowed him into her bed a year ago, but bonding? That was a commitment on a whole other level, one she wasn't sure she was ready to tackle. An alpha's mate had to be a partner. Hard to be an equal if your mate felt you needed to be protected from everything. She could bend if when needed, but if she gave herself entirely to him and he wouldn't reciprocate, or couldn't, would there be anything left but ashes when all was said and done?

"What triggers the bonding?" Warrick and Ethan finished their conversation. Her brother raised a hand to her, and she blew him a kiss. Warrick began to walk toward her.

"No one knows for sure." Ryuu's answer was low, probably trying not to let Warrick hear. "Most bonding stories I've heard involve a life threatening choice for one partner or the other."

A flash of memory hit her—fighting off the evil invading tendrils of Lizbeth Chavez's soul-destroying magic. An eternity passed before her struggles had begun to weaken, a clear signal she had run out of time. Desperate, she had reached out and touched a piece of amber lightning.

Recognizing Warrick's magical imprint, she had grasped hold of what she had thought were the pack ties, too wounded to tell differently, and tried to apologize for not being able to hold on any longer. The magic had burned through her and seared its way to her soul. The power of it created a new bond while dragging her back to the land of the living. When she opened her eyes, she found herself irrevocably tied to the Northwest Alpha.

Warrick stopped in front of her, pulling her from her memories. He ignored Ryuu and reached out to gently trace the delicate markings on her face. She closed her eyes and leaned into his familiar touch. With a low rumble, he pulled her close and wrapped his arms around her. Needing the comfort of his touch as much as he obviously needed to touch her, she went pliant.

Above her head, he spoke to Ryuu. "Why don't you go join up with Sebastian and make sure things are moving along?"

Ryuu straightened and stretched. "Where are you going?"

"I'm going to have Xander take me to Taliesin's offices."

"Late night meeting?" Her voice was muffled against his chest.

"I need to follow up on something."

"Oh, goody. Can't wait," she muttered drily.

Looked like her evening wasn't over. With Ryuu off helping Sebastian, it was up to her to provide her alpha's protection. She sighed and pulled back, putting some distance between her and Warrick.

The two men exchanged a few more words, then Ryuu took his leave.

Silence descended between her and Warrick, stretching until it played along her nerves. Slowly, like a door creaking open, he loosened his end of the bond. Her wolf began to settle as it sensed his. He studied her, and she could see both the wolf and man in his eyes. He reached out, but she stepped back and caught a fleeting sense of hurt and confusion. But she couldn't allow his touch to weaken her resolve.

"Why are you running scared?" His question was stiff.

"Let me ask you something," she said. When he gave a short nod, she continued. "Why did you bond us?"

"You were dying." His voice was gruff, almost angry. "I —we need you."

Need, not love. His choice of words scraped over her heart leaving her chest tight. "Need?"

"If we lost you, the pack would be devastated."

"What about you, Warrick?" she whispered.

"An alpha can't have a weakness, Xander." Regret colored his voice, but he gave her the brutal truth.

It hurt, so much she almost rubbed her chest. "So you consider a mate a weakness?" This just got better and better. What made her think she could make this relationship work?

"Did you forget what happened with Chavez?" He rubbed the heel of his hand over his chest.

His movement made her realize she was projecting her pain through their bond. Furious with herself, and with him, she reeled in her emotions. "Chavez's mate was crazy."

"He covered for her because he loved her, and now his pack is in upheaval."

She wanted to punch him. The urge was so powerful, she curled her hands into the leather of her bike's seat behind her. "So it's not a mate that you consider a weakness, but the emotion behind it?"

"No," he denied. "You should never give an alpha wolf someone of his own."

Confusion momentarily overrode her anger. "Wait. Why?"

His lips thinned and his jaw tightened. "An alpha is the ultimate protector. Protection of our packs is a natural directive. We will do whatever is needed to protect what is ours. Even if they don't want to be protected."

"Even a mate?" She kept her tone careful as an inkling to why he was so damned determined to keep his heart out of her reach formed.

"To protect a mate, some would burn the world," Warrick answered in a curiously flat voice. "Even at the expense of our pack. Chavez is proof of that."

"Warrick—" she started.

He snarled and ran a hand through his hair in obvious frustration. "My wolf recognizes you as our mate." Possessiveness stormed down their bond confirming his words.

Mate. A deep thrill hummed through her at his claim, but her heart ached because there was more to it. Dreading his answer, she asked, "And the man?"

"Is torn." He face was grim. "Claiming you protects and strengthens the pack, but increases the danger to you." His 'and me' was left unsaid.

"You think you can claim me, but keep me at arm's length? As if that will somehow keep me safe?"

He didn't answer, but she could feel the belief in his screwed up logic.

She and her wolf took exception to his assumption, and there was no stifling her growl as feminine fury rose and burned against his male arrogance. "I don't need you to keep me safe, Warrick. I need you to accept me for who I am."

Her challenge was the last straw and she practically heard his control break. Swearing, he trapped her between his body and the bike before she could blink.

Being caged brought her wolf snarling to the fore. Claws broke through and she swiped out, leaving thin bloody lines across one cheek before he captured her hands in his.

He snarled back and took her lips with savage intensity. Ravaging her mouth, he took sharp bites of her lower lip before laving the stings with his tongue.

Neither she nor her wolf wanted to calm, even as desire and deep-seated need rose in a wave. Riding the fine edge between anger and passion, she got her own nips in, refusing to back down.

He settled his body over hers, hot and demanding.

She jerked her arms against his hold, twisting her wrists until she was free. Then she raked her nails over his back, unsure if she wanted to mark him or hurt him. His hiss of indrawn breath was lost in the storm raging between them.

She continued to nip at his lips, his chin, determined to leave her mark on this stubborn male who couldn't see what he held. She wasn't a weakness, but a partner, the one person he should feel safe with, something both woman and wolf agreed upon. Until Warrick and his wolf acknowledged them as such, there would be no accepting the bond fully, regardless of the impact on the pack. But maybe—just maybe she could buy them some time to figure this out. If he could answer her questions.

Decision made, her body softened. Her hands relaxed, sharp rakes turning into long, petting strokes. Biting kisses gentled into a soothing tangle of tongue and lips. Her acquiescence quieted both the man and the wolf so determined to make their point.

"Warrick," she gasped as he released her lips and made his seductive way down her neck. "We have to stop." There was nothing wrong with making out in a poorly lit parking lot, but her alpha was a bit more private than most. This unrestrained passion masquerading as dominance play revealed another mark of his fraying discipline.

He lifted his head, sexual hunger flushing his skin. Those amber eyes, so at home on his wolf but so startling in his human face, smoldered. "Mine." The word came out on a growl.

She didn't drop her gaze. "Probably, but not completely. Not yet." She continued to pet him. Where her words alone may have raised his hackles, her body language kept him calm.

He leaned in and pressed a chaste kiss against her lips before pulling back, putting much needed space between them.

The loss of his heat left chills on her skin. Her claw marks on his cheek caught her attention. They were already healing, but seeing them made something inside her tremble. She dragged in a shaky breath and picked her words carefully. "How many bonded couples do you know?"

He stiffened, turned, and then paced a few feet away, running a hand over the back of his neck. Tense silence stretched between them as he retraced his steps back to her. She began to worry he wasn't going to answer her. Then he said, "Two."

"That's not a lot."

He gave her a wry look. "Bondings are rare among the Born."

"Bondings are the happily-ever-afters for shifters."

He gave a short laugh. "Those aren't your words."

She let a small smile curl her lips, struggling to hold the nonchalant stance against her bike. "Nope, my mom's. So fair warning." When he winced, she laughed. "Did you think I could hide what happened from my mom?"

"One could only hope," he muttered, his shoulders

hunching slightly. It was funny to watch the big, bad alpha squirm at the prospect of facing her mother.

"You'll survive," she teased. Her humor faded as she brought their conversation back on track. "You said 'rare among the Born.' What about the Bitten?"

Bitten wolves were an exception not a rule. Contrary to popular myths, a mere scratch or bite wouldn't change a mortal into a shifter. It took a savage attack that left the victim near death. Even if the individual made it through the initial attack, their new reality tended to shatter most mortal minds. Those that actually managed to survive for any length of time fought a constant battle for control and never reached the power levels of those born to it.

"I can't think of any Bitten wolves that are bonded. The few matings between a Bitten and a Born have always ended badly. Maybe there's not enough balance between wolf and man for a Bitten to hold such a bond."

"That's depressing," she said.

"It's truth," he answered, watching her.

"Okay, fine," she said. "If bonding needs both wolf and man to agree to a relationship, how did we end up like this?"

His soft snarl echoed through the night. He didn't like her question. "Like what?"

"Stop it," she chided. "No games."

His lips slowly uncurled. "No one's been able to explain why bonding happens. Hell, even those sharing one tend to have a hard time putting what it is into words." He moved until he stood next to her, brushing against her. "I do know that I couldn't do it alone. If you hadn't wanted us, you would be dead."

She ignored the implications of his astute observation.

"Which one triggered the bond, Warrick? You or your wolf?"

"You're pushing, Xander." His scowl deepened the shadows on his face as he shifted his weight forward.

"You're the one who tied us together. Now deal with it." Maybe she could get him to see what was so clear to her. If his wolf accepted her, why couldn't the man? If she didn't figure out how to open his damn eyes or heart, this tie would rip more than the pack apart. "Since your wolf already considers me yours, I'm betting on him."

"We aren't two separate beings."

"Yes, you are. Just because you and your wolf have a thinner line than most doesn't change that. There's Warrick the alpha and Warrick the wolf. Which one decided to save us?"

"Both," he snapped.

She tried to keep the relief washing through her hidden, knowing he wouldn't appreciate it.

Before she could comment, he continued, his words scraping her sore heart. "The wolf thinks you're his to protect. If he could, he'd keep you locked away from anyone who'd try to hurt you or use you to hurt him or the pack. The man—" He paused, carefully choosing his words. "The man knows you can protect yourself. You wouldn't be a Wraith or a Tracker if you couldn't, but—"

"But I'm a weakness the man—the alpha—can't afford," she repeated his earlier comment, understanding his logic. Not that it made it hurt any less. "If someone managed to get to me, you'd be distracted."

"Distractions can get you killed," he confirmed.

It took courage, more than was pretty, to ask the next question. "Do you really want this?"

"If I didn't, you wouldn't be here." His answer was a strangely gentle reminder of the choices they both made.

"You can't keep this—," she waved a hand, chest height, back and forth between them, "—closed down. It's causing issues." Unfortunately, the bond worked both ways, which meant emotional exposure happened at both ends. Her stomach clenched at the thought. "You won't be able to hide from me." She tried to temper the accusation behind her statement.

"I haven't hidden anything from you."

She pressed her lips together, trapping the heated response hovering on her tongue. Arguing would get them nowhere. Or more precisely, it wouldn't get them where she needed them to be. Folding her arms, she studied him. "So how do you know this stuff?"

"My parents were bonded." It came out reluctant, the ice in his voice a warning she stumbled onto an emotional minefield.

She picked her way forward. "Were?"

"They died within hours of each other."

She heeded the cold distance in his answer and changed directions. "What happens if I reject this?"

Her nose twitched at the sharp bite of anger suddenly flooding the air. Deep inside, a fragile hope strengthened. If he really thought she was a weakness, her question shouldn't have provoked such a volatile reaction.

"There will be no other mate for my wolf," he gritted out, tension tightening his body.

There was no silencing the devil inside her. "And the man?"

He growled, clearly at the end of his patience.

She let her grin free and cut him some slack. "Nice to know I wouldn't be the only snappy one around."

Truth was, if they couldn't make this work, she couldn't stay with the pack. Even if he never took another lover, she wouldn't be able to remain near him and not want to be with him. Not after spending a year at his side. Besides, hadn't her choice really been made weeks ago when she had reached out to the lifeline he offered? The question wasn't whether she could accept the bond, it was whether she could accept the fact that Warrick might never allow her all the way in. She buried the knowledge that this man was hers, deep in her heart, determined not to let him see how much it would scar her soul if he refused to change.

She turned away and began to unfasten the helmet strapped to her bike. She wasn't sure she could get the next bit out while facing him. "There have to be ground rules, Warrick." She took the first hesitant step to bridge the gap. They might both be dominants, but he was an alpha. The fact he had given her the last few weeks without pressing for a decision was remarkable. And telling.

In the corner of her vision, she saw his shoulders tense. "What kind of ground rules?" Wary caution colored every syllable.

Putting the helmet on, she snapped the chinstrap closed and let a wicked grin curl her lips, knowing it would make him leery. "So worried, alpha mine? Scared of a little pixie?" She handed him the second helmet her brother produced from his trunk of preparedness and stepped to the other side of her bike.

He took it, his shoulders relaxing, and a rare grin flitted across his lips. For a moment, he appeared years younger and her heart sped up, just a little. "Last week, you got Ryuu into plastic pants and a purple wig then dragged him into that human club, Drucilla's. There were pictures of him posted on Facebook."

Her smile widened as she put her hands on the bike's seat and leaned forward. "Hey, not my fault his team couldn't manage to hold a football during their last game."

"He was dancing on a table."

"He made almost a hundred bucks."

Warrick finished securing his helmet and shook his head. He reached over the bike's seat to gently trace a finger down her jaw. "I'd be stupid not to be cautious about your ground rules. I've learned not to underestimate you."

"Smart man." She cleared the huskiness from her voice and turned serious. "If we're going to make this work, you have to stop shutting me out of the bond."

He frowned. "I wasn't aware…"

A distant look crossed his face as he trailed off. A kaleidoscope of emotions cascaded down their connection, making her stagger under the impact. It rolled her under. Flashes of images and feelings too fast to process seared across her mind and heart. She struggled to surface, unable to secure her mental footing in the swirling mass. It slowed, like a receding tide, leaving her gasping.

Warm hands gripped her shoulders, offering an anchor in the aftermath. She was grateful for his support, her arms trembling as they pushed against the bike's seat.

A rumbled apology echoed in her ears and in her mind as Warrick adjusted the bond until the emotional flood leveled. "It's not intentional," he said. "Better?"

She gave a short nod, as the bond found its balance between them. Even now, when he was trying to keep it open, she could sense parts still blocked from her. But it was a good start and better than before.

She took a breath, steadied, then laid out the rest of her rules. "No others. If you're mine, you're mine." It took concentration not to let her claws free to curl into the leather beneath her hands.

He arched an eyebrow. "There hasn't been anyone else in the year we've been together. Why would it change?"

She ignored his question. If he wanted to remain blind to the females who tried their damn sneaky best to get in his bed, so be it. "You're mine, therefore I'm free to defend that claim however I see fit."

He studied her. "It goes both ways."

"Fair enough," she agreed. "You can't interfere if I'm called in by Mulcahy for a job."

Ryan Mulcahy was the Captain of the Wraiths—the Kyn's black-ops group. There were no rules of engagement, other than to protect the Kyn and humans from the nightmares lurking in the shadows. The elite group was generally regarded as a myth even among the Kyn, and she had been part of them for years.

Warrick frowned. "I've never interfered with your Wraith duties."

She snorted and pulled back. "Any male that claims a mate becomes damn possessive. They try to shelter their little female from the big bad uglies of the world. Problem is I'm part of the group that keeps those big bad uglies in check, regardless of who my mate is." She caught his gaze. "Tell me it doesn't bother your wolf that my job puts me in danger."

"I can't," he admitted. "But both man and wolf know exactly how dangerous you can be. We're counting on that to help keep you safe." The feral protectiveness leaking through their connection stole her breath. "Don't make me regret that faith."

"As long as you know it's mutual."

Surprise flashed across his face. "You don't have to protect me."

Stupid, stupid male. "If I'm your mate, those who threaten you, will answer to me."

Suddenly, the cinnamon and clove spiced scent she associated only with him filled her nose, a seductively dark edge weaving through it. Her words had triggered a definite response in the man watching her.

He clenched a fist in frustration. "Ryuu and Sebastian are my Second and Third for a reason."

She straightened, fighting back the urge to shake him. "If we're a couple, then I will have your back. They can't be with you twenty-four-seven."

"Neither can you."

His dismissive tone hurt, but she dropped it for now. She could probably beat his stubborn ass to a pulp and he'd still think he was indomitable. Fine, there were other ways to make him see her as a partner instead of a weakness.

"Last rule." She fought to keep her tone level. "No lies. Ever." On the other side of the bike he remained silent, watching her. She met his gaze and let him see just how serious she was. "No keeping things from me." Her voice was laced with steel. "No giving me part of the story, no hiding the truth to protect me."

"Or?"

"Or I leave now."

His face darkened. "And go where?"

"Vegas." Quiet conviction rang in her answer. Never threaten an alpha unless you meant it. It would rip her heart out, but she'd do it. "Their alpha, Jeanette Claison, would have no problems accepting a Tracker." Xander could handle his need to protect her, his asinine belief that he was invincible, but she'd be damn if she'd stand beside someone who didn't believe in her strength, who lied in his misguided attempt to keep her safe.

The silence stretched and she thought she finally asked for something he couldn't give. She held her breath, bracing for the pain beginning to etch itself over her heart.

"Xander."

Her name in that low voice had her blinking and meeting his amber-flecked gaze.

"I will do my best to never lie to you, but I can't promise that I won't deal with it myself if I think the threat to you is great enough."

"Would you tell me first?" She pushed the question past the tightness of her throat.

He paused. "I don't know."

His honesty stung, but she had asked—no, demanded—it, so she couldn't complain. She swallowed past her dry throat and made her decision. "Fine. Then I'm yours."

She would have to accept this was what he could give her, for now. The rest, she'd have to fight for, but then that was nothing new.

CHAPTER 6

Xander shut off the Ducati's engine, the rumbles fading into the night as Warrick unwound his arms from her waist. Light spilled from the glass front of the seven-story building that housed Taliesin Security, a national leader in security. Talicsin also served as the public front for the Northwest Kyn. Here, the Kyn held jobs, utilizing their unique skills while providing a believable cover to their human counterparts.

Locking the helmets to the bike, she followed Warrick past the night security guard to the elevators. When the door slid shut, she took a moment to let her spine slump against the back wall. Using the reflective surface of the elevator's doors, she watched Warrick from under her lashes. The soft, interior light smoothed the ragged edges of the night's stress on his angular face. He leaned a shoulder against one wall, his attention seemingly focused on the ascending floor numbers.

"Why are we here?" She almost regretted breaking the comfortable silence.

His attention shifted from the glowing numbers to her,

but she kept her relaxed pose. "I'm hoping to get some answers on what happened with Eilers tonight."

She raised an eyebrow. "How?"

Before he could answer, the soft ding heralded the elevator's arrival to the top floor. He led the way through the simple but lushly appointed reception area and the deserted front desk. Entering the security code, Warrick pulled open the door leading into the interior offices and held it as she passed through. Subtle lights ran along the floor, casting heavy shadows down the hall. Together, they continued past darkened offices and conference rooms.

The hall ended, branching left and right. Turning to the right, where Warrick's rarely used office was located, she came to a halt when he quietly called her name.

Turning, she saw him continue down the left corridor to where a swath of bright light cut across the gloom. Sighing, she reversed course and followed in his wake, catching up in time to see him stop in an open doorway.

"Hello, Raine."

"Dammit, Vidis. Whatever you dragged me in for better be damn important."

Xander couldn't stop a grin spreading across her face at the familiar, feminine, disgruntled snarl. She ducked around Warrick's body and threw herself into a chair. A warm toned wooden desk fought for space with leafy green things tucked into the corners. No pictures graced the walls, and the standard computer screen and keyboard were huddled on the far corner of the desk, as if trying to put as much space between Raine McCord and their delicate mechanical parts as possible.

At Xander's entrance, Raine straightened and flashed her a smile, before resuming her frown that etched small furrows between her startling gray eyes. Her black hair, with newly acquired glints of silver, was pulled back, and her hands were curled around a cup, with the telltale string of a tea bag hanging over the edge. Part Fey and part mixed bag of tricks, thanks to some twisted science experiment, Raine was an enigma in the Kyn world. Yet, the lethal warrior had been honed in the hellish fires of her past, leaving behind the pure blade of a survivor. Becoming Raine's friend required delicate handling, much like the temperamental leopard she could shift in to.

"Hey, Raine." Xander propped her boots against the edge of the desk. "How's things?"

"Things were fine, until your summons arrived," Raine sent Warrick a dark look.

Needing to ease the tension of Raine's unintentional challenge, Xander laced her fingers behind her head. "Hmm, was Gavin giving you a cooking lesson?"

Raine had mentioned her lover and partner, Gavin Durand, was sharing his culinary secrets.

The distraction worked and a hint of color rose over Raine's high cheekbones as she turned her attention back to Xander. "He's damn good in the kitchen." She raised her cup to take a sip of tea, not quite hiding her small smile.

"I bet." Xander met her gaze with a feminine smirk, squashing the small twinge of jealously at her friend's telling gesture. Raine and Gavin recently figured out how to make their complex relationship work. Not an easy accomplishment by any means, since both were members of the Wraiths. Yet, the fact that they found a way gave Xander the slim hope that she and Warrick might find their own path. "Thanks for coming in."

Behind her, Warrick gave a sub-vocal growl and without thinking, Xander sent an admonishment through their shared connection. *"Knock it off."* She jumped as the impression of snapping teeth came barreling back.

Raine's gaze sharpened over the rim of her cup. Setting it down with care, she leaned back in her chair. "Feel free to have a seat, Vidis," she invited.

Warrick pushed off the doorframe and took the other chair. "My apologies for the lateness of my call."

Inwardly, Xander heaved a sigh. Around others, Warrick tended get all formal. It could be attributed to his status as an alpha, but she thought it had more to do with his age. Over the last year, she managed to knock some of his crustiness loose, but still...

"I'm sure you have your reasons," Raine said.

"I'd like you to see something." Warrick's voice betrayed nothing. Yet, through their connection, Xander could feel his subtle rise of tension.

"Do I get any more information?"

Warrick shook his head. "I'd rather not skew your perceptions."

If she hadn't been watching, Xander would have missed Raine's flash of interest that was there and gone with Warrick's pronouncement. Leave it to Warrick to trap Raine with her own curiosity.

"Fine." Raine sighed, pushing to her feet. "I'm assuming this means a trip?" When Warrick nodded, she pulled her jacket off the back of her chair.

As Raine prepared to leave, Xander dropped her feet and stood up. She moved out into the dimly lit hallway, Warrick behind her. As much as she wanted to know what he was up to, there was no way she was going to parade her ignorance of his objectives in front of Raine. Nope, she'd wait until they were alone, then call him on it.

"So, where are we headed?" Raine punched the call button for the elevator.

As it was Warrick's show, Xander let him answer. "Chinese Gardens."

The elevator arrived and as they stepped inside, Raine hit the button for the bottom floor before turning to Warrick. "Correct me if I'm wrong, but isn't it a little past visiting hours?"

The grin Warrick sent her was more teeth than amusement.

Raine's gaze flickered away. As realization of what her small action admitted, her lips curled back from her teeth and Xander cut in before her friend could do something truly stupid. "This is not something you want to fight the crowds to see."

Raine's attention shifted to her, and Xander fought the urge to squirm under that unnerving gaze. Behind those gray eyes lurked a ruthless but patient predator. Xander's wolf padded forward and together they showed the cat in front of them that they were not prey. Not even close.

Raine gave a slow blink and the cat retreated.

Satisfied with their silent victory, Xander's wolf receded.

A slow smile twisted Raine's lips. "I'm not much for crowds in general."

"Ain't that an understatement?" Xander drawled.

In the parking lot, they parted ways, with Raine heading to her SUV while Warrick and Xander stood beside her bike. As she tightened the strap of her helmet, Xander turned to Warrick. "Do you suffer from short term memory loss?"

In the midst of unfastening the helmet from the bike, he stopped at her unexpected question. "Pardon?"

She stepped in close, took the helmet from his unresisting grip, and stretched up to place it over his head. She ignored the momentary stiffness that straightened his spine when she took the helmet. When her movement remained non-threatening, he slowly relaxed. She kept her tone even, no hint of her inner irritation leaking through. "What part of not shutting me out, did you not get?"

Genuine puzzlement painted his face. "The bond is still open."

Helmet secure, she let her hands rest on his shoulders as she met his gaze. "There are more ways to shut me out than to lock down the bond." The last of her irritation died a quick death at his continued confusion. Her alpha was so use to making decisions on his own that the idea of sharing was completely alien to him. "Would you like to share your plan with me?" she prodded.

Understanding chased the confusion away. "What's the one thing your friend can do that others can't?"

Ah, she thought as pieces began to fall into place. During their time in Arizona, Raine's unique ability to see magical signatures helped to identify and defeat the Soul Stealer. "You're going to see if she can identify any magical traces."

"If we're lucky, it may shed some light on what happened with Eilers."

"Wouldn't it be better to get her to Eilers's body?" She dropped her hands.

"There's no way Division will let us anywhere near his body. No matter how good your brother is," he said. "So we'll take her somewhere Division isn't."

"And if there's nothing at the Gardens?"

"Then I'll make Ethan earn every penny I've paid him."

She snorted. "He's good, but I'm not sure even he could get through Division."

"Then we'll go around them." There was no give in his statement.

She opened her mouth to respond, but the lick of frustrated uncertainty that didn't belong to her, had her closing it without saying a word. Pressing the matter would do nothing but spark an argument, and the night had been long enough already. She really wanted to find her bed before the sun rose. Or his bed, she amended, sliding a sidelong glance at the man next to her. As much as she missed their physical relationship, the thought of sleeping, just sleeping, in his arms again, left both woman and wolf yearning for a quick resolution at the Gardens.

She knew better, though.

She stepped up to the bike, threw her leg over and started the engine. Warrick waited until she was settled, before getting on behind her. As his warmth and arms wrapped around her once more, she guided the bike into the night.

CHAPTER 7

After stashing her bike in an empty parking lot, Xander and Warrick dashed across the quiet street running along the Chinese Gardens. Heavier pockets of darkness pooling under trees guarding the back wall of the Gardens shrouded their movements. When they reached the agreed upon spot, a figure stepped free of the shadows.

"I really hope you have bail arrangements set," Raine said softly. "Because I can damn well guarantee Mulcahy won't shell out a dime."

"My brother's a lawyer," Xander responded drily. "He'll give us a family discount."

Before Raine could answer, Xander leapt and grasped a sturdy branch extending over the wall. Pulling her body up, she didn't bother waiting for the other two as she dropped into the Gardens. As soon as Raine, then Warrick, landed next to her, Xander made her way into the concealing foliage.

She could barely hear the stealthy movements of the two behind her as she led them to the rocky grotto where Eilers's victim had been hidden. Knowing there wasn't enough room for all three of them inside the small alcove, she stepped to the side.

Raine moved past her into the shallow cavern and though her voice was pitched low, Xander caught every word. "Am I looking for something in particular?"

Warrick stood outside the entrance. "Anything unusual."

There was a faint snort. "You realize we're dealing with magic, right?"

Xander grinned, enjoying Raine's needling of Warrick. It would be good for him to realize, sooner rather than later, that not everyone would walk carefully around him.

Faint sounds of traffic mixed with the natural night choir as the minutes stretched. Xander started to get antsy. The longer they stayed in the Gardens, the higher the chances were that the human security patrolling the grounds would stumble across them. "Can you tell who or what attacked him?" she finally asked.

"You know, this isn't exactly a science," Raine muttered.

"Do your thing before we find out how much bail is required for trespassing," Xander shot back.

"There's no rushing perfection, my friend."

Warrick's low growl silenced both women until only the incongruent sound of the merrily tumbling water from the grotto's falls remained. Magic pulsed like a low electrical current in the night air, raising the hair on the back of Xander's neck. Once, she asked Raine what she saw when she did...whatever it was she did. Knowing how private her friend was, Xander was surprised when Raine actually answered. "It's like looking at a living tapestry, where each person's magic is a different colored thread."

Tempted though it was to ask what Raine saw when she looked at Xander and Warrick, Xander never found the courage to ask. She could admit, if only to herself in the darkest night, that she was scared of what Raine would say. It would suck to have indisputable proof of Warrick's inability to ever fully accept their bond. She wasn't sure she could recover from such a blow.

"Vidis, I'm not sure what I'm looking at." Raine's voice carried a distracted note.

Warrick shifted, leaning his head into the cavern. "What do you see?"

"I've got some traces of a magic user. I think it's a shifter, a really angry shifter, but I'm not sure."

"I thought the colors were fairly distinctive," Xander said.

The shadows thinned as Raine stepped out of the cavern and stood next to Warrick. "Generally they are, and from what little I've seen until now, shifters tend to stick to more natural earth tones. Something about how close you all are to the more natural world resonates in the colors your magic reflects. But this—" She frowned, obviously trying to pick the correct words. "The closest way to describe it would be a moth-eaten piece of ripped fabric."

Xander tried to understand Raine's explanation. "So it's full of holes?"

Raine shrugged. "That, or whatever was holding it together, is unraveling."

Unraveling didn't sound good and, considering the spurt of Warrick's worry winging through their bond, she wasn't the only one concerned.

The sharp crack of a branch under foot had all three freezing in place. The searching beam of a flashlight swept over the heavy foliage between the grotto and the walking path. Security was making its rounds. Xander met Raine's gaze. Using hand signals familiar to every Wraith, she outlined a quick escape. When Raine nodded, they simultaneously grabbed Warrick's arms.

Unsure of how clear Warrick's psychic reception was, Xander sent a quick warning down their bond. *"Hold on!"*

He barely tilted his chin in acknowledgement when she and Raine pulled the Northwest Alpha onto the Shadowed Paths of the volatile world existing between the magic and mortal realms.

Shadow Walking was a rare, but vital skill, one those few Wraiths with Fey blood sought to master. Unfortunately, Warrick was a pure blooded Lycan. Xander, on the other hand, carried enough Fey blood to Shadow Walk, thanks to the roving eye of some randy male, generations back. But it still ruffled her wolf's fur every time she did it. Right now, it was going to save not just her ass, but Warrick's as well.

Xander let her surroundings melt away. They were replaced by the icy winds and twisted terrain that made up the eerie landscape. She ignored Warrick's rising tension under her grip as he stepped onto the warped pathways. She tightened her hold, praying he had enough discipline to keep his wolf from bolting. If she and Raine lost their hold on him, she wouldn't have to worry about the repercussions of their bond because he would be forever lost in a world that would drive him insane.

Using a mental countdown, Xander kept a sharp eye on identifiable landmarks as she and Raine pulled Warrick along. Arctic winds lashed around her, whipping against her insubstantial form. She sensed him along their link. Like faint film images, she caught snatches of his wolf, back arched, tail and head down, trying to identify the unseen threats. In answer to his uneasiness, her wolf rose and took her place at his side, trying to ease the tension. Xander sent a fervent prayer to whoever was listening that Warrick the man could hold his wolf in check for a few more moments.

Between one breath and the next, she and Raine stepped off the Shadowed Paths and onto the cold concrete of downtown Portland. Streetlamps cast soft pools of light around the nearly empty parking lot they now stood in.

Warrick jerked away from the two women and strode over the asphalt.

Raine moved to follow, but Xander stepped in front of her with a sharp shake of her head. "Let him go. His wolf didn't like that trip."

"Whoever does?" Raine looked around. "At least we didn't have an audience."

"Even if we had," Xander tilted her head toward their surroundings, "it wouldn't have mattered."

Across from them, sitting under a mural painted on the wall, the white letters, proclaiming *Keep Portland Weird*, seemed to glow softly against the bricks. Xander didn't catch Raine's answer as a sharp spike in the connection she shared with Warrick had her moving. "Stay here," she threw over her shoulder at Raine.

She raced to the darkest corner of the parking lot, knowing she was going to be the only thing standing between an unsuspecting downtown Portland and a very unsettled wolf. She skidded to a halt at the warning growl. She lowered her head, hunched her shoulders and kept her posture as non-threatening as possible. Slowly, she approached the wolf standing among the shredded remains of jeans and a T-shirt.

Stiff legged, with his ruff standing on end, Warrick's wolf was deadly, but beautiful. His shoulders reached Xander's waist, his body much larger than his wild cousins. With his narrow chest and heavily muscled legs, he was a viciously quick hunter. His fur ran from white to burnished copper, covering the spectrum from blond to brown, with the darkest coloring appearing on his muzzle and spine.

Right now his lips were pulled back, revealing sharp canines as a continuous stream of growls vibrated from his chest.

Stopping a foot away, she crouched down until her head was below his. "I know you're not happy, but this really isn't a good time to come out and play." Keeping her voice even wasn't hard. She learned early on how to project the necessary calm to appease the more dominant members of the pack.

Scattershot images burst into her mind. *Unseen wolves harrying the pack. Broken bodies of those he promised to protect. A flash of her wolf snapping and snarling, not allowing him to stand between her and those who threatened her. The unfamiliar feeling of being pulled into a strange world, twisted beyond comprehension, while enduring the biting stings of unseen attackers who hid behind a whirlwind of chaotic magic. Frustration in knowing that danger stalked her, again.*

Understanding sparked and she sent back a wordless apology to both the man and the wolf, her heart hurting. She hadn't considered how the culmination of the evening's events would impact Warrick and his wolf. "Shadow Walking's never fun." She spoke slowly, hoping her words would pull the man back into the driver's seat. "If we had another choice, I swear we would've taken it."

After an uncomfortable couple of minutes, his growls quieted, then he came closer. When she felt the press of his warm breath as he nuzzled her hair, she knew Warrick was on his way back. The subtle tension locking her muscles began to drain away. He pressed against her, knocking her on her ass, so she crossed her legs Indian style and looked at him.

He came forward and nudged her again. She reached up to scratch behind one tufted ear. He tilted his head, encouraging her attention. Catching sight of the shredded remains of his clothes, she sighed. He rested his chin on her shoulder so it didn't take much to turn and meet the bright slits of amber peeking beneath half-closed lids. "You realize we have a problem?"

A deep canine groan answered her as she scratched a particular-y sensitive spot. As a mental image of driving a naked Warrick on the back of her bike through the city streets burst into full technicolor life, she was tempted to echo the groan. Instead, she leaned her head against his. "You're clothing optional, alpha mine."

Warrick settled to his haunches, his tail brushing across the rough ground.

"There's a mission a couple of blocks over." Raine walked toward them. As she got closer, there was no missing the grin edging her mouth. She offered Xander her hand. "Want to bet that there are some donation bags left in the back?"

Taking her hand, Xander let Raine pull her to her feet. "You're enjoying this way too much."

"Karma's a bitch." Raine studied Warrick. "Damn! He's bigger than I had imagined."

A hundred inappropriate responses rushed to Xander's tired mind, but she kept them under verbal lock and key. Unfortunately, one must have made its way down the connection she shared with Warrick, because his solid bump to her hip was followed by a warm tendril of very satisfied male amusement. An unfamiliar heat stained her cheeks. "Clothes would be good," she muttered, doing her best to ignore Raine's very knowing, full-blown grin.

They made their way out of the parking lot, Warrick walking between them. Between the late night hour—or early morning, depending on your point of view—and the dimly lit streets, Xander hoped they could pass Warrick off as a really large dog. The skim of warmth as his shoulder brushed her waist made her snort. Yeah, that was a long shot.

The trip to the mission gave Warrick a chance to settle and think. Each time a pair of headlights pierced the darkness, Xander and Raine tried to disguise Warrick's figure in the shadows. It was laughable, but he let them try. Walking next to Xander, he let his wolf wallow in the presence of his mate.

Coming out of the Shadowed Paths, his wolf had been nearly rabid. The distorted magic had been hard to handle. Even with Xander's wolf standing beside him, it took every thing he had to hold his wolf back until they stepped back into the real world. Her determination to protect him gave him the added edge he needed to endure.

There was a warm glow of pride for the courage of the small warrior walking next to him. A contradiction of lethal efficiency and feminine mystery, she intrigued him from the start. Her fierce independence and wicked humor had captured the man and the wolf, tempting them with glimpses of what could be. It wasn't until he almost lost her that he recognized how far she had crept in.

Earlier, when she asked who choose to save her, the man or the wolf, he gave her the truth. Both. Neither one could bear to let her go. Yet, life taught him some harsh lessons. Love did not conquer all. And sometimes love, no matter how strong, could warp and break even the strongest couples.

Savage memories rose, seeking cracks in his emotional walls. He ignored them, focusing on the issues Xander pointed out in their discussion. She wanted him to leave his end of the bond open, but there was no way he could drop all his barriers. Not even for her. She was the only one who looked at him as if he were whole, as if there was more to Warrick Vidis than alpha of the Motoki Pack. He couldn't lose her. If he let her see every inch of him and his wolf, she would realize how little of the man really existed and just how in control his wolf really was.

An alpha did not remain an alpha because he was compassionate. An alpha was, to borrow Neil's words, the top dog because he was ruthless, conniving, and would protect his wolves through any means necessary. And for the one they considered their mate, there was no line they wouldn't cross.

Xander was a warrior, ruthless in her own way, but under it all, lay a core of loyalty and compassion that kept him warm. She would protect her mate and children against all threats, just as she did the pack. Her need to be his partner echoed through their bond, but even if his human side understood, his wolf's primary drive was to keep her safe. She was his to protect.

If he let her stand beside him, their enemies would target her to get to him. And therein lay the problem. Xander would always be his weakness. It didn't matter if she could hold her own against all sorts of foes, it would take just one mistake on his part and she'd be gone.

The incident in Arizona drove that fact home. He had

been subconsciously tracking her through his pack ties. Uneasy and tense, he had paced for hours before she let him in. Her fear at facing something threatening not just her life, but her connection to the pack sent him running. He left the pack without notice, traveled hundreds of miles to invade another alpha's territory, and raced into an unknown situation because she was in danger.

He hadn't been thinking about the pack as he cradled her broken body. As his rage turned into a living, encompassing demon he hadn't given a thought to the repercussions of invading Chavez's territory without Ryuu or Sebastian. But when Raine killed Chavez's deranged mate, Warrick had gloried in the vicious satisfaction flooding his veins. He sure as hell hadn't considered the consequences of bonding Xander to him, heart and soul.

Xander's hip brushed his shoulder again. He leaned in a little, needing her touch. What was done was done. Now he needed to figure out how to deal with the woman beside him without destroying them both.

Raine and Xander herded him across the dark street. They moved past the semi-clean front stoop of the mission and down the side of the building to the narrow alley behind it. The alkaline scent of stale urine mixed with rancid trash, seasoned with a hint of kerosene, drifted from partially empty brown bottles nestled along the alley's edges. Warrick sneezed as the nauseous brew stung his nose and his ears flattened.

Xander met his baleful look, ignoring the glee Raine didn't bother hiding. "Beggars can't be choosers."

He chuffed in disagreement.

White trash bags leaned against the rusted steel door. Grabbing the first one, Xander made quick work of finding a pair of ripped jeans and an oil stained T-shirt, with a drunken clam printed on the front. Setting them aside, she cupped his face, making sure he was paying attention. "Hurry and change," she told him. He stood there, watching her tug Raine out to the alley's entrance. "C'mon, Raine, the smell is making me sick."

Like it was any better for him? He turned to look at the outfit she had chosen and leaned down to sniff at the clothes. A faint scent of detergent teased his nose. At least whoever left these had washed them first. He turned back to see Xander give Raine a push as she slouched against the brick wall. She looked at him and mouthed, *Hurry up*, before giving him her back.

He sighed and reached for the shift. The familiar wrenching of muscles and sinew didn't interfere with his ability to eavesdrop on the conversation between the two women.

"So." Raine tucked her hands into her jacket pockets. "Finally forgave him, huh?"

Xander closed her gritty eyes and let her head bump against the brick at her back. "There was nothing to forgive."

"Good."

The wealth of sincerity in that one word had Xander blinking her eyes open. All signs of Raine's earlier humor were gone, replaced by an unnerving intensity. Puzzled, Xander asked, "What am I missing?"

Raine shook her head. "Nothing. It's just..." She dropped her gaze and hunched her shoulders. "Even if I had realized what Vidis was going to do, I wouldn't have stopped him."

Her lips clamped tightly closed and she lifted her head to met Xander's gaze almost belligerently.

It took a moment for Raine's seemingly out of context statement and ill-at-ease body language to click. Raine, who never apologized for anything, was looking for forgiveness. She and Gavin were the ones to find Xander in Arizona. Between the two of them, they held her body and spirit together until Warrick's arrival. Warrick tried everything to keep Xander with him, but when it looked as if he was going to lose her, he used Raine's unpredictable magic to repair the damage the Soul Stealer had done to Xander's spirit. As with most things Raine touched, the results were anything but normal. When all was said and done, Warrick and Xander were indelibly linked.

For some reason, Raine now thought she had to apologize for her actions. Xander racked her brain for some pithy comment to snap the uncomfortable tension, but drew a blank. As the only two females in the Wraiths, girly heart-to-heart talks weren't easy for either of them. Yet, Xander's friendship with Raine was an unexpected boon. In the predatory warrior, Xander found a kindred spirit, someone who understood the bloodier aspects of their world but was just as much at a loss when it came down to the whole male-female relationship thing.

"I'm glad you didn't stop him," Xander finally answered.

Although Raine tried, she didn't fully succeed in hiding her relief at Xander's response.

Xander bit back a small grin and turned her attention back to the night-shrouded street. "Can I ask you something?"

"Sure."

"Do you and Gavin—" Xander stopped, uncertain how to continue. Trying again, she said, "You and Gavin share…"

When the pause began to stretch, Raine prodded, "A love for good food? A taste for sharp-edged weapons? What?"

Her flippant questions caused Xander to choke back a laugh. "No, you idiot. The tie between you two, how do you manage?"

When Raine didn't immediately respond, Xander turned and met Raine's shrewd gaze. As if that was what she had been waiting for, Raine finally asked, "Manage what?"

Xander grimaced. "To stay separate. To stay…you."

"Trial and error."

The simple answer set her back. "That's it?"

"What? You were expecting Dr. Phil?"

Before Xander could respond, the sound of a quiet male curse cut through the night. She and Raine turned to the alley in time to watch Warrick limp toward them as he pulled the T-shirt on over his head.

Xander sucked in a breath. No man should look that good in torn jeans and a ratty T-shirt. Even as the thin material drifted down to hide the sculpted muscles of his chest and stomach, images she stuffed in a box over the last few weeks began to leak out. They teased her with tactile memories of running her fingers and tongue over that intriguing map.

"Shoes."

The word emerged as a growl, jerking her gaze up only to be caught by the flash of answering heat and hunger that added a wickedly seductive element to his savage stare.

"You're drooling," Raine said, sotto voice.

"Don't care," Xander muttered.

"Do you remember what I asked you in Arizona?" Raine asked, a hint of laughter in her voice.

"You asked a lot of things in Arizona," Xander said.

"Smart ass." Raine bumped her shoulder into Xander's. "So has your answer changed?"

Dragging her gaze away from Warrick's hypnotic pull, she wracked her brain to remember what Raine was referring to. "Answer to what?"

Raine tilted her head, all traces of her earlier humor wiped away. "Is it worth it?"

As Warrick came to a stop in front of them, she looked right at him, knowing he heard every word. "Yes."

CHAPTER 8

AFTER LEAVING RAINE AT HER CAR WITH PLANS TO MEET UP AT Taliesin the next morning, Xander led Warrick over to her bike. "So where to next?"

"Home."

At his abrupt answer, she stilled for a moment and narrowed her gaze, fighting not to turn around. "Home?"

He stepped closer, trapping her between him and the bike. Even though he kept a deliberate sliver of space between them, the heat of his body wrapped around her. It tempted her to lean back, to let the night's events catch up and pull her under, safe in the knowledge he'd be her anchor. That seductive promise of safety was part and parcel of his draw as an alpha. They were the ultimate protectors.

But who would protect him? The insidious whisper left behind a tendril of worry. They were no closer to identifying the threat or the mastermind running the show.

Behind her, Warrick leaned in, setting his hands on the bike's seat and locking her in a cage of skin and heat. A fine tension sang through her. Against her shoulders, she could feel his muscles bunch as he nuzzled the patch of skin where her neck and shoulder met. Exposed by the too-large sweatshirt, it was vulnerable to the onslaught of his warm breath and the whisper-soft brush of his lips. Her pulse skipped a beat.

Hungry for the small touches she had denied both of them for so long, she closed her eyes, resting her head against his shoulder, granting him even more access. Her body melted into his.

He wrapped an arm around her waist, anchoring her as sweet sensations piled one on top of another, dragging her into a world where only his touch mattered. A helmet hung forgotten in one hand as she curled her free hand over his wrist, digging her nails in as he hit a particularly sensitive spot that wrung a low groan from her throat.

"Home," he whispered. Her lashes fluttered open as he grasped her chin and turned her face to his. His skin was flushed with a nearly violent need. "No more challenges." The command was given against her lips.

With a purely feminine thrill at his show of dominance, she let him take what he wanted, offering no resistance as his lips crushed hers. Lips and tongues dueled as she met each of his demands with her own, until they were both breathless. Her exhaustion, worries, and fears were crushed beneath a wave of intense desire.

When he finally let her go, she dragged cool night air into her lungs, hoping to clear her haze of need. Her lips felt swollen and her skin flushed. She blinked, trying to focus beyond their combined hunger.

He didn't back away, crowding so close she could see the individual pinpricks of amber in his brown eyes. With no way to hide from the wolf or man, she didn't try, standing still under his intense study.

Releasing his wrist, she cradled his jaw, shivering at the rasp of stubble against her palm, It took her two tries before she could clear the huskiness of want from her voice. "Let's go home, alpha mine."

At her capitulation, his eyes lit with a fierce satisfaction, while a devastatingly wicked grin warned her of the dangers ahead. He gave her enough room to get on her bike, before he settling in behind her.

Nervous excitement warred with an almost painful need, causing her hands to shake as she started the engine. Terror and desire sent her pulse racing as they sped through the darkness toward home. Tonight, Warrick would claim her, and she him.

Years ago Xander fell in love with Warrick's house. The custom built log cabin sat at the end of a winding gravel drive on prime acreage nestled next to Forest State Park and acted as the pack's central gathering place. His nearest neighbor was a couple miles away, and the isolation suited not just the man, but the pack as well. The old-growth forest gave plenty of room for hunting and playing under the light of the moon.

Tonight, she was grateful for the privacy as the Ducati's engine fell silent. Her fingers trembled as she locked the helmets into place. Warrick's heat at her back, and the soft brush of his lips against her neck rekindled the erotic storm from earlier.

"Warrick." Her protest was drowned out by her groan as his teeth found a particularly responsive spot. Dear gods, it had been so long. Now she and her wolf wanted to bask in his touch, but first— "Inside. We have to get inside."

He answered with a wordless hum as his quick hands delved under the baggy sweatshirt and wrapped around her bare waist.

She twisted until she could turn and face him. Curling her hands around his jaw, she dragged his head up, forcing him to meet her gaze. "I want a bed." The words were breathless but clear.

Her demand broke through his desire and his eyes sparked. A wolfish grin curled his lips. "Fine." His agreement was too close to a growl but at least he listened. He shackled her wrist and drew her behind him as he unlocked the front door and pulled her inside.

The interior was bathed in deep shadows. It was a good thing shifters could see well in the dark, because he wasn't even taking the time to turn on any lights.

She barely noticed her surroundings as Warrick drew her past the living room and up the stairs to his bedroom. Her pulse began to pound as needy hunger coiled low and tight. She followed his broad back through the double doors of his bedroom. Stopping, she twisted her wrist, forcing him to let go.

He took a couple of steps forward then, with one rough move, yanked the stained T-shirt over his head, tossing it on the floor. She sucked in her breath as moonlight cast intriguing patterns over his back. The borrowed jeans barely held their place across his hips and clung to his very tight ass.

Before he could turn around, she closed in and curled her hands around his bare waist. Running her nose along his spine, she followed the teasing touch with little open-mouthed kisses. The feel of his skin under her hands and lips set every nerve on fire. She missed this. The freedom to touch, to taste.

His head fell forward and his hands covered hers as he let her play, his soft groan urging her to continue.

His back was an erotic canvas, his skin stretched across broad shoulders, defining the underlying muscles that flexed with his every move. With her hands trapped under his against his flat stomach, she pressed closer, using the only weapon left to her, her mouth.

She nipped and licked the taut expanse of his back. Her breathing roughened and desire spiked, threatening to shatter her fragile control. Soul-deep want rushed through her like a wild fire, searing away her emotional confusion. Sensation and emotions coalesced into a knee-weakening brew.

Tugging her hands free, she mapped each dip and rise of his muscled abdomen. Slow. She needed to take this slow, to savor each touch. It didn't matter how touch-starved she and her wolf were, or how temptation sang along her veins, demanding she gorge—she needed to take her time.

Every delicate brush of skin over skin, every damp kiss drove the heat higher, sinking sensuous teeth deeper. Tonight, she and her wolf would take their mate and cement their bond because this man, this wolf was theirs.

Her emotions roared down their connection. A shudder went through Warrick and he looked over his shoulder, his voice rough. "Xander."

Even in the dimly lit room she could see the taut line of his jaw and the red flush running along his cheekbones. His answering wave of need, want, love, and possession flowed back, causing her breath to catch at the whirlwind of his emotions, Yet the chaotic brew settled inside her and she held the precious gift close. For the first time, she caught a glimpse of what they could share as their bond flared into brilliant life.

Amazingly, she could feel an echo of her touch and his need for more even as he held back, not wanting to scare her. Silly man. As if the erotic pictures rolling through his mind weren't giving her ideas. It was wildly exciting to feel what she did to him. Heeding his reactions she gentled her touch here, deepened it there, making sure to discover what set his blood on fire. The storm of desire strengthened, becoming a force of nature. She let it take her under, uncaring if she broke under the pressure.

Instead, he broke first, capturing her exploring hands and turning to face her. With her wrists trapped in one hand, he cupped her face with the other. She tilted her head, burrowing deeper into his touch, nipping at his palm, craving his warmth.

He brushed his thumb over her bottom lip, causing her breath to catch and stutter. Her audible reaction drew a slow, tantalizing smile from him.

She shuddered as the pads of his fingers traced over the intricate lines of her tattoo, slowing when he found the rougher ridges of old scars hidden among the design. She tried to evade his touch, but stopped at his low growl.

He released her hands and cradled her face. "Someday, you're going to tell me the story of these."

Unable to look away, she managed to get out, "Why? It's not that important."

His smile faded and he nipped at her lower lip. "It's part of you. It's important."

She blinked against the sudden pressure of tears his answer caused, and turned her face into his hands, hiding how deep his words hit.

His fingers brushed along her face once more. As

whisper soft as his touch was, the depth of emotion behind it burned through skin and blood, leaving an indelible mark on her soul.

She licked her lips in a telling move, her tongue flicking over his finger as it completed its path.

His eyes darkened and his gentle touches disappeared. His need surged and a low growl escaped. He lowered his head and took her lips, deliberate seduction lost under their rising wild hunger. His mouth plundered, wiping away any traces of rational thought, leaving behind only primal urges and soul-deep needs.

She twisted in his hold until she could grasp his shoulders and drag him closer.

He released her mouth and, with a muttered curse, gripped the edge of her sweatshirt to drag it over her head.

Cool air swept across her over-heated skin, leaving chills behind. Beneath the concealing lace of her demi-bra, her nipples pebbled. A scorching whip of want lashed at her, driving her cravings higher. The room took a dizzying turn as he lifted her off her feet. Instinct had her legs wrapping around his waist as she tried to crawl closer, ravenous need taking the driver's seat.

His bed's thick comforter pressed against her back and her tight hold loosened enough to allow him to pull back. He rose above her in the moonlight, his lips trailing over her shoulder and down the slope of one breast.

She arched under him, whimpering.

His constant growls, rumbling in his chest, created a vibrating wall of heat against her sensitive skin as he shifted his weight to one arm. His movement drove his hard length against her, making her core weep with want. Keeping the pressure steady, even as her body began to writhe beneath him, he traced one finger along the lacy edge of her bra.

Captivated, she watched his face tighten with lust as she followed his delicate movements, mesmerized.

His tongue swept over his bottom lip, anticipating the feast awaiting him.

She wanted to feel the damp heat of his mouth suckling the aching nipple he was currently teasing. She needed—no, craved—more than his careful touch. He was driving her crazy. "Please, Warrick." Her plea fractured as his finger dipped beneath the lace.

His low chuckle rasped over her sensitized nerve endings, sliding under her skin and twining around her heart. Slowly, he brought his slumberous gaze to hers, never stopping the butterfly movements that left her squirming. "You are mine." His voice was rough, as his ability to form coherent words disappeared.

Through their bond, a wave of protective love, pride, worry, tenderness, and wild need tumbled to her. Cautious joy shimmered through her. Maybe they could really make this work.

She stilled his delicate touch by curling her fingers around his wrist. "Yes, but—"

His body tensed in a moment of predatory stillness.

Her emotional uncertainty flared through their bond, but she wasn't a dominant for nothing. Assured of his full attention, she released his wrist and raised her hand to the nape of his neck, tangling her fingers in his thick hair, pulling him down to her mouth. Just before their lips met, she snarled softly, "You're mine as well."

Her claim was met with male pride. Their emotional connection deepened as both human and primal sides collided in a storm of passion, want, need, and desire.

Setting her teeth into his lower lip, she and her wolf made their claim in complete harmony. He was hers. Releasing her hold, she sealed her promise with a kiss. She and her alpha might not have it all worked out, but she would fight tooth and nail for him. For his wolf.

The flare of satisfaction in his eyes was her only warning as his passion stepped off the feral edge. With a low growl, he reclaimed her mouth as he tore the fragile lace of her bra, baring her to his touch. Cupping her breast, he released her lips and captured one swollen peak in the heated cavern of his mouth. His tongue curled around the tip as he drew her deep.

Erotic heat sent her arching into his consuming touch while broken sounds fell from her mouth. Words fled, leaving her gasping as fire roared through her. Determined to drag him into the same shattering storm, her fingers fumbled at his waist, tearing open his jeans, and he returned the favor.

A confusing flurry of movement ensued, then both were blessedly naked. The luxurious sensation of finally being skin-to-skin tore what few remaining restraints existed free.

Following the frantic path of her hands with her mouth, she set her teeth into his neck, leaving her mark, claiming him. His groan was answered by her soft laugh. Her nails left behind red marks as she dragged them from his shoulders to the rise of his ass.

He used his heavier body to press her into the mattress as his mouth wove a destructive path from her neck, over her breast, and lower. Their storm of passion raged, destroying rational thought, leaving behind riotous sensations in its wake.

Her mindless demands of "More!" were met by low,

answering growls. Their hands slid over and around sweat-dampened skin, rediscovering familiar territory and blazing new ones. Their tongues tangled in frantic need as judiciously applied teeth added a carnal bite to their play that turned a shared wildfire into an inferno.

The love she tried to push away broke its lock and surged forward, shattering through their shared psychic tie, leaving her vulnerable. Her insecurities and fears were washed under the initial, vicious wave of need created by their weeks-long separation. As her body burned in the sensuous inferno, she gorged on the ability to connect to the man who lived in her soul. For the first time, his wolf and hers were in alignment, with no barriers between them. The connection between them strengthened, illuminating the possibilities.

Their caresses gentled and lingered. Kisses turned from desperate to drugging and somehow Xander managed to get Warrick at her mercy. His body lay stretched before her as she cupped his strong jaw in her hands. Straddling him, she leaned forward to sip from his lips. Determined to tease them both, she let his heated length slide along her dampness, increasing their hunger and drawing it out. She kissed her way down his chest and lower. Her heart raced, causing her breath to turn short and choppy as she gloried in her ability to indulge.

She didn't stop until she knelt between his thighs. Dragging her nails down his ribs in a light caress, she watched in feminine pride as he arched under her touch. Bending forward, she pressed a trail of small kisses over his thighs, deliberately avoiding his straining erection.

His hands burrowed into her hair. "Dammit, Xander."

She gave a low laugh and let him pull her to where he wanted her most. Wrapping her hand around him, she flicked her tongue and traced the velvet-covered steel in her hand. His hips rose with an undeniable demand. Desire coiled, dark and needy, wiping away her laughter until only want remained. His spicy scent swirled around her, dark with desire, and she gave up the fight, craving his taste.

Taking him into her mouth, she closed her eyes, savoring his addictive taste. Their bond was wide open and she followed the images in his mind. Paying attention to what drove him crazy, she tightened her lips and flattened her tongue. His groans were music to her ears. She lost herself in his pleasure until she couldn't tell where hers began and his ended. When she couldn't take anymore, she lifted her head, waiting until his eyes fluttered open.

Carnal need and unspoken demands swirled in his dazed amber gaze. With a small smile, she adjusted her position until she rose over him. Muscles flexed and coiled as took him in one slow, torturous inch at a time. His rigid length began to fill her, and her breath stuttered as she fought not to break their visual connection. Holding his gaze, she rotated her pelvis, using small controlled movements to take him in.

His eyes blazed as his hands went to her hips to help her torture them both. Inch-by-agonizing-inch, she took him, until he was seated so deep the sensation rode the line between pleasure and pain. She stopped, savoring the edge. Bracing her hands on his thighs behind her, she arched her spine, pushing him deeper. Her soft, hungry cry broke free, her eyes fluttering closed. He shifted his hips, giving a gentle push, rocking her forward. Her hands flew to his chest to brace herself. "Not yet," she begged. "I need—"

"Me." He wrapped one hand around her neck, the other holding her hip as he rolled her under and took over.

Her broken cries filled the heated darkness as he held

her hips still and pulled his shaft out with deliberate slowness, dragging his thickness against her most sensitive spot.

White lightning sparked through her veins, tightening the coil of need to a new breaking point. Her body writhed under his, trying to get him to move.

He pulled back until only the tip of him was inside and her hips bucked against his restraining grip, trying to recapture him. His low chuckle was her only warning. He plunged deep, wringing a short scream from her. He didn't stop, pulling back only to drive forward again, setting a demanding rhythm she greedily answered.

Lost in the dance, in the spiraling sensations threatening to shatter her she willingly gave in to the tempest, trusting him to hold her. Together, they rode the cresting wave, the rise and fall of their bodies accompanied by soft murmurs and muttered demands. Sensations piled upon each other until her world burst apart in a violent explosion of ecstasy. Her cry of release was joined by his deep shout as he followed her.

Embracing the shuddering man, who held her heart in his hands, she basked in the wonder of their connection. She could feel him, every aspect of him and his wolf. The soul-deep sense of precious completion brought tears to her eyes and hope to her heart. Her arms tightened as their bond burned like a star. Their breathing began to slow and, as the minutes passed, the nova of their connection dimmed to a warm ember.

Fear fluttered across her heart and she closed her eyes, fighting back useless tears and tucking her emotional hurt away. As their bond settled, his barriers reformed, locking pieces of him out of reach. Faced with his inability to trust her, hurt more than she wanted to admit.

Warrick rolled to his side, tucking her against him. He brushed a loving hand over her short hair before dropping his arm around her waist.

She burrowed against his chest, unwilling to reveal her pain.

He nuzzled her neck and pressed a soft kiss to her jaw. "Sleep, pixie girl. I've got you."

CHAPTER 9

Warrick snapped awake, his wolf prowling under his skin. Careful to keep his breathing low and even, he lay in his bed with Xander's warm weight sprawled across his chest. Silence lay heavy and deep, broken only by Xander's soft exhalations. It took a second to identify what had disturbed him and set his wolf on edge.

It was too quiet.

The normal white noise of the nighttime chorus from the woods surrounding his home was absent, replaced by an uneasy stillness. He didn't need his wolf to recognize the signs of a hunt. He tightened his hold on the curvy form in his arms and the slight movement caused her boneless body to tense. He brushed a soft kiss over her tousled hair, feeling the silky strands under his lips.

"Company." His warning was a mere thread of sound.

She tried to push away from his chest, but he tightened his grip, stilling her movements. She jerked her head up. Sparks of amber gold cut through the normal green of her eyes. The resulting glow, set among the delicate lines of ink, gave her an exotic appearance.

Her gaze jumped to the window overlooking his balcony, the blinds partially open. The faint sound of the intruders softly landing had her lips curling back in a silent snarl. The beginnings of a sub-vocal growl vibrated her chest against his. As the immediate threat closed in, the warrior replaced the woman. Her nails curled into his shoulders leaving a stinging bite behind.

Following her gaze, he caught the slightest edge of movement in the sporadic moonlight. His wolf charged to the surface and his vicious snarl filled the night as he reversed their positions. He raised his body giving Xander room to roll out from under him and off the bed. The window shattered as something dark and heavy crashed through the blinds and skidded across the wooden floor.

Fury tore through Warrick. *They dared to threaten him? In his home? With his mate?* The change swallowed the man in seconds, leaving an enraged wolf behind. Muscles coiled and nails dug into the rumpled sheets as he lunged for the attackers.

The sounds of snarls and growls filled the dark bedroom as Xander crouched on the floor, her hand sweeping around her until the brush of fabric met her touch. Snatching Warrick's discarded T-shirt, she dragged it over her head, keeping her gaze focused on the closed door. Flickering shadows danced along the small gap at the base of the door. There were more intruders besides the jackass that crashed through the window.

Next to her, the bed shuddered as the fighting wolves slammed into it. Though the noise behind her drowned out all other sounds, there was no hiding the nose-wrinkling scents wafting from the hall. Warrick could handle the one in the bedroom. She would deal with whoever lurked on the other side of the door.

Keeping her focus on the gap, she gauged the shifting shadows as she stalked forward. Her wolf rose, preparing for the change. Inching closer to the door, she caught the bite of cordite and oil seeping through cracks in the doorframe. *A gun? The fucking cowards brought a gun?*

A gun meant she needed hands, not paws. Cold practically allowed her to control the familiar ache of the change. Her muscles quivered in anticipation as she allowed only her canines to lengthen, her nails to thicken, and her senses to sharpen. Partial shift complete, the night lost some of its secrets.

Across the room, a sharp, unfamiliar yip proved Warrick scored a hit. The shadows under the door paused.

She slid into the space to the left of the door, pressing her back to the wall, falling into a hunter's stillness. Like the intensity before a lightening strike, the build-up of the intruder's anticipation on the other side coiled her muscles. Her lips curled in satisfaction. *That's right, come on in.*

The crack of a foot hitting wood sent the door crashing against the opposite wall. As moonlight glinted off metal, Xander exploded into movement. Grasping the barrel of the shotgun, she used surprise and momentum to yank the shooter through the doorframe. He got a shot off, but she ignored the burn of the metal under her palm as the barrel bucked and a slug rammed into the ceiling.

Jerking the gun down and across her hip, she pulled the intruder forward and straight into her fist. The short but powerful strike to his temple loosened his grip on the weapon and sent him stumbling back into the rebounding door and out into the hall. She followed, yanking the shotgun out of his hand before slamming the stock into his chin. His head snapped back and he crumpled to the floor.

She kicked his body away and looked up in time to see a third form charging down the hall. She switched her grip until the shotgun became an improvised baseball bat. Once again, she swung the gun and the impact of the stock meeting flesh and bone reverberated through her arms and shoulders. Her attacker staggered back, the muffled groan music to her ears.

Her grip on the barrel tightened, the metal creaking as it gave under the pressure. She tossed the now useless gun away and began to stalk her prey. Sporadic moonlight fell through the high windows, shrouding the corridor in patches of shadows.

Her assailant was still on his feet, one hand clutching the railing, the other wrapped around his ribs. He shuffled back, retreating, his breathing harsh as he avoided the shafts of moonlight.

"Bet it hurts, uh?" Menace left her a voice a vicious purr. "Probably broke a few ribs."

She stalked closer, matching him step for step. The hair at the nape of her neck began to rise in warning. She stopped, and so did the man veiled in shadows.

She scented the air and her wolf went wild. Power, dark and twisted, rose and gathered strength. *A spell?*

This was no wolf, but a wizard.

Keeping this one alive was no longer an option. The darker counterparts to witches, wizards were bad news. Everything they touched, everything they did, ended in pain and suffering. It didn't matter who the spell was meant for, it had to be stopped. Only the wizard's death could break the magical storm hovering in the air between them.

"Go ahead, bitch." His words were gritted out between shallow breaths. "Let's see who'll make it first." He let go of the railing and stepped into a pool of moonlight. The building magic deepened, and she recoiled as the perverted tendrils raked against her spirit. Ignoring the discomfort, she shoved the nightmarish memories of another's deviant magic and focused on her target as she inched forward a step at a time.

A brief surge of satisfaction coursed through her, Warrick's, and then his triumph howl echoed through the house. *Two down, one to go.*

The wizard paled, his gaze darting nervously to the entryway behind her.

Using his moment of distraction she lunged, clearing the space between them in an instant. Her lethal nails ripped across fabric and skin, blood blooming in dark ribbons across his stomach and chest. His horrified screams rent the air, but her attack broke his concentration, shattering the building spell.

Her wolf took over, instinct guiding her actions as the overriding urge to eliminate the threat consumed her. The wizard stumbled back under her fury. When he raised an arm to keep her from his throat, she raked her nails across his unprotected stomach. He doubled over and she went for his throat. Hot blood flooded her mouth, sparking a savage joy. The force of her attack slammed the wizard into the wooden spindles of the railing and, with an ominous crack, the hand carved wood broke leaving the man teetering over open air.

Even as she felt him fall, she refused to release him. Her hind claws scored the floor, her teeth locked in his throat, her fore claws digging deep into the soft tissue of his stomach as his weight pulled him down. The all-consuming need for his death, allowed her to ignore the ringing blow when he managed to land a solid punch to her face.

A freight train slammed into her, yanking her away from her prey. Snarling, she swung to face the newest threat. Adrenaline rushed through her veins like a firestorm and it took precious seconds for the familiar scent of cinnamon and cloves to pierce her mindless fury. As the haze dissipated, she realized she was lying on the hallway floor with Warrick's wolf straddling her. His amber eyes locked on her, his dark muzzle close to hers as his snarls and hot breath fanned her face.

She pushed her own wolf back, forcing her body to fully reclaim her human shape. She held Warrick's furious gaze as her teeth and hands returned to normal. Panting, she pushed against the fur-covered chest above her. "Get off me!"

He dipped his head to nuzzle the skin between her shoulder and neck.

"Warrick." The underlying warning in her voice was hard to miss.

He raised his head, his tongue swiping out to lick her chin.

She slapped his shoulder. "Get off."

He stepped back, letting her struggle to a sitting position. She wiped a hand over her bloody mouth, wincing as she brushed a rising bruise from the wizard's hit. She peered through the gap of splintered spindles to living room below.

The wizard lay in a twisted, lifeless heap in the middle of a slowly spreading pool of blood. If his fall hadn't been interrupted by the thick edge of the coffee table, he might have survived. Maybe.

"We need a cleanup crew," she muttered.

A skin-prickling sensation heralded Warrick's change from wolf to man. His tanned hand appeared in front of her. She grasped it, ignoring the blood streaking her skin, and let him pull her to her feet. He wrapped his arms around her, surrounding her with his heat.

Closing her eyes, she let her forehead rest against his bare chest while her arms wound around his waist, finding comfort in his hold. Adrenaline receded, leaving her chilled and her voice soft. "What the hell is going on, Warrick?"

"We'll find out." His hand stroked over her spine. "I'll get my phone and call Ryuu."

She sighed and gently pulled away. "Great. Now I'll have to pay up."

Warrick cocked an eyebrow. "What bet do you two have going now?"

She felt the color creeping along her skin. The blush had nothing to do with the temptation his nakedness presented. Nope, not at all. She just wanted to make it down the stairs and end this conversation. "I'll tell you later." She tugged at the edge of the blood-spattered T-shirt she wore, as if another fraction of an inch would help her not feel so exposed.

"Tell me now," he said, stepping close. His nostrils flared, his eyes darkening as her blush deepen. He curled his hands around her waist, closing that last minuscule space between them.

"Not a chance." The bite of feminine frustration sharpened her tone. She would push him away. In a minute. Maybe.

"Now you have me curious." His head lowered, the warmth of his breath brushing against her neck. Soft kisses trailed over her sensitive skin.

Some days it just sucked to be a shifter. She could never hide her reactions. Even when her mind knew it wasn't the right time or place, her body had other ideas.

"Too damn bad." Her hands rose to his chest, reveling in the flesh covered steel. Raw scratches and ragged bite marks marred his otherwise smooth skin. She brushed her lips over a particularly deep scratch. Against her stomach, she felt him jerk, hot and hard, in response. Yep, in just a second she was going to pull back.

The sharp nip of his teeth against her neck had her doing just that. "What the hell?"

He raised his head, a rare grin curling his lips. "I want to know about the bet."

"Don't you think the dead bodies might trump something as trivial as a bet?" He was too close. Every damn breath she took was drowning in his scent. "Go call Ryuu."

"Fine." He leaned in and gave her a quick kiss before letting her go. "I'll make him tell me then."

Watching him walk away, she smothered a sigh. Coming or going, Warrick was a hell of a man. "Put on some sweats," she muttered, knowing he'd hear her.

She turned and made her way down the stairs to see what she could figure out from their not-so-friendly neighborhood wizard.

CHAPTER 10

Stepping around the body lying inside the bedroom doorway, Warrick's faint grin at Xander's last comment faded. Instead, as the iron-rich odor of blood washed away the familiar scents of his bedroom, his earlier anger retuned. He stopped next to the bed, grabbing one of the end posts as every muscle stretched taut. His wolf clawed against his skin, demanding to be let loose, to hunt down those who dared to threaten his mate and invade his home.

He almost lost her. The choking wave of rage and fear rose, as thick nails burst from his fingers, leaving deep gouges in the wooden bedposts. He dropped his head, closed his eyes, and fought back the constant growls rumbling in his chest. That damn wizard had almost taken her with him. She and her wolf were so far gone, neither had realized how precarious their footing was.

His need to protect her was going to tear him apart.

She wanted a partner, not a protector. He was bonded to a warrior and not just any warrior, but one of the most lethal fighters in the Kyn community. She was a Wraith, a premier hunter of monsters. Dammit, he knew she could handle herself, but the prowling animal inside wasn't easily calmed.

Reining his emotions in, he locked them away from the connection with Xander. He didn't want her to see how close he was to losing it. He forced his fingers to uncurl from the bedpost. Teasing her about the damn bet had given him a touchstone, keeping the man in the driver's seat, while covering his wolf's desperate need for the reassurance of her touch.

He grabbed a pair of sweats from his dresser before stepping over the mangled nude body lying amongst shards of glass from the shattered window. He pulled the sweats on then picked up his cell phone from the nightstand and flicked on the lamp. The warm light pushed back the room's shadows as he tucked his cell between his shoulder and ear then crouched next to the body.

On the fourth ring, Ryuu answered. "Yeah?"

"How soon can you make it to my house?" Warrick demanded.

There was a pause. "Fifteen minutes."

"Good. I had some unexpected visitors tonight." He turned the body over, inspecting it.

Ryuu snarled softly. "How many?"

"Three. Two wolves, one wizard."

Warrick studied the slack face, ignoring the gaping hole where a jugular once resided. He didn't recognize this wolf. Under the gore, the body bore numerous scars. Amidst the ragged marks of claws were the telltale puckers of several bullet wounds.

"A wizard? Do you need me to arrange a meeting with Cheveyo?" Ryuu asked.

"No," Warrick ground out.

The name of the most powerful witch in the Northwest

left Warrick's wolf lunging against the man's restraints. He picked his way through the miasma of emotion roiling under his skin, trying to unravel why Cheveyo riled his wolf. *Was Cheveyo a threat?* A soft growl vibrated across his spirit. A flash of Xander standing between a shadowy evil and Cheveyo seared his mind. He flinched. The small movement left him mentally snapping at his wolf.

He pinched the bridge of his nose. This damn bond was driving him and his wolf crazy. "No," he repeated. "Not just yet."

Maybe there was something more going on than what he could see right now. Xander was safe downstairs with the dead wizard. Cheveyo was the logical choice to go to for information, but unease whispered through Warrick. Cheveyo was recovering from his battle with the Soul Stealer, and his position as head of the Magi House was precarious at best. If someone wanted Cheveyo's seat, now was the best time to strike because it would drive a wedge between the houses.

"Warrick, whoever it was sent three against one," Ryuu said. "They weren't playing around."

"Three against two," he corrected.

There was a pause then, "Damn it, Vidis! Your woman's gonna wipe out my bank account. She just couldn't wait until the next full moon?"

Lifting his head, Warrick adjusted the cell. "You were betting on when we'd have sex?"

Ryuu chuckled softly. "Actually the whole pack has a pool going."

Warrick shook his head, fighting the small grin tugging at his lips. "Get over here, Ryuu, and bring a couple of helping hands. Oh, and be prepared to pay up."

He hung up without waiting for an answer. His pack

was betting on his sex life? Didn't they have anything better to do?

He rose to his feet and went to his dresser. Pulling open a drawer, he grabbed the pair of yoga pants Xander left behind months ago. Ryuu and a couple of other wolves would be here soon. As much as he enjoyed seeing Xander in only his discarded T-shirt, he wasn't in a sharing frame of mind. Turning, he headed to the door. Fierce pride filled him and his wolf as he stepped over the second body. Xander had managed to break the fool's neck. She was beautiful, lethal, and his.

Xander was crouched beside the dead wizard when Warrick, now wearing sweats and nothing else, joined her. He held out a pair of soft yoga pants, too small to be his. She must have left them here on a previous visit.

"Anything?" he asked.

She took the pants from him. "I don't recognize him."

Staying on the edge of the cooling pool of blood, Warrick crouched as well, his arms resting on his knees. "Doesn't mean he's not one of Cheveyo's."

She snorted, bracing herself against Warrick's shoulder as she pulled on the pants. "Are you really that paranoid? What in the hell would Cheveyo gain by destroying our pack?"

"That's what I'm determined to find out," Warrick said. "Besides, I'm not being paranoid if the threat is real."

"Oh it's real, but it's not from Cheveyo." She straightened and moved around to the other side of the body. "If Cheveyo wanted to challenge you, he wouldn't send some two-bit wizard after you in the middle of the night. Maybe we should call him and see if he recognizes him."

"No." Warrick's sharp denial snapped her head up.

She narrowed her eyes. "You're just looking for any reason to not ask for help."

"Not true," he gritted out between clenched teeth.

She guessed she was starting to ruffle his fur the wrong way. Poor baby. "Prove it."

He stared up at her for a moment, the muscles in his jaw tensing. "How?"

"If you won't go to Cheveyo, then ask Raine to examine the bodies. Maybe she can find a link between the rogues and this wizard."

"Hell, no!" he snarled. "Even she admits her talents are unpredictable."

"What's your problem, Warrick?" Xander snapped. "You had no issue dragging Raine to the Gardens a few hours ago. What changed?"

He glared at her. "If Cheveyo's involved, I can't afford to bring Raine in."

Despite her resolve to stay calm, her voice rose. "You need answers, and the only way to get them is to ask. Someone is using rogues to attack our pack. They're altering the Bitten. How long before they decide to take a pack wolf?"

A muscle jumped in his clenched jaw. "Pack wolves are safe," he argued.

"Why? Because of pack ties?" she pushed. "You think that whoever's experimenting on the Bitten, won't figure out a way to interfere with the ties? If they can alter the magic that controls when a Bitten shifts, the ties will be a cakewalk."

"The ties are not my wolves' only protection." He rose to his feet.

"What?" she challenged. "Do you have every wolf tagged with a GPS chip or something?" She knew as well as he did that implanting electronic devices in any Kyn was a waste of time. Mixing electronics and magic never ended well.

He opened his mouth, but she held her hand up, cutting him off. "No, enough! No matter what I say, you'll find some reason not to reach out." She paced away from him then turned, trying to scrape her fraying patience back together. "We need help here, Warrick, before it's too late."

"Once I know it's not Cheveyo, I'll consider going to him."

Damn stubborn ass! Fear and frustration seethed together, making her sick to her stomach. Some instinctive sense screamed he was making a mistake. If he didn't reach out for help now, someone else would pay. "They know you won't ask for outside help,"

His jaw firmed and his lips thinned.

She didn't need the spark of irritation echoing through their bond to know he wasn't happy with her comment. Tough shit. "They're counting on it."

His hands curled into fists, his eyes dark. "What does that have to do with anything?"

"You're one of the most powerful Northwest Kyn, Warrick." She struggled to keep her frustration out of her voice. She wasn't challenging her alpha, or lover, right now. She was trying to understand potential threats. "But you're also the most isolated. It's common knowledge that you never wanted to be the head of the Lycos House."

His nostrils flared as he frowned. "Nobody wants the damn position."

She sighed. "I know, but you will always be the best one for the job. Political power games don't interest you, so you tend to be the most logical voice among the houses. That impartiality sets you apart from the others. They watch their step with you because you're fiercely protective of what's yours and you make a terrible enemy. If someone wanted you out of the way, for whatever reason, all they needed to do is start picking off your wolves, one by one. To do that, they'd have to shatter your connection to pack. Your guilt and grief would cripple you." She reached up and cupped his cheek, refusing to back down because this was too important. *He* was too important. "You've said it yourself, you're our alpha, and we are your weakness."

He gazed down at her, arrogance etched in the fine tension running through his body. She recognized the look, it was one he used when dealing with other Kyn and their leaders—distant and cold. It hurt to see it here, when it was just the two of them.

She and her wolf reached down the link they shared, only to come up short at the wall he erected. Bitter disappointment had her throat aching. Even her wolf was pulled up short by his stinging rejection. The emotional hit burrowed deep. "Don't," she whispered.

She dropped her hand and stepped back, out of his reach. She wasn't doing this. If he didn't want to listen, so be it. She didn't need to stick around and try to pound some sense into his thick head. So much for trying to make this whole bonding thing work. The first time she pushed, he shut her out. It wouldn't be long before she was going for his throat just to get a reaction.

"Xander," he rasped, but she ignored him.

The sound of tires on gravel cut through the tense

silence. Warrick glanced through the windows behind her as headlights flickered over the walls.

She moved deeper into the shadows. She tried to stop the trembling in her hands. Hurt filled anger sent cracks through her normally steady control. As her emotions rioted, her wolf crept forward. *They could leave*, her wolf whispered. *Run wild and free, and not come back.*

It was a tempting offer. She snuck a glance at the front door. With Ryuu here, Warrick wouldn't need her. And if he didn't want to listen, fine. But it didn't mean she couldn't go hunting on her own. There was more than one way to protect the pack. The scent trails of their attackers would be relatively fresh. Maybe she'd find something to use there. Plus, she could use the time away from the constant need to make him see her as more than a warm body and rebuild the barriers around her heart.

"Stop." Warrick's low command made her pause.

Without realizing it, she had inched her way to the door. The sound of approaching footsteps kept her focus on the door, waiting for her chance to escape.

"Stop." This time his command held a push of power behind it.

She gritted her teeth as her body obeyed her alpha, freezing in place. Her inability to move spiked her fury, and her wolf snapped and snarled. Striking out in the only way left to her, she sent the firestorm of anger and hurt roaring down their bond. *He would dare use this against her?*

Behind her came a low growl, and the invisible hold on her body disappeared.

As soon as she was free, she spun on her heel and leapt at Warrick.

He raised an arm to block her upraised fist, wrapping his hand around her wrist, and tried to pull her off balance.

Undeterred, she used her momentum to spin her body behind him. With her wrist locked in his grip and her arm wrapped around his waist, it didn't stop her from using her foot to rake a punishing kick against the inside of his knee.

He stumbled forward, but didn't loosen his grip and she fell with him. As his knees hit the floor, she landed, draped over his back, their legs tangled together.

The sound of the door slamming open barely pierced her fury. Startled exclamations sounded behind her, but she ignored them as well.

Before she could free herself, Warrick grabbed her T-shirt and shifted his grip.

Then she was flying through the air to land with a bounce on the couch. Momentarily stunned, she blinked at the shadowed ceiling above her.

Between one blink and the next, his wild face filled her vision. His hair was a riot of blonds and browns, while a red flush ran under his tanned skin. His eyes sparked between wolf and man and his lips were peeled back from his teeth.

She tugged against his hold as he pinned her wrists to the cushion. Before she could get a leg up to push him off, he dropped his lower body, trapping her.

"Knock it off!" he roared.

She stilled, silence settling like a heavy blanket around them. "Don't you ever pull that shit again or, so help me, I will rip your throat out," she whispered harshly, struggling not to scream at him.

No one, not even this man, had the right to take away her free will. Her wolf clawed at her, demanding freedom, and she fought her back down before this situation became any more screwed than it already was.

"I'm sorry." His soft words were followed by someone's sharply indrawn breath. His unexpected words brought both the woman and wolf up short. Alphas didn't apologize for anything. He studied her and something that felt perilously close to fear, trickled through their bond. His fear, not hers. "You were going to leave."

It took effort to set aside her anger and hurt, to listen, really listen to what was coming through that damn bond. Like a radio tuned slightly out of frequency, she picked out his emotions from the chaos of her own.

He held her, saying nothing, but let her explore their connection for answers.

Frustration, anger, need, want, and through them all the cutting edge of fear that she would leave. That she would run and not come back. Neither wolf nor man wanted to take the chance of her leaving when they just managed to get her back. Using his power as alpha to stop her was instinctive. She wasn't able to tell if it was his decision or his wolf's, or both together. However, it didn't matter who made the decision, only that it had been made.

"Never again." She ignored the lump in her throat as she tried to untangle herself from his part of the bond. She met his wary gaze, letting him see that this was a line he would never again cross. "Swear it."

They watched each other, ignoring the audience staring at them from the front door. Emotions flitted over his face as he struggled, wrestling with his need to keep her safe at any cost and her demand. Finally, he gave her a solemn nod. "I swear, Xander. Never again."

She blinked back tears, refusing to allow them to fall. "Get off. You're heavy."

Instead of obeying, his body settled closer, blanketing hers. He dropped his head until it rested against a throw pillow, burying his face against her. His warm breath whispered across her neck. She felt the gentle press of his lips against her pulse then heard his muffled, "No."

"No?"

"No, not moving just yet." He released her wrists and wrapped his arms under and around her, holding her tight.

"I hate to break up this Hallmark moment," Ryuu's voice cut in, "but we have a mess in aisles three and five to clean up."

Warrick's long exhalation sent goose bumps racing down her spine. Tension tightened his body as he slowly released her. He rolled to his feet with lithe grace then held his hand out to her.

She thought about ignoring it but after sneaking a peek at his face, decided against it. Once on her feet, she tugged her hand from his. One of the things she honed through the years was her ability to compartmentalize her emotions, but right now, it was a struggle. Between her and Warrick, the stupid bond was a tangle of frustration, anger, worry, resentment, and helplessness.

He shot her an unreadable look before turning to face his Second and the two wolves with him. "Where's Sebastian?"

"Still cleaning up Neil's mess," Ryuu answered. "I brought Saul and Zeke."

Xander moved out from behind Warrick. "Hey, guys," she greeted casually, pretending nothing unusual had happened.

"Evening, Xander," Saul said, his gritty voice a great addition to his stout frame. An older wolf, he helped train the younger ones and worked with Ryuu wherever their skills could be best utilized.

Zeke crouched next to the dead wizard. "Your work?"

"Gravity's a bitch," Xander answered.

"Not as much as you, darlin'." He sent her a wicked grin, avoiding his alpha's glare, but not Saul's smack to the side his head.

A massive flirt, Zeke had cut quite a path through the younger females. Xander found him amusing. In a few years, he would challenge for the position of the pack's Third. When he did, she'd happily start the betting pool and place her money on him.

"Give me a few minutes before you all head upstairs," she said. "I need to make sure I have the scent of the two in the bedroom."

Turning toward the stairs, she stepped over broken bits of railing and spindles as she headed up. She forced herself to focus on what needed to be done, because somewhere in this mess lay the hints that would set her on the trail of whoever was threatening Warrick.

CHAPTER 11

T HE RISING WIND BLEW THROUGH THE HOLE WHERE WARRICK'S bedroom window once stood, as Xander stepped over the body sprawled in doorway. A hint of rain teased the air but she set it aside and concentrated on gathering the intruders' scents before they disappeared.

Burnt oil with a touch of pine for the one she killed. She moved around the bed and crouched next to Warrick's kill, being careful to avoid the shards of glass littering the floor. Old wood laced with musk.

The scent triggered a memory.

Closing her eyes, she titled her head, trying to bring the elusive scent closer. The slight scrape of a foot against the floor had her opening her eyes and raising her head. Warrick stepped into the bedroom, Ryuu behind him.

"Ryuu, do you remember that situation in Canada a couple years back?" she asked.

Something dark crossed his face. "The one with the woman and little boy?"

She nodded. "I think we just found her ex-husband."

Warrick leaned against the doorjamb as Ryuu made his

way over. She rose and stepped back, giving Ryuu space to confirm the wolf's identity.

He settled on his heels, his eyes narrowing as he studied the body. "I'd have to pull the photos on file, but I think you're right."

"You know him?" Warrick asked.

"Kurt Stevenson," Ryuu answered. "From the Jasper Pack."

"And an all-around bastard," Xander added.

Ryuu got to his feet, his lips curling in disgust. "Used his wife and son as punching bags."

A flash of fury burst through their bond, causing Xander to flinch. Warrick straightened, his eyes bleeding to burning amber. "Why didn't Jasper's alpha step in?"

"He tried," she said. "Unfortunately, Kurt recruited a couple mavericks to ambush the alpha. They put him in a coma for three weeks. Their Second called us. Ryuu sent Sebastian and me up to help."

"You came home with a broken arm," Warrick growled.

She blinked, shocked that he remembered. "Uh, yeah. Sebastian and I got the two recruits, but we got called home before we could corner Kurt. We gave Jasper's Second all the information we had and left it to him to track Kurt down. Last I knew, Kurt had gone maverick."

"The wife and child?" Warrick asked.

"I moved them to a different pack," Ryuu answered. "So long as Kurt was out running around, they needed to be somewhere safe." Calling for outside help meant the Jasper Pack relinquished any say in Ryuu's decisions on the matter.

"We should probably check on them," Xander said.

Ryuu gave a short nod and stepped away, pulling out his cell phone.

A cool push of air through the gaping hole caused her to shiver. Refusing to look at the man in the doorway, she let her gaze skim over the room. Heat rushed to her face when she caught sight of the torn green satin of her panties bunched in front of the dresser. She sliced a quick look at Ryuu's back. Damn it, there was no way he had missed that. She stalked over to snatch them up and stuffed them in the wastebasket against the wall.

A soft male chuckle jerked her head up.

"Come here." Warrick's low demand stroked over her skin.

She curled her fingers until her nails bit into her palm, trying to ignore the urge to walk closer. "I'm fine where I'm at, thanks."

"Don't trust yourself?" he mocked softly.

"Don't trust you," she spat back, her earlier anger burning through her emotional dividers. *It wasn't fair!* Even with his rejection still stinging, she wanted to walk over and bury her face in his chest, and have his arms wrap around her. Memories of their earlier encounter taunted her, ripping at her heart. Damn him for tempting her with the unattainable. Damn her for believing it.

"Little liar," he said.

"They're fine." Ryuu drew their attention. "No threats. No signs of Kurt being anywhere near them."

She folded her arms across her chest and leaned against the dresser, shoving her inner turmoil away. "So why now? Why wait two years to strike back?"

Ryuu shared a look with Warrick. "I'm not so sure he did."

The silent exchange left her stomach tight. She turned to Warrick. "What are you two seeing that I'm not?"

Warrick didn't pay her any attention. Instead, his gaze

was fixed on Ryuu. She could feel the tension in the room rising.

"You want to explain it to her? Or do you want me to do it?" Ryuu's verbal challenge surprised her. Especially after he already read her the riot act for pushing Warrick.

A low, vibrating growl trickled from Warrick, but it failed to drown out Ryuu's next words. "Two wolves and a wizard says they aren't fucking around, Vidis. They want you dead."

"Who's they?" When the two men continued to stare at each other, she stalked to Warrick and shoved her palms against his chest. It didn't even rock him. "Who's they?"

The two men remained silent.

Keeping her frustration in check, she shuffled the bits and pieces together from the last few weeks. "The ones I've had to hunt? They're part of this?" A picture emerged, creating a frustrated fury, underlined with a sinking fear. "Explain to me how tonight is connected to that mess, Warrick."

He flicked his gaze to her but remained mute.

"Start talking before I kill you myself," she hissed.

He wrapped his hands around her wrists, holding her palms against his chest. "We don't know for certain it's connected."

She tugged against his grip until he let go. "You promised no games." She rubbed her wrist absently, stepping back to watch the two men. "That phone call—" Warrick crossed his arms over his chest and remained silent, but she wasn't fooled. "Whoever called you, they're using the Bitten to challenge your leadership." She arranged and rearranged the puzzle pieces. "There's something more, something I'm missing." It teased her, but remained illusive. "'A real alpha protects the pack. Who are you protecting?'" She repeated the words that had echoed through their bond back at the club. There was more, she could hear the whisper of it.

"'How many deaths will it take?'" Warrick's voice was flat as he gave her the rest.

The ominous question drew a chilling finger across her soul. It spoke of someone who wanted Warrick to suffer, to bleed before they took his place. A straight-up challenge she could understand. But this, this was personal. She fought back the fear that this time she may not be able to protect her alpha. "Who would hate you so much?"

Something bleak and heart-rending flashed over his face, so fast that if she wasn't watching him, she would've missed it. "There's no one left who feels that deeply toward me."

His words ripped tiny holes in her heart. He was so wrong. Whether he knew it or not, there was someone who hated him as much as she loved him. Yet, arguing with him would gain her nothing, so she looked to Ryuu. "Why ask a question like that?" she asked him, ignoring Warrick—for now.

Ryuu raised an eyebrow.

"They asked who he was protecting." She began to pace, her brain picking through the facts. "An alpha is the ultimate protector. Pack is their priority. So, why?"

Following her line of reasoning, Ryuu asked, "Better question, who else do they think he's protecting?"

"He's the head of the Lycos House, so maybe the Kyn?" she offered.

"Humans." Warrick's rough answer had them both turning toward him.

"Humans?" She shook her head. "That does not make

sense. Anyone who knows you knows the pack always comes first."

"Unless the pack member used to be human," Ryuu said.

"The Bitten were once human." She stopped next to the second body and faced Warrick. Her alpha's face remained blank. "So whoever they are, they're taking the Bitten to experiment on as a challenge to you. The first three were mavericks, but from the threat, it sounds like the next victim could be a pack member. It's like they're trying to warn you before they attack."

Warrick winced but said nothing.

"We don't have any Bitten in our pack, which is why they've targeted mavericks." Pieces came together, but she was still missing something. "Could it be a maverick who's behind all this?"

"Doubtful," Ryuu answered. "What would they gain? Mavericks rarely work together without self-destructing." He gestured to the two bodies in the room. "Besides, they'd have no compassion for a Bitten wolf. If anything, they consider them a lesser creature."

"Or prey," Warrick added.

Ryuu shrugged. "Perhaps. Regardless, it would take something huge to unite the mavericks."

"Because working together requires a level of trust the mavericks have never shown," Xander said.

"Right." Ryuu drummed his fingers against his thigh. "But it's not just the mavericks we have to worry about." He snuck a look at Warrick before continuing. "We think whoever's behind the phone calls is also behind the partial shifts." He looked at the body at their feet and grimaced. "There've been a few rumors floating around."

That was news to her. "What kind of rumors?"

"The kind that lead to false hope," Warrick answered, his voice cutting. "Claims that there's a cure to being Bitten."

She understood his anger. The Bitten were the most vulnerable wolves of any pack, and for someone to prey upon that weakness was unforgivable. "Who's making the claims?"

"We're trying to find out," Ryuu said. "The problem is, without knowing who's behind it, we don't know where to start looking."

She studied both men, noting their tension. A few more pieces clicked into place. "You think the Talbot Foundation has a hand in this, don't you?"

Warrick shrugged. "We may not have physical proof, but we know they're still experimenting on other Kyn. What's stopping them from taking a run at shifters?"

Only months ago, she had helped Raine rescue Gavin from a demented scientist determined to unlock the genetic secrets of the Kyn. She watched as Raine reduced the hidden lab to a pile of rubble and terrorized the scientist into a blathering mess. Together, they delivered Dr. Lawson to Warrick and the Tribunal for judgment. "Have you looked into Jonah Talbot?"

Jonah Talbot was the power behind the Talbot Foundation and the former employer of the late Dr. Lawson. Even though it was never proven, it was strongly suspected that he might have encouraged Lawson's little science experiments.

Warrick shook his head. "You're starting to sound like Raine. Talbot isn't the only powerful human who would dearly love to replicate the strengths of the Kyn for his own use."

"Perhaps not," she said, "but it's a logical starting point."

"It's not him, Xander," Ryuu said. She turned to him but he held up a hand before she could speak. "I looked for a tie, and there isn't one that I can find, at least right now."

She blew out a breath. "Fine." She studied Kurt's body. "Then we start here and find out what ties these three have to the three Bitten. They have to connect somewhere." She raised her head and met Warrick's gaze. "We find the connection, we find out who wants you dead."

CHAPTER 12

Over an hour later, Mother Nature was vying with Warrick for the top spot on Xander's shit list. She had shifted into her wolf form to better track the scent trail of the attacking wolves, yet the rain was quickly washing away the lingering traces.

The first pale streamers of dawn began to strip layers off the darkness, lending a surreal aspect to the dense foliage and gray clouds. She padded farther into the damp forest surrounding Warrick's home. Beside her, Ryuu's idea of back up, kept pace.

"You know, Xander," Zeke drawled, adjusting his backpack with her clothes in it, "getting some is supposed to put you in your happy place, and you don't seem to be anywhere near your happy place."

She let a low growl trickle out of her throat as she continued tracking the delicate traces of scent hiding in patches along the ground. The combined scents of fur and magic led her to a fallen log, where the smell was stronger. She followed it, winding her way through thick tree trunks, ignoring Zeke's muttered complaints as he scrambled to keep up.

A gust of wind whipped the light rain directly into her face. She sneezed and shook her head, frustration rising as she lost the scent again. Water beaded over her fur, and she lifted her head to scan her surroundings. The rain might be washing the scents away, but that wasn't the only thing she could track. No matter who, or what, made its way through the forest, there would be visible signs of their passing.

Meticulously, she quartered the area. Over by one tree, she found a clump of dark fur caught in the ragged bark. She snagged Zeke's attention with a sharp yip.

"What is it, Lassie?" Zeke dropped into a crouch next to her, dropping an arm around her neck. "Did you find Timmy?"

She gave his chin a sharp nip. Dear gods, she was going to gut this boy wonder someday. Seriously, how did anyone manage to work with him without killing him?

"Hey now," he said, jerking back. "Where's your sense of humor?"

Too bad she couldn't roll her eyes in wolf form. Instead, she bumped her head into his arm as he rubbed his chin. Then she set a paw on the tree trunk near the clump of fur.

His humor faded and his eyes narrowed as he scanned the area around them. He pointed at a spot a few feet away. "There's broken branches over there."

Sure enough, thin branches, about shoulder height, were sporting the white marks of recent breaks. Someone hadn't been at all careful as they barged their way through the forest.

She bumped her head against his shoulder again, then pawed at the backpack. It was time for her to get back on two feet.

Zeke shrugged off the pack. "I'll wait for you over there." He turned and walked away.

She was grateful for his small courtesy. Most shifters had no problem with nudity, but maybe she'd been on her own too long, because she preferred privacy when she shifted. Xander waited until his back was turned then called the change. The twist of bones and muscles sliced hot fire across her nerves as she regained her human form.

It wasn't as fast or as smooth as normal, since she was functioning on roughly three hours of sleep and her battered body was still repairing the damage she sustained earlier. Yet, only minutes passed before she was crouching naked as a jaybird, as the drizzle turned into a downpour, flattening her hair against her skull. Grumbling under her breath, she scrambled into the yoga pants and another of Warrick's T-shirts before pulling on one of his sweatshirts. Her boots were at the house, which meant she would have to go barefoot. She grabbed the backpack and made her way over to Zeke.

"I think we're close to the road." She tossed the backpack at the younger man when he turned to face her. "They were staying on the outside edge of the park, instead of utilizing the heavier cover inside. Chances are there's a car out there."

"Not exactly smart, were they?" Zeke slipped the backpack's straps over his shoulders.

She cocked her hip, tilted her head and tapped her chin with a thoughtful finger. "Let's see. They decided to attack the Northwest alpha with a pair of wolves, a shotgun, and a wizard." She straightened and grimaced. "I'm thinking intelligence wasn't their strong suit."

"They weren't pack." Zeke's statement was certain, serious.

She slanted him a look. "No, they weren't."

She made her way through the forest, careful to note the small signs indicating the earlier passage of the dead trio. Broken branches, smears of dirt against a rock, crushed leaves—each an indicator they were on the right path.

The forest thinned and the dark ribbon of the road began to peek through the falling curtain of rain. They continued on in silence for a bit longer until they paralleled the road. The wind had picked up, causing the rain to lash out in bursts. She caught sight of the car, even as Zeke touched her shoulder. He shrugged off the backpack, pushing it under the thick brush.

Motioning for Zeke to take the right, she moved to the left. The older nondescript sedan seemed lifeless, surrounded by an abandoned air. She was fairly certain no one lurked in the predawn shadows nearby, but it never hurt to be on the safe side.

Together, she and Zeke moved up opposite sides of the car, staying low to keep out of the rearview mirrors' line of sight. The rain was becoming bothersome now, the heavy downpour obscuring her vision. Peering through a fogged window, she tried to see inside but couldn't make anything out.

Reaching the driver's door, she turned just enough to slide her fingers around the cold edge of the handle then yanked the door open. The outside air swept through the car, bringing hints of stale sweat, fur, and the ionic sting of magic. Aside from the sound of the rain pinging against the roof, silence greeted her. "Clear," she called to Zeke.

"Clear," he responded from the back passenger side.

She rose to her feet and looked at him across the glistening roof. "That was anticlimactic."

He gave her a wicked grin. "Two times in one night? You must be so disappointed."

She flashed him a smile that was all teeth. "I think you're jealous."

"Jealous?"

"Yep, because I got some and you didn't."

"Please!" he snorted, but a tint of red rode his cheeks before he ducked inside the car.

Her smile softened, becoming more natural, as she slipped into the driver's seat, closing the door behind her. She pulled down the visor, hoping to find a rental agreement, something, and got...nothing. "I dare you to tell Warrick he's anticlimactic." She watched Zeke through the rearview mirror.

"Yeah, I think I'll pass." His voice took on a sharp edge as he said, "I'll let you do it. He's got enough people pissing him off lately."

She stilled and turned around to meet his gaze. "Including me?"

Shock widened his eyes. "I didn't say that! I'm not suicidal, Xander." He dropped his gaze from hers and rubbed his neck.

She waited, not blinking.

He blew out a short breath, squirmed a bit, then settled. "Look, whatever's going on between you and Vidis, that's between you two. But there's something more happening around here."

Zeke's answer made her wonder what he'd seen that she hadn't. "Explain."

"I'm not blind, and contrary to popular belief, I really do pay attention to what's happening." His chest expanded as he took a deep breath. "You've killed three wolves in two weeks. I was on the second clean up crew. I saw what was left." Sympathy flashed across his face and she knew she hadn't been able to hide her wince from him. "They weren't normal Ferals, so what the hell is going on?"

Wariness nipped at her. She shifted in the seat to face him and folded her arms, studying the younger wolf. It was pointless to lie, he'd smell it, but that didn't mean he needed the whole truth. "Someone's promising the Bitten a cure."

His mouth dropped open in shock. It took him a second before he asked, "A cure? Seriously?"

She nodded and settled with her back to the steering wheel.

He gave a low whistle. "Wow, that's…"

"Cruel?" she offered.

"I was going to say twisted, actually." His gaze narrowed. "That would explain why Ryuu has me hacking into some of the Bitten's chat rooms."

She blinked then frowned. "Chat rooms?" Zeke was brilliant with computers, which was why he worked in Taliesin's IT Investigation department.

"I forgot, you were in Arizona." He leaned forward and folded his arms on the passenger seat's headrest. "A couple of months ago, Taliesin had a group of us start monitoring online groups they suspected might be Kyn. The goal is to make sure these groups don't reveal too much."

"I bet that's going over well."

He rubbed his chin back and forth over his forearms. "Yeah, like a lead balloon. I know the older generation hates change, but…"

"But soon the world will be too small to hide the Kyn," she finished softly.

"Right." He sighed. "The thing is, a month later, Ryuu

asked me to start monitoring some chat rooms frequented by known Bitten wolves."

"Smart man."

He flashed her a small grin. "He likes to utilize my awesome nerd powers." He paused, studying her as rain continued to pound against the roof. "If what you're saying about a cure is true, it would explain some things."

"Like what?"

"A few weeks ago, there was a conversation centered around some science paper. It was published years ago in an obscure medical journal and discussed the possibility of mutating DNA to create specific characteristics. The conversation began to get into more recent scientific discoveries and morphed into a what-if discussion."

She frowned. "What-if what?"

"What if science could create an antidote to a werewolf's bite."

"Seriously?"

He nodded, all earlier traces of humor gone. "There was even one thread that branched out into conspiracy theories of possible government research using Kyn as test subjects."

Even as chills ran down her spine, she kept her tone even. "That story has become an urban myth for the Kyn."

"Sort of like a secret black-ops group of Kyn that takes out the trash, right?" he chided, certainty making him appear years older.

Xander held his gaze and said nothing.

He shrugged. "Look, normally I'd agree with you, but right before Vidis headed down to Arizona, the members starting dropping off line."

She bit her lip, thinking. "Most Kyn would never put themselves at the mercy of the human government."

"You forget, Xander," Zeke said, his voice unusually serious, "the Bitten aren't really Kyn. They're humans who've been changed into what they consider monsters. If everything you ever were, was taken away, and you were given an option to get it back, wouldn't you take it, regardless of the consequences?"

In a heartbeat—and that was the problem. Someone out there, human or Kyn, was exploiting that hope, using it to lead the Bitten to a horrific death. "Is there any way to get the names of those who were in that chat room?"

"Unfortunately, the ones we've been able to track were logging in from public computers," he answered.

Another dead end. Every time she thought they might have something solid, it disappeared in a puff of smoke. She sighed. "Let's see if there's anything here that can help."

The next few minutes passed in silence as they systematically searched the car. The glove compartment contained a map, but nothing else. She ran her hands between the seats, finding only a few petrified French fries and an empty gum wrapper. Behind her, Zeke was stretched along the back seat as he searched under the front passenger seat.

"Found something." His excitement was muffled against the faux leather.

She turned around to face him as he pushed upright, holding a small black rectangle in his hand. "What's that?"

"GPS." He grinned. "Which means if I can get this back to Taliesin, I can get you a map of everywhere they went."

She reached between the seats and grabbed his face to give him a loud smacking kiss on his forehead. "You rock, Zeke!" Maybe they had finally caught a break.

He pulled back, a red stain spreading under his skin as he squirmed in the back seat. "Um, yeah, I try."

She turned back around, hiding her smile at his reaction. "Let's head back. If I'm lucky I can make it home in time to change before I have to report in to the office."

They headed back out into the rain and made their way back to Warrick's. Zeke stopped and picked up the backpack. "You know," he said. "If you and Vidis had waited two more days, I would've won the pool."

She lunged toward him with a growl, but he darted off, his laughter trailing behind him.

CHAPTER 13

A few hours later, Xander stood with her eyes closed, half dozing under the pounding spray of a hot shower. Tight muscles slowly unclenched and the exhaustion dogging her began creeping in, leaving her in a semi-conscious state. She and Zeke had returned to Warrick's to catch the tail end of the cleanup operation. Saul and Ryuu took the bodies away to an undisclosed location. Since Warrick's presence was required at Taliesin's that morning, he had, after much growling, agreed to take Zeke with him so the boy wonder could start pulling information from the GPS unit.

Xander was grateful for the reprieve, even more so when she realized she wouldn't have to sit through a meeting with Taliesin's head honchos. Normally, standing at Warrick's side while he dealt with the other three Kyn head of houses was an enjoyable challenge. This morning, her head was a mess and she needed space and time to get it straightened out.

"Wake up, baby, and come down for coffee," her mother's voice called through the door.

Sighing, she turned off the water, opened the shower

door and grabbed a towel. She could have gone home, but her mom's place was closer.

The scent of freshly brewed coffee, baked cinnamon, and icing curled around her, though the luscious scent of cinnamon brought a cascade of images of Warrick and their night together. Her body trembled under the memory of his possessive touch and the needs he managed to bring to life. For a moment, she indulged in the delicious memories before shoving them into their imaginary box and slamming the lid tight.

She finished toweling off and dragged on the clothes she left behind a couple months ago. The black fitted cargo pants had decorative straps with bronze buckles down the legs. They went well with the black-and-red stripped T-shirt she pulled on before using her towel to wipe the condensation from the mirror. She finger-combed her wet hair and sighed. There was no way to hide the dark circles under her eyes or the washed out tone of her skin, which meant her mom was going to pry.

Folding the towel over the edge of the shower door, she opened the door and headed into the kitchen. Stepping onto the cool tile, her toes curled. "Sorry, Mom. Long night."

Standing a few inches taller than her daughter, with hair a pale, ash-blonde, Talon Cade set down the cup of coffee and rose to embrace Xander. In a periwinkle-blue sweater and light-blue jeans, she could easily be mistaken for Xander's older sister. Most Kyn looked younger, some by decades, than their actual age. If a shifter managed not to get themselves killed in a dominance fight, they could live hundreds of years.

Her mom's arms tightened as Xander buried her face against her mother's neck. For just a moment, she wasn't the pack's Tracker or a dreaded Wraith, but a very loved daughter. Emotion rose in a choking wave and she squeezed her eyes closed.

Talon held her, rubbing small comforting circles on her back. As Xander loosened her arms, her mother pulled back and cupped her hands around Xander's face, cradling it. "You're going to tell me what happened." Maternal love and demand, all tied together.

Xander gave a jerky nod.

"Good." A gentle pat then she was moving to the counter. When she turned back, she handed Xander a cup of coffee. "Go sit at the table. I'll bring you a roll."

Xander settled into one of the spindle-backed chairs as her mom set a freshly baked cinnamon roll in front of her.

"Eat," her mom ordered before taking the seat next to her.

Xander obediently took a bite. The roll melted the moment it hit her tongue. She groaned. "Why didn't I inherit your ability to cook, instead of Dad's nose for scents?" She tried to cook but, even with her mom's help, her attempts at culinary creations turned disastrous.

Talon's lip curved. "It's not who you are, baby." She took a sip of her coffee and watched her daughter, letting the silence settle.

Xander picked up her cup and took a sip. She let her eyes close as the caffeine-infused ambrosia hit her tongue.

"So how was Warrick?"

Her mother's quiet question had her snorting coffee through her nose as she choked. She got herself under control and glared at the woman smiling serenely back at her.

"You're just down right evil, Mom," she muttered.

Talon's soft chuckle reminded Xander of all those times

she and Ethan had thought themselves so smart, only to find out their mom was still a step ahead. "I may not have your dad's sensitivity to scents, but it was a little hard to miss who you've been spending time with, dear."

There was no fighting the blush that bloomed in her cheeks. "He's fine," she mumbled.

"Yes, he is," her mom answered with a hum.

Horrified, she stared at her mother. "Oh gods, Mom! You're mated!"

"Mated, not dead." She took a sip of her coffee, her teasing grin fading as she set her cup on the table. "But you, sweetheart, are bonded to the most powerful male in the Northwest. I'm worried."

Xander dropped her gaze to her cup, turning it in place on the table. Here, in the home she grew up in, safe with the mother who stood beside her through so much, she admitted, "So am I."

"I'd be more concerned if you weren't, baby," her mother chided. "There's a part of me that wishes you had chosen someone less..."

"Complicated?" Xander stopped her restless movement to look at her mom.

Talon shook her head. "No, I think dominant is the word I'm looking for."

Xander didn't bother to stop the small smile that broke through at her mother's choice of word. "He's an alpha, Mom. Dominant is one of the requirements for the job."

"Yes, it is," Talon answered. "But you put two strong-minded wolves together and no matter how much they love each other, someone has to bend or they both break. I just don't want to watch you break."

A mix of resentment and love rose, leaving Xander floundering. She dropped her hands to her lap to hide her clenching fists. "I don't break," she said, pushing the words past her tight chest.

Something close to sympathy flashed over her mother's face. "That wasn't what I meant."

"Then what did you mean?"

Talon sighed. "Do you love Warrick?"

Frowning, Xander sat back in her chair, crossing her arms across her chest. "That's a stupid question, Mom. Of course, I do."

"Do you love him enough to be the person he needs you to be?"

Confused, Xander said, "You're not making sense."

Talon studied her daughter, the rare seriousness in her expression sending a nervous tremor through Xander. "I love you, Xander."

"I hear a but in there," she muttered.

"But," her mother continued, "you've spent your life walking your own road, answering only to a few. You do what you feel is right to protect those around you."

"And that's a bad thing?"

"No, baby, it's not. But it makes me worry that you won't be able to allow your mate to lead if you think he's in danger. Warrick's not just our alpha, but *the* alpha. His every action, every decision is under constant scrutiny by those under him and by those holding the same position in the Kyn community."

Xander bit her lip, starting to understand what her mom was getting at. "And you think I weaken him?" It hurt like hell to think that those who loved her best saw her as Warrick's weakness. How many others saw her this way? How many other pack members saw Warrick's decision to bond with her as a horrible mistake? Maybe he was right to keep distance between them. Maybe he saw the same thing.

Something must have shown in her face, because her mom made a noise and was out of her chair before Xander could blink. Talon knelt in front of her and caught Xander's face in her soft palms, keeping Xander's gaze on hers. "You listen to me, Xander Cade, you are not a weakness. Do you hear me?"

"But you just said—"

"Don't you put words in my mouth, child." Talon's pale green eyes bore into hers.

"I don't understand," she whispered.

Talon leaned her forehead against Xander's. "You're too protective. That's what I'm trying to get you to see. You'd try to protect him at the risk of your own life."

Xander blinked, trying to process how that was such a bad thing.

Pulling back, her mother sat back on her heels. "Do you think I don't know?"

Confused, she asked, "Don't know what?"

"Bonding occurs when one wolf's life is in danger and their mate ties them together to save them. Who was dying, Xander?"

There was fear in her mother's voice and Xander suddenly realized she hadn't hid things quite as well as she had thought. "Me," she admitted on a whisper.

Talon closed her eyes and took a shuddering breath. "That's what I was afraid of." She opened her eyes, and Xander could see the tears fiercely held in check. "You're my daughter and I could have lost you. Who were you protecting?"

"Him," Xander answered with brutal honesty. She hadn't wanted what was happening to her to touch Warrick. It had been her choice to start cutting pack ties, not his.

Her mom tilted her head. "I'm assuming he had a few issues with that."

The wry comment tugged a small grin free. "Just a few."

Her mother rose and wrapped her arms tight around her. "I'll forever be grateful he chose to save you." Releasing her, Talon stepped back and grasped Xander's chin. "You need to let him protect you as much as you need to protect him."

"It's not that easy, Mom."

Talon smiled blissfully. "Nothing worth having is easy, baby. Remember that."

Before Xander could answer, her cell phone rang. Rising from her chair, she gave her mom a quick, fierce hug then snagged the phone off the counter. "Cade."

"Hey, Xander. You up for a little fun?" Raine asked.

"Depends on your definition of fun." She turned and blew her mom a kiss before heading back down the hall.

"Let's start with some B&E."

Xander pushed into her old room and sat on the bed, cradling the phone between her ear and shoulder as she pulled on her boots. "And where will this little soirée be taking place?" She stood and reached for her jacket as Raine rattled off an address. "Why does that sound familiar?"

"It's Eilers's place," Raine answered.

Xander stilled. Neither she nor Warrick had given Raine much information the night before. "Raine, how'd you get his name?"

There was a snort from the other end of the line. "I got my ass pulled into the office this morning and informed by his royal furriness that I was to go with you to this particular address to uncover what ever I could." Raine's exasperation came through loud and clear. "Would it hurt him to say please occasionally?"

"Probably." Xander wasn't sure how she felt about Warrick's order.

"So you in?"

"As if you have to ask," she said, the familiar excitement of the hunt beginning to bubble in her veins.

"Great. I'll meet you there in about fifteen?"

"I'll be there."

Raine hung up without saying goodbye, and Xander grabbed her keys from her dresser. Running down the hall, she gave her mom a quick kiss. "Work. Got to go."

"Be safe, baby."

She flashed her mom a wicked grin. "Always."

CHAPTER 14

Warrick had only been in his office at Taliesin a couple of hours and already his wolf was clawing in an agitated bid for freedom. He hadn't wanted to leave Xander, not when things were so...strained. Damn it, he'd been so sure that once he sated himself with her scent and skin, this itchy need to keep her close would become more manageable.

He pushed out of his chair to stalk over to the window overlooking the backside of Taliesin. Mother Nature crowded the parking lot, blocking out the neighboring buildings, and providing the illusion of isolation.

As the Chief Financial Officer of Taliesin Security, he could have picked an office with a better view. Yet, he enjoyed the one he had. The fact that his office was as far away from the other executive offices as possible was an added bonus. It limited the amount of interruptions he was forced to deal with whenever he decided to make an actual appearance.

If the choice had been his, he wouldn't have left the comfort of his home office. Unfortunately, remnants from this morning's altercations were still being cleared out.

Besides, his pending meeting was better served in the impersonal confines of Taliesin than the security of his home.

His wolf pushed forward, edging out the man. He could feel the change hovering. Between his lack of sleep, his chaotic emotions where Xander was concerned, and trying to unravel the bloody puzzle behind the threats, his civilized veneer was starting to crack.

Starting to crack? Those fissures were so deep, he wondered how anyone could miss them. It took so little lately to widen the gap between animal instinct and human intellect, it was a wonder he wasn't spending all of his time furry and on four feet.

He ran one hand through his hair and blew out a breath, recalling Xander's furious face as he kept her from leaving his house. That was one prime example of his unraveling control. Forcing compliance was a great way to show your mate how much you respected her.

He turned from the window and moved back to his desk, taking his chair. He propped his arms on the desk and lowered his head into his hands. Even now, though distance separated them, he could feel her. It amazed him that, even through her lingering anger at his actions, she was trying to find an excuse for him. He couldn't bear to tell her that there was no excuse.

He groaned. He was going to lose her. A sickening sense of emptiness flooded his stomach and he closed his eyes. His need to keep her safe meant he would continue to make mistakes. How many more would she forgive before she left for good? Pressing his fingers against his closed lids, he fought back his urge to howl with frustration.

The buzz of his phone cut through his thoughts and earned a heated glare.

"Yes?" He didn't try to hide the edge of the wolf riding his voice.

Unperturbed, Taliesin's ever-efficient receptionist, Rachel, answered smoothly, "Your ten o'clock appointment is here, Mr. Vidis."

He glanced at the wall clock. Fifteen minutes early. Interesting. "I'll be available in ten." He carefully set the receiver back in the cradle.

Leaning back in his chair, he considered the situation. The man currently cooling his heels under Rachel's watchful eye wouldn't be pleased. No dominant wolf liked to be made to wait. However, he was in Warrick's territory. His territory, his rules.

Except that Ryuu, who was still out with Saul on trash duty, had made him promise to call in reinforcements, just in case. Considering how shaky his control was, it was probably safer to follow his Second's advice. Safer for this visiting maverick, at least.

Warrick punched in Sebastian's extension. After two rings, his Third's voice came over the line. "Hey, boss man."

"Sebastian, you available for the next hour?"

"Sure. What do you need?"

"There's a petitioning maverick waiting up front. Would you be so kind as to show him in at ten o'clock?"

"Ten o'clock?" Sebastian asked. "You got it."

Warrick hung up the phone and pulled over the file Ryuu had prepared on his pending visitor. It was thinner than Warrick would have liked. The request to meet had been rather abrupt, and Warrick knew Ryuu wasn't happy with the limited timeframe he'd been given to research the man.

He opened it and began to scan the report. Dan Vicks. No photo. Ryuu had been pulling the maverick's passport photo when Neil Eilers had decided to hunt down his ex-girlfriend.

Dan had made his way to Oregon via northern Canada. He had chosen to live outside pack and taken the path of maverick. His work history was fairly straightforward. He appeared to be a contracted consultant with a large technical company, working up and down the coast. Single, no family listed as emergency contact or dependents.

Even with the short time frame, Ryuu managed to touch base with wolves in some of the other Canadian packs. One wolf in British Columbia's Kenai Pack had described Dan as "a tough son of a bitch who seemed friendly enough." A wolf from Alaska's Stonehammer Pack had offered his two cents, calling him "a hard-working fellow."

Neither Kenai's nor Stonehammer's alphas relayed any problems. Ryuu noted that Dan tended to gravitate to other mavericks, but that wasn't unusual. Most lone wolves were more comfortable around non-pack wolves.

Warrick closed the folder. Chances were good Dan Vicks was simply looking for permission to stay in Motoki's territory as he conducted business.

Normally, Warrick would have no problems granting such a request, but the last few weeks were far from normal. Neither he nor his wolf, were happy about letting an unknown maverick into his territory.

The sound of footfalls moving down the hallway had him tucking the folder into a desk drawer. He stood up and walked around his desk as the footsteps stopped in front of his door. He took a deceptively relaxed pose, leaning against the desk's edge, his hands resting behind him as Sebastian's firm knock sounded.

"Enter," he called.

The door opened, Sebastian's broad-shouldered body

blocking Warrick's view. Sebastian stepped forward, moving aside to let the man behind him through.

The half-remembered scent hit Warrick first, like a fist to his solar plexus. His breath stilled as shock rocketed through him. Every muscle locked into place as he fought not to visibly react. There was no way to stop the drastic rise in tension as Dan Vicks stopped inside the office, watching Warrick warily.

Under his skin, where Sebastian and Dan couldn't see, Warrick's wolf laid his ears flat and curled his lips back from his teeth. Warrick felt his nails burst through his skin and dig deep into the underside of the desk's edge.

It took every shred of discipline he possessed not to lunge at Dan and sink his teeth into his throat. The faint brush of Xander's wolf gave him breathing room.

"Sebastian, leave." Warrick forced the command past his pounding fury. He didn't take his stare off the wolf standing across from him, even as the door shut with an audible click. The tension in the office rose to a screaming pitch and still Warrick didn't trust himself to react. Instead, he began to restrict the bond between him and Xander, his attention centered on the man standing in his office.

"Warrick." The man nodded without breaking eye contact, his dark brown hair, streaked with black, shifting with the movement.

Unprepared for the stinging slice of pain at hearing his name from a voice he long thought dead, Warrick's anger rushed forward, burying the heartache deep.

"Dan Vicks?" he ground out, refusing to look away from the eerily familiar, hazel gaze.

"Would you have agreed to see me if I had given you the name Dmitri Vidis, brother?"

"I have no brother," Warrick snarled. "My brother died the day he betrayed our parents and the pack."

The skin around Dmitri's eyes tightened. Amber flashed briefly before he finally dropped his gaze, conceding Warrick's dominance. "Betrayal is a matter of perception, isn't it?" The rough edge of his question revealed the predator crouched under human skin.

Half-remembered resentment and pain flared, and Warrick bit out, "You chose to turn your back on us."

"I recall it more the other way around," Dmitri said coldly. "My family and pack turned their backs on me."

Warrick stared unblinkingly at him.

Dmitri's lips twisted into a bitter smile as he looked at Warrick, his gaze just beyond Warrick's shoulder, offering no challenge. "We shall agree to disagree."

Warrick made a conscious effort to uncurl his hands from the desk's edge, forcing his wolf's presence back. No matter how tempted he was, he couldn't rip Dmitri's throat out. No challenge had been offered. The slick bastard managed to escape an execution all those years ago because there had been no evidence of his supposed actions. And afterward, when the bodies had been buried and a new alpha installed, Warrick found no trace of his brother. Eventually, he assumed the traitor had taken his place among the numerous causalities.

Too damn bad he couldn't have stayed dead.

For a moment, Warrick cursed his sense of honor that kept him from destroying the wolf standing in front of him. "What do you want?" he bit out, hanging onto civility by a hair's breath.

"Not to rehash history," Dmitri answered.

Warrick straightened and his wolf was pleased when the other wolf took an involuntary step back. "I'm uncertain if you're arrogant or just a fool for coming here."

Dmitri scowled and lifted his chin, but didn't rise to the taunt. "I'm here to petition the Northwest alpha." Forced neutrality coated every word.

Warrick swallowed his rage, stuffing it into a tight, dark spot in the corner of his soul. Mentally, he reached out and grabbed onto the familiar detachment he used in his dealings with the other heads of house and humans. The cold logic was unexpectedly comforting.

"I'm listening." He gestured to one of the chairs in front of his desk. "Have a seat." He waited until Dmitri was seated before he forced himself to move around his desk. The hair on the back of his neck stood at attention as he turned his back on his brother.

He took his time settling behind his desk. With his riotous emotions ruthlessly held in check, he studied Dmitri.

They had always been close in height, with Warrick standing a bit taller and Dmitri carrying more muscle through his chest and shoulders. Where Warrick had their mother's unique blend of browns and blondes, Dmitri echoed their father's darker blacks and browns. It was hard to look into the shared hazel eyes and not feel something.

Yet, where Warrick could easily blend into the crowd, Dmitri would stand out. Even now, he feigned a relaxed pose, stretching his legs to cross at the ankles and folding his hands over his stomach. Dressed in linen slacks and a silk shirt, he carried himself with a casual elegance, unmarred by an edge of arrogance. That arrogance had been the motivation behind Dmitri's choice to leave their old pack in Russia and go maverick.

Questions surged in Warrick's mind. Questions he

didn't dare let loose, because once he did, there was no way either of them would leave this office without bloodshed. His wolf prowled against his self-imposed restraints and he forced himself to think past his emotions.

Setting his elbows on the desk, he laced his fingers under his chin, and kept his face blank. "Are you petitioning as Dan Vicks or Dmitri Vidis?"

"Dmitri no longer exists," he answered. "Dan Vicks is a legitimate businessman."

"What does Dan Vicks want from the Northwest alpha then?"

"Recognition."

Warrick raised an eyebrow but said nothing.

"I've been approached by a group of mavericks and elected as their representative."

"Representative? Since when have the mavericks needed a representative?"

"Since this particular group of mavericks decided to create their own pack," Dmitri answered smoothly.

Warrick dropped his hands and leaned back in his chair. Dmitri's request was highly unusual and not one Warrick could have predicted. "Why the change of heart? Mavericks are lone wolves for a reason. Pack structure isn't to their liking, nor do they do well within it. Why do they feel the sudden need to establish their own pack?"

"It's not sudden, nor are they considering it a change of heart. More as a strategic move."

"Why?" Warrick asked, suspicion beginning to creep in.

"Protection," Dmitri answered. "The world has become a much smaller place, making it harder and harder to live our lives undetected by humans. There are six of us who would like to establish a formal pack with our own territory."

Paranoia raised its ugly head. Dmitri's request on the heels of the current shitstorm was making him twitchy. "How are your fellow wolves coming to the attention of the humans?"

Dmitri snorted. "Do you have any idea how difficult it is to find an isolated area to run in?"

Warrick raised an eyebrow. "Isolated areas aren't hard to find on this coast."

"No, but it would be simpler having our own territory, where we didn't have to worry about some nosy human and their camera phone."

"If that's the case, why doesn't each maverick just petition the local alphas?" Warrick pressed.

"Too many politics. We're dominants and you know as well as I do, how many issues bringing in an outside dominant will cause. No local alpha's willing to risk the possible upheaval in their packs." He paused. "And none of us want to disrupt the local packs."

Warrick studied Dmitri. He wished he could believe Dmitri's altruistic answer, but their shared history made him wonder. "It's never stopped you before." Heat curled around the edges of his words.

Dmitri pushed out of his chair and to his feet. "I'm not here to revisit old arguments."

Warrick leaned back, deliberately keeping his body relaxed in the face of Dmitri's aggression. "As an alpha, it's my job to ensure the safety of my packs. I know Dmitri Vidis, but I don't know Dan Vicks." He caught sight of Dmitri's fists curling as his words found their mark.

"If I had to come to you as your brother, you would've torn out my throat," he growled, temper rising along his cheekbones. "I haven't forgotten that day either, Warrick. You wanted to kill me."

No matter how hard he tried, Warrick could no longer keep the storm of memories locked behind ice. He shoved his chair back so violently it hit the wall behind him with a resounding thunk. Pressing his palms flat against the solid wood of his desk, he fought the urge to leap over the wide surface and take his brother down in a hail of teeth and claws. "I should've killed you."

Dmitri rocked to the balls of his feet and leaned forward. "For what? For begging our father to save my mate? He was a hypocrite!" he growled. "Had it been Mom in the same situation, he would've moved heaven and earth, worked with whoever or whatever it took to save her. But because my mate was human, he refused!"

"You're a fool," Warrick snarled. "You chose a human for a mate. You were so blind you couldn't see the threat right in front of you. She set you up and you fell for it."

"She had nothing to do with those who attacked our pack," Dmitri argued. "You have no more proof now than you did all those years ago."

"How would you know? You disappeared!" Warrick snapped. "You chose her over our family. Our parents' blood is the only proof I've ever needed."

Dmitri spun away from him, muttering Russian oaths under his breath. He stalked to the windows, his shoulders rising and falling as he visibly fought for calm.

There was an ache in Warrick's chest and it took him a moment to recognize it—the urge to comfort. It was startling to find the need to reach out still existed. But then he remembered the brutally butchered bodies of his parents awash in the rivers of blood from fallen wolves and squashed it relentlessly.

"It was a mistake to come here," Dmitri said, his back still to Warrick.

Blowing out a breath, Warrick tried to reclaim the impartiality of being an alpha. If they had been human, the past would remain the past. But they weren't. They were Kyn and sixty-five plus years wasn't as long as it sounded. Old suspicions and simmering resentments lingered, and he didn't think Dmitri's sudden reappearance would bring the answers any closer.

If he couldn't let this go, Warrick would lose the last member of his family. Again. They might never be close—there was too much between them for that—but perhaps a truce of sorts would work. The image of his mother's face swam before him, her voice chiding, "You are brothers, *moy volk*, never forget that."

"We'll agree to disagree," Warrick repeated his brother's earlier words.

Dmitri turned from the window, wary suspicion narrowing his eyes. "The petition?"

"I'll consider it." He held up a hand when Dmitri opened his mouth. "I'll need to run it by the other alphas to get their input. Then we'll have to decide where a possible territory can be created."

Dmitri shut his mouth and gave him a short nod. "How long before we would have an answer?"

"A week, maybe a little longer."

"Thank you." The words were gruff. Dimitri made his way back to the front of Warrick's desk. They eyed each other over the wide surface as the silence stretched. "I was surprised to find out you had taken this position."

Warrick didn't respond, uncertain where his brother was going.

A wry smile played along Dmitri's lips. "Do the other leaders know they've asked the wolf to guard the henhouse?"

"Is that how you see it?" Warrick asked.

A short laugh escaped Dmitri. "You never had the patience to deal with fools or the subtleties of politics. How did you end up the public face of the Northwest packs?"

"No one else wanted the job," Warrick answered dryly.

His brother laughed, stepped back, then inclined his head. "I'll wait to hear from you. I'll leave my number with your receptionist."

Warrick watched his brother open the heavy door and walk out. Sebastian, who was waiting in the hall, slipped inside and leaned against the doorjamb, enabling him to see both the hallway and the office.

He waited until they could no longer hear Dmitri's footsteps. "Is everything okay, Vidis?"

Since the office was soundproof, Warrick could keep his unexpected family reunion a secret. At least for now. He considered Sebastian's question. Was he all right? If his chaotic emotions were anything to go by, the answer was definite no. He couldn't tell if his wariness was a result of Dmitri's sudden reappearance or a warning.

"I'm fine," he answered absently, knowing his Third would likely see through the lie.

Sebastian didn't say anything, just waited.

"I'll be fine," he growled. The walls of his office seem to close in as his wolf pushed against the confines of his skin. He needed space to unravel his emotions from his logic.

"You've got another meeting," Sebastian said, his tone deferential, a reminder that other responsibilities required his attention.

Later, Warrick soothed his wolf. The beast paced, then sent the image of Xander, running in wolf form next to them, in silent demand.

The reminder of his mate had him checking the bond.

He winced. It was shut down tight. She was going to be beyond pissed. He relaxed his psychic hold and his jumbled emotions filled the bond. He felt her pause and he waited, unconsciously holding his breath. A second ticked by. Then another. Air shuddered out of his lungs as warm tendrils of acceptance echoed back, calming his heart and mind.

Warrick's shoulders relaxed and his wolf settled.

"Ready?" Sebastian asked.

He gave his waiting Third a nod and followed him out the door.

CHAPTER 15

XANDER PULLED ONTO THE DIRT DRIVE AND PARKED NEXT TO THE mud-splattered green SUV in front of Neil Eilers's trailer in Holbrook. She shut the Ducati's engine off, removed her helmet, and waited for Raine to make her way over. The taller woman stood next to her as Xander straddled her bike. Together, they studied the structure in front of them.

"Not quite what I expected," Xander commented.

The trailer tried to hide its age behind artfully arranged flowerbeds and a relatively new layer of siding. The yard was neatly tended, indicating someone tried hard to make it a home. There was a small sitting area tucked next to the tiny porch. A potted flower nestled in the middle of a round metal table. Similar trailers sat on either side, showing the same care and pride.

Raine cocked her head. "Didn't he just move here?"

"Yeah." Xander got off her bike. "The information I had said he was working construction and moved in about seven months ago. Before that, he bounced around."

Raine glanced around as they moved toward the door. "We have a lookie-loo on the left."

Xander let Raine get a step ahead, just in case. The squeak of a screen door cut through the quiet morning. Xander turned and watched a little blue-haired old woman purposefully make her way down her steps. Dressed in dark slacks and a delicately patterned shirt, she walked across her lawn until she stood at the edge where grass met gravel.

"Young ladies," she called.

Raine's quiet snicker as she continued to work on the door lock made Xander grin.

"Yes, ma'am?" Xander answered. Her mother would have been so proud of her manners.

"Mr. Eilers isn't at home. Is there something I can help you with?" The older woman's gaze switched between Xander and Raine.

"No, ma'am." Xander kept her tone respectful as she faced the elderly neighbor. "I'm sorry, Ms..."

"Mrs. Peterson."

"Mrs. Peterson," Xander repeated. "Unfortunately, Neil's not coming back."

Mrs. Peterson's face paled, her lips thinning as she brought her hands up to press against her stomach. "What happened?"

Xander reached out to lay a gentle hand over Mrs. Peterson's tightly laced fingers. There was no mistaking her worry as anything but genuine. "Have the police stopped by to speak to you yet?" She felt the tremor that ran through the papery skin under her hands, spreading until Mrs. Peterson began to shake. "Come on," Xander urged, wrapping her arm around the frail shoulders. "Let's sit down." She guided the older woman to one of the chairs beside the metal table.

On the porch, Raine got the door open and now paused. Xander looked up and gave a short shake of her head. She could hear Raine's sigh as she leaned against the doorjamb. It was probably a bit over cautious, but she didn't want her friend going inside alone.

With Mrs. Peterson safely ensconced in the chair, Xander sank into a crouch in front of her. The older woman tightened her grip on Xander's hands, effectively trapping her.

"What happened to Mr. Eilers?" Mrs. Peterson asked shakily.

"He was involved in a bar fight last night." Xander stuck as close to the truth as she could knowing Division would spin the entire incident. "Unfortunately, he was killed."

Mrs. Peterson sucked in an audible breath. "Oh no, that poor boy." Tears swam in her faded eyes as she searched Xander's face.

"Were you two close?" Xander kept her voice gentle. Although not evident, Xander couldn't miss Raine's impatience. It rode the air like an impending electrical storm, setting her wolf on edge. When Mrs. Peterson dropped her head and pulled a handkerchief out of her pocket to dab her eyes, Xander sent Raine a quelling glance. The uncomfortable sensation backed off and Xander returned her attention to the older woman.

"He was always doing little things for me," Mrs. Peterson said. "He spent the winter clearing my steps and driveway when it snowed. He even offered to do my shopping when it was so cold out." She sniffed. "Are you family?"

"Friends," Xander answered. "I'm Xander, and that's Raine. Neil didn't have any family."

Mrs. Peterson nodded. "I remember he mentioned that once." She paused, twisting her handkerchief. "I knew something was wrong, but I didn't want to pry."

"What happened?"

"I don't know."

Something in her voice had Xander and her wolf coming on point. There was something here, some clue. "But you have an idea," she guessed softly.

Mrs. Peterson nodded. "It was those boys who were coming over." Fear tightened her skin, lending her a pinched look. "They scared me," she whispered. "I could never put my finger on it, but they made me so uneasy."

It amazed Xander how often humans failed to listen to their instincts. Kyn or human, that personal warning system was a gift from Mother Nature. She was grateful her own nature didn't allow her to ignore such signs. "Do you remember their names?"

Mrs. Peterson shook her head. "I was coming over to ask Mr. Eilers for help moving a mirror, but when I went to knock on his door, I could hear voices arguing inside. They were quite loud and I wasn't comfortable interrupting."

"When was this?"

"About two weeks ago," she said. "After that, I didn't see much of him." She studied Xander. "You should let the authorities handle this, dear."

Xander smiled. "We're just here to check on his things."

Mrs. Peterson patted her hands. "Good." Her gaze dropped to Xander's tattoo. She leaned forward and dropped her voice. "You know, I don't know why you chose to cover such a lovely face."

"It's a family tradition." She ignored Raine's snort.

Mrs. Peterson blinked at her, too polite to say anything more. "Well then, I should leave you to it." She got to her feet. Xander wrapped a hand under the older woman's elbow and helped her to her door. As Mrs. Peterson opened her door, she turned. "Thank you for being honest with me."

"Of course." She paused. "Mrs. Peterson?"

"Yes, dear."

Xander pulled out a card and held it out. "If those boys come back, will you let me know?"

The older woman nodded and took the card. "Taliesin Security?"

"Yes, ma'am. I'm a private investigator."

"Are you sure you'll leave this to the authorities?"

"I'll be careful. Promise."

"See that you do, dear." She closed her door and Xander turned to make her way back to Neil's place.

She jogged through the yard and up the steps as Raine straightened and opened the door. "I'm wondering how a nice young man, who helps his elderly neighbor, suddenly decides to indulge in a headline inducing bloodbath." She stepped inside, Xander on her heels.

"It's what we're trying to figure out." Xander shut the door behind them.

The curtains were drawn, leaving the interior in shades of gray. A small ball of light popped into existence, hovering behind Raine's shoulder.

Its sudden appearance tripped Xander's pulse. "Nice trick," she muttered.

Raine slanted a mocking look over her shoulder. "Better than leaving our prints all over the light switches."

Xander stepped up beside her, scanning the room. The trailer was fairly straightforward. An open living room, set apart from a small kitchen and dining area by a waist high wall and broken by a wide entryway. To their left, the shadows disappeared into a narrow hallway, no doubt leading to the bedrooms since the kitchen and living room took up the remaining space.

There was a leather couch to Xander's right, some of the cushions slightly askew. A hand-crocheted blanket in shades of brown lay across one arm. A scarred wooden coffee table supported a large flat screen TV. There were two bookcases on the back wall.

Xander walked over to them. The books were lined along the shelves, one or two slightly out of place. A pile of magazines rested on top of the books on the third shelf. The top one had to do with woodworking. On the other bookcase, CDs were stacked three deep. There were a couple of framed photos. A young Neil with a surfboard in one hand, his other wrapped around the waist of a tall, laughing woman. In the next photo, a smiling Sara beamed from the safety of Neil's arms, snow skis poking up behind them like bunny ears.

Those happy snapshots added fuel to the simmering anger Xander held deep inside. Someone had destroyed Neil's life. And for what? It was such a waste. She straightened the picture of the young couple so it lined up with the older photo.

"What're we looking for exactly?" Raine asked from behind her.

"I don't know." Xander frowned and stepped back from the bookcases. Something was off. She did a slow turn, taking in the living room once more. "Raine, is it my imagination or does it look like someone's done a thorough search?"

Raine flicked a finger against one of the misaligned couch cushions. "It's possible." She paused. "On the other hand, it's just as possible that the kid wasn't completely anal about housekeeping."

"Maybe," Xander muttered.

Narrowing her eyes, she drew in a deep breath, dragging in the scents of the room. She sorted out Raine's unique blend of trees and wind, tinged with a faint feline musk. Under that was a very faint trace of rose water, as if the one it belonged to hadn't been there recently. Mrs. Peterson. Over it all was the scent of chipped wood, tinged with a curl of smoke and something wild, something not right. Neil's.

Deep inside, her wolf came to attention, ears perked. She wanted Xander to move forward. Not catching whatever it was that was triggering her wolf, Xander began quartering the room. It took her a few minutes but she finally realized what was wrong. There were blank spaces by the couch, bookcases, and leading down the hall. "What the hell?"

The absent of a scent was disturbing. How would someone erase their scent? She had never run across such a situation. She'd tracked those who had masked their scent, but erased it? It just shouldn't be possible.

"What?" Raine asked, dragging her attention back to Xander.

"There's a trail, but there's no scent to go with it."

Raine tilted her head. "Is that even possible?"

"I didn't think so," she answered.

Whatever Raine said next was washed away in a sharp, bright blast of pain. Xander sucked in her breath and reached out blindly, her hand finding the edge of the low wall between the living and dining rooms. Starbursts exploded across her vision. *Warrick. Something was wrong with Warrick.*

Frantic, she and her wolf raced down their psychic connection, only to slam against a solid wall. *Damn him!*

Hurt and bitter disappointment rose, choking her. She could feel the press of carpet under her knees and knew she had fallen to the floor in the real world. Hands were on her shoulders, as Raine tried to figure out what was happening.

As the piercing needles from the abrupt closure of the bond receded, Xander dragged in a deep breath, forcing air into her lungs. She had to think past her emotions. Warrick was many things but he wouldn't deliberately go back on his word. If he shut down the bond, there was a reason. She just had to find it. She reached for calm and shared it with her wolf until both of them could think.

"Xander, damn it! What the hell's going on?" Raine's voice was tight with tension.

"Warrick," she croaked. "Something's going on with Warrick."

Hands fumbled at her pockets and she slapped them away.

"Knock it off," Raine snarled. "I need your phone to call Taliesin."

Grateful, she closed her eyes and let Raine pull out her cell phone while she concentrated on breathing. She could hear Raine talking, probably to Rachel.

"Xander."

She blinked her eyes open to find Raine crouched in front of her, her silver eyes worried. "Rachel says he's in a meeting with a client and Sebastian. She was told not to disturb him."

"Okay," she said. "Okay." Some of the dread pulled back. She could feel her wolf prowling back and forth. "Give me a second."

She raised her knees, folded her arms on top of them then laid her head down and closed her eyes. With her panic pushed back and the shock of the unexpected disconnect, she took her time trying to figure out what was going on. As her mind quieted, she and her wolf were able to sense the faint tendrils of anger, shock, and hurt seeping from Warrick.

Relief flowed thick and hot through her veins. He was okay, physically. Emotionally, she wasn't so sure. She pushed against the bond and felt it loosen. The faint brush of Warrick's wolf against her hip nudged her back and helped settle her stomach. She stopped pushing, opened her eyes, and raised her head.

Raine sat in front of her, a small frown creasing her forehead and Xander was caught by the molten quality of her eyes. Normally, they were a cool silver, but she could swear there was a slight glow going on now.

Raine blinked and the weirdness disappeared. "Welcome back."

Xander's legs shook and she wrapped her arms around them. "Thanks." She rubbed her chin on her knees.

Raine inclined her head. "You okay?"

Xander nodded.

"And Vidis?"

"For the most part." Xander released her grip on her legs, and let her head thump back against the wall behind her. "He should be okay, but..."

"But?"

Xander sighed and got to her feet. "Do you still have my cell?" She held her hand out.

Raine reached out and let Xander pull her upright. Then she retrieved the small phone from her pocket and handed it over. "I really don't think you'll be able to get past Rachel."

Xander punched in a number. "Don't you know if you can't get through a wall, you might as well go around it?"

"It's more fun to go through."

Raine's quip left Xander grinning. The phone rang three times before it was picked up. "Don't tell me you have more bodies, Xander," Ryuu said in lieu of a greeting.

"I wouldn't want you to get bored," Xander shot back.

A low curse then, "Seriously?"

"Actually, no." Xander let the humor fade from her voice. "I need you to answer a question for me."

"Okay."

"Who was Warrick meeting with this morning?"

Ryuu picked up on the tension in her question. "A Dan Vicks. Why?"

"Is he human or Kyn?"

"Kyn." Ryuu jumped on her quick inhale and asked sharply, "Why?"

Xander flicked a glance at Raine, knowing her next question would lead the woman in front of her to demand further explanations, but she had to make sure Warrick was safe. "Is he a witch?"

"No, wolf. A maverick actually." There was an ominous silence and she knew Ryuu was following along. "You think he has some tie with last night?"

"I don't know." In front of her, Raine shifted her weight, anticipation rising and Xander knew she was picking up both sides of the conversation.

"What do you know?" he snapped. "Sebastian should be with him. I made him swear to take one of us into the meeting."

"He did. According to Rachel, Sebastian's with him."

"Xander, stop screwing around and tell me what happened."

As a Second, Ryuu's need to protect his alpha would override everything, including his friendship with her.

"Stop snarling at me," she hissed. "I don't know what happened. All I know is something went down with him and now I can't get him to answer me."

"Oh, for the love of—" She heard Ryuu blow out a breath as if reaching for his patience. "You scared the shit out of me because he decided he wanted a little privacy?"

Xander pulled her phone away from her ear and looked at it, unwilling to believe Ryuu had just blown her off. She put it back to her ear as his casual dismissal lit her temper. "Listen up, you arrogant ass," she growled. "You ever speak to me like that again and I swear to all the gods I will turn your hide into a fur rug. This has nothing to do with my relationship with my mate. Something or someone just threw our alpha into a killing temper. After last night's visitors, I refuse to take chances with his safety. So if you don't want to meet me in the Challenger's Circle, you'll get your ass over to Taliesin and find out what the hell is going on."

She hung up before Ryuu could answer. She clenched her phone, fighting the urge to throw it across the room. *What in the hell was wrong with everyone?* Warrick was trying to go all "fang and fur" in the middle of a business meeting, Ryuu was treating her as if she was some half-brained idiot, and if she had to hunt down one more deranged wolf, she was going to prove just how bitchy a female wolf could get.

"Maybe it's a full moon," Raine said.

Xander spun around, hearing the laughter under the words. "Maybe they need to be neutered," she snapped.

"You could do that," Raine offered dryly. "But then you might regret it later."

Xander's laugh escaped before she could stop it. "Yeah, I might." She tucked her phone in a pocket. "We might as well check out the rest of this place." She moved down the hall.

"Xander," Raine called, stopping her. "You want to tell me who your visitors were last night?"

Xander hunched her shoulders and turned back to her friend. If she shared with Raine, Warrick would be furious. But instincts told her they were running out of time. Too much was happening on too many fronts. Whether Warrick wanted to admit it or not, they needed answers. Since she couldn't get him to go to Cheveyo to find out who would have the power to interfere with a shifter's ability to change, then she would go around him. He could get as furious with her as he wanted, but when all was said and done, protection of her pack and her alpha was primary. If he was her mate, then he would have to deal with her need to protect him as much as he needed to protect her.

Her decision didn't stop the butterflies of worry from scraping against her heart. When Warrick found out—there was no if in this equation—the emotional fallout could really hurt. She reached out to her wolf, seeking reassurance. Determination and acceptance answered.

"Xander?" Raine prompted.

"Two wolves and a wizard stopped by last night." She leaned against the hallway wall, her arms crossed over her chest. "They were under the assumption that Warrick would be home alone."

Raine frowned. "Correct me if I'm wrong, but if you plan to take out an alpha, don't you just slap them with a white glove or something?"

Her question loosened the tension in Xander's stomach. "If a wolf wants to challenge for the alpha position, he or she has to move up the ranks."

"Which means?"

"You have to fight your way up a chain of dominance. If you can't defeat an alpha's Third or Second, there's no way you'll ever be top dog."

"So besides the fact they brought along a wizard buddy, this wasn't a challenge."

Xander shook her head.

"Assassination attempt?" Raine ventured.

"Maybe," Xander answered then she plunged in. "The body we had you look at last night—" Dear gods, had it only been last night?

"The one with the magic full of holes."

Xander nodded. "That's the third wolf I've had to hunt down in the last two weeks."

Raine raised an eyebrow. "Is that normal?"

"Hell no," Xander said. "If it was, there's no way I could hold a job and be a Wraith. There just wouldn't be time."

"So it's a relatively new development?"

"Yeah, you could say that." Xander pushed off the wall and paced a few steps back and forth.

"What was the common factor?" Raine asked.

"All three were Bitten wolves."

"Is that the only thing tying them together?"

"No," Xander said. "The Bitten can only change during the full moon, and they can only change into full-wolf form. The ones I tracked, they were this weird mixture of human and wolf. It's not natural."

Raine held up a hand. "Hold on. I've seen some of you running around in wolf-man form."

"Warrior form," Xander corrected. "Half human, half wolf. Only Born can obtain that."

"So someone's screwing with the Lycos House?" Raine paused. "The wizard? Vidis is worried he's one of Cheveyo's."

Xander winced and Raine gave a soft curse. This was why Xander wanted Warrick to share with Raine. In all the years she'd worked with Raine, she noticed her friend never failed to be able to put together a fairly solid picture of any given situation, even if there were missing pieces.

"Damn it, Xander." Raine spun away and stalked to the living room.

Xander followed until she stood in the little entryway. "Don't damn it me, Raine. If it had been my choice, I would've dragged your ass over to the house last night."

Raine turned and glared at her. "Vidis wouldn't let you," she guessed shrewdly.

"You were choice number two, Cheveyo was choice number one. He outright refused both."

"What happens when he realizes you told me?" Raine asked.

Xander shrugged, forcing her pulse to hold steady and hide her uncertainty. "He's going to rip me a new one."

"Is that all?"

Xander grimaced. "I think that'll be more than enough, thanks."

Raine stared at her, her gaze steady and unblinking. Xander's breath caught and held, but she refused to look away. Finally, Raine blinked and started muttering under her breath. She began pacing back and forth through the small living room. "I'll have Gavin check into the wizard."

"I don't have a name," she paused, thinking, "or a body at this point."

"Won't need it," Raine said. "Gavin's great with ferreting out secrets."

"And Cheveyo?"

Raine stopped in front of Xander. "Maybe we can wait until we see what Gavin uncovers before we drag Cheveyo into this." She waved her hand in the direction of the hall. "Let's go check out the bedroom."

Xander led the way down the hall and into the bedroom that encompassed the back end of the trailer. "Thing is, I don't think we're going to get a choice."

She stepped into the room and moved to the side, letting Raine in. Together, they began to search the bedroom.

"What do you mean?" Raine rifled through the nightstand tucked on the far side of the bed.

"Unless you know enough about magic to tell me how someone can alter a wolf's change, Cheveyo's the only one I can think of who might have the answer," Xander explained.

Raine stopped and faced Xander across the bed. "Do you think Cheveyo's behind this?" Her question was quiet, dangerous.

"Honestly? No." Xander knelt on the floor, running her hands under the mattress. Nothing.

"But Vidis does," Raine said.

Xander shook her head. "Not really." She got back to her feet and put her hands on her hips, looking around the room. "Warrick has to put the pack's safety before everything else, so it means he's naturally paranoid."

She dragged in a deep breath, sorting scents. Again, she found the same thing in the bedroom as she had in the rest of the trailer.

"Anything?" Raine asked when Xander opened her eyes.

"Yeah, there are blank spots in here, too."

"Maybe a concealing spell, which means someone's already been through here." Raine sighed. "They're good. There's nothing here that shouldn't be."

"Except for that nonexistent scent," Xander muttered.

"Guess we're done then," Raine said. They headed out of the trailer, Raine locking the door behind them.

Xander gave a little wave at the flutter of curtains from Mrs. Peterson's trailer.

"You heading back to Taliesin?" Raine stood next to her as she swung her leg over her bike.

"Yep," Xander answered. "Besides making sure Warrick hasn't eaten someone for a mid-morning snack, I need to find out if he knows anything about removing scents."

Raine nodded. "Gavin and I will do what we can, but I'm going to have to go to Cheveyo," she warned. "Probably sooner rather than later."

Xander settled the helmet on her head. "I know."

Raine met her eyes. "I'll give you as much of a head's up as I can before Cheveyo faces him down."

"Appreciate it," Xander said.

Raine shook her head. "I hate politics."

Xander laughed as Raine headed toward her SUV. Before Xander could start her Ducati, her phone rang. Using the Bluetooth in her helmet, she answered.

Raine stopped and turned.

"Xander?" came Zeke's voice through the helmet's speakers.

"Hey, Zeke. What's up?"

"Are you coming into the office any time soon?"

"Yeah, I'm on my way over now." Tension crawled up her spine. Zeke's voice sounded strained. "What's wrong?"

"I think I found a connection between the three Bitten," he answered.

"What is it?"

"The thing is, I'm not sure it's real."

"Why?"

"It doesn't make sense." She could hear the worry in

Zeke's voice. "I'm going to check something out, but it shouldn't take me too long."

Apprehension curled in her stomach. "Zeke, don't go poking into something without back up."

He huffed out a laugh. "I'll be fine. Besides, I shouldn't have to leave the offices. Do you have time to meet later this afternoon?"

"Sure, just let Rachel know when you need me. I'm heading to Warrick's office now. Ryuu should be there soon as well if you need him."

"Gee thanks, mom," Zeke drawled. "I'll be fine. See you later."

"Later."

Raine walked over. "Everything okay?"

"We may have a break." She studied Raine. "Before we headed out to Arizona, Taliesin's IT Investigations department was looking into a couple of online chat rooms. A month ago, they found a conversation thread centered around a possible cure to a werewolf's bite."

Raine's eyes narrowed and her face went carefully blank. "Who was in the chat room?"

"Bitten wolves and possibly some humans."

Raine's hands curled into fists. "Kyn experiments." Her jaw tightened. "Is Talbot involved?"

"I don't know," Xander answered. "The conversation was purely hypothetical. Then the members began dropping offline."

Raine turned away, her back rigid. "If humans are running the experiment, chances are Jonah Talbot is involved somewhere."

Xander understood Raine's anger. Jonah's father had used Raine as his own personal guinea pig, and when a top scientist in Jonah's company had injected her lover, Gavin, with some strange drug, Raine had taken violent offense. Unfortunately, those experiences tended to color Raine's perceptions.

"Raine." Xander waited until Raine turned back to face her. "The problem is we don't know if the one behind this is human or Kyn."

Raine's snarl was impressive, but Xander ran with a much more intimidating crowd. "No sane Kyn would sell out another to the humans."

"Don't be too sure," Xander said.

"For gods' sake, Xander—"

"Once I would have agreed," Xander cut in. "But as someone recently pointed out to me, the Bitten aren't really Kyn. They're humans who've been torn out of their lives and forced to live in a world that they always thought was some fairy tale. They've been turned into monsters. What do you think they would give to get their humanity back?"

Raine didn't answer but stalked back to her car.

Xander sat there, watching her friend tear out of the driveway. Sighing, she went to turn on the engine when she felt a give in the bond. Her hand stilled and she held her breath. Inside, she followed her wolf down the bond. Before they could hit the wall Warrick had erected, they were met with his wolf. He stood before them, head and tail down.

Xander could feel Warrick's emotions. The chaotic blend of confusion, anger, hurt and, over it all, worry. The tentative brush of his wolf under hand seared through her, the silent apology her alpha was sending her unmistakable.

Relief left her smiling. Emotionally, she dropped to her knees and wrapped her arms around his neck. Her wolf crowded close, brushing along her mate while Xander buried her face in his ruff, letting him feel her acceptance of his apology.

His reaction to whatever had happened in his office hadn't been a rejection, but a misguided attempt to protect her. Changing his instinctual reactions wouldn't happen over night.

She tightened her arms briefly before letting him go. She left the two wolves curled up together as she came back to the real world. Finally starting her bike, she tried not to dwell on what his reaction would be when he realized what she had done to protect him.

CHAPTER 16

Xander was grateful to make it to her office without running into anyone. Zeke left a message he would be available to meet after three. In the middle of listening to Rachel's voice inform her that her presence was required in the large conference room at one, a sharp knock sounded on her door.

"Come in," she called, cutting off the recorded voicemail.

The door swung open and Ryuu's wave of suppressed aggression sent Xander's wolf rushing to the surface. She forced herself not to jump to her feet. Instead, she took her time standing up, never taking her gaze off the very real threat hovering in front of her desk.

Without dropping his gaze, he swung the door shut. He stood behind one of the padded chairs facing her desk and gripped the back, the padding denting under his nails. There was no missing the amber tint to Ryuu's normally dark eyes, or the wolf in his voice. "You hung up on me."

"You were being an asshole," she gritted out.

With an almost casual movement, Ryuu threw the chair

into the wall. Xander didn't even flinch as wood cracked against drywall. Instead, she rocked forward on her feet, the muscles in her thighs curling in preparation of a leap. She couldn't let her human skin slip or the lethal nails of her wolf slide out. This wasn't a fight to the death. Her earlier action caused Ryuu to question who was more dominant—his alpha's mate or him.

When Ryuu took a step forward, it looked like they were going to figure out the answer. She rolled to the balls of her feet, shifting her balance forward in anticipation. The office was small, but she was strong enough to send him back through the door and to the floor of the hall, if need be.

His muscles curled and bunched under his T-shirt.

Her focus narrowed as she waited.

"Give it your best shot," he snarled.

She was airborne before his last word hit the quivering air between them. She cleared the desk and slammed solidly into his chest, sending them both crashing through the door into the hallway.

Ryuu wasn't Second for nothing. He got his feet into her stomach and his hands wrapped in her shirt, sending her over his head. As he released his grip, she continued the roll until she got her feet under her, her hands pressed against the floor. Keeping the momentum, she spun out with her leg, getting a solid hit to Ryuu's shoulder as he pushed himself up.

In the narrow confines of the hallway, her kick knocked him back into the wall. He stumbled, but didn't go down. So she continued her spin, arm set for a sharp left hook. Before she could connect, Ryuu's hands came up. The sharp slap of flesh resounded through the hall as he blocked her punch and sent her face first into the wall. Even with her arm numb from his hit, she got both hands between her chest and the drywall as he came in tight behind her, wrapping his arms around her.

The problem with using the same sparring partner was that over time they eventually got to know all your tricks. Hell, Ryuu even taught her a few. So they stood there, Ryuu's heavy breathing in her ear, his arms squeezing, holding her immobile.

"Submit," he growled.

Xander was a small female in a world populated by bigger, stronger males. If her years as a Wraith and a dominant had taught her anything, it was that you used whatever tricks you had to get your point across. No matter how dirty. She bared her teeth at the wall, hooked her foot behind Ryuu's, and snapped her arms wide, breaking his hold. As his arms released, she spun and slammed her palm into his nose.

He howled in pain and she caught the sharp scent of fresh blood. She stepped to his side and fisted her now free arm to nail him in the crotch. He stumbled back. She didn't give him a chance, turning into him and delivering a series of lightning quick strikes to his stomach, forcing him to give ground.

He retaliated by trapping one of her fists against his abdomen and driving a bruising hook kick to her thigh.

She twisted her wrist, freeing it and using her other hand to aim a palm strike against his jaw.

He snapped his head back, avoiding her hit.

Using the space she'd gain as he took a step back, she lashed out with a back kick.

He blocked it and went in for his own series of strikes. As his arms whipped out, she blocked his first strike.

Deflecting his second strike, she looped her arm over and under, capturing his wrist in both hands then twisted her body. Caught in her arm bar, Ryuu had no choice but to follow where she took his wrist. She kept twisting until she had him on his knees next to her.

Panting, she grinned. "Submit."

Blood smeared bright red against his dusky skin, but his grin was as fierce as hers. "This time."

Triumph burst inside her and escaped with a laugh. Whether he deliberately let her win or she managed to get the better of him due to luck didn't matter. It hadn't been a real battle for position. She had no desire to take Ryuu's place, but at least now he'd listen to her first. She leaned closer until their foreheads touched over their entangled arms. "I can't believe you fell for that."

He tugged on his arm and she released him. Then he touched her face briefly. "Nice moves."

She rose to her feet, offering him her hand. "Thank you."

"Are you two done?" The dry question had Ryuu and Xander spinning around. Standing in the hall was Gavin Durand, Raine's lover and partner. Hair, the color of good bourbon, was tied back at the nape of his neck, his long legs encased in faded jeans, and his broad shoulders covered in a dark T-shirt. The shirt's image showed a dog chasing a cat and below that the caption *Fast Food*.

Xander snickered. "Let me guess. Raine's idea?"

Gavin looked down then pulled the material out and away from his body. "Yeah." He looked back up. "She dared me to wear it to work."

"What did you dare her to do?" Ryuu asked. "Wear a skirt?"

A speculative light lit Gavin's eyes. "Not yet, but you know, that might not be such a bad idea."

Xander made a mental note to warn Raine and, if

necessary, make sure to drag her friend to that little leather shop down on Hawthorne. There was this one skirt that had caught Xander's eye, but on Raine...hmm. "What brings you over to our wing?"

Gavin and Raine's offices were on the other side of the building. Since Warrick decided to take the office all the way on the butt end of the building, she and Ryuu ended up picking the offices closest to him.

Gavin gave a pointed look at her door, which was valiantly trying to maintain a hold on its frame by one lone hinge. "Your little discussion could be heard all the way to Rachel's desk. I left her soothing our guests and decided to see if another opinion was needed."

"Nope." Xander took a step forward. She winced as her thigh protested. Ryuu's kick was going to leave a bruise. She rubbed it and kept moving, leading Ryuu back to her office.

As she stepped past Gavin, he caught her upper arm in a gentle grip, bringing her to a stop. She turned to look at him.

"Does Vidis need to know?" he asked softly.

She gave him a patronizing smile and patted him on the chest. "Down, boy. Ryuu and I were just exchanging points of views."

Gavin turned his serious gaze to Ryuu and let her go. "You sure?"

She grabbed a box of Kleenex from her desk and tossed it to Ryuu, who started mopping up his face.

"We're good," he told Gavin. "Besides, I'm sure Vidis already knows."

Leaning against her desk, Xander folded her arms, watching Ryuu make a bigger mess of his face. "Oh for gods' sake, Ryuu, come here." She stepped up, snatched the wad of Kleenex from him, and began wiping away the worst of the blood. "Which guests are out with Rachel, Gavin?"

"Sector Chief Osborn and some other suit," he answered. "Once you two are cleaned up, your presence is requested in the large conference room."

Hands stilling, Xander turned and glanced behind her at the clock on the wall. She winced. Ten to one. Damn it. Turning back to Ryuu, she asked, "Do you have another shirt in your office?"

He shook his head. "No, but I can get one out of my locker in the gym." The fourth floor housed a gym utilized for training and after-hours workouts. "I'll be there as soon as I can." He gave her a mock scowl. "Next time, leave my damn nose alone." He turned and began to walk out of the office.

"Aww, don't worry, you can tell your lady friends some big biker dude did it."

Ryuu didn't look back, just gave her a one-finger response.

She laughed.

"You know," Gavin said as Ryuu disappeared, "until today, I thought the fact you and Raine were friends was just strange."

"Why?"

He grinned. "I was under the impression you were somewhat sane."

Grabbing her jacket, she waved him out of her office. "You must have been fooled by my demure appearance."

"Nope," he said as they walked down the hall. "I think it's more that everyone believes you're the one person who can tame Vidis."

She snorted, stopping outside the restroom. "Tame and Warrick will never exist in the same sentence." She slid

Gavin a glance under her lashes and gave him a wicked smile. "Besides, I like him wild."

She left Gavin laughing as she went into the bathroom to make sure she was presentable.

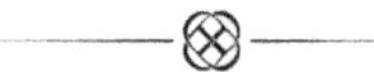

An hour later, she was seated next to her brother, Ethan, at a large oval table while the tension in the room was thick enough to choke on. Not only was he Warrick's lawyer, but his position as a senior legal advisor for Taliesin made his attendance mandatory. His yellow legal pad was filled with his chicken scratch. She wondered if it they were actual notes or just doodles. Knowing her brother, it could be either.

Across the table, Section Chief Victor Osborn and Special Agent in Charge Reynolds were trying their hardest not to flinch under the stares of the Kyn sitting across from them.

"Chief Osborn, are you informing us that your government is seriously considering making the existence of the Kyn public knowledge without our permission?" Ethan tapped his pen against his pad.

"No, Mr. Cade, I believe my exact words were, 'there are rumors that some individuals are starting to discuss exposing the Kyn.' Individuals, not the government." Xander was impressed with how Osborn kept his tone patient and level.

"Are these same individuals aware that such a move is a direct violation of the Agreement signed in 1946?"

"Whether they do or not is beside the point," Osborn said.

"We beg to differ." The melodious voice belonged to

Natasha Bertoi, the petite Chief Marketing Officer and deceptively beautiful head of the Amanusa House. Humans had misnamed them demons, even though most could walk down the street without raising an eyebrow. But if you could shatter their tightly held reins of discipline their human masks would slip, showing the predator lurking within.

Osborn shook his head, his voice grave. "If you continue to have such public situations as the massacre at the club last night, it's not the politicos you'll have to worry about, but Joe Q. Public who's going to plaster it all over the internet."

"Last night's situation was highly unusual," Warrick cut in.

Xander caught the flex of muscle under Ryuu's arm, a sure sign of a clenched fist under the table. Obviously, she wasn't the only one sensing how close Warrick was to throwing Osborn out a window.

The first half of the meeting had been quite civilized, as various strategies were devised to deal with the public relations fallout from last night's disaster. Coordinating a unified story between the Kyn and Division had been an exercise in creative writing. It never failed to amaze Xander at how good Natasha was at her job. The woman's thought processes were downright scary. No wonder she enjoyed her work. Her ability to obscure reality was phenomenal.

It was all fake smiles and civil tones until Osborn decided to warn the Kyn that their time behind the curtain might be coming to a close faster than they realized. Which meant Xander would be cooped up longer than anticipated. She kept her sigh to herself.

"We understand that." Osborn shook his head. "Hell, I understand that, but it doesn't change the fact that maintaining silence on the Kyn's existence is coming under fire." He sat back in his chair, his fingers beating a restless rhythm against the table. "To be honest, I'm impressed that the government managed to keep you all behind the scenes as long as they have. As helpful as the Kyn have been in the past, the fact remains that when you're outed, the American people are going to find out their government has been keeping some very dangerous secrets."

"That shouldn't be breaking news." The dry comment came from Gavin who was sitting in as Ryan Mulcahy's representative. As CEO of Taliesin Security to the humans and Head of the Fey House to the Kyn, Mulcahy also carried the title of Captain of the Wraiths to a few very select Kyn. The man was a bit busy, and since Gavin was here, Xander figured he must have drawn the short straw for today's meeting.

Osborn's sidekick, Reynolds covered his smile with a quick cough when his boss frowned at him.

"Chief Osborn," Ethan redirected Osborn's attention. "Forgive me for asking, but why are you sharing this information with us? Won't that put you in direct confrontation with your superiors?"

Osborn's lips curved in a grim little smile. "I've worked with the Kyn for years and I know just how good you are at keeping secrets. I have no fears you'll keep my name out of things." He met Warrick's gaze directly. "If the actions of a select misguided few threaten the relationship between the humans and the Kyn, I want to make sure you know who the instigators are."

Xander gave the human points for courage. He managed to hold Warrick's gaze longer than most. It helped that there was no acrid scent of lies behind his words either.

Warrick studied the Division agent for a moment and when Osborn finally dropped his gaze, the tension etching lines around Warrick's mouth lessened. "We appreciate the warning."

Osborn gave him a short nod and stood up. "Thank you for taking the time to meet with us today. I'll make sure these statements are released to the press by tonight."

Next to him, Reynolds stood as well, his escalating pulse telegraphing his relief at their impending departure. Xander couldn't blame either one. She watched both men make their good-byes and wondered how much longer the Kyn could depend on Division for help before fear set in.

CHAPTER 17

Warrick hadn't missed Ryuu's bruised face or Xander's slight limp when they came into the meeting. There was a moment before Rachel showed in Osborn and Reynolds where his wolf had come to attention, trying to get him to open the bond. Since he had been in the midst of a conversation with Natasha Bertoi, he gritted his teeth and ignored him. It hadn't been easy. In fact, he had to remind himself and his wolf that Xander was perfectly capable of taking care of herself. Something she was continually reminding him. Since his wolf reluctantly settled, he forced his attention back on task.

Now, thanks to Osborn's little bomb, it would be even longer before he could get some answers.

"Well, that was fun," Xander said into the silence left in the agents' wake.

Ethan snorted and began packing up his paperwork. "I'll get to work on getting this all documented and to our chief legal officer, Ms. Iver."

"I especially like the usage of airborne hallucinogens on the club-goers as their explanation for seeing a 'big hairy wolf dude.'" Gavin added finger quotes around one eyewitness's description of Neil.

Natasha gathered the loose papers in front of her and carefully placed them in a leather binder. "It was more believable than trying to insinuate they were too drunk to see straight." She rose from her chair and turned to Warrick. "We need to meet with Cheveyo and Mulcahy immediately."

Frustration nipped at Warrick's heels. He didn't want to be stuck in another meeting. His wolf was gnawing at his restraints, thanks to his earlier meeting with Dmitri. The need for action raked its claws deep. Besides, his to-do list was growing at a frightening rate. First, he had to find out what the hell happened between Xander and Ryuu, then he needed to track down the illusive puppet master behind the trio of idiots now calling six-feet-under home, and if he was lucky, he might figure out how Neil and the other dead Bitten fit in. Add in his brother with his headache-inducing demands, and dealing with the amorphous threat of the human government could damn well wait.

Unfortunately, Natasha was still waiting for his response and ignoring her had never really worked in the past. "Tomorrow," he said, struggling to keep his impatience in check. He rose from his chair and turned away.

"No, Vidis. Today."

Her not-so-subtle order brought him to a stop. Obviously, he'd done too good of a job of hiding his fraying patience since Natasha felt free to push. His wolf surged forward. His head lowered and he slowly, carefully turned back to her. Noticing her whitened fingers wrapped around her binder and the bright avarice light in her eyes, he revised his earlier assumption. Natasha knew she was provoking him. She just didn't care.

He let his wolf out a little more, no longer caring what such an action revealed. His lips curled back and a low, hair-raising snarl escaped. "Tomorrow." It was hard to push the word out.

Instead of giving ground like any sane individual, Natasha gave him a condescending smile, queen to peasant. A thin ring of red appeared around her periwinkle blue irises as she let her own predator out to play. "We don't have the luxury of indulging your temper tantrum, Vidis. If the humans decide to turn against us, we must have a plan in place, or we lose all we have managed to gain over the years."

He hadn't realized he had moved to lunge forward until his chest collided with Xander's back. Somehow his mate had managed to get between him and the demon queen. That, more than the feel of her small form holding him back, had him pulling up short.

"Okay, time out," Xander said, addressing Natasha. "Warrick is in the midst of investigating what caused Neil's public display of temper last night, Natasha. We need to get that resolved before we can help with the possible fall out of Chief Osborn's intel. It won't hurt things to wait till tomorrow, will it?" Her tone was conciliatory.

Natasha fixed Xander with an unblinking stare. Warrick growled, faintly aware of Ryuu moving up on his far side and Ethan rising from his chair. Right now, he didn't give a damn if they were preparing to help him or stop him. If Natasha didn't stop eyeing his mate like she was considering how to dissect her, it would take more than Ryuu and Ethan to stop the impending carnage. No one threatened his mate, not even the Demon Queen.

"Natasha." Gavin's voice was mild, but effective in redirecting her attention to him. "Mulcahy and Cheveyo may not be available today. Tomorrow would be best for all involved."

Endless seconds ticked by before Natasha blinked. The looming presence of her true character winked out of existence, allowing Warrick to pull his wolf back though he didn't make the mistake of taking his gaze off of her. Instead, he continued to watch her as she flexed her bloodless fingers against her binder.

She tilted her head to Gavin in acknowledgement. "Fine, tomorrow then. I'll give Rachel the time." She turned back to Warrick, giving him a lethal bearing of teeth. "Attendance is mandatory." She didn't wait for an answer, but swept from the room.

"What a bitch," Xander muttered as soon as the blonde disappeared down the hall.

"I think that gives bitches too much credit," Ryuu said, sotto voice.

"It's what she's best at." Gavin rubbed a hand over the back of his neck. He glanced at his watch and rose from his chair, deliberately avoiding Warrick's gaze. "I've got to head out, too."

Ethan shot his sister a raised eyebrow and Warrick felt the brush of her silky hair against his chin as she shook her head. Ethan sighed and said, "I'll follow you out."

As the two males left the room, Warrick's wolf finally stepped all the way back, letting the man resume the driver's seat. He shook his body like he was flinging off water and caught Xander's hips in his hands. He pulled her back until she was leaning against his chest. Drawing her scent into his lungs, he turned his gaze to Ryuu. "Now, what the hell happened between the two of you?"

"Nothing." Xander stepped out of his hold until she could turn to face him.

"Try again." He switched his gaze back to her, his hands curling in an attempt not to shake her.

She flicked a glance to his Second then back to him. When she raised her chin, he knew he had a choice. Either badger her until she answered, or find another way around her. He took the path of least resistance and said to Ryuu, "I'm only going to ask once more. What happened?"

Ryuu held up his hands in a placating gesture, retreating a step. "We were only reestablishing our communication techniques."

"And?"

"Our lines are all clear."

"She kicked your ass, didn't she?" A warm glow of pride unwound a few knots in his stomach.

Ryuu's lips twisted in a wry grin. "Yeah, but I let her." Then he laughed and dodged the punch Xander threw. "Look, I need to head out. I've got some urgent emails awaiting my attention. You two play nice."

Ryuu bumped shoulders with Xander as he left, the small, affectionate movement reassuring Warrick the two truly were okay.

When they were the last two in the conference room, the tension drained from his body. His wolf still rode under his skin, wanting to run, but the need wasn't as suffocating.

"Warrick?"

Hearing the hesitancy in Xander's voice softened the ice-cold barrier he locked his emotions behind. His voice was gruff when he answered, "Yeah, pixie girl."

"If you give me a few minutes, we can duck out and go for a run at your place." She made the offer as if expecting him to reject it, or her. "I just need to call Zeke and push our appointment out a little later."

Her unusual show of insecurity made him frown. Was it his fault she felt this way? Stupid question. Of course it was. Initially, he shut down their connection to give her time to come to terms with the changes his decision had created. Instead, she'd taken it as a personal rejection. The truth was, part of him needed her to want to be with him, so much so he'd been worried he'd pressure her into accepting their bond. Unfortunately, he found keeping their connection open now was proving more difficult than he had expected.

He reached out and cupped her face, his fingers finding and tracing the delicate lines of her tattoo. The familiar texture of the hidden scar tissue under his fingertips reminded him how much he wanted to know the story behind the artwork. But not now. Later, when things weren't quite so...hectic.

"I'd like that," he answered.

Her smile lit up her face and there, where she would be horrified to realize he could see it, was a wealth of emotion. Just for him.

He kissed her, stepping close, bringing his body in so he could feel every inch of her. The heat of her seeped through his clothes, his skin, and slowly began making its way through that layer of emotional ice. Need, want, and softer emotions he refused to name rose, drowning all his good intentions. He took her over, and she let him. Would she understand how much that meant to him? That she, a dominant wolf, would submit to him? Not because he was her alpha but because, at some level, she felt safe enough with him to trust him? It humbled him even as it raised his passion higher.

As much as he wanted to strip her bare and make use of the conference table behind them, he pulled back. It took an ungodly amount of discipline to gentle their kiss until he could raise his head. Her face was flushed, her breathing ragged, and her nails sharp little bites against his shoulders. He smiled, both wolf and man happy with their accomplishment.

"Okay then," Xander managed to choke out. "I'll—um —meet you in about five."

He let her go. A sense of anticipation simmered in his bones, holding back the myriad of problems surrounding him. This run meant more than just a chance to let his wolf out, it was a gift. Her gift to him, a chance to step outside his position as alpha and take a moment for just the two of them.

Hours later, rain and shadows obscured the moon as Xander pulled into a parking lot. The run with Warrick had done her and her wolf a world of good. She felt calmer, more centered. And Warrick? Well...She grinned as she recalled how he had chased her through the forest this afternoon. They had indulged in a wolf version of tag, slipping in and out of the heavy foliage to nip and pounce on the unsuspecting it. For a few blissful hours, they simply played. It was so rare for Warrick to do that, and it had been fun.

Now, it was time to dive back into the waiting problems. First up, meeting with Zeke.

She parked her bike under the Morrison Bridge. The small parking lot was half full. Tucked in an industrial area most would probably avoid, if given the choice, sat

Montage. The squat, red brick building didn't look like much, but the quirky pub served spectacular dishes, if you didn't mind a little spice. Personally, she preferred the alligator gumbo.

The street lamps stood watch outside, valiantly attempting to illuminate the darkness and drive back the night. Like a pied piper, the sounds of music and laughter seeped around the iron-barred door, beckoning visitors to take a chance despite the worn exterior.

She pulled open the door and stepped inside, letting the warmth and smells wash over her. Looking around, she took in the crowd. Burly bikers, white-haired grannies and gramps, too-cool college students, casual professionals— Montage welcome them all. No judgment, just good food and great beer. It was one of her preferred meeting places.

She caught the attention of one of the waitresses. Mitzi smiled as she finished setting a bowl of gourmet mac and cheese in front of an elderly couple. It took her a few moments to work her way around the tables, but once within earshot, she told Xander, "There's a spot in the back. Will that work?"

Xander nodded and followed her back. "Thanks, Mitzi." Xander scooted into the booth.

"You want your usual?" the Rubensesque brunette asked.

Xander shook her head. "Not tonight. I'll just stick with the gator bites and a coffee. I'm meeting someone." She gave Mitzi Zeke's name and a brief description, then sat back to wait.

She wasn't too early, maybe ten minutes. Normally, Zeke was fairly punctual. She passed the time people watching. It was always fun here. She spotted an intriguing couple.

The man looked like he'd gotten dressed in the dark. Skin tight pants, done in vertical stripes of green and blue, clashed horribly with the paisley-patterned shirt resembling a refugee from a seventies sitcom. His companion was bit more together. Her batik skirt at least matched the shirt. Xander would bet good money that her shirt was made from organic cotton, just based on the Birkenstocks and mass of dull-brown dreadlocks. If those weren't a clue, the distinct musk of body odor would have been. Sometimes having a sensitive nose just sucked.

She amused herself by creating their background story. She left off once Mitzi brought her coffee and Cajun-seared gator tails with black bread. She closed her eyes, inhaling the stomach-awakening aromas. Her stomach grumbled—loudly.

She caught Mitzi's chuckle. Opening her eyes, she gave her favorite waitress a wry grin. "I've been stuck in meetings all day."

"Hungry work, meetings," Mitzi agreed. "You need anything else, sugar?"

"Nope, I'm good. Thanks."

Another quick grin then Mitzi was off, buzzing around the other tables.

Xander picked up her coffee and took a sip. The subtle blends of cinnamon and spice hit her tongue. Lovely. She dug into her food. About twenty minutes after the gator tails had made their last descent, her good mood started to sour. Zeke was late. Her fingers drummed an impatient beat against the table and her gaze kept straying to the door, as if that would encourage him to walk in.

On the table in front of her, her cell phone began doing its Mexican jumping bean impression. She snatched it up. Ryuu, not Zeke.

"Hey," she answered.

"Hey back," he answered, sounding distracted. "Let me talk to Zeke."

"Would love to, but he's not here."

"What?" Ryuu shot the word out.

Uneasiness stretched awake inside her, causing her stomach to protest the pile of food she had just dumped on it. "He's not here," she repeated.

"He left over forty minutes ago." There was nothing distracted about Ryuu now. "Where the hell is he?"

"Did he mention stopping somewhere else first?"

Don't panic. Not yet. There could be a reasonable explanation. Just because everything seemed to go to shit in a hand basket lately, didn't mean Zeke was in trouble. Too bad her roiling stomach wasn't buying it.

"No," Ryuu answered. "Did he tell you why he wanted to meet?"

"He said he had found a connection between our three —" She stopped. There was no way a human could eavesdrop on her conversation, but still, it never hurt to be safe. "—chew toys," she finished.

Ryuu's growl registered loud and clear in her ear. "And you didn't think to let me know that one of my employees was going to pull some Sherlock Holmes stunt?"

"First off, he wasn't planning on leaving the office," she shot back, knowing it was worry making Ryuu an ass, but still. "Second, when I spoke to him after the meeting, he was still working on it. At. His. Desk."

"Okay, okay," he muttered. "I'm going to see if I can get into his computer and find out what he was working on."

"What's he driving?" she asked then tucked her phone between her shoulder and ear as she began digging money out of her pocket. She threw it on the table, grabbed her jacket, and left Montage. As she hit the door, she was almost running.

"An old green pickup truck," he answered. "You won't be able to miss it. He's been putting it together piece by piece, so it's a patchwork of primer and olive green. I think he's got a headlight out as well." He blew out an audible breath. "At least it wasn't working this morning when we were at Warrick's."

"So GPS is out then," she said, getting on her bike. "I'm going to backtrack his possible routes and see what I can find. See if you can track his cell." She didn't wait for his response, but hung up and shoved the phone in her jacket pocket. Tugging on the helmet, she started the powerful bike and roared out of the parking lot, her heart in her throat.

CHAPTER 18

Xander followed the most direct route from Montage to Taliesin, scanning the steep drop offs and surrounding traffic. Oregon's Department of Transportation obviously had something against streetlights because they were few and far between. It never bothered her, until now, when she could have used the extra light. Since the shadows created their own black holes along the roadsides, she concentrated on any signs of a vehicle going off the road.

Her frustration mounted and the uneasy feeling from earlier had morphed into a full-on ball of dread. It wasn't until she hit the road tucked in the forested area just past the Terwilliger Curves that she struck pay dirt.

She carefully pulled in behind the parked pickup sitting on the side of the road. Her headlight illuminated the obviously newly dented bumper and the partially open driver's door. She sat there, studying the truck, her bike's quiet rumbles magnified under the heavy foliage. Someone had hit the vehicle, hard enough to leave one taillight hanging by a wire like a dangling, bloody eyeball.

Tension crawled down her spine. She turned off her

bike's engine, but left the headlight on so she could study the damage. As the engine's echoes faded, an oppressive silence snuck in and the feeling of being watched crawled over her.

Making her way to the truck, she tried to scan her surroundings without being obvious about it. Between the wind blown clouds cutting in front of the moon and the swaying trees, the shadows took on ominous over-tones.

Up close, she could see the flecks of darker paint etched into the scraped metal of the bumper and, through the windshield, confirmed the cab was empty. Crouching down, she ran her finger over the marks. She studied the paint chips on her finger under the light of her bike's headlamp. Blue or black, maybe. She couldn't be sure unless she got some better light. Even with her exceptional eyesight, it was a muted shade of dark. She brushed her finger off on her pants, rose to her feet, then did a slow perusal of her surroundings.

If someone was out there, they were holding prenaturally still. Walking around to the passenger side of Zeke's abandoned truck, she sucked in a deep breath, hoping to catch a scent. Wood, winter, wet dirt, the sharp bite of gasoline, and something that stung her nose. It got stronger as she moved toward the front of the truck. She sneezed. Antifreeze.

Frickin' fantastic. Zeke's radiator must have blown. Unfortunately, the astringent smell just rendered her nose temporarily useless. It would take a few minutes to clear it out.

She placed a hand against the hood, the metal cold under her touch, increasing her worry. She crouched down and sure enough, there was a pool of antifreeze painting the dirt with a light luminance. Half-hidden behind the front wheel well, she was able to see under the truck and to the other side. The faint snap of a branch had her breath stilling and her muscles coiling. She watched the bare ground on the truck's far side. Leaves blew gently across the earth, but nothing else moved.

She couldn't stay in this position long or whoever was out there would know they had her attention. She pasted a worried frown on her face and stood up. "Hey, Zeke? You out there?" She kept her voice quiet. Let her watcher think they had her fooled. She made her way around the front of the truck until she stood next to the partially open driver's door, presenting a tempting target.

There was no way she was giving that forest her back. Right now, she was scent blind and although the night was a spectrum of grays, the shadows were thick.

A soft moan drifted through the night, raising the hair on the back of her neck. Was it Zeke? Had he been disoriented from the hit and stumbled off in the wrong direction? Or was it a lure? She stared into the heavy foliage. Only one way to find out.

She picked her way down the slight slope and into the trees, letting her wolf slide under her skin, taking comfort in her reassuring presence. Her steps quieted and her muscles flowed as she made her way deeper in. Again, that soft moan echoed through the night. She tilted her head, swiveling around to pinpoint the direction. Definitely sounded male. She altered her path until she was downwind.

There, through the patchwork of branches and ivy-covered tree trunks, she finally found her prey. Hunched over, a hand on a thick pine, she still couldn't tell if it was Zeke. Whoever it was, was facing away from her and seemed to be completely unaware of her presence.

She held still, watching, waiting.

The figure gasped then stumbled forward.

She rolled to the balls of her feet, poised to jump closer, except the capricious wind changed its direction.

The figure straightened with alarming speed, one arm coming up then down.

Pure instinct had Xander jerking her body to the side and spinning behind the nearest tree. The blade swept by so close she could taste the bite of silver in the air. She rounded the trunk, lethal nails ripping through her fingers, the bright pain lost under the rush of adrenaline. She managed a couple of steps before he was on her, cutting off her route.

Muscled arms wrapped around her waist as a shoulder plowed into her stomach. He managed to lift her off her feet but she twisted enough to keep her arms free. Still, not a good position to be in. He used his weight against her, slamming her against the tree.

Pain exploded across her back and ran down her spine. Unable to brace for the impact, her vision became dotted with white stars as her head snapped back with a solid thunk. The shock of the hit may have stolen her air but it flipped her internal switch.

Time seemed to slow and the night erupted into crystal clarity. Her pain faded under the melding of her intellect and her wolf's instinct.

She cupped her hands and slammed them over his ears, shooting an explosion of air down his eardrums. To make her point, she dug the sharp tips of her nails into his scalp and skull and dragged them down. The arms around her waist loosened and her feet hit the ground. A painful yowl ripped through the night as he stumbled back. Not hesitating, she kicked out with her leg, nailing her attacker in the ribs.

He stumbled back, shaking his head and flinging his blood like sweat. The furrows from her nails left strips of flesh hanging around his head like strands of gory hair. His yowl morphed to a furious growl. "Stupid bitch, I'm gonna make you pay."

"You're welcome to try," she snarled.

He was a big guy. Thick arms, even thicker chest, no neck, and huge hands. If she was lucky he'd be slow and awkward. He stepped closer, his arms up in classic boxing stance, and snapped out a left jab.

She barely had time to twist to take the hit on her shoulder. So much for that theory. She was facing an experienced fighter.

Using her twist, she continued her spin and snuck in a strike on his unprotected ribs as she came back around. She ducked his right hook and went in low, raking her nails across his stomach. The scent of fresh blood marked her hit and her nose coming back online.

The bright burst of scent was quickly followed by another. Her attacker's. A now familiar smell of Feral wrongness washed over her. Whoever this was, he was tied to Neil and the two other Bitten wolves. The unexpectedness of her discovery left her open and she took a solid hit to her stomach. Doubled over his arm, she clamped her shifted hands on his flesh and sank her claws in deep, fighting for air.

He roared, trying to yank his arm back.

Her nails tore through his skin and muscles, shredding his arm to the bone as he tried to pull it back. She dodged to the side, letting him go to avoid his hastily thrown right hook aimed at the back of her head.

He stumbled, off balance, and hunched over, his mutilated arm cradled against his stomach.

It was an opening and she took it. Sucking in short, shallow breaths, she moved in, counting on her small size and speed. Before he could avoid her, she hammered her fist against the base of his skull then darted out of reach. The shock of her hit sent him to his knees.

She lashed out with a kick to his jaw. Dazed or not, he still got his hands up to block the kick and slapped her leg away. But it wasn't enough. She used the movement of her right leg to mask the actual strike from her left. Her foot snapped just under his ear, hitting hard against his carotid artery. The shock of her strike ran up her leg, but she didn't have time to gloat. Her right leg crumpled under her as she completed the kick, giving her an up close and personal view of the ground.

She forced her body to roll out of range of his possible retaliation then struggled to her feet. The majority of her weight rested on her left leg as her right took its sweet time to relearn how to hold her weight. It didn't matter. Her attacker swayed on his knees. His left arm was braced against the ground while his right hung uselessly at his side dripping blood.

She limped over until she stood directly in front of him. It wasn't a smart move, but there was a chance he was about to keel over as his heart tried to pump blood through his smashed artery. But she couldn't be certain. Most shifters who encountered such damage could heal it. They'd just endure some woozy moments. Problem was, if he was anything like the wolves she'd been dealing with lately, he may not make it. Before he checked out, she needed some damn answers.

He lifted his head, his eyes trying to focus on her.

She sighed and considered crouching down but her right leg was still bitching. She told it to shut the hell up and awkwardly knelt down. "Where's Zeke, asswipe?"

Dull incomprehension stared back at her.

She grabbed his square chin and held him steady. "Where. Is. Zeke?"

He mumbled something, but she couldn't make it out then his eyes slid close.

She shook his jaw. "Wake up, Sleeping Ugly, and focus here." She pulled the dominant card and shoved the command at him.

His eyes flickered open and she didn't need her wolf's sudden wariness to know something had just gone horribly wrong. The dull gaze was replaced by a gut-chilling Feral glow and his lips pulled back, revealing too sharp teeth.

She barely jerked back in time to avoid having a chunk of her face torn off as he lunged forward. When he went to put his weight on his hands, his mangled arm collapsed beneath him, slowing him down.

She scrambled back, trying to get to her feet. Her wolf didn't give her a chance to choose but ripped through her, shifting her form. Her change was so fast, she was still reeling from the shock, even as her wolf surged forward and took control.

She flung the remnants of her clothes clear. There was no waiting for her attacker to regain his feet. Instead, she laid her ears flat and used the muscles in her four legs to clear the space between them. He might have worn human skin, but only the animal remained. He scrambled to his hands and feet, moving on all fours with a disturbing grace.

They circled each other, the werewolf and the man-wolf.

He lunged.

She dodged.

His weight slammed into her haunches instead of her side like he had intended. When he stumbled, off balance from the misjudged hit, she surged forward and sank her teeth deep into his unprotected throat. His blood filled her mouth and savage satisfaction rose. He was prey. He was dead.

A deep growl rumbled in her chest as breath rattled in his. He began to panic. His wild hits rained along her spine and shoulders, but she clamped her teeth tighter and yanked her head to the side. Warm blood splattered across her muzzle. Her prey stopped fighting and slowly collapsed in front of her. She dropped the metallic-tasting meat and took a cautious step back. Then another, never taking her gaze from the crumpled form in front of her.

She backed away and when the night's sounds returned to normal, relaxed her ears before dropping into a sitting position. With the immediate threat removed, she felt a familiar presence tugging along that bright connection. *Mate. Worry. Inquiry.*

She wagged her tail and shared her satisfaction of a job well done, a challenge accepted and won. Then her human was there, soothing the ruffled fur of her mate and gently blocking their shared connection. She let her eyes drift closed as Xander's quiet thankfulness and acceptance ran over her like gentle fingers stroking through her fur. She huffed out a sigh. They were safe, so she relinquished control to Xander.

The change was much, much slower and a hell of lot more painful this time. When she was done, she lay on the ground naked and panting. She could still feel Warrick's concern and did her best to keep him calm. She forced her worries about Zeke to the back of her mind, where Warrick wouldn't see it. There was nothing he could do and she just needed a few minutes to get a grip on what the hell was going on.

Warrick would've never known what had happened if her wolf hadn't decided to reach down that thrice-damned bond and pull on his power. Since shifting on the fly wasn't one of her usual talents, she had no doubt that little feat was all him. Hell, she didn't even know she could do that. A small smile escaped. It could come in handy though.

Then her muscles contorted, protesting her recent changes and her smile turned into a grimace. Unfortunately, the aftermath left something to be desired.

She rolled to her back, feeling the cold from the ground seep along her spine. She breathed through her protesting muscle cramps and assorted aches and pains, keeping her gaze on the moon playing peekaboo with the windswept trees. When the cramps slowed to a dull throb, she turned to her side and carefully pushed her body into a sitting position. The world around her took a quick, stomach-curdling dip before leveling off.

In front of her, face down in a pool of blood, lay her attacker. The wind reached out with chilly fingers and her skin erupted in goose bumps. Not wanting to chance a face plant, she slowly crawled forward. Somewhere around her had to be what was left of her clothes, right? Thinking back to the fight, she knew they had to be close. Carefully turning her head, she scanned the surrounding trees until she spotted the pitiful remains of fabric.

Damn it. Please, gods, let her phone be all right. Adjusting her direction as the wind picked up, bringing with it the smell of impending rain, she stopped, brought up short by a scent. She raised her head, drawing the air in through her nose. It made her ribs ache, but she ignored the discomfort.

Maybe she had been hit harder than she thought because this scent couldn't be here. It didn't make sense.

She stretched her neck as she followed the faint traces. It was so light. She closed her eyes as she held onto the elusive trail. Where was it coming from? It took her a minute but she caught it and tracked it down.

She opened her eyes to find her nose scant inches from her attacker's body. His jacket covered shoulder to be exact. She leaned in, until her face skimmed the material. There, under the musky not-quite-right smell, lay the unique blend of citrus and cloves.

Shocked, she sat up, her mind whirling. What the hell was going on? This scent shouldn't be here. Scents were like fingerprints, each one belonging to a specific person. This one belonged to one wolf—Sebastian Riner, Motoki Pack's Third.

CHAPTER 19

By the time Xander found her phone, buried under a mixture of material scraps, wet leaves, and bits of wood and dirt, the damp chill had sunk bone deep. She hunched her back and cradled the electronic device protectively while soft rain slid down her back. As the phone flickered to life, her finger hesitated over the screen.

Calling Warrick was out. What could she tell him? She had no idea where Zeke was and as for Sebastian? Other than the faint traces of scent, there was no direct evidence he had anything to do with Zeke's disappearance. Not to mention the whole motive question. Despite her personal feelings, her mind struggled with tying Sebastian to this mess.

She stared down at the screen, shivers wracking her hands. Warrick had enough on his plate. Whatever happened in his office earlier left him badly shaken. Which was why when they were out running earlier, she deliberately stifled her questions, wanting to give him a much needed break from whatever it was that left his fur ruffled.

She could call Ryuu. She shook her head. Nope, no calling Ryuu. Not only was Sebastian one of his closest friends, but the same reasons applied. No concrete evidence and no logical explanation.

Which left her with...who?

The muscle in her hip cramped, and she shifted her weight, which brought the battered body back into the line of her sight. She narrowed her eyes as she considered someone who might be able to see more than she could.

It took her three times to get her numb fingers to hit the right buttons.

"McCord."

"Raine, it's Xander. I need your help."

"Where are you?" Concern lent Raine's voice a sharp edge.

"Just pass the Terwilliger Curves. Um—" Xander clenched her teeth to block another violent shiver before continuing. "—I'm about a mile and half down on Dowlings Road."

She heard Raine mutter the directions to someone else. "How bad are you hurt?" There was a dull thud of a car door closing, then an engine revving.

"Not hurt," Xander got out through chattering teeth. "Just freezing my ass off. Do you think you could bring me some clothes?"

There was a pause. "Wow, I'm impressed. I never thought Vidis would be one to indulge in roadside sex."

Despite the grim circumstances, Raine's wry comment made Xander smile. "Jealous?"

"Nah, I prefer the kitchen floor. It's warmer."

Xander choked on a laugh then groaned as her ribs protested. "Warrick's in a meeting, I think."

"You are hurt." Raine hadn't missed the pain-filled sound. Her voice was wiped clean of any teasing. "We're about ten minutes out. Do I need to call Vidis?"

"I'm fine," Xander reassured her. "A little bruised and battered, but fine. And don't call Warrick. I need you to check something out first."

Another pause. "Does this have to do with our earlier conversation?"

Xander studied the scene before her. *Did it?* "Maybe," she answered slowly. "I'm not sure."

"Okay, hang tight. We'll be there in a few." The line went dead.

"Yeah, not going anywhere," Xander whispered. She huddled under the relative shelter of the huge trunk and waited.

Warrick stood in his office, his back to the room, listening to the voices arguing behind him on the speakerphone. Half of his mind tracked the conversation of his alphas as they discussed the pros and cons of allowing the mavericks to establish their own pack. He sighed. Things were going exactly as he had suspected. No one wanted to give up territory, nor was anyone very happy about adding another pack to the Northwest. If he pushed this, he was in for a hell of a fight.

Problem was, he wasn't sure he wanted the fight. Dmitri may be his only surviving family, but a part of Warrick wished his brother had stayed dead and gone. Dmitri's presence was a complication Warrick didn't want, or need, right now. Not to mention the dark tendrils of unsupported suspicion starting to twist around the emotional storm his brother had left behind.

He wished he could blame his uneasiness on their shared history, and maybe that was some of it. But it was hard not to listen as that coldly logical voice pointed out how Dmitri's appearance, just as Warrick faced an unknown threat, was too coincidental. He couldn't decide if the voice was a result of his own personal feelings or a warning. He continued to stare blindly out the night-shrouded window.

"Vidis," a deep voice called his attention back to the conversation continuing behind him. "How well do you know this Dan Vicks?"

Warrick turned his head and glared at the phone. "Considering I just met him today, that seems an asinine question, Mike."

Strained patience and a sigh echoed down the line as the other voices fell quiet, listening. "Is it? A maverick you don't know, who wants land and power in your territory, approached you. I'd be an irresponsible wolf if I didn't point out to my alpha that something doesn't smell right here."

"Besides," chimed in another voice, "these are mavericks, Vidis. These wolves couldn't cut it in a normal pack. They're unable to submit to an established alpha. What makes them think they'll be able to bare their throats to you now?"

"The fact that they've made an effort to submit a legitimate request," Warrick said, "indicates their willingness to try. We can do no less than give their request fair consideration." Disgruntled rumbles erupted over the phone. "Gentlemen." Warrick kept his tone level, even as the urge to snarl rose. "I'm not asking for a decision tonight. I'm asking that you consider the request then send me your valid concerns as soon as you can."

There was no ignoring the whip of command in his tone. One by one, the men on the phone murmured their reluctant agreement and rang off.

Mike Bradley, alpha of the Kenai Pack, stayed on the line. He waited until everyone else had hung up before saying, "Vidis, I don't like this."

Warrick stepped back from the window and made his way to his desk. "Which part, Mike?" He dropped into his chair and stared at the phone. "Being asked to give up land or the fact that we're considering giving a bunch of renegade wolves their entree into pack politics?"

"Both," Mike answered. "I know if you decide to do this, the land will come from me or Philippe."

"It's not like Alaska or Alberta are lacking land," Warrick observed dryly.

Mike's answer was an inelegant snort. "That's not my biggest worry. My gut syas there's something more to this than protection from human detection."

"Mine, too," Warrick admitted. "Until I can find out what that is, we'll follow through on the petition process."

"Politics as a stalling measure," Mike said. "Nice."

Warrick's smile felt grim. "Their choice to come play with the big dogs. Now let's see if they can hold their own."

"Well then, as long as you know what you're doing," Mike said. "I'll send you my two cents in the next few days then." He rang off.

Warrick sat at his desk, rubbing his temples in a futile attempt to erase the ache behind his eyes. He hoped Mike's faith in him wasn't displaced. His path wasn't as clear as he'd like. In fact—

Xander.

His thoughts were abruptly cut off as a whip of lightning streaked across his soul. Xander was in trouble. He didn't hesitate, but opened himself to their bond. There was as sharp snap as she pulled on his abilities. He breathed through it, his fists clenching on the desk, giving what he could. His wolf surged to the surface and raced down their connection, only to find a breathless silence.

He concentrated on dragging air into his lungs and shoving it back out. His wolf paced back and forth, like a dog on a leash. Together, man and wolf waited. Warrick refused to let his dread gain the upper hand. Xander was a warrior and she would let him know if this was something she couldn't handle. Wouldn't she? He shoved the question back, focusing on his wolf.

He had no idea how long it was before savage satisfaction of a battle won, joy of being with their mate, and a tendril of gratitude for respecting their independence broke through, calming man and wolf. This time, Warrick reached out to Xander, needing to know what was happening. He was met by her gentle rebuff. He could sense she was okay, but handling something. He retreated.

He wanted answers and if he couldn't get them from her, he'd go around her. He picked up the phone and dialed. On the other end, the phone rang once then went to voice mail. "You've reached Ryuu Kern. Please leave a message."

"Call me," Warrick growled then slammed the phone down. What the hell was going on?

Xander jerked awake at the sound of gravel under tires. A swath of light cut across the trees and left her blinking. She got to her feet like an old woman, muscles protesting every movement, and used the tree trunk behind her for balance. The slam of car doors was followed by the sound of her name being called.

"Here," she answered, her voice rough.

Moments later, Raine stepped out of the night, her silver gaze taking a quick inventory of Xander and the sprawled form between them. She half turned and called back, "Gavin, stay put for a second." Then she continued forward and stepped around the body. She held out a bundle of clothes to Xander. "Here. Put these on before that blue becomes a permanent addition to your skin tone."

Xander grinned and grabbed the clothes.

Raine winced. "And don't do that."

"Do what?" Xander dragged on the oversized sweatshirt that must belong to Gavin since it fit her like a dress and carried his scent.

"Smile like that."

Puzzled, she lifted her head as she finished pulling up the stretchy workout pants, her body shuddering with pleasure as the material provided much needed warmth. "Huh?"

With one finger, Raine made a circular motion near her mouth in response.

Xander reached up and felt her face. Dried blood crusted her skin.

"It looks like some kind of gruesome facial," Raine muttered.

Xander dropped her head to hide her smile. Funny how such a small thing unsettled the unshakable Raine. Xander fiddled with the tie on the pants until she was sure her humor was under control. "Thanks for the clothes."

Raine knelt by the dead body, her arms resting on her

knees. "No problem." She studied the corpse. "What happened?"

Gavin stepped clear of the trees. "I turned off the lights on your bike."

"Thanks." Xander dropped her phone into her pocket and gathered the shredded remains of her clothes. She had turned the phone off after Warrick's second attempt to reach her. She had no idea what to say to him. She tried sending reassurance down their bond, but if the answering wave of male frustration was any indication, it wasn't enough.

She picked her way over to Raine. "The truck belongs to Zeke."

"Zeke's the one who was looking into things about the chat room, right?" Raine asked.

"Yep. He was supposed to meet me at Montage, but never showed. Ryuu called, looking for him and we got worried."

"So you decided to see if you could track him?" Gavin held out a hand for the bundle she held.

She handed him the pathetic ball of cloth and watched as he stuffed it into a plastic bag. The man must have been a Boy Scout to be that prepared, unless...She shot a speculative look at Raine's bent head, wondering again about the strength of the connection she shared with Gavin. "Someone ran his truck off the road. And I found this one," she motioned to the body, "hanging around."

Gavin quirked an eyebrow. "Waiting for you or on clean up duty?"

"I think I interrupted his clean up duty." Xander used a bare foot to nudge the body. "I don't think whoever sent him thought anyone would be looking for Zeke so soon."

"Gavin, help me turn him over." Raine duck-walked

until she was at the body's shoulders. Gavin squatted down and helped flip the dead weight over.

Xander winced as the extent of the damage was revealed.

His arm was nothing but torn tendon and bone. There was a gaping hole under his chin, and his nose was obviously broken. Even the moonlight couldn't soften the impact of the deep furrows along the sides of his head.

Gavin let out a low whistle. "Damn, Xander. For such a little thing, you pack a hell of a punch."

Before Xander could react, Raine reached out and smacked him on the arm. "Don't be such a male."

Gavin caught her wrist and gave her a small tug. "It was a compliment."

"Whatever," Raine muttered.

Xander caught the hint of a blush running under Raine's skin and wondered what she missed.

Raine got to her feet, her hands going to her hips. "What do you need from me?"

Now came the tricky part. "I need you to read his magic."

Raine watched her. "Are you going to tell me what I'm looking for?"

Xander looked back at the body, thinking. "I think there's a connection between this wolf and Neil."

"What kind of connection?" Obviously, Raine had filled Gavin in on the situation.

Xander shrugged. "I'm not sure yet." She forestalled Raine's impending question by raising her hand. "Look, I found traces of someone who shouldn't have any connection with this."

Raine tilted her head. "How does my reading the magical traces help?"

Xander blew out a breath, trying to still the roiling of her stomach. "I'm going to see if we can match it to someone else."

"You suspect someone," Gavin said flatly.

Xander dipped her head in a short nod. "I do, but until I'm certain, I'm not naming them."

Silence fell. Xander paced a couple steps away then came back. Maybe her personal feelings were finally getting in the way. While she waited for Raine, she turned the situation around and around, trying to connect the faint threads to actual reasons. Sebastian could be a real bastard. His opinion on the female gender was outdated—Neanderthal, at best—but being a chauvinistic dick didn't automatically make you a betrayer. There was a slight chance that a reasonable explanation could be found—maybe. The thought of accusing a trusted member of her pack made her ill, but it wasn't going to stop her from following this. Wherever it led.

"Fine." Raine broke the quiet, sharing an unreadable look with Gavin. Xander got the impression she was missing parts of a conversation. "I'll do what I can, but you're going to do something for me."

Xander stilled. "Like?"

"You're coming with us and meeting with Cheveyo."

Xander instantly started shaking her head. "Oh hell no, Raine. You don't know what you're asking."

"I know exactly what I'm asking."

"Do you?" Xander bit out. "You're asking me to go behind Warrick's back and share pack information with someone he doesn't trust."

"No," Raine countered, "I'm asking you to protect the stubborn ass that you love and start using the resources available to you, since he won't."

A coldness, that had nothing to do with the night chill and everything to do with the fragile line she walked with Warrick and their relationship, crawled across her heart. "No," she repeated, her voice hoarse.

"Xander," Raine said with a conciliatory note. "You're not betraying him. You're protecting him."

"That's not protection," she argued.

"Isn't it?" her friend asked with brutal practicality. "You don't want to name your suspect, probably because he's someone close to Vidis. But you need something to tie this all together if you want to find Zeke. Not only that, but chances are Cheveyo can offer some valuable insight into why someone would hire a wizard to assassinate an alpha. You know as well as I do, that Cheveyo had nothing to do with it, but from what you've said, there's not a chance in hell that Vidis will ask for his help."

Xander spun away as Raine's words hit with unerring accuracy. Damn it, Raine was right. The problem was if Xander did this, if she reached out to another head of house without talking to Warrick, he'd never forgive her. He was so concerned with not looking weak and protecting those he considered his from any and all threats that he isolated himself. And that was another conversation, which would end in an argument if their first one was anything to go by.

Plus, she couldn't talk to Warrick without revealing her suspicions of Sebastian, and the gods knew she better have some solid damn proof before she set Warrick on his Third. If she was wrong, it would destroy more than her relationship with Warrick. It would devastate their entire pack.

But she couldn't let this go, not so long as there was even a slim chance there was something to this.

Choosing between her need to protect the man she

loved and her desire to honor his trust was going to tear her apart. Either she did her duty, following every lead to protect her pack and alpha, or she bowed to her mate's demands. Rubbing her fist against the dull ache in her chest, she admitted she was screwed either way.

The last time she put her emotions before duty the end results had cost the life of her best friend and her unborn cub. Memories pressed close—her friend's tear-stained face as she cradled her stomach in a futile attempt to protect her unborn child from her mate, who's sanity was lost to the feral nature of his wolf, and Xander, hesitating to do what needed to be done.

She brushed her fingers over the scars hidden under the ink on her face. Her wolf rose, offering what comfort she could, crowding the painful memories back so Xander could think. As Tracker, she knew what her decision had to be, but it left that hidden part of her raw and torn.

Gently, she closed the door on those softer emotions and took a deep breath. She couldn't let her pack and her mate pay for her inability to make a decision. There was no way to prepare for the fallout when Warrick found out. When he did, because there was no doubt he would, he would be furious. That she could handle. It was the other reactions he may not admit to that worried her. After demanding he be honest with her, did she have the right to ignore his concerns? Even if she was convinced it would keep him safe? Keep their pack safe? She reached out to her wolf, needing comfort and strength as she considered her options. Protection of their mate was paramount.

And if we lose him? She buried her face in the familiar fur of her wolf as she whispered the heart-rending question.

Her wolf's answer was clear. *Protect our mate.*

Tears burned and her shoulders hunched as the dread

in her stomach left bile rising. She was going to risk it all because the thought of harm coming to Warrick was more devastating than watching him walk out of her life.

Sucking in a breath, she shoved her emotions back, straightened her spine, then turned around. Hollow pride rose when her voice didn't shake. "Fine. Let's get this done."

CHAPTER 20

"How long do you think you can keep Vidis out of this?" Ryuu asked, all business.

Xander pressed the phone to her ear, grateful for her friend's temperate disposition. Which was kind of an oxymoron when you thought about it. Instinctual by nature, a shifter being able to maintain a level head was nothing short of a miracle. *And you're doing a wonderful job of avoiding his question,* a snarky mental voice that sounded a lot like Raine's piped up. Except Raine was standing with Gavin just outside the range of the SUV's headlights.

"Just a little while longer, Ryuu." Xander rested her head against the SUV's window. Tucked in the back seat, she was trying to keep this conversation somewhat private. "I may have something, but it's not making sense."

The sound of Ryuu's sigh echoed down the line. "I can give you an hour then I'm heading over to get the scene cleaned up, that's it. He's already called once."

She closed her eyes, her fingers tightening around the phone. "I know. He's been trying to reach me as well."

"You're blocking him?"

"I'm trying."

"Fan-fucking-tastic," Ryuu muttered. "That will make things oh so much better."

She choked back the snarl threatening to escape behind gritted teeth. "Dammit, Ryuu." Like this was easy for her.

"Don't," her friend snapped, no longer her friend but the Second of the Motoki Pack. "I don't know what the hell's going on, Xander, but you better be damn certain that whatever you're hiding won't threaten our alpha or pack when it comes to light. Because, mate or not, I'm done watching you two tear at each other."

The urge to smash the phone into the glass until one or both shattered made her hand shake. But it wouldn't accomplish a thing. Even she could hear her wolf in her voice as she said, "This isn't me being pissed at my mate. I'm doing my job as Tracker. Threaten all you want, but I will not make an accusation without proof." Her teeth were clenched so hard she had to drag air in through her nose. Forcing her jaw to unlock, she continued, "Right now, I need a little room to follow this lead with Raine, then I will meet you at Warrick's in two hours."

"Fine." Obviously, Ryuu had reached the end of his patience because he bit the word out like his teeth were wrapped around her neck. "I'll see if I can get ahold of Sebastian and get him to help. Then we'll discuss this entire mess at Vidis's." He hung up before she could respond.

She choked back the bile rising in her throat. If her suspicions were right, Ryuu would be showing up alone. Jerking the door open, Xander fairly leapt from the SUV. She could feel the press of fur under her skin. Her volatile emotions and the lure of the moon made for a potent combination. Stalking over to where Raine and Gavin were waiting near Zeke's truck, she clenched her phone.

"My, Grandma, what big eyes you have," Raine said, her arms folded across her chest as she stood shoulder to shoulder with Gavin.

"You should see my teeth," Xander growled, literally.

A small smile flashed over Gavin's face.

Raine pushed off the truck and studied her with a critical eye. "You sure you can handle the ride back to Taliesin?"

Taliesin, where, at Xander's request, Cheveyo was going to meet them. Xander winced. That would be a fun meeting. She blew out a breath. She must look a little rougher than she thought for Raine to ask. "Yeah, I'll be fine." Because really, she had no choice.

The sound of plastic cracking had her looking down to where she held her phone. She made a concentrated effort to relax her fingers and get a damn grip—emotionally speaking. What she wouldn't give to be able to lose herself to her wolf. A long, hard run under the light of the moon would do more to help her find her balance than what was waiting for her tonight. Ryuu's attitude might ruffle her fur the wrong way, but if she was being fair, and she was the one on the outside looking in, she'd have to wonder about her critical thinking skills when it came to Warrick. Hell, the emotional roller coaster of the last couple days would rival any amusement ride.

It took a moment for Raine to give her a slow nod. "All right, let's go see what your little friend can tell us." She turned and headed back toward the body.

Gavin waited for Xander to follow Raine before falling into step beside her. "How long do we have?"

"An hour."

"Should be more than enough," Raine threw over her shoulder. Coming up to the body, she stepped around until she could crouch at his head. "So you want me to match his magic to Neil's?"

"Pretty much." Finding a spot on a fallen log, Xander went to take a seat. Her thigh was still one big throbbing ache, which made bending down awkward. Not to mention the number it played with her balance. Before she could face-plant, Gavin was there with a steadying arm. "Thanks." She settled on the log with his help. "It won't be exactly the same."

Raine cocked her head. "What do you mean?"

Xander flicked her fingers at the body. "I think this one isn't a Bitten, but a Born. His change was too fast."

"So then, why do you think Raine will be able to link him to Neil?" Gavin moved over to Raine's side.

"Same scent of wrongness." When they both looked at her, she gave a small shrug. "His scent was just...wrong. I'm not sure how else to explain it."

"Works for me." Raine turned her attention back to the body. "Okay, let's see if my eyes can back up your nose." She slid Gavin a quick look. He moved behind her then crouched down until he could brace her back, his hands resting on her waist. Only then did she close her eyes.

It was weird watching Raine do her thing. Xander had been through this with her before in Arizona, but it was still fascinating. Being around Raine was like hanging out with a lightning bolt, the sense of roiling energy she carried like a second skin, and you never knew when it would sneak out and shock your ass. Yet, when she did this...whatever it was...all that energy just disappeared. As a matter of fact, if Xander hadn't been sitting right across from Raine, she wasn't sure she would have even known Raine was there.

Every shifter possessed enhanced senses—smell, hearing, sight—but none of them would help her track

Raine when she was pulling on whatever magic she used to examine someone's magical signatures. It was as if she stepped out of the physical world and melded into the psychic one. Very weird. Xander wondered if she should tell Raine about the strange phenomena. Maybe later. Right now, they had other things to worry about.

Wind blew through the branches, chasing leaves and trailing chilly fingers against her skin. The faint sounds of traffic from the highway interrupted the night's natural chorus, a reminder that no matter how thick the trees were they were a fragile protection from prying eyes.

Long minutes passed before Raine finally spoke. "Okay," she said, her voice low as if she was concentrating on something. "I've found what I think is his normal weave."

The way she phrased that left Xander puzzled. "You can't tell?"

Raine opened her eyes and turned her head toward Xander, her normal gray eyes now glowing silver. "It's a mess in here." She dropped her gaze back to the body. "And he's dead, in case you've forgotten. Means his traces are starting to fade, which makes it harder to figure out what the hell's going on." She went quiet, her fingers moving in a restless pattern. "Need to move a little deeper," she muttered.

The hair on the back of Xander's neck began to rise. She struggled to her feet, ignoring the twinge in her thigh and rushed to her friend's side, her hand out as if that would hold her back. "Raine, stop!"

Gavin's posture turned from supportive to protective in an instant. Whether in response to Xander's warning or because he was acting as Raine's psychic shadow, Xander had no idea. He wrapped Raine in his arms, pulled her to his chest, then dragged her a few inches away from the body, but Xander knew he was mimicking the move on the psychic plane. It was there, in the fierce concentration etching his face in harsh lines and in his coiled muscles.

"Raine!" There was no mistaking the sharp command in his voice. "Step back, now!"

Xander found she was holding her breath as she fought back a frustrating sense of helplessness at not being able to protect her friend from whatever she faced.

Raine's body jerked in Gavin's arms then her eyes flew open. The strange glow wasn't there. Instead, the normal gray was back, a fact that helped Xander breathe. Her abused thigh finally gave out and she sat down hard. Whatever had tripped her warning system into shrieking life was gone. "What the hell happened?"

Raine leaned back into Gavin, one hand gripping his wrist as if she needed an anchor. Her face was even more pale than usual. "Got too close."

"To what?"

"A big, psychic black hole." Her grin was forced. "Apparently, if your magic is too damaged when you die, it starts to disappear into bits and pieces, leaving nothing behind." Raine turned her head away and buried her face against Gavin's chest, a shudder visibly running over her.

Confused, Xander just looked from her to Gavin.

"Think of magic like a piece of cloth." Gavin's voice was even, but traces of anger lay just under the calm tone. "Every aspect of who you are and what you can do makes up the threads that, in turn, create the material. His material was ragged and torn. When Raine went closer to examine it, it began unraveling faster than she expected. It left her with nothing to hold on to."

"That can't be good," Xander said.

"It's not," Raine's voice was muffled against Gavin. She

turned her head to look down at Xander. "But the good news is you were right. Whatever's behind the new and so-not-improved version of your wolves leaves a distinctive destructive pattern behind. He and Neil were definitely linked." Raine straightened and pulled away from Gavin's hold. He dropped his arms and let her move.

Proving the connection should have made Xander feel better. Instead, her disquiet became louder than ever. "So it's a spell? No science involved?"

Above her, Raine offered Xander a hand. "Spell, yes. Science? I don't know enough to be sure."

Xander grabbed Raine's hand and let her friend pull her to her feet. She brushed the collection of dirt and detritus from the stretchy material of her borrowed pants. "Would Cheveyo?"

Raine didn't immediately answer, but stared at the body for a minute. "Maybe, but I think messing with someone's magic will be a hell of a lot easier than proving science had a hand in this." She shook her head and met Xander's gaze. "Besides, science has never played well with magic." Old horrors darkened her eyes.

Xander curled her hands to keep from reaching out in comfort. She kept her voice soft. "Maybe that's the why behind all the damage you're seeing."

Raine gave a short nod, turned away, and headed to the cars, leaving Xander and Gavin behind.

"Will she be okay?" Xander asked the man who moved to stand so silent beside her. Watching her friend walk away, she knew she wasn't the only one still trying to find her way back after Arizona.

Gavin brushed her shoulder. "She will be." He began following in Raine's wake.

Watching his broad back disappear into the shadows,

Xander sighed. She dragged her hand through her hair and wished this night was over. Even if Cheveyo confirmed their suspicions on the spell and its effect, they had no idea who was behind it or why. Discovering Sebastian's scent on the body hadn't helped either. It just raised more questions. Questions she wasn't sure she could ask without hurting those she was sworn to protect.

The night clouds shifted and the moon's light fell over her, offering a soft song of promise. She closed her eyes and lifted her face, taking a moment to bask in the comfort. Her heart ached. Her pack was being stalked by an unknown enemy, her mate was being singled out, and Zeke was out there alone somewhere. Fate's cosmic clock was ticking away and Xander had the feeling she was running out of time.

Xander and Raine headed to Taliesin, leaving Gavin behind to ensure no one else decided to drop in before Ryuu came to clean up the after party mess. There was no need for conversation on the ride over. Raine's stereo was filling in the blanks quite nicely, the volume nowhere near as ear-destroying as normal.

Xander propped her bare feet against the dashboard and let her muscles relax into the seat. The insipid yellow streetlights played peekaboo with her battered pedicure. *Now you see the dirt, now you don't.* She'd have to take advantage of the fifth-floor showers before she met with Cheveyo. She looked out the window. Much like her battered feet, the reflection of her blood-spattered face flickered across the glass like an old film reel.

An unexpected, impatient tug on the bond connecting

her to Warrick raked across her psychic skin. Flinching at the underlying demand for a response that was coming through loud and clear, she let her head fall back against the seat. She kept her face turned away from Raine, just in case. Warrick wasn't going to be patient and she couldn't keep him out forever.

Not that she wanted to, but she had no idea how much he could see when she let him in and that worried her. For three weeks, she kept him out and he hadn't pushed. Now he was done playing patient predator, demanding she let him in. Her wolf stirred, offering a solution. Xander took it. Loosening her grip on the bond, she let her wolf take the lead. In the dark glass, a low amber light flickered. Her pupils expanded and rounded, until her wolf stared back.

Her lids fell to half-mast and she sank deeper into the essence that was her wolf.

Warrick's relief when Xander finally released her grip on the bond was short lived. He hoped to get some answers as to what in the hell was going on. Instead, he found himself face to face with her wolf. His wolf surged forward to rub his body along hers, tangling noses in greeting. Somewhere deep inside, a bittersweet ache bloomed. One he refused to allow to surface. Frustrated anger edged out the worry, sliding over the ache. She was avoiding him.

The brush of fur under his clenched fists was followed by the warm weight of her wolf brushing against he legs. He looked down at the distinctive blend of blacks, grays, and whites that made up Xander's fur. Her short ears were covered in black fur that blended into a mask for her amber eyes and ended in her white muzzle.

His hands relaxed, and even though her head reached his waist, he crouched down until they were eye level. He cupped her beautiful face in his hands and stared into her eyes, catching sight of the woman behind the wolf.

"I know you're in there, Xander." He kept his voice level. They had never verbally communicated through the bond, but he hoped she could hear him. "I don't know what's going on but whatever it is, hiding from me isn't going to help."

He waited.

Her wolf licked his wrist. *Not hiding.*

"Yes, you are." There was no way to miss the rough edge in his voice.

Her wolf whined. *Need time.* There was a pause. *Please.*

He dropped his forehead until it rested against hers. No matter what she said, he knew something was wrong. She was trying to protect him. Again. He wanted to yell at her for putting herself in-between him and whatever she considered a threat, but—he had promised to trust her, trust her judgment. The problem was the niggling feeling that things were about to go to shit fast was bearing down hard.

He lifted his head and held hers immobile, forcing her to look at him. "You will be careful." He didn't bother hiding the demand of the alpha and the man. Her ears perked forward. "Two hours max, Xander. That's all I can give you."

She answered with a small yip then her tongue swept out over his chin. She spun around, nuzzled his wolf and trotted back down the connection. Warrick and his wolf watched her black-tipped tail disappear as she gently blocked her end of the bond.

He had no doubts that whatever course of action she

had decided on, he wasn't going to like. Xander wasn't known for backing down from what she thought was right. The fact she used her wolf to run interference meant she was really worried that what she was doing was going to piss him off. Therein lay the real issue. When everything was said and done, would he be able to see past her actions to her intentions? For the first time in a very long time, he didn't have an answer.

CHAPTER 21

Xander's two-hour time limit was almost up. Warrick was pacing the floor in front of the large stone fireplace in his living room when a car's headlights splashed across the windows as the sound of gravel grinding under rubber joined the show. As he watched a dark SUV make its way up his drive, his stomach clenched.

The temporary calm he found from their earlier shared run had long since disappeared. He tried reaching Ryuu or Sebastian for the last few hours with a frustrating lack of success. Neither his Second nor Third were bothering to return his calls, regardless of his very explicit messages. And although Xander's earlier visit had helped, he was now having a hell of a time accepting everyone's decided lack of communication. Whatever was happening was going to be bad.

Car doors thumped closed and he didn't move as he heard at least three people make their way to his front door. The tension curdling his stomach rose another notch. Unless it was Xander, Ryuu, or Sebastian, he was in no mood for company.

A sharp knock broke through the quiet, snapping the leash holding him still. He was across the room before the echoes of the knock faded away. A familiar scent had him wrenching the door open to see Xander, flanked by Raine and Cheveyo.

Under his skin, his wolf drew back his lips and snarled at the invaders, yet outwardly he knew the only visible reaction to his growing suspicion would be his eyes flaring to wolf amber. After a quick glance at the individuals behind her, he focused on Xander.

Relief flowed through him and he tightened his grip on the doorknob.

Her long-sleeved black T-shirt and jeans were an abrupt departure from her normal eye-searing color choices. Yet, strangely, the lack of color etched a beautifully lethal picture. He caught the hint of antiseptic soap and shampoo, indicating she showered at Taliesin. A bruise was coming up along her cheek and she held her weight off one leg. The urge to drag her into his arms and check for other injuries clawed at him, but there was a careful distance to her as she faced him. A distance that disturbed both the wolf and man.

"We need to talk." Her words were soft as she met his burning gaze with stubborn resolve.

He captured her arm and gently pulled her over the threshold, bringing her close to him. Not saying a word, he ignored the others, keeping her trapped in his arms. He tugged her close until he could feel her slight tremors as she wrapped her arms around his waist and burrowed closer. He closed his eyes and dropped his head over hers protectively.

Someone gave a soft cough and Xander stiffened in his hold before reluctantly stepping back. Inside, his wolf gave a soft, mournful howl. Instead of joining in, he took a deep breath and faced his visitors.

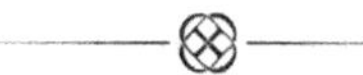

Watching Warrick straighten, his alpha persona falling into place, Xander felt the first cracks start in her heart. *Maybe,* her foolish heart had whispered when he held her, *maybe he'd understand why she had to do this.* Now cold logic gave a harsh laugh. Warrick the man might, but Warrick the alpha would see only betrayal.

"Come in," he said.

She stepped back, letting the other two enter the house. She barely restrained the urge to flinch under Warrick's unreadable gaze. He turned and headed back into the living room, leaving her to follow behind.

A large U-shaped sectional took up the majority of Warrick's living room. Wolves loved to sprawl out and since an alpha's home tended to be a gathering place for the pack, lounging space was a necessity. The high-end flat screen TV hung above the river-rock fireplace, a roughly hewn piece of oak providing a sturdy mantle.

Warrick crossed the thick, patterned rug, covering the wooden floors, and waved the others to take a seat. He watched Cheveyo take a seat on the nearest couch before taking his own seat across from him on the opposite section. Raine stopped in front of the large painting hanging on the wall.

Xander limped her way past Raine and across the living room. No sign of last night's deadly confrontation remained, other than the broken banister above her.

As tempting as it was to take a position behind her alpha, there was no way some leather and wood would protect her from the upcoming confrontation. She stifled a little sigh and carefully lowered her aching body into the corner seat, nearest the fireplace. There was a good two feet between her and Warrick. It would have to be enough. She settled into the plush leather as Raine turned away from the art and perched on the cushion next to Cheveyo.

"Nice art, Vidis." Raine studied the fall forest scene where wolves peeked from behind trees as if playing hide-n-seek with the viewer.

"Thank you," Warrick answered. "However, I'm sure you're not here to appreciate my artistic tastes."

"Not really." Raine crossed her arms over her chest. A tense silence curled around the large room.

Warrick raised an eyebrow. "I thought not." He leaned back, stretching his arm along the back of the couch, and Xander became hyperaware of his hand lying mere inches from her. He turned his attention to Cheveyo. "I'm surprised to see you here."

The most powerful witch in the Northwest inclined his head, a small grin playing around his mouth. "The rumors of my death were greatly exaggerated."

Not by much, Xander thought, considering the still-pale undertones to Cheveyo's normal burnished skin. A physical reminder of his recent ordeal in Arizona. Between the straight black hair brushing his collar, the sharp planes of his face, and his piercing obsidian eyes, the Native-American blood running through his veins wasn't in question. However, standing six-foot-six, Cheveyo's ancestry included some European somewhere along the line. It was a compelling combination, if you didn't mind dating a giant.

Warrick shot a withering glance in Xander's direction. "Considering the unusual silence of my wolves tonight, I'm eager to hear why you've come." There was a snap to his voice, as he bit off each word.

Raine opened her mouth but Xander cut her off, "Zeke's missing." She ignored the frown Raine sent her. "I think whoever was behind last night's attack now has him."

Warrick turned to her, the beginnings of anger thinning his face down. "Why?"

"He was checking on possible links to last night's attack," Raine answered.

Warrick swung his head around. "Excuse me?" His voice was so soft it raised every hair on Xander's body.

"You know, the two wolves that helped redecorate your house and the wizard who was tagging along?" Raine drawled. "Your missing wolf wanted to meet with Xander, share some information he found. Problem was he never made it to the meeting."

Warrick rose to his feet in a fluid motion, the wolf evident in every movement. He turned on Xander before anyone could react. With one hand on the back of the couch and the other on the padded arm beside her, he trapped her in place.

She fought for calm and met his barely restrained fury head on.

Ignoring the others, he leaned in. "You defied my orders?" The lethal edge of his question no way diminished by his deceptively gentle tone.

"I did what I felt was necessary to protect my alpha and my pack." She managed to keep her voice equally quiet.

His low growl didn't completely cover the sound of leather tearing under his claws. They stared at each other for an endless moment before he pushed away.

As he stalked over to begin pacing by the large windows behind her, she let out a shaky breath and closed her eyes.

There was a choking lump in her throat, but she fought past it. Opening her eyes, she caught a flash of sympathy before Raine could hide it. Xander looked down and curled her fists in her lap.

"Did you call in Ryuu or Sebastian to help search for Zeke?" The cold edge to Warrick's voice cut her to the bone.

"Ryuu was tracking from the office, and I retraced Zeke's possible path to the pub. I found his truck abandoned on Dowlings Road. He'd been run off the road."

"You know this how?"

"There was damage to the bumper, his radiator was busted, and there was blood on the steering wheel."

"Not to mention the welcoming party left behind," Raine chimed in, unhelpfully.

"How many?" Warrick's question, snapped from directly behind Xander, made her jump.

Furious over his petty move, she used her sudden spike of temper to bite back. "One." She deliberately took her time to face him. His face was inches away. Fleetingly, she wondered what he'd do if she nipped his chin in punishment for his behavior. Seeing the furious light in his eyes, she figured he'd probably rip her head off.

He pushed off the couch and paced a couple of steps.

"Can you contact your missing wolf through your ties, Vidis?" Cheveyo's quiet question stilled Warrick in mid-step.

Warrick flicked her an unreadable glance before turning his back on the room and its occupants to face the large windows.

She watched him. For a minute, he stood there unmoving. Then he slammed his end of the bond brutally shut and she flinched under the impact. She dropped her head to the back of the couch to hide the tears springing into her eyes while her wolf whimpered at the abrupt loss of their mate's presence. *Gods, it hurt.* More than she had imagined.

She breathed her way through the shocking pain. It was going to get worse before it got better. Bit by bit, she began compartmentalizing. Find Zeke, confront Sebastian, and eliminate the threats to Warrick. Pack first. Falling apart into a thousand broken pieces would wait.

"Who's this?" Warrick snapped.

Xander lifted her head to see lights streak across the window. She cleared her throat to get her voice to work. "Gavin and Ryuu. I told them to meet us here when they were done."

"Are you sure about this, Xander?" Cheveyo's question was soft, but it snapped Warrick's spine rigid.

Xander knew what Cheveyo was really asking, but her decision was made as soon as she called him in. She watched Warrick for a moment then turned to face the others. "I'm going to need Ryuu's help."

"Can you trust him?" Raine asked.

Warrick didn't turn. "More than any other."

Xander couldn't stop the small flinch at his answer and all that it implied.

"Vidis." Cheveyo waited. Xander heard the small brush of cloth, as Warrick must have turned to face the witch. "Can you feel your missing wolf?"

"No." It surprised her how much emotion one word could hold.

"Then we have a very serious problem," Cheveyo said.

Before Warrick could answer, the door opened, bringing in cold air along with Gavin and Ryuu.

Ryuu gave the others a quick nod. "Vidis," he greeted,

before dropping down to sprawl next to Xander. "Got Zeke's truck and your bike at my place."

She gave him a small grateful smile. She hated leaving her bike unattended, but she was in no shape to ride it back. Hopefully, she could catch a ride with Raine or even Ryuu when they were done here. Considering what she was about to hit Warrick and Ryuu with, Raine was probably the better bet.

"The truck's going to need some work." Gavin took a seat on the padded arm of the couch next to Raine. "We were lucky to get it as far as we did."

"Before I forget." Ryuu straightened his legs and tilted his hips as he dug his hand into a back pocket. He came out with Xander's keys. "Here."

She took them with a quiet, "Thanks." She could feel the weight of Warrick's gaze behind her. Tension crawled up her spine. It was time to get this conversation back on track. "Anything come back on the body?" She knew Ryuu had run her attacker's prints while she was meeting with Cheveyo.

Ryuu frowned. "Not much, actually. The only reason I found anything was because his prints were buried in an old incident report."

Her pulse skipped. "Buried?"

Her question was quickly followed by Raine's. "What kind of incident?"

Ryuu looked between them, no doubt picking up on the underlying tension in their inquiries. "He was a minor witness in an investigation of an underground cage match that used wolves to hedge their bets."

"Hedge their bets?" Raine repeated. "Are you telling me someone was stupid enough to let wolves fight with humans?"

Surprisingly, it was Warrick who answered. "In that particular case, yes. There was a maverick who convinced a couple of other lone wolves that stacking the deck against the human fighters was a sure way to make some money."

Raine frowned, puzzlement clear on her face. "Wouldn't that be overkill? I mean, a wolf could take out a human with no problem."

"But they can also take more of a beating," Warrick explained, coming to stand behind the couch. "Makes for higher odds if the human seems to dominate in brutal fights and then suddenly goes down under one solid hit." He shrugged. "For a short while, it worked."

"Who took the report, Ryuu?" Xander didn't want to ask Warrick, choosing to keep her focus off of him.

Ryuu studied her before answering. "Sebastian."

She exchanged a knowing look with Raine. When her friend went to say something, she gave a short shake of her head, warning her off.

Unfortunately, Warrick was paying attention. "You want to tell me what's going on, Xander?"

No, actually she didn't. Wasn't it enough that she had to sacrifice her relationship with him to keep him safe? Did she have to be the one to rip apart one of his few friendships? Between her imagined betrayal and what she was beginning to fear was a very real one, would Warrick ever take a chance on believing anyone again? She wanted to tear something to pieces, preferably Sebastian. Instead, she sat there, stubbornly silent, unwilling and unable to hurt him any further.

"Perhaps we should go back to why your pack ties aren't working," Cheveyo offered. Relief at the offered reprieve had Xander looking up, only to encounter Cheveyo's steady regard. He shifted his gaze to Warrick. "To interfere with such a connection would require a great deal of magic."

Warrick rested his arms on the back of the couch and leaned forward. "A great deal of magic? Similar to what a wizard could wield?"

A tight smile creased Cheveyo's face. "Possibly, but—" he held up a hand, "—until I have Raine study the magic's weave, I won't know for sure."

Energy flared around Warrick and Xander's skin suddenly stung with hundreds of small stings. His wolf hadn't like that. Slowly, the sensation faded. "You're asking me to put my pack at risk by letting her in that deep."

Raine snorted. "Trust me, Vidis, the last thing I want is to mess with your—" Gavin deliberately coughed, and Xander got the impression Raine made a quick change in her word choice, "—pack."

"As much as I appreciate your offer, I'm going to decline. I've seen firsthand how unpredictable your magic is, Raine." He still spoke to Raine, but Xander felt the lash of his comment. Yep, her alpha was one seriously pissed off puppy right now.

She refused to give him the satisfaction of reacting. Instead, she cradled the beginnings of her own temper. "You can't afford not to let her check it out." She was grateful how calm she sounded as she challenged Warrick, even as she refused to look at him.

Next to her, Ryuu looked at her as if she'd lost her damn mind. And maybe she had, but she couldn't sit here while her alpha risked not only his wolves, but himself over some misguided paranoia.

"Are you sure you want to challenge me, little wolf?" The question was asked in a dangerously soft tone next to her ear.

She closed her eyes, fighting to hold still and hide her rioting emotions. With his hot breath curling over her scalp and neck, it was obvious his wolf was too close, allowing him to move faster than the eye could track. She wasn't fooled by his seeming control. "I'm thinking of the safety of all our wolves," she ground out, keeping her eyes shut and fists clenched in her lap. "I'm willing to do whatever it takes to bring Zeke home safe."

His snarl sent a primal fear spiraling through her, drying her mouth. "Are you saying I wouldn't?"

She forced her eyes opened then, using every ounce of courage she had, she slowly turned until mere inches separated them. It was so hard not to let her voice shake, but she managed three words. "Let. Her. Check."

He held her gaze for an interminable moment, his wolf holding her stare but she refused to back down, resigned to losing him. This was too important. She didn't know what he saw but something had him giving her a slight frown before all emotion smoothed away and he pulled back, breaking their staring contest.

Straightening, he visibly got himself back under control. He took his time as he made his way around the couch and took a seat on the section facing the fireplace. Once situated, he looked at Raine. "Don't harm me or mine, and I won't harm yours."

This time the growl came from Gavin, who'd risen to his feet and stood in front of Raine. "Don't threaten her, Vidis."

Warrick's smile was anything but humorous. "I don't make empty threats, Durand."

"Neither do I," Gavin snapped back.

"Enough." Raine's soft reprimand was followed by a tug on the back pocket of Gavin's jeans, until he retook his previous position. When he was once again seated, she turned to Warrick. "I give you my word, no intentional harm to you or yours." Something unreadable passed between the two.

Xander forgot to breathe as Warrick considered Raine. No Kyn gave their word lightly, and Raine was smart to word her vow so carefully.

"No harm," he agreed.

The pressure on her chest lifted and Xander tried to quietly suck air into her lungs.

Ryuu stirred, but Warrick stilled his movements with a small shake of his head. The small spike of energy tingling along Xander's skin was a clear indicator that Warrick was telling his Second something. Reassurance, probably. It didn't seem to be working because Ryuu frowned and folded his arms.

"Do you need anything?" Xander asked Raine, remembering the candles and salt circle they used in Arizona to help Raine make the transition from the real world to the one that existed in-between.

Raine flicked Cheveyo a quick look before shaking her head. "No, I—we've been practicing." She leaned back into the couch, closed her eyes, and took a deep breath. Gavin reached out and captured her hand, his protective move proclaiming loud and clear where he stood.

Warrick had settled back into the couch as well. Xander could make out the subtle amber glow that flickered like candlelight under his half-closed eyelids. Even though he kept the bond locked tight, she sat there, poised to do whatever it took to protect him, while her wolf paced back and forth deep inside. Neither one of them thrilled with their inability to sense what was happening. She took small comfort from Gavin's presence, knowing he provided Raine a measure of control.

The sound of a clock ticking away somewhere in the house became overly loud in the quiet. When Raine finally spoke, Xander jumped. "Okay, I think I've found it." Her voice was slightly distracted.

"Describe what you're seeing." Cheveyo leaned forward, his arms resting on his knees. His attention going from Warrick to Raine.

"I recognize Vidis's colors, but I'm not sure what pack ties would look like."

"They would be bundled, like a multi layered cord," Warrick answered, showing he was aware of what was happening.

"Ahh..." Raine fell quiet. Xander caught the restless movement of her friend's fingers, as if she was sorting through something. "Okay, I think this is it." She paused, her head tilted to the side and her brow wrinkled.

When a few more quiet minutes past, Cheveyo said, "Raine, you need to tell me what you're seeing."

Raine's eyes opened, their eerie glow caused Ryuu to startle. "You could have come along for the ride," she grumbled, and Xander caught the flex of Gavin's grip.

Cheveyo's lips tightened and a fine tension stiffened his shoulders. "We already discussed this, and it's best if I stay out of your magic for a bit."

Since Raine and Gavin managed to drag the witch's spirit from the clutches of a Soul Stealer, Xander didn't blame him for not wanting to go back in. Hell, she wasn't sure if she could let Raine near her and her wolf, considering how things turned out last time.

Raine huffed out a sigh. "Fine." Her head swiveled toward Warrick. "Most of your ties kind of disappear the farther they move away from you." She shifted on the couch as if she was going to get up and step closer. Gavin held her in place. "If I follow them, I think they lead back to your individual members. But there's a couple of ties that seem to be blocked from the rest."

When Raine addressed him, Warrick had opened his eyes and now he watched her. "By what?"

"I'm not sure. It keeps slipping away," she murmured. "I'm going to go a little closer..." Her voice trailed off.

Tension rose from Raine and spread through the room, until Xander wanted to scream.

"Well, that's not good," Raine finally said.

Xander reached the limit of her patience. "Plan on sharing?" she snapped, the coiling tension making her muscles hurt.

Raine turned her freaky gaze on Xander, her lips curling in a very unhappy smile. "I would if I knew what I was looking at. Every time I get close it slips away like a shadow."

"What does the magic weave look like?" Cheveyo broke in.

Xander knew, from her conversations with Raine, that when she looked at an individual's magic she not only saw various colors but individual weaves as the magic wove together, creating distinct patterns as unique as fingerprints.

Raine closed her eyes, her concentration evident. "I'm not sure, but I think we're looking at a shifter."

"Why?" the witch pushed.

"It's like Vidis and Xander, but not." She raked her hands through her hair. "Hard to explain."

Cheveyo studied the ground between his feet, thinking. "Whoever cast a spell on the ties is using their connection to Vidis to fuel it, so if we try to break what's holding it closed, chances are it will come back on Vidis."

"What if I try unweaving the threads," Raine offered.

"I don't think that would be wise," Cheveyo answered.

"Why?" Warrick asked.

Cheveyo's mouth tightened and he shrugged. "We don't know enough about this spell to know what will happen if Raine touches it. It sounds as if it's constructed to feed off of existing connections and the fact it seems to hide from her, gives me a very bad feeling."

"I have a missing wolf, Cheveyo," Warrick said. "He's mine to protect and mine to bring back home. A bad feeling isn't going to keep me from using what I can to find him."

"No." The sharp denial escaped before Xander could call it back. When everyone, including Warrick, looked at her, she could feel the weight of their stares. It didn't matter. "No one is going to mess with whatever it is until you can guarantee Warrick won't be harmed."

"I'm with Xander," Ryuu chimed in. "We can't afford for you to screw around with Vidis or the pack ties."

Warrick held up a hand to stop both Xander and Ryuu. "Not your decision." He stared at them both.

"That's not your only problem," Raine broke in and all three wolves turned to her. She looked worried. "Whatever this is, I think it's killing your missing wolf."

CHAPTER 22

Raine's announcement reverberated through the room. Shock left Xander reeling. "No. There's no way they can do that without you knowing." She turned to Warrick, panic raking through her and her wolf. "Right?"

"The pack ties should be inviolate. The only person who should be able to impact the pack ties is the alpha who creates them. The fact that someone managed to block my connection with any of my wolves shouldn't even be a possibility." He growled and rubbed a hand over his face. "What the hell's going on, Cheveyo?"

Cheveyo raised his head and narrowed his gaze on Warrick. "The only way someone can influence your connection to any of your wolves is if they shared a connection to you and the rest of your pack."

Warrick stiffened. "You think it's a pack member."

"It's the only explanation that makes any sense," Cheveyo confirmed.

"My pack is loyal!" Warrick shot back, but Xander caught the creeping doubt as his temper spiked.

"Someone's playing you."

Gavin's quiet comment brought Warrick up from the couch in a strangely liquid movement, revealing how close his wolf was. He brushed past her to the open space by the windows. Her gaze followed, her heart aching as he began to prowl back and forth.

She watched, her stomach clenching so hard it hurt. The more they talked about this, the more her suspicions solidified. But if she had problems making sense of it, it would be a hundred times worse for Warrick.

Ryuu's nudge brought her attention back and he jerked his head toward Warrick in a silent demand. She frowned. Did he really think Warrick wanted her anywhere near him right now? Even as locked down as the damn bond was, she could feel the tendrils of anger, betrayal, pain, hurt, love, and denial seeping around the edges. Each one a stinging lash across the psychic heart of her and her wolf. If such delicate touches hurt this much, she dreaded what sat behind that tightly locked door.

Ryuu's wolf flared, rounding his dark eyes with an amber light, and he gave her a silent snarl. She snapped her teeth back at him, frustrated and worried that her overtures would be shot down in front of everyone. This wasn't about her. This was about Warrick and if they wanted to untangle this mess, they needed to take a real in-depth look at someone they trusted.

It took her a minute to uncurl from the couch, her abused thigh muscle having stiffened from being in one position too long. She couldn't miss the expectant looks on the faces surrounding her. All of them—Raine, Gavin, Cheveyo, even Ryuu—foolishly thought she'd be able to... what? Calm Warrick and his wolf down? Maybe she should warn them that what she was about to tell Warrick would do anything but calm him.

Carefully, she made her way over to Warrick and stepped directly in his path. His head swung up and he towered over her. It was hard to meet his gaze, but she did. All those feelings, leaking around his block in the bond, were swirling in a furious storm of amber and gold. Funny how the same body that could make her feel so safe could also make her feel so small.

This close to him, there was no way to mistake the roiling energy surrounding him. It pressed against her like the heated winds before an electrical storm, making it hard to drag air into her stuttering lungs. Keeping her movements slow and careful, she laid her hands palm down on his chest. "There was a scent on the guy who jumped me tonight."

His heart thundered under her touch. "Whose?"

She swallowed tightly. "Sebastian's." She heard Ryuu's sharp intake of breath.

Warrick didn't take his gaze from Xander, and she got the impression their tenuous connection was the only thing keeping him on two feet. "No."

Tremors shook his frame and, standing inches away, she watched as the change ran under his skin, bones shifting slightly. A disturbing sight but she didn't flinch. As his control began to crumble, hers solidified. She couldn't let his wolf rise in front of Cheveyo and the others. He'd never forgive himself.

"There has to be an explanation."

"Maybe." But even she could hear the lack of belief in her answer.

"Sebastian wouldn't betray Vidis," Ryuu's snarl sounded behind her.

He must have leapt over the back of the couch, but she wasn't sure because she didn't dare break her visual connection to Warrick. Right now, if the muscle twitches and minuscule shifts under her hands were any indicators, that connection was the only thing keeping Warrick grounded.

"Why not?" Gavin asked.

"Sebastian is Vidis's Third," Ryuu said. "Besides strength, loyalty, and trust are necessary parts of holding that position. Seb loves Warrick and has always protected him and the pack."

Something flickered in Warrick's face, something she didn't understand. "Maybe he still is," Warrick said, releasing her and slowly stepping back.

"Maybe he still is what?" she asked, unable to see where Warrick was going. Under her skin, her wolf turned frantic, picking up on something Xander was missing.

"Protecting me, protecting the pack." There was a decided lack of emotion in Warrick's voice, but he didn't take his gaze off of her.

Her vision began to narrow as her pulse picked up and her limbs began to numb. The voice in her head was screaming at her not to ask, but she ignored it. "From what?"

"You."

His one word answer hit her as hard as any punch and she stumbled back, reeling. Someone reached out to steady her, but she spun away, unable to bear any touch. It wasn't so much his answer but the wave of accompanying emotions he finally allowed to seep through that was flaying her to the quick. On some level, Warrick blamed her.

"Someone needs to start talking in clearer sentences real damn quick."

The fact that Raine's voice was crystal clear meant she was close. Xander opened eyes she hadn't realized she'd shut and found Raine standing between her and her pack mates.

She had to bury her emotions where he couldn't find it. She dragged every damn block she could find and threw it at the thrice-damn bond she shared with her alpha until she could finally breathe. It took precious minutes, but she managed to get some distance between her ravaged emotions and what was happening around her.

"Sebastian has had some issues with Vidis and Xander becoming mates," Ryuu offered when Warrick showed no signs of ceding to Raine's demand.

Sharp-edged fury rose and cut through all the emotional bullshit like a heat-seeking missile. "Did you not stop to think I might want to know this?" Xander demanded of Warrick as she stepped around Raine.

"He's entitled to his opinion."

His unruffled response just about sent her and her wolf springing for his throat. Only the fact that she knew Ryuu would step between them held her back.

Unable to deal with Warrick, she turned her attention to Ryuu. "How many others were upset with the mating bond?"

He shrugged uncomfortably. "There were some grumblings from some of the lesser wolves."

"Why?" Raine was trying to run interference.

But Xander knew the answer. "Because they think my refusal to accept the bond makes Warrick appear weak." Her burst of frustrated fury left her head pounding. The sick sense of failure rose in its place. Once again, her lack of action was going to get someone killed.

"No," Ryuu cut in. "No matter what he thought about your relationship, Seb would never go after Zeke. They were friends. He would never betray the pack."

"Then explain his scent on the body," Xander demanded, wrestling her sense of failure back to focus on the here and now. "Explain why he's not here." She didn't look at Warrick, couldn't look at him. "His position is beside you and Warrick, but he's not here. Don't tell me you haven't tried to reach him all night."

Color swept over Ryuu's face and his lips tightened but he didn't deny her accusation.

"A scent is not absolute proof." Warrick's voice was cold as he stood beside Ryuu.

His position wasn't lost on her. More than physical distance now stood between them. "No, scent is not absolute, but his absence is a bit damning."

"I am not condemning my Third based on circumstantial evidence." The angrier Warrick got, the more reasonable his voice became. "He has never given me a reason to question his loyalty." His unspoken condemnation shattered more than her heart.

She sucked in a breath. "And you think I have?"

He deliberately looked over her shoulder to Gavin, Raine, and Cheveyo then returned his gaze to her. His non-answer was hard to miss.

Her bitter laugh cut through the uncomfortable silence. "I see."

She ignored Raine's outstretched hand and glided up to Warrick until she stood inches away. She studied him and felt her heart shred under his unemotional mask. By going to Cheveyo without his permission she had bet against the odds and lost. She would crumble under the pain later, after she confronted Sebastian, got Zeke back, and eliminated the threat to her alpha. Until then, she would do her job.

"You are entitled to your opinion, alpha." There was no

trace of affection in her use of his title. "However, I demand an answer from your Third."

Something rose behind those eyes, too fast for her to read. "Ryuu will talk to Sebastian. You will stay the hell out of it."

Her smile was all teeth. "I don't think so."

He leaned close until his face blocked out everything else. "I haven't officially claimed you as my mate, so you have nothing to support your demand."

His softly spoken words streaked like silver bullets, leaving devastation in their wake. He could tear her apart, but she wouldn't break, not from this, not yet. "I'm not asking as your mate, Alpha Vidis. I am insisting as your Tracker."

"Vidis," Cheveyo interrupted their staring contest. "Considering the complex spells being used against you and yours, the threat may be bigger than what we can see."

Warrick watched her for another uncomfortable minute before turning his attention to Cheveyo. "Spells? There's more than one spell involved against the pack ties?"

Unable to stay near Warrick, Xander moved toward the fireplace. She put as much distance as she could, without actually leaving, and listened to the conversation.

"No," Raine answered. "There's another spell behind your sudden influx of out of control shifters. Based on what I found tonight and when you dragged me to the Gardens, someone is out there messing around with the magic that controls how your wolves change."

"Oh, for gods' sake," Ryuu cut in. "You're telling me there's a spell that influences a wolf's change? No." He made a sharp movement with his hand. "If that was the case, it would have been used years ago."

"Maybe it's a recent discovery." Cheveyo watched

Warrick. "It's obvious from what Raine and Xander have shared that whoever is behind this is still perfecting the spell."

Ryuu looked from Cheveyo to Xander. "And you think Sebastian is mixed up in this?"

She could read his need for her denial and it hurt to nod her head. She watched her answer sow the seeds of doubt as Ryuu began to wonder.

"I don't think you all have time to wait around," Gavin said. "You need to track down Sebastian and find out what he knows about Zeke's disappearance. According to Raine, you're running out of time."

"I need to make a few calls and see if I can get some more information about the origination of these spells," Cheveyo said.

"We can do it from my place," Raine offered. "It's closer." She turned to Gavin. "You, Xander, and Ryuu should head over to Sebastian's."

He nodded.

"No." Warrick's voice stopped everyone's movements. "Xander and I will head to Sebastian's. Ryuu, take Gavin back to Taliesin. I need you to unearth whatever information Zeke found."

"I'll drive," Ryuu muttered and headed for the door, Gavin following close behind.

"Ryuu," Warrick stopped his Second. "This time, stay in touch." He looked at Cheveyo. "You as well." His gaze slid to Xander standing still by the fireplace. "No more surprises." He turned to the door, leaving everyone to follow.

CHAPTER 23

THE LAST PLACE XANDER WANTED TO BE WAS LOCKED IN THE PLUSH interior of Warrick's luxury sedan with him, but obviously, he wasn't taking requests. Under her skin, her wolf clawed her bloody. Too much had happened tonight and her control was shot to hell. Her vision kept flickering to her wolf's gray-scale version and her muscles were coiled so tight her bones ached. Even the tinted glass couldn't mute the siren call of the moon. She didn't dare reach out to turn on the radio in an attempt to break the screaming silence because she was scared if she moved, she'd shift.

They'd been in the car about ten minutes, with another fifteen to go since Sebastian's place was located over on the west side. The loss of her connection to Warrick, the verbal wounds he inflicted, and her own demons managed to drive her wolf into a near feral state. Her whispered promises that they'd be all right fell on deaf ears and the pressure to change edged into dangerous territory.

She stared out the window, blind to the scenery, all her focus centered on the prowling monster housed inside her skin and bones. When she felt the sting of her nails lengthening, she curled her hands into the seat and tried to breathe the ache in her body away.

She shuddered, fighting her body and her wolf. Her jaw was clenched tight, trapping the howls rumbling in her chest. The wildness living and breathing inside of her, smashed with relentless force against the barriers of her control. Desperate to escape the emotional storm, her wolf wanted out. Low growls filled her ears and her control cracked.

She clawed at the seatbelt, the thick material shredding under her nails. The sounds of a trapped animal began to replace the growls, then the scent of cinnamon and cloves wrapped around her. The unexpectedness of it halted her frantic movements.

"Xander, stop." The command acted like a brake, holding her and her wolf on the edge of her impending change.

She blinked and Warrick's face was in front of her. Vaguely, she realized he'd pulled off to the side of the road. Her door was open and he was crouched in front of her. His hands were cupped around her face, forcing her to look only at him. The feel of his touch seared through the madness, giving her a chance to claw a deeper hold on her crumbling control.

"Let me go." It was hard to get those words out.

"No." His denial shattered her fragile hold.

She knew he was saying something else but she couldn't hear it over the howls of her wolf. Her bones and muscles contorted, stealing her breath and her mind. A howl of triumph sounded as Xander faltered under the dual impact of her wolf's demands and the pull of the moon.

Then, like a switch being thrown, her wolf went quiet, leaving her gasping for breath. The suddenness was a brutal relief. The sound of air being dragged into her lungs was overly loud. It took her a second to realize her face was pressed against warm skin, her arms wrapped around Warrick's neck. His scent seeped into her lungs and acted like a tranquilizer, slowing her pulse and bringing her rioting body back to normal.

She didn't dare move, for the first time in a long time worried she might not be able to control her wolf if she did. The repeated brush of his hand against her spine made her throat tighten. As her mind cleared, knowledge filtered in.

This sense of calm, of protection, of safety was an alpha's gift. One he could share with his wolves. The ability to bring a wolf back from the cusp of change could be painful or, as in this case, not. That decision belonged to the alpha and the situation. She had watched Warrick use it on the younger wolves who were adjusting to the change, and rarely had she seen him use it as a punishment to prove his dominance.

Minutes passed, neither of them moving. It was the sound of a car whizzing by that finally had her dropping her arms and pulling back. He let her go, his hands sliding until they rested on her knees. But she refused to meet his gaze, needing what protection she could get from him. Her emotions were too raw and she needed time to deal with them.

"Better?" His question was quiet, and the concern she heard puzzled her but she refused to look at him and dipped her head in a short nod.

"Xander," he began.

She held up a hand, flicked a quick glance at him, and let it skip away. "Don't. I can't right now. Let's just get to Sebastian's." She could feel the weight of his stare and ignored his silent demand. "Please," she whispered, barely able to get the plea past her tight throat.

His fingers curled into her knees before he sighed and let her go. He got to his feet, shut her door, and made his way back to the driver's seat. This time when they pulled out onto the road, she kept her attention focused out the window, working not to think. The silence that wrapped around them once more was strangely mournful.

Warrick flexed his fingers against the steering wheel, dividing his attention between the deliberate movement and the road. It wasn't what he wanted to do, but everything was such a damn mess. From the corner of his eye, he could see the back of Xander's head as she pretended to be enthralled with the passing scenery. A sharp pain shot up his jaw and he forced his teeth to unclench.

He knew he'd hurt her. He didn't need their bond to figure that one out. Not that it was working. He slid her another glance. He doubted she knew just how tight she had shut down the bond between them. His fingers tightened until his knuckles pressed against his skin. After relying on their connection for the last few weeks, to not feel even a whisper of her left him feeling hollow.

He wasn't apologizing this time. Not after she had deliberately gone behind his back and sought out Cheveyo. She was his mate, dammit. Her loyalty belonged solely to him. Instead of sharing her suspicions with him, she had blindsided him. She had gone to another male for help. Not him. Then she had the audacity to challenge him in front of outsiders. What had she expected him to do?

Listen.

Screw that, she hadn't listened when he had specifically explained why he hadn't wanted Cheveyo in his business.

But she was right.

He snarled at that insidious voice. Maybe this time. But next time? She made a big deal about communication and trust, but it seemed to be a one-way street. How was that supposed to work? If she didn't respect his decisions, why should he bother explaining himself? He'd taken the time to share his reasoning, and she still went ahead and did what she damn well pleased.

If you wanted a submissive bitch...

He never said that.

Then why are you so angry?

His internal, schizophrenic conversation ground to a halt as he considered the question, turning it over and over. From the start, Xander had drawn both halves—man and wolf—to her. She kept him off balance. He hadn't known what to expect from one moment to the next. She didn't react like the majority of females, bending the minute he pushed. Instead, she held her own with him. Intelligent, stubborn, opinionated, quirky as hell, and lethal, she was an intriguing puzzle he knew he'd never fully solve.

Her decision to go to Cheveyo was a given. He knew that. She had listened to him and tried to discuss it, but he shot her down because the thought of her going to another male drove his wolf crazy. And her going after Zeke? She was a dominant wolf, who just happened to be a tracker. Protecting her pack would always come first, before him, before her own safety.

And there it was. The real bitch. Underneath the thin veneer of a modern man, lay the soul of his wolf. He needed to protect his mate, to shelter her, and keep her safe from everything. But that wasn't who she was.

"If I am your mate, those who threaten you will have to answer to me." This time the voice in his head was Xander's, an echo of the promise she had given him the night before.

He sighed softly. His mate was a protector, through and through. She would stand beside him against any threat and, if tonight was any indication, stand in front of him when she thought he was too blind to see the full picture.

No matter the cost.

Xander wasn't some newly changed wolf at the mercy of her emotions. The fact that she nearly changed in the car worried him and his wolf. Not to mention how far she was shut down.

Considering the upheaval resulting from tonight's debacle, he began to consider just how big of a price Xander might have paid for her decisions to protect him. Earlier, when she reassured him she was okay, she had hid behind her wolf. He'd bet good money she had just discovered Sebastian's scent on her attacker. She wasn't one to make accusations without solid proof, and to get that proof she'd used whatever sources she could. Including the one he had warned her not to use. To find Zeke, to protect the one she considered hers, to protect her pack, Warrick had no doubt Xander would do whatever it took to find the answers she needed.

Which meant the only person he needed to protect her from was herself.

Nestled in a small bedroom community, Sebastian's house was one of many tucked back off the quiet roads. By the time Warrick brought the car to a stop in Sebastian's driveway, Xander had managed to shove all the messy emotional crap to the back of her mind, thanks to Warrick's Prozac routine. There would be time enough to lick her wounds privately later.

She pushed her door open, not waiting for Warrick, and got out. Closing the door behind her, she rounded the hood. Warrick made his way to the front door and she followed, keeping a deliberate distance between them. The less he touched her, on any level, the better off she and her wolf would be.

A cement walkway wound its way behind a wall of small trees and bushes, standing guard between the carefully tended front yard and the off-white siding of the older home. The neighborhood was quiet and dark. Not surprising, considering it was past midnight and streetlights seemed to have been skipped in this particular section. Somewhere, a couple of dogs were discussing their day in short canine exchanges. A combination of wood smoke and the burnt remains of someone's dinner laced the air. Some of the surrounding homes had left their porch lights on, creating little pools of welcome in the night.

Warrick stepped up to the door and knocked. Light peeked from the edge of the drawn curtains covering the large front window, but nothing moved inside.

Xander retraced her steps and found the walkway curling around to the back of the house. A little peeking around revealed no sign of Sebastian's truck. A weathered wooden fence surrounded the small backyard. The gray boards ended just above Xander's head, so she reached over to flip open the latch on the gate. A light shove and it swung open, the hinges quiet. Stepping through, she kept a hand on the rough wood and eased the gate shut behind her.

The back of the house was dark, but there was enough ambient light between the moon and the neighbor's house to make out a couple of old oaks, watching over the patchy collection of grass. A metal shed huddled in the far corner. In moments, she was up the cinderblock steps to the slab of concrete masquerading as a patio. The glass sliding door didn't provide much of a challenge and, with a few deft maneuvers, she slid it slowly open, careful not to set the vinyl strips of the blinds clattering like plastic bones.

She held still, waiting for any signs of life, but other than the hush of the heater, it was quiet. Gathering the panels of the blinds in one hand, she dragged them aside and stepped in. She paused, listening for the hum of one of those home alarm systems. Getting in was too easy, but then again, if you could sprout fangs and claws, a standard alarm system became redundant.

Satisfied nothing was going to come screeching to life, she slid the door shut and let the blinds go. The light from the front room bled through a square walkthrough to the kitchen, stopping just short of the round wooden dining table. To her right, shadows played along floor-to-ceiling shelves, sharing wall space with the typical-guy, big-screen TV. A blanket-covered couch and a couple of recliners gathered around a coffee table.

Warrick's sharp knock got her feet moving, but the feel of something crumbling underfoot was followed by the soft cracks and pops of glass breaking. Looking down, she lifted her foot off the pile of whatever lay broken on the floor. Skirting around it, she crossed to the front door.

She undid the deadbolt and pulled open the door, catching Warrick in mid-knock. The porch light left his face in a mask of shadows but she caught the flare of amber before it was snuffed out. Not saying a word, she turned away to finish searching the house and left him to follow. At the end of the hallway, she and Warrick split. She took the right and he the left.

The first room doubled as a home gym and a storage closet from what she could tell. Skis were propped in one corner while a bike hung from one of the walls. A stereo sat on top of some boxes stacked against another wall, and taking center stage was a freestanding punching bag.

Behind door number two was a bathroom, and door number three revealed a master bedroom. Even if the unmade king size bed hadn't clued her in that this was Sebastian's room, the strength of his familiar clove and citrus scent would have been a dead giveaway. It didn't take her long to check the bathroom and narrow walk-in closet. She stood in the doorway between the bedroom and bathroom when Warrick appeared.

"He's not here." She let her gaze roam over the room.

Strangely, other than the messed-up bed, the rest of the room was meticulously neat. Either Sebastian had a maid or he was raising the bar on male cleanliness. Knowing Sebastian, she went with the maid.

Warrick leaned against the doorjamb and crossed his arms over his chest. "There's an office at the other end."

"Find anything interesting?" As the words left her mouth, her attention returned to the bed. *There was something...*

"What is it?" Warrick asked, the sharpness of his question jerking her gaze to his.

The impact of meeting his gaze shook her. As long as she didn't look at him, really look at him, she was fine. But now her throat swelled, making it hard to squeeze her voice around the lump inside. Worried she would open her mouth and everything that was boxed away would escape, she looked away. "Nothing," she choked out.

"Don't lie to me." His voice was flat, cold.

That tone was just what she needed to slap herself back in line. Her temper reignited with an almost audible sound, snapping her spine straight. No matter what he thought of her actions, she would not bow her head and let him disrespect her. She stalked toward him, making sure she put enough swagger in her walk to make a dead man sit up and take notice. The burn of frustration and feminine ire provided enough emotional armor to let her get in his face.

He didn't move from his position, even as she stopped in front of him with no more than mere inches separating them. She tilted her head to the side and in a very deliberate, very soft voice told him, "I don't lie. Ever."

"Really?" His lips curved into a small half smile, and his lids slid to half-mast.

Her heartbeat picked up as his scent crowded in until she swore she tasted cinnamon. Her tongue swept over her lower lip. He focused on the revealing move and she could feel the tension tighten between them. "Really."

"Then tell me, Xander—" His voice dropped and he bent his head closer, until the carved angles of his face blocked everything else from sight and they were practically breathing the same air. "Why did you really go to Cheveyo?"

Because you were being a stubborn ass, was the first answer that popped to mind, but she stuffed it back. There was an intensity to his question that made her hesitate. She searched his face, trying to determine what was really behind the question. Hadn't he already decided the answer for himself? Unable to read his inscrutable countenance, she heeded the quiet nudge of her battered heart and gave him the truth he hadn't wanted earlier. "To protect you."

Her answer turned his half smile into something infinitely tender.

"Silly girl," he whispered before he took her lips with a gentleness that rattled her.

The heat of his mouth on hers seeped under her skin and bones and began to wrap around the cold wounds from earlier. When he raised his head, her pain and confusion were still there, waiting to be addressed, but now they were tempered with a fragile hope.

She took a careful step back.

He let her go, watching her. "Tell me what was bothering you about the bed."

With a lessening of the awful tension between them, Xander found it easier to focus on the matter at hand. Turning away, she walked over to the bed. She lifted the bunched up comforter and flipped it back. "It's just that the sheets are shredded." Leaning closer, she traced the deep rips with a finger and added, "Not just the sheets, but so is the mattress."

Warrick went and stood at the foot of the bed. "Claws don't only come out when you're fighting."

Heat washed over her face as last night's memory of his skin under her nails danced in her head. "This isn't about sex."

"Maybe it was good sex."

She gave him the look every female used when a male was being dense. "I don't think so."

Warrick quirked an eyebrow.

"Single toothbrush in the bathroom, no unexplainable underwear lying around, and the only scent I've been picking up in here is his." She glanced back down and frowned. "I don't know, maybe bad dreams? Unless he's an extremely restless sleeper." She shook her head, unable to pin down why such a small thing was bothering her. "Never mind." She made her way around the bed until she stood next to Warrick. "Did you find anything in the office?"

"Nothing out of the ordinary." He motioned her ahead of him. They both headed back down the hall. "There's a password-protected laptop on the desk."

"We can call Ryuu and see if he can help us crack it."

Warrick wrapped his hand around her wrist, stopping her before she entered the office. Turning her head, she looked at him.

His face was grim. "You really believe Sebastian would turn on the pack?" *On me?*

There was no missing his unspoken question. "Maybe there's another explanation," she offered, trying to give him something.

"But it's not looking good," he growled.

"No, it's not," she said.

His jaw tightened, but he gave her a short nod before letting her go.

CHAPTER 24

Twenty minutes later, Warrick was wearing a path in the beige carpet in front of Sebastian's desk as Xander followed the last of Ryuu's instructions.

"Okay, I think that's it," she said and hit Enter. The black and white text on the screen disappeared, only to be replaced with a heavily muscled troll-like figure hefting an overly large ax and standing on top of a pile of blood-soaked bodies. "Lovely," she muttered.

"You should be in."

Even over the tinny speaker of the phone she could hear the grimness in Ryuu's voice. He wasn't at all pleased with their poking around in Sebastian's business. Good thing Warrick was with her. Otherwise she would've wasted time arguing with him.

Xander figured if she was wrong, she could apologize later, but for now, she'd rather piss off Sebastian by violating his privacy than risk Zeke's continued good health. "Yeah, I am."

"Did you find anything on Zeke's computer?" Warrick

asked from the other side of the desk, his steps measured and deliberate.

Unsurprisingly, he was driving her crazy with his pacing, so she hissed at him. He raised his head and she frowned pointedly then gave a sharp shake to her head. He stopped directly in front of her, leaned his hands on either side of the laptop, and curled a lip. She raised an eyebrow, smiled sweetly, then went back to scanning the contents of Sebastian's laptop.

"Maybe," Ryuu answered. "Gavin and I have been running Zeke's history from today and he was poking around in some old reports and files. One of the reports was the one on the cage fighting incident."

"And the others?" Warrick asked.

The pause on the other end of the phone was damning. "Another was the incident report on the rogue, Kurt Stevenson. Zeke had also pulled files up on each of the dead wolves. He was following Sebastian's activity log."

"Sebastian could have been trying to find a link between the attack and the dead wolves," Warrick said.

Xander peeked at Warrick from under her lashes. His voice may have been bland, but with him so close, she didn't miss his nails gouging the desk's surface. Unable to resist, she covered one of his hands and gave it a soft squeeze. Under her touch, his fingers flexed.

"Ryuu, look at this," Gavin said. There was the sound of a chair being rolled across a floor and some shuffling.

Xander let go of Warrick's hand and went back to the laptop. Opening Sebastian's email, she began combing through the various messages and folders.

A string of curses had her fingers halting and she looked at the phone. "Ryuu?"

"Dammit, Xander," his voice came back, taut with tension,

She winced at the underlying layer of pained betrayal in those two words. "What did you find?"

"Zeke traced an online chat room identity back to Sebastian."

Validation of her suspicions didn't make her feel any better. Instead, a sick sensation crawled into her stomach and made itself at home. "Which chat rooms?"

"One of the ones that went dark before Warrick headed to Arizona."

"The same one the Bitten were discussing possible cures in?"

"Yeah," Ryuu said flatly.

"But that doesn't make sense." She met Warrick's gaze. "Sebastian's a Born wolf, not Bitten. Plus, you said he was upset because you chose me as your mate, but the bond happened in Arizona. So if that was his trigger, what was he doing in the chat rooms before that?"

"Because he knew I was going to choose you before Arizona." Warrick straightened and resumed his pacing as if I hadn't just dropped a bomb.

Stunned, Xander got up from her chair and rounded the desk until she was directly in Warrick's path.

He stopped in front of her.

"You want to explain that?" she asked quietly.

His jaw tightened, a hint of color rising along his cheekbones, and his shoulders straightened. "You've been mine for a while now, Xander." When she stood there, silent, he continued. "We'd been together for over a year. Neither my wolf nor I would waste our time on someone we didn't want. The damn bond is a bonus, but I'd chosen you as my mate long before that."

Instead of being offended at his propriety statement, she found herself stifling a smile that threatened to bloom at the sound of his growly, put-upon tone. She held the proof of her importance to him close, letting it sooth some of her ragged edges, and cleared her throat. "Nice of you to let me know."

Whatever Warrick planned to say was cut off by Ryuu. "That wasn't all Zeke found. That GPS unit you two found in the rental, he managed to get a printout of the route."

Warrick's gaze shifted to the phone. "And?"

"There were a couple of stops before they hit your place. One was a hotel in downtown Portland, the other is an address."

"They could've checked into the hotel," Warrick offered as Xander went back to the desk to bend over the laptop.

She pulled up Sebastian's Internet and went to Google Maps. "Give me the address."

"4327 SW North Shore Drive, Gaston."

"Son of a—" Her bitten-off curse had Warrick coming up behind her.

"What?" Ryuu asked.

"Sebastian's definitely linked to the address. It's the last place he mapped." As the proof of Sebastian's betrayal mounted, disbelief and fury began to build.

There was the clatter of computer keys through the phone line. "Gavin's checking property records to see who it belongs to now."

Xander pulled out her phone and began typing in the address. She and Warrick would need it.

"Xander, was there anything else on the laptop?" Ryuu asked.

"Nothing glaringly obvious," she answered.

"If you bring it back with you, I'll go over it." Based on

the sharp edge of Ryuu's voice, there was no more hesitancy in invading Sebastian's privacy.

"It'll have to wait until we check out this address," Warrick cut in, leaving no room for arguments.

"Vidis, I don't think the two of you should head out there without some back up. We have no idea who Sebastian's working with or why."

"Or what that spell can really do," Xander added under her breath.

Warrick's glare and warning snarl made Xander wince. He shifted his fury to Ryuu. "I'm not sitting around and leaving Zeke alone with that bastard longer than I have to. He's not expecting us to be able to track him so soon. Once you have a name, you and Gavin head over to the hotel and see what you can find out."

Ryuu knew when not to argue with his alpha. "Fine, but you keep your cell phones close. I'll call you as soon as we have a name on the property." The drone of the dial tone filled the room.

Xander clicked the phone off and shut down the laptop. "Do you really think Sebastian has Zeke?"

It was hard to get the question out. Warrick's fury led off of him like a dark wind. It took everything she had to keep her hands steady and her wolf under control. Rarely had she been in his presence when he was this angry, generally making a point to stay out of his way when his temper was riding him hard. But she was his mate, which meant her place was beside him. So she sucked it up.

"If he doesn't, he's going to tell us who does," he snarled before stalking out of the small office.

As he and his anger swept out of the room, she sighed. Yeah, this was going to be fun.

Warrick's sedan bumped over the weather-beaten asphalt as they followed the GPS as it took them away from the edges of Haag Lake and deeper off the beaten path. They made the normal thirty-minute drive in just under twenty. Xander was amazed that Warrick's blatant speedracer impression hadn't attracted the attention of the police.

"Pull over here," Xander said when the dot representing them on her phone came to the last bend in the road. "If Sebastian's really there, no point in letting him know he has visitors."

Warrick didn't answer, but carefully pulled his sedan off to the side of the road. When he turned off the engine, she shot Ryuu a quick text that they made it, then stashed her phone in a pocket. She reached for the door before realizing that Warrick hadn't moved. He was sitting still, staring out the windshield, his hand flexing around the steering wheel.

"Warrick?" she called his name softly, worried by his unusual reaction.

"I don't like this."

The words were squeezed out, as if by keeping a tight rein on his voice, he could choke back whatever emotion was riding him.

"I'm not a big fan of it either, but we don't really have a choice," she said, uncertain what was going on.

In a very wolfish manner, he cocked his head toward her. She sucked in her breath as she found herself staring into the eyes of the wolf. "Not this plan. Having you here."

She bit her lip, hard. It stopped the urge to snap that this wasn't the time for his possessive side to come out to play. Even her wolf wanted to claw at him in frustration. They were mates. Mates stood together. When was he going to get that? It was only when her wolf reached out to make her feelings known that Xander realized how tight she had locked down their bond.

Warm fingers grasped her chin, forcing her to meet his gaze. "I want you here, but we—" he tapped his chest, "—want to keep you safe. This isn't going to be safe."

"You need to let him protect you as much as you need to protect him." Her mother's earlier words whispered in her head and resounded in her heart, shedding a new light on their earlier argument.

If she continued to snarl and claw against Warrick's nature, she would destroy any chance they had at making their relationship work. She had a choice—walk away, or learn to meet him halfway. Considering how vital this man was to her, her decision wasn't that hard.

She dismantled the barriers she erected and let the bond flow open between them. Piece by piece, she felt each thread slip back into place. A sense of coming home, of finding her center swept through her, smoothing over the ragged edges of hurt feelings. There were still parts of him that were walled off, but she could wait. Her alpha had waited weeks for her to accept their bond and patience wasn't a virtue most alphas possessed. It was time to step up and take her place at his side. She couldn't expect Warrick to be anyone other than who he was, which meant if it was her turn to wait for him to figure out how to let her be a partner, then so be it.

Reaching out, she cupped his face. "It's not safe for either of us, but if you watch my back, I'll watch yours. Deal?"

The taut lines in his face softened as he turned his lips

into her palm and pressed a warm, chaste kiss against her skin. "Deal," he said, his voice husky with emotion.

Warrick and Xander approached the dark house, careful to stay downwind. It helped that the threatening rain finally decided to make an appearance. The steady downpour covered the sounds of their approach and washed away their scent, giving them a welcomed edge.

Together, they decided to approach on two feet instead of four. Even if her nose wasn't as sharp in human form, she couldn't argue that opposable thumbs came in damn handy when you were trying to sneak around. Besides, Warrick had reassured her that it wouldn't take much for him to call his wolf, should the need for fangs and claws come into play.

The house was a long, rectangular ranch style. The blind eyes of the windows looked over the bare porch, spanning the front. As they crossed the oil-stained gravel driveway, no signs of life sputtered from within.

Warrick worked his way around the back while Xander crept up onto the porch, keeping to the darker patches of shadows. She made her way to the door, carefully stepping across the weathered boards of the porch. The dull metal of the front door's handle was within reach when the low groan of a warped board moaned under her foot. She froze and held her breath, waiting to see if the noise triggered a reaction. The muffled din of the rain against the porch's tin roof continued without missing a beat. When no other sounds joined in, she let her breath slide out in a soundless exhale.

Wrapping her hand around the cold metal, she twisted

it. Locked. She considered breaking in, but before she could make the decision, a silent call resonated under her skin. Warrick had found something.

Sliding under the wooden porch rail, she dropped to the gravel and made her way around to the back of the house. Rounding the side, she met Warrick. He touched her arm then pointed. Set back, closer to the tree line, was the darker outline of another building.

As she followed in Warrick's wake, the lines morphed into the shape of a barn. Not the A-frame type, common out this way, but another long, low rectangle. Unlike the house, this one was occupied. There were no visible windows but lines of electric light escaped from sporadic gaps along the walls. Wood never did well in the Northwest. Eventually, years of exposure to the elements left it warped.

Even yards from the barn, the rain drowned out any scent or sounds. As they closed the distance, she caught the signs of movement from inside, the light flickering as someone moved across it.

As she and Warrick closed in, they couldn't miss the sound of Sebastian's voice. "What the hell were you thinking?" Stress and anger made his words sharp, but underneath was a frantic note that worried Xander.

"I was doing my damn job!" The snarled answer came from someone she didn't recognize.

"I don't remember telling you to dose him!" She recognized the meaty sound of a fist meeting flesh. There was a grunt and something heavy slammed into the wall, shaking the building.

Using the noise as a cover, she and Warrick burst through the door, turning it into jagged splinters. Their explosive entrance brought the fight inside to a shocked halt, giving her necessary seconds for her eyes to adjust to the light.

Sebastian stood with one hand twisted in a dingy white wife beater that was stretched across the barrel chest of a stocky bald man she'd never seen before. As Warrick sprung across the dirt floor, Sebastian pushed the other man away to face the lethal threat bearing down.

The guy stumbled back, trying to find his balance. Xander closed in, using her shoulder to hit him just under his ribs and drive him into the wall. His breath whooshed out but it didn't slow him down. Even as she nailed his kidney with a short jab, numbing pain spiraled down from her shoulder as he landed a solid blow.

He managed to score a glancing hit along her jaw before she turned into him, her back to his chest. He brought his arm down for another blow but this time she managed to capture it, and hold it over her shoulder. Using a wrist lock, she twisted his arm until her sore shoulder sat just above his elbow and yanked down. The sharp snap of bone was followed by his howl of pain.

Knowing it wasn't smart to stay within reach, she smashed his foot under the heavy sole of her boot, grinding her heel as she spun out of his reach. His breathing was rough, his broken arm hanging uselessly at his side, but his focus didn't falter as they circled each other. Amber washed over the brown of his irises and was quickly followed by his hair-raising growl.

Behind her, she could hear Warrick and Sebastian fighting but she didn't take her gaze off of her opponent, even when his bones began to shift under his skin. Normally, she'd have no problem matching the speed of his change, but thanks to the fact she already changed once tonight, her wolf was slow to respond. It left her at a distinct disadvantage when he rushed her. In warrior form.

Grim realization struck. This was another Born wolf, not some experimental Bitten.

Change complete, he struck.

Sucking in her stomach as he swiped out with his claws, she heard her shirt rip and felt the stinging kiss as his nails raked her skin. She retaliated, raking out with half-formed claws at his throat.

He ducked his chin, letting her rip the skin along his square jaw. Sharp white teeth snapped at her wrist, catching it in a brutal grip. He jerked his head to the side, breaking it.

Her wolf surged to the fore as the burst of white-hot pain radiated up her arm. Instinct had her swiping out with her other hand. He released her wrist and tried to bring his hands up to protect his face, but he was too slow. Her thick nails ripped into the skin above his ear and tore a bloody path across the side of his face. His pained roar wasn't as satisfying as the feel of his warm blood splattering her face. Freed from his bite, she stumbled back and ducked under his blind swing.

Her breath came in short ragged pants as waves of agony resonated up her arm. She needed to end this quickly. She scanned the area around them for anything she could use as a weapon. Along the wall, behind Baldy, hung a line of rusted tools.

A low growl brought her attention back to the wounded wolf in front of her. His spine was hunched, his hand covering the side of his face. When he lowered his hand and raised his head, she smiled. She managed to do some serious damage with her last strike. His eye was nothing more than a gory mass sitting inside the strips of torn skin.

"Bitch!" he hissed, a deadly light entering his remaining eye. His muscles coiled. Using the speed inherent to all shifters, he sprung.

She leapt out of the way and made a beeline for the tools. Even half blinded, he still managed to rake his claws over her back. She hissed at the pain. She slammed into the wall just as her uninjured left hand closed around the splintered wood handle of the nearest tool. Ripping it down, she brought the tool around in an awkward swing, using her broken wrist to propel her body until her back was to the wall and not the raging wolf behind her. The reverberation as her strike met Baldy's skull sent slivers of wood into her palm. The sting of those small wounds was lost under the scream of agony as the broken bones in her wrist ground against each other. Her vision began to gray.

Baldy staggered back from the blow and dropped to his hands and knees.

Gritting her teeth, she fought her way through the pain and tightened her grip on the tool's handle. Now or never. Raising her makeshift weapon, she brought it down once more. Only as the metal's edge sliced into the base of Baldy's skull, cutting deep and driving him face first into the ground, did she realize she had grabbed a shovel.

The shovel came to an abrupt stop as the metal met his spine, the shock of it shuddering through her. For a second, she stood there, letting the tool hold her up, and tried to remember how to breathe. A burst of coppery scent heralded fresh spilt blood and brought her head up.

Warrick and Sebastian had both chosen the half-wolf, half-man warrior form. Even though Sebastian's bulkier warrior form topped Warrick's by a couple of inches, it wasn't turning out to be much of an advantage. Leaner and faster, Warrick moved with blinding speed and accuracy.

Blood seeped between the ragged remains of Sebastian's shirt and dripped onto the churned up ground at their feet as he and Warrick circled each other, looking for an opening.

There was a slight hunch to Sebastian's shoulders, indicating there were more wounds on his front. They turned, Warrick coming into view, and some of her tension faded. Although his shirt was decorated with rips and tears, the claw marks she could see didn't seem to be bleeding very heavily, nor did they seem to be slowing him down.

Even as she forced her hand to let go of the shovel as she slowly straightened, Warrick and Sebastian closed in once more. For all its violence, their fight was a lethal ballet of grace and speed set against their heavy breathing and occasional grunts. There were no loud growls or yips, as most shifters had learned to fight in the modern world in relative silence.

Sebastian was tiring, evident in the slight drag of his foot and his jerky movements as he tried to stay clear of Warrick's sharp claws. She needed to be closer, in case Sebastian tried something. Desperate wolves never followed the rules. The pull and sting of her various injuries made each step a revelation on the many nuances of pain.

Halfway to them, a muffled whine jerked her attention to a shadowed edge along the far side of the barn. *Zeke!* She turned and scanned the shadows hovering by the wall then altered her course. Inside her head, her wolf growled and she snarled back. Warrick could take care of himself. They needed to get to Zeke.

As she got closer, the shadows resolved into a definite form. Her steps picked up until she was in a stumbling run. With thick chains wrapped around his wrists, Zeke was strung up between two heavy posts that used to frame an interior stall. It wasn't until she was in front of him that she caught the scent of burnt flesh.

Her growl was low and vicious. *Damn bastards had used silver.*

"Zeke?" She touched his face. His skin felt cool to the touch and her heart stuttered. She pressed her fingers against his neck, searching for his pulse. Her breath wheezed out when she felt the reassuring beat, but it was too slow. "Just hang on, okay?"

It took her a few seconds to study the chains holding him. A padlock, nestled on each post, linked the ends of the chains. She grabbed one, only to snatch her hand back as the lock seared her skin. Where in the hell did they come up with silver padlocks?

She scanned the area around them for anything to use to break the lock and found a whole lot of nothing. She considered dashing back across the barn and grabbing one of the rusted-out tools. Curling her fist, the sharp bite of wooden splinters made her reconsider. She doubted the old implements would be able to withstand the pressure needed to break the lock. She glared at the post and chain, frustration clawing at her. She had one hand, the other completely useless. There was no way she could tear the chains apart.

Desperation and frustration boiled over. She couldn't leave Zeke and she didn't dare wait for Warrick. Furious, she snapped out a kick at the post and was rewarded with a sharp crack. Inspiration dawned. She struck out again, nailing the post in the same spot with the strongest kick she could manage. The wood visibly split. Encouraged, she continued to pummel the post. Pushing aside the resounding choir of pain her body began to sing, she concentrated on turning the aged wood into splinters.

CHAPTER 25

IT TOOK LESS TIME THAN XANDER THOUGHT BEFORE A SHARPER crack sounded and the post broke. She snapped out another kick, creating more space between the two pieces. Then she used her good hand, ignoring the burn of silver, and began pushing the chain down the wood. When she finally got the first layer of chain to drop, the rest followed, slowly slithering into a pile on the ground. It gave her enough time to catch Zeke's unconscious body as it began to collapse.

She got her bruised shoulder and left arm around his waist then gently shuffled him toward the other post. It was difficult to propped him against it with his still-chained wrist but, with some judicious grunting, she managed. She stood up, only to have her leg cramp viciously and collapse under her. Strong hands caught her before she could get up close and personal with the ground.

"Are you okay?" The words were growled close to her ear.

Worried about freeing Zeke, she had missed the conclusion of the fight behind her. Leaning into Warrick for support, she let her head fall back against his shoulder and concentrated on breathing through the spasms in her leg, ignoring his question.

"Is Sebastian dead?" she asked.

Normally, when a wolf died the pack ties ensured everyone in the pack knew. Unfortunately, they were as far from normal as they could get lately.

"Not yet," he said grimly.

"I need your help to get Zeke unchained." She stepped away from him and tested her leg. Her muscles still protested, but she could work around it now. "It's silver and I'm down to one hand."

Warrick made short work of the lock and chain. She tried to ignore the scent of his skin burning as he gently untangled Zeke's wrist from the silver. When he was done, he gathered Zeke in his arms and stood with deceptive ease. He turned to walk away and she sucked in a sharp breath.

His back was a mess of claw and bite marks, some still seeping blood.

"Dammit, Warrick," she choked.

He turned his head and looked at her over his shoulder. "I'll be fine, pixie girl."

A low groan switched their focus to Sebastian's battered form. Warrick's spine stiffened. "Chain him," he snapped. "I don't want him going anywhere."

"I'll take care of it," she answered. "First, I'm calling Ryuu."

Warrick nodded. "Have him meet us at the house."

Something in his voice made Xander's heart skip a beat. "Warrick?"

He didn't answer and she watched as he took Zeke out of the barn. She wanted to help, but for now, she needed to ensure sure their enemies wouldn't circle around and attack. She kept an eye on Sebastian as she pulled out her battered phone. One-handed texting was easier than trying to field the questions Ryuu was bound to ask if she called. When she was done, she dropped it back in her pocket.

She considered the pile of silver chain and the distance between it and Sebastian. There was no way she was dragging Sebastian's ass over to the chain, nor did the prospect of burning her hands fill her with joy. It took her a few minutes to get her T-shirt off, leaving her in a dark blue bra and black jeans.

Wrapping her sore left hand in the T-shirt, she managed to drag the silver chain over to Sebastian. Then she manhandled him until he was lying on one end of the chain. As the silver touched his skin, he arched up, an agonized howl escaping his throat. His body convulsed, but the damage Warrick inflicted left him helpless and dazed.

She jammed a booted foot over his throat, holding him in place. She had no qualms about causing him untold agony. As it was, she and her wolf would have happily torn his throat out without batting an eyelash. The only thing holding them both back was how much a quick death would piss off Warrick.

It was awkward and difficult, but she managed to get the chain around Sebastian by rolling the wolf along the ground and letting the chain curl around him. When she was done, the scent of burnt flesh had deadened her nose. Silver chain was coiled around Sebastian from shoulder to waist, his arms trapped against his body. He was panting, his body jerking in little spasms as his heels scraped the ground.

Task done, she tugged her shirt back on and stood over him. *How to keep him in place?* He wasn't really conscious but his body was twitching under the kiss of silver.

The sound of tires on gravel had her doing a strange

limping run to the door of the barn. Sebastian wasn't going anywhere soon and Warrick was with Zeke in the house. There was no telling who was coming up the drive.

Slipping outside, she was halfway to the house when she heard Ryuu's familiar voice. "Vidis? Xander?"

"Here." Shifter hearing being what it was, there was no need to raise her voice.

Ryuu burst around the side of the house, another form on his heels. As they cleared the shadows, she saw it was Gavin. "How'd you get here so fast?"

"Never went to the hotel," Ryuu answered. "Where's Vidis?"

"Inside with Zeke," she said. "You need to go help him." As Warrick's Second, he would be able to help channel both the alpha and the pack's power.

Ryuu gave a short nod then spun around and headed to the house. She stood there, watching him go.

"Xander?"

She jerked at the sound of her name and blinked, realizing Gavin was standing in front of her. Her snarl was instinctive.

He raised his hands and dropped his gaze to her shoulder. "Sorry, you were about to topple over."

It took her a moment to fight her wolf back. Exhaustion, pain, and worry were setting her on edge. "Sebastian's in the barn. Can you watch him?" Her attention was focused on the house. Warrick was drawing on the pack ties and the call of her alpha was insistent.

"Go," Gavin said, brushing past her.

"Don't kill him," she threw over her shoulder as she headed toward the house. Then she stopped thinking about Sebastian.

Warrick had kicked in the back door, and she followed

the pull of her pack into a living room. There was a camping lantern on the floor next to a worn couch. The shattered remains of something was pushed into a pile next to Ryuu, who was kneeling on the floor at one end while Warrick sat on an old wooden crate at the other. To an outsider it would seem as if the two men were simply watching the one on the couch. The crush of magic that surrounded them told a different story.

She dropped to her knees between Ryuu and Warrick, reaching out and placing a hand on Zeke's bare stomach. As soon as her skin touched his, the magic sucked her under. She offered all she had to Warrick and Ryuu as they tried to reconnect Zeke's tie. She could sense them working together, but couldn't see what exactly they were doing. All she could do was add the strength of herself and her wolf. Her forehead rested against the nappy edge of the couch's cushion and she closed her eyes, letting Warrick and Ryuu take what they needed.

Minutes or hours passed—she wasn't sure which. At some point, Warrick reached out to the entire pack for additional strength. Their pack was small, with fewer than forty wolves spread throughout Washington and Oregon, but each one responded with no reservations. Together, they held onto Zeke with dogged determination.

One of the greatest strengths of the shifters was their packs. Together, they were more lethal, more powerful than they were as individuals. Packs' ties allowed the alpha to utilize those individual strengths to protect and defend his wolves. As Warrick pulled on each wolf, she felt the normal barriers existing between individual pack members fade. It was the strangest sensation as the varied collection of strengths reformed around Warrick.

For the first time, she caught a glimpse of what it meant

to be an alpha. Even as she answered his call, the part of her connected to him through the mate bond sat like a quiet shadow next to him, watching in wonder.

There were common traits shared among their wolves —protectiveness, compassion, loyalty, love, and family. Right now, each one was just as determined as their alpha to save Zeke. Together, they formed a thick band of light that wrapped around Warrick, who sat cradling a weaker, thinner strand. That strand was tangled with a black cord. There was another band of light trying to connect to the one in Warrick's hands by slipping through the gaps between the black threads. It finally connected, its hold precarious.

As if from a distance, she heard Ryuu's voice, "I think I have him."

"You need to hold it because that damn spell won't let me in." That was Warrick.

"You have to hurry, Warrick." Ryuu's voice sounded grim.

She blinked her eyes open and turned until her cheek was rest-ng on the sofa. Warrick was still sitting in the same position at Zeke's head, his eyes closed.

"I'm trying," Warrick answered.

Xander frowned. His lips hadn't moved.

"Warrick!" With Ryuu's sharp cry, it clicked. The mate bond was allowing her to listen in on their conversation through the pack ties.

There was a sharp wrench, as if something was being torn from her. Her vision whited out then she was back on the psychic plane next to Warrick. The black bands had turned into a writhing mass, swarming over Warrick's hands as he held onto Zeke's thin strand, moving toward the thick thread that belonged to their pack. Evil permeated the strands. They rapidly worked their way up Warrick's arms, around his waist and up his chest. Blood ran in rivulets where each dark strand touched.

"Warrick!" she screamed as terror filled her.

In a flurry of teeth and claws, she and her wolf attacked the shapeless mass, trying to drive it away from the thicker band. It was like fighting greasy smoke. There was nothing to dig their claws into, nothing to tear into with their teeth, but she tried. Forcing it back from the pack, she and her wolf stood between the dark mass and Warrick and Ryuu. She wasn't sure what was happening, but there was no doubt in her mind if she didn't keep this thing back, she'd lose everyone—Warrick, Zeke, Ryuu, and the pack.

She could feel Warrick and Ryuu doing something behind her, but she didn't dare take her gaze off the threat in front of her. Her wolf stood stiff-legged next to Warrick's, guarding his body and harrying the writhing mass of the spell. She was grateful that here on this plane she and her wolf could act as two separate beings because it gave her a chance to study the spell.

It took her valuable moments to finally see where the spell was anchored. Remembering Cheveyo's earlier observation that the spell would need to use an existing connection, she located Warrick's link to Sebastian. When she found it, uncertainty and dread left her limbs trembling. She looked back and saw that the threads seem to be thicker now, and Warrick's chest and arms were painted red. Grim resolution solidified.

Reaching through the surrounding threads of the spell, she ignored the sting of their touch against her skin and the dull agony of her broken wrist. Gritting her teeth, she wrapped her hands around the spell. Stomach churning, the sense of sickening wrongness sent her to her knees, but she didn't let go. Not understanding why or how, she called on the bond she and Warrick shared and began to tear apart the thread holding Sebastian to the rest of the pack.

It was like trying to tear apart a thick length of silver, but somehow she knew if she let go, it would be disastrous. The searing burn seeped through her skin and nerve endings. By the time it hit bone, she was screaming.

Fury and desperation lent her additional strength and she dug deep, calling on everything she had. When the strand finally snapped under the pressure, she was thrown back, as if some huge fist had punched her in the stomach. She landed on her back, trying to relearn how to breathe. Her hands were numb from the pain overload and her body felt as if it had been pounded with a meat tenderizer.

"Xander?" Warrick's voice finally penetrated the abnormal white silence in her head.

"Fine," she muttered. "I'm fine." She rolled over to her hands and knees, the pressure on her battered palms and broken wrist reawakening her nerve endings. Yanking her hands up, she rocked back on her heels, swaying slightly as she crouched in place. It took a moment to find the strength to get to her mental feet and turn around.

Her heart sank. The whirling mass of the spell was nothing but a gray pile of broken threads, but the light that was Zeke was almost translucent. Warrick sat bloodied but unbowed between their two wolves, his face a mask of determined concentration. She was able to make out a faint outline of Ryuu kneeling in front of him. Together, the two men worked with quiet desperation over the fragile thread.

On the psychic plane, she stumbled forward and dropped to her knees next to Ryuu. She wanted to reach out and help, but was worried her touch might do more harm than good. Under Warrick and Ryuu's hands, Zeke's light began to flicker.

Her mouth went dry as fear filled her and her pulse began to race.

"He's convulsing." That was Ryuu's voice. "Xander, you're going to have to hold him down. We can't leave him here."

She didn't answer, just forced herself out of the psychic plane and back into the physical world. She blinked her eyes open. The feel of Zeke's body jerking under her touch had her moving before her vision cleared. She threw herself across his chest, trying to hold him in place so he wouldn't fall to the floor. She buried her face against the faint pulse in his neck and whispered reassurances to him.

His body arched violently, almost throwing her off. She lifted her head and readjusted her hold, dismissing the flare of pain in her broken wrist. His spine bowed and his eyes flew open, meeting hers briefly. Bones shifted with brutal intensity and Zeke screamed until it warped and changed into an agonized howl. The sound chilled her soul. His body slammed back down on the couch and she scrambled to cradle his face in her hands, ignoring the horrific spasms of bone and muscles beneath her palms.

"Stay with me, Zeke. Please," she cried, her voice choked with tears. "Please!"

His eyes opened and found hers again. His mouth moved but no sound came out.

"I'm right here, Zeke. You have to fight," she whispered. "You can't leave us."

He lifted a hand with an effort and touched a tear rolling down her face. "Hurts."

"I know," her voice shook. "Just a little longer. Give Warrick a chance to help you."

Before she could finish, another violent convulsion wracked Zeke. This time, his howl was accompanied by the sound of bones snapping. Under her hands, his face began to change in sections. But when the seizure passed, he was no longer recognizable as wolf or human.

"Zeke?"

His eyes fluttered open and met hers. "Sorry," he slurred.

"No! No, dammit! You hold on." Frantic, she watched the light in his eyes dull. "No, Zeke!" She cried, but it was too late.

One last breath of air passed his lips then the tension seeped from his twisted body. Zeke was gone.

CHAPTER 26

ZEKE'S DEATH REVERBERATED THROUGH THE PACK AND THE resonating wave of sorrow and loss rocked Warrick. He needed to be able to function, so he released his draw on the ties, letting his wolves drop away, one by one. Opening his eyes, he found Xander kneeling by his side, her head resting on Zeke's chest. A wash of tangled emotions flowed over him and he slid to the floor behind her, gently pulling her away from the still form on the couch.

For a moment, she struggled then turned in his arms and buried her face against his chest, one arm wrapping around his waist. Settling on the floor, he rested his chin against the silky strands of her short hair as the heat of her tears dampened his chest. What was left of Zeke was a horrific amalgam of human and wolf. Warrick tamped down on the soul-deep rage trying to rise.

He kept one hand on the back of Xander's head, holding her next to his heart, while the other stroked down her spine. She didn't make a sound, which somehow made her sorrow worse. He blinked away the burning pressure in his eyes and fought to think beyond the cresting wave of grief and rage at his lost wolf.

He could feel Ryuu behind him, waging his own internal battle. Tonight, the pack had lost two wolves, Zeke and Sebastian. Whatever Xander had done, and he'd try to remember to find out exactly what it was later, had severed the ties of his Third to the pack. For all intents and purposes, Sebastian no longer existed within the Motoki Pack. Normally, Zeke would have stepped in and picked up the slack as he was next in line.

He tested the strength of his pack and was shocked when the expected gap from Sebastian and Zeke's absences wasn't there. Instead, a new presence sat in its place, helping to maintain the strength and security of the pack. He took a closer look and when he identified the wolf sitting in place of Third, he tightened his arms around Xander. Dropping his head to bury his face in her hair, he breathed out a soft sigh of relief. Briefly, he wondered how she'd handle having her brother, Ethan, as his acting Third.

"What happened?" Xander's question was muffled against his chest.

"The combination of the spell and the drug was too much," Warrick said.

When she made a slight move against him, he raised his head and dropped his arms. She didn't move away, but turned until she was once again facing Zeke. He watched as she traced Zeke's unrecognizable features, then her hand dropped into her lap.

"How did you know how to destroy the spell?"

Ryuu's question had Warrick looking behind him. Ryuu sat on the floor with his back against the couch, his hands resting on his knees, staring across the room.

Xander didn't turn. "Something Cheveyo said about the

spell having to be tied to one of the pack." She paused. "I thought only an alpha could break the pack ties."

Her comment sparked the answer Warrick was looking for at her unexpected action. He brushed a hand over the back of her head in an effort to offer comfort. "For all intents and purposes, you're my mate, which means you can act in my place."

She gave a small nod.

On the couch, Zeke's body shuddered. Ryuu sprung to his feet, Xander and Warrick following his example. Like some invisible wave, the grotesque changes that left Zeke broken melted away. When the strange energy finally faded, the outward signs of his forced change were gone, leaving a deceptively peaceful mask in its place.

Xander reached out, her hand visibly shaking, to touch the heartbreakingly young face. "I want blood," she said, nothing fragile in her cold voice.

"Answers first." Ryuu had moved to stand next to them.

"Answers first," Warrick agreed, and he knew just where to start.

As if reading his mind, Xander finally faced him. "No. You'll kill him."

He dropped his gaze pointedly to the wrist she was cradling close to her stomach. He knew it was broken. He could feel every ache and pain she bore through the bond, and the only reason she wasn't feeling his was because he was holding it back. She had enough to deal with.

"It'll heal," she snapped. "He's bound in silver and Gavin's out there, so I'll be fine."

"We're going with you," Ryuu growled.

She turned her glared on him. "If you go, you two are going to stay the hell back. If either of you get in his face, he'll bite his tongue off before saying anything to you. He knows neither one of you will listen, so death would be an easy out."

Ryuu got in her face. "And just why would he talk to you?"

Going toe to toe with Ryuu, her answer was a study in cold control. "Because he thinks women are stupid creatures and no matter how beaten he is, he believes he's smarter than me."

Ryuu shook his head. "You think he's going to spill his guts to you because you're a female?"

"No," she answered, backing away. "He'll tell me because he believes this is all my fault."

Warrick caught the edge of her soul-deep guilt and knew she believed it, too. He shot Ryuu a look to back off and reached out to pull her back into his arms. Tugging her close, he dropped his head until his lips were next to her ear. "It's not."

When she went to close her end of the bond, he growled a warning. She stopped and tilted her head until she could meet his gaze. He'd let her search for whatever answers she needed. He didn't blame her. Sebastian's decisions were his own. If anything, had he been paying closer attention to his wolves, maybe he could have stopped all of this.

She lifted her hand and brushed a gently stroke along his jaw. "I guess we could all play the blame game." She dropped her hand, pulled away, and faced Ryuu. "I know you don't want to, but you have to stay quiet and let me do this. We have to stop whatever the hell is going on before it kills anyone else."

Ryuu's hands curled into fists and he shot a rage-filled look at Warrick. Understanding his Second's need to spill blood all too well, he put his trust in his mate's judgment. He knew himself well enough to know it wouldn't take much for him to tear out Sebastian's throat right now. He gave Ryuu a small nod.

Taking a deep breath, Ryuu touched Xander's cheek. Warrick walked up behind her, dropped a kiss to the top of her head. Ryuu held the door open for her, Warrick at his side. She forced her feet away from Zeke and out the door.

The rain from earlier left the grass between the barn and the house glistening with droplets. Xander came to a halt where the light from inside the barn met the night as it poured through what was left of the barn door, Ryuu and Warrick silent shadows behind her. Her wolf was so close, almost too close, wanting to rend the flesh from Sebastian's bones, one strip at an agonizing time, and she was okay with that. Hell, she could almost taste his blood in her mouth, so real, she could feel the sharpness of her canines heralding a change.

Gods, how had she managed to fool Ryuu and Warrick that she could do this without killing Sebastian? Staring at the splintered wooden planks in front of her, she fought for control. Her wolf objected, strenuously, fighting her every inch of the way, but in the end, Xander prevailed, backing her wolf down. When her mind cleared, she considered her approach.

Sebastian was a misogynistic bastard, so drawing his resentment and anger wouldn't be hard. Her mere presence would set him off. The trick was getting him to reveal who he was working with on that damn spell and what he hoped to accomplish. That would require some serious manipulation.

Based on the bits of conversation she had caught

earlier, she'd bet good money that Sebastian hadn't wanted Zeke harmed. Since he was no longer connected to the pack, she wasn't sure how much he knew of what had happened. Self-centered ass that he was, he'd find someway to pin Zeke's death on her, though. The sharp pain in her chest reminded her that, no matter how much she masked it with edgy fury, her guilt was alive and well, gnawing at her heart.

Enough! Her lip curled in a silent self-directed snarl. *Time to grow a pair and get some answers.* Straightening her shoulders, she pushed her own battered emotions into a little corner of her heart, with a firm reminder to shut the hell up, then locked the proverbial door, and focused on the task in front of her.

Lifting her chin, she stepped into the barn. As she made her way to Gavin, who stood over Sebastian, she could feel Warrick and Ryuu slip into the heavier shadows draping the edges of the barn. Sebastian lay in an unmoving silver-covered heap, his face battered and bloody, his eyes closed. Above him, Gavin watched her approach and arched one eyebrow in question, a silent inquiry on Zeke. She gave a short shake of her head. His jaw tightened, his mouth thinning, and she swore the air around him darkened. Then again, maybe it was just the crappy lighting in the barn.

She stopped and nudged Sebastian in the ribs with the toe of her boot. All it produced was a low groan. Her thigh was one throbbing ache so crouching down was going to be a bitch, but she could deal. Besides, she'd be able to hide her damaged wrist that way.

It wasn't graceful, but she managed it for all of ten seconds. When her leg vigorously voiced its objections to her position, she shifted until she was sitting cross-legged on the dirt. Resting her wrist in her lap, she reached out with her left hand and grabbed a handful of Sebastian's short hair, using it as a handle to lift his head.

"Wakey, wakey." She gave his head a sharp shake.

He groaned again, but this time his eyes fluttered open. He stared at her with a dazed blankness.

Needing him awake and aware, she reached out and pulled on Warrick's power, hoping it would still work even though Sebastian's link to the pack was cut. "Open your eyes, Sebastian."

The surge of strength behind her command was breathtaking. What was better was the fact that Sebastian was now very aware of her, if the level of fury evident in his eyes was anything to go by. He lunged for her, obviously forgetting the massive amount of chain wrapped around him like some silver boa constrictor. His movement dug the chain in deeper, burning its way through his skin. The combination of anger and pain sent him writhing in a jerky dance.

She watched him for a minute or two, taking pleasure in his evident agony. Unfortunately, she knew if she was going to get the answers she needed, she would have to cut his little temper tantrum short. She reached out, keeping clear of his snapping jaws, and pressed a gentle finger against his sweat and blood-streaked forehead.

"Stop." And thanks to her ability to draw on her mate's position, Sebastian did exactly that. She dropped her hand.

For a moment, the temptation offered by the unexpected strength of the alpha's mantle and dominance spun through her head. A whisper of caution crept in, not belonging to her, but to Warrick. Heeding his warning, she dropped her dark line of thought and contemplated the man before her.

Amber replaced Sebastian's normal brown eye color, his

irises rounding, a clear indicator that his wolf was rising to the fore. They couldn't afford to have the man hide behind the wolf. The longer she could keep him riled up, the longer it would take for him to realize nothing tied him to the pack or Warrick.

She held his gaze. "Either pull your wolf back or I will. Your choice."

"You don't control my wolf!"

She leaned forward, her answer all the more threatening for its softness. "I'm the alpha's mate, and you answer to us."

Under the bruises and cuts decorating his face, he flushed white then red. "I don't answer to you, bitch."

She sat back and let a small smile curl her lips. "Would you rather I let Ryuu talk to you?" Wariness flickered as his gaze darted around. "Or maybe Warrick?" she added.

This time, she caught the sharp spike of acrid fear before he hid it behind his anger. "Vidis's head isn't in the game."

"Considering he just kicked your ass quite nicely, I'd say his head is completely in the game."

He sneered, reopening a cut in his lip. "He's blinded by his dick. If he hadn't been so focused on fucking you, he'd have stepped in a hell of a lot earlier."

She widened her eyes in mock innocence. "I had no idea you thought so highly of my charms, Sebastian."

Her taunt hit its mark. He lunged toward her, only to jerk as the chain bit deep. "Fuck you, Xander!"

"Temper, temper." She wagged a finger in front of his face. "If you're thinking of taking Warrick's position as alpha you better learn some control."

His snarls and growls reverberated with mindless fury

and spittle ran down his chin. He seemed unable to control his small jerky movements against the chain.

Dispassionately, she watched him. He reminded her of a rabid dog wearing a human face. "You'd never survive as alpha. Not only do you lack the control needed, you'll never have the respect of the pack."

Stilling, he gave her a twisted smile. "And you think Vidis does? After you've been nothing but a cock tease for months, acting as if he's not good enough for you? But even that wasn't enough to stop him from running out on us the minute you got yourself in trouble in Arizona. He chose you over the pack. I'm not the only one who thinks we're better off without you. You've made Vidis weak. An alpha's priority is his pack, not some piece of ass!"

She choked back the churning maelstrom his rant ignited. "What would you know of priorities?" she bit out. "You've preyed upon our weakest members, promising them something that doesn't exist, for what? Some idiotic plan to undermine Warrick's authority?"

"They were mavericks, outsiders!" he sneered. "They aren't pack. They'll never be pack. Besides, they weren't true wolves, just a bunch of worthless humans who were too stubborn to die."

"And that makes it okay to use the Bitten as guinea pigs?"

"I wasn't going to let that shit anywhere near our wolves." Despite the chains, he still managed to shrug his shoulders. "If it wiped out a few freaks, all the better."

"But it wasn't just the Bitten mavericks who suffered," she pointed out, watching him.

"So a few humans bit it." His supreme indifference set her teeth on edge. "They're like Starbucks, there's one on every corner." He bared his teeth in a savage grin. "Consider them collateral damage."

She reached out and snagged his chin, her nails digging into his jaw as she held his face still. Leaning in, she hissed, "So Zeke was collateral damage?" Sebastian's eyes widened as his skin paled, his contemptuous disdain bleeding away, but she didn't stop. "Zeke's death is on your hands. The same hands that led at least three Bitten to their deaths, uncaring of who got in the way. You betrayed your alpha and your pack, unnecessarily exposing our world to the humans. For what?" She gave his jaw a sharp twist. "Jealousy? Ego? Power? What was so damn important it was worth the life of your friend, the respect and trust of your pack and alpha?"

She let go of his head, letting it thump to the ground.

Fear edged out his anger. "Zeke isn't dead. You're lying!" He fought against the chain. "You're lying!"

"Do I reek of lies to you?"

His voice rose. "Vidis was here! He was here! He could use the pack to heal Zeke! He wouldn't let him die."

"He didn't let Zeke die. You did. Your spell, your drug. The combination of the two kept the ties out of Warrick's reach."

"No, you're wrong!" he yelled, his voice frantic. "There's no spell that can interfere with the pack ties."

She captured his gaze, held it, knowing he would hear the truth in her answer. "There is, a nasty one. It's the reason Warrick couldn't save Zeke from your actions. It's the same one that kept him in the dark about your treacherous deeds."

He shook his head, dragging it through the dirt. "No, that's not possible."

There was no scent of deceit in his answer. Uneasiness

rose. Something didn't add up. If Sebastian had nothing to do with the spell then it meant there was another unknown threat out there. Someone who was using Sebastian without his knowledge. Was that even possible? She needed to ask Cheveyo.

"Then give me another explanation," she demanded, her patience unraveling.

Desperation seeped from him. "Maybe it was the drug,"

She gave him a nasty smile. "The drug? Why don't you share what nasty shit was in your little 'cure'?" she crooned.

He couldn't hide his wince at the dangerous edge in her tone. "I don't know."

"Who gave it to you?"

"Some lab rat." Some of his old arrogance began making a reappearance. He was going to play dumb.

In no mood to screw around, she asked, "Gavin, do you have a knife I can borrow?"

Sebastian paled as Gavin handed her a beautiful black blade, edged in silver.

Leaning forward, she brought the ultra sharp tip up until it rested against the soft skin under Sebastian's eye. He sucked in a breath and his eyelid fluttered. "Careful there, I'm not as steady with my left hand," she warned, letting him see how badly she wanted to dig the blade in. "Name."

"Brant—Brant Sutler."

"And this Brant, he made the drug?" She let the blade pierce the skin, drawing a small ruby bead forth to tremble on the tip.

"I—I don't think so." Sebastian's throat worked as he swallowed convulsively. "But I think he knows who did."

"You're going to tell us where we can find Brant, aren't you?"

"Ye—yes," he stuttered, unable to move for fear of impaling his eye on her pretty new toy. Tears seeped from the corner of his eyes as he rattled off an address. She committed it to memory, even knowing Warrick and Ryuu would do the same.

When he was done, she pulled the knife back and handed it back to Gavin. Ignoring Sebastian, she waited until Gavin slipped the knife back in place before saying, "I need Cheveyo."

Gavin offered her a hand to pull her to her feet. "I'll call him."

As she rose, Sebastian began to jerk at her feet. "You can't turn me over to that witch!"

Not bothering to mask her disgust or contempt, she looked at him. "Watch me."

"You can't do that!" Then something behind her caught his attention. "Tell her, Vidis. I'm pack. We don't turn pack over to outsiders."

"You're not pack, Sebastian." Cold satisfaction filled her as she said the words. "You're nothing. You're less than nothing."

Watching his rising panic was fun. Not as much as tearing him apart piece by piece, but close. Warrick and Ryuu came to stand beside her, their silent judgment lying heavy on the air.

She knew the moment Sebastian realized he was no longer connected to any of the wolves because his face went slack then horror wiped everything else away.

"No!" he screamed. "What did you do, bitch?" He began to thrash against his bonds. "I'm going to kill you! I'll rip out your throat and feast on your guts!"

She let his words wash over her, waiting until his fury had run its course.

He lay panting, his body twitching involuntarily under the chain. Brutal realization was a crushing mistress, wiping out all of his earlier arrogance and anger. Sebastian stared at her, a dull light in his eyes. "Why?" he asked hoarsely.

Standing over him, she felt hollow. There was no misinterpreting his question. A pack wolf without a pack was a living ghost. "Killing you would be too easy."

He closed his eyes and turned his face away.

Maybe Cheveyo would have some success in figuring out who used Sebastian to set the spell, but for her, there was nothing more to learn from him. Turning, she stood before Warrick, heart sick and exhausted. "We need to give him to Cheveyo and figure out who's using him."

Warrick didn't answer, just stared over her head, his attention focused on Sebastian. This close, the roiling emotions he battled pressed against her like a thunderstorm.

She snuck a glance at Ryuu, who wasn't in much better shape. Sighing, she decided to pull out the big guns. Leaning into Warrick, she wrapped her good arm around his waist. "Take me home, Warrick. I hurt and I'm tired."

Without a word, he picked her up and left the barn.

CHAPTER 27

Xander and Warrick left Sebastian with Ryuu and Gavin,
who promised to take him to Taliesin where Cheveyo
waited. She didn't argue when Warrick had Ryuu set her
wrist. Considering how fast shifters healed, she'd rather
have the bones in place now, rather than re-break the wrist
later. The makeshift splint lessened the dull ache, but did
nothing for the one in her head.

When Ryuu was done, Warrick actually carried her back
to the sedan. He set her on her feet before opening her door.
Once settled inside, he leaned over to fasten her seat belt.
Worried by his continued silence, she reached out and
touched his face, turning him toward her. Small starbursts
of amber lit his eyes, and there was an edge to him she
couldn't pin down.

"Want me to drive?"

Instead of answering, he dipped his head and caught
her lips in a tender kiss. The taste of him filled the last of
the hollow places inside her, spreading heat and need. Even
as exhausted as she was the urge to burrow into his
warmth and strength was tempting. When he drew back,

something tight inside loosened in her chest, allowing her to finally breathe.

He ran his thumb over her lower lip. "No, just rest." He closed the door and slid into the driver's seat. Headed back down the winding road, he asked, "How's the wrist?"

"Better." She tried to relax in the seat but couldn't find a comfortable position. "Can you lean my seat back?"

A small grin appeared. He fiddled with something on the side of his seat and hers began to recline. She sighed with relief and settled in, facing him. "How long before we'll have to meet Cheveyo, do you think?"

Sporadic moonlight played tag with the shadows, adding interesting new angles to his face. "Four, maybe closer to five hours."

The clock on the dash read just after three in the morning. "I'm going to need more caffeine."

"Food first," he countered, sliding her an unreadable look. "Then sleep."

She smiled to herself. Her alpha was kind of cute when he tried handling her. "Drive-thru?"

"Home."

She held up her bandaged hand and his smile made a comeback. "I'll cook," he offered.

She closed her eyes and let her lips curve up. "I could get use to this."

"What?"

"Having you take care of me." A yawn caught her, cracking her jaw.

His chuckle was soft. "Sleep, pixie girl."

Exhaustion wrapped her in soft arms and dragged her down.

Xander woke when the white noise of the engine cut out. She blinked blearily as the dull thump of Warrick's door sounded. During the short ride home, her body's various aches and pain had morphed into a stubborn stiffness that left her feeling as if she had aged twenty years. Her door opened, and the cold early morning air chased the enclosed warmth out of the car.

Before she could get her bearings, Warrick picked her up and made his way to the house. She hooked her arm around his neck, letting the splint rest on his shoulder.

He paused at the door. "Can you get the keys out of my hand?"

It was awkward, but she managed to snag the keys without falling out of his arms. She fumbled left-handed and got the key in the lock. She pushed the door open and Warrick kicked it shut behind them. He took her straight to the living room and placed her on the couch. "Stay put. I'll grab a blanket and bring you some food."

She caught his hand as he turned away, holding him captive. "I was joking, you know."

He looked back at her, one eyebrow raised. "About?"

Heat rushed over her face. "You don't have to take care of me. I'll come help with the food."

He turned back, crouched in front of her, and gently took her hand. "Let me." The intensity in his gaze had her squirming. "I like taking care of you and you so rarely give me the opportunity to indulge."

"Okay." Her voice sounded breathy, and only when he had risen to his feet and left her alone did she drop her head into her hands. *Oh gods, lame response.* She wasn't some fainting flower! But there was no denying how his words and actions touched her heart, healing some of her emotional hurt from earlier. Having him there made this gods-awful night bearable. At least she wouldn't be sleeping alone with only her nightmares for company.

Weighted warmth drifted over her, and she opened her eyes to find a hand-crocheted blanket in various shades of green covering her. She tilted her head back to see Warrick standing behind the couch. "Thanks."

"I've got food heating, but there's time for a shower if you want," he offered.

She considered how much effort it would take to make it up the stairs and weighed it against the grimy feel of her blood-soaked clothes. "A shower would be great."

She pushed the blanket off and swung her feet to the floor. Testing her balance, she gingerly pushed her battered body upright. Warrick moved around the couch to provide additional support if needed.

"I'm good." She waved him away. "Go keep an eye on our food. I don't want you to burn anything."

"Xander," he growled.

She held up a hand to stop whatever he was going to say then shuffled like some elderly woman toward the stairs. "I'm fine. I got this."

He didn't move but watched as she began the climb. She was grateful he didn't rush to help, knowing the more she moved, the easier it would get. She made it up the stairs, breathing a sigh of relief when she reached the top. Gripping the railing, she leaned over and gave the man waiting at the bottom a grin. "See? All in one piece."

Warrick leaned against the newel post, his arms crossed over his chest. "You're looking a little pale there, love."

No surprise there. Her legs felt like wet noodles and she

had a feeling the only thing keeping her upright was her grip on the railing. "It's the lighting." She paused. Another round with the stairs would knock her on her ass. "But maybe we could eat up here?"

Laughter lessened the lines on his face. "Go. I'll bring the food up." He turned and made his way to the kitchen.

She stopped just inside the double doors to his bedroom. It was pitch black and she felt along the wall until she found the light switch. With the light on, she realized why his room was so dark. Boards covered the broken window. Had that only been a day ago? Dear gods, it felt so much longer.

At least the glass shards were gone. Moving around the room, she snagged one of Warrick's T-shirts and headed into the bathroom. Rummaging through the cabinets finally produced a plastic bag she could use to cover the make-shift splint on her arm. It wasn't pretty but it would work.

Standing in front of the mirror, she studied the remnants of her clothes in dismay. There was no salvaging her shirt. Damn it, at this rate she would need to replace her entire wardrobe. The pants needed a few sessions with the washer, but they should survive. Streaks of rusty brown had long since replaced the purple dye in her hair and bruises in various stages of healing left her looking like the victim of some over-enthusiastic, deranged make-up artist.

Sighing, she turned away from her reflection and used the handy-dandy rips in her shirt to pull it off completely, dropping it to the floor. She kicked the ragged pile into the corner, then turned on the shower, letting the water warm up. Only having one hand made getting her boots off challenging and, after much cursing and a few creative contortions, she won the battle. They joined the shirt, quickly followed by the rest of her grungy clothes. Finally naked, she stepped into the shower.

When the warm water hit her skin, she flinched until her body recovered from the shock. Slowly, her muscles uncoiled, leaving her in a near comatose state, her head resting against the wall as water sluiced over her back, her wrist cradled protectively at her waist. Steam rose around her, adding to the time-out-of-time feeling. As her body let the night's tensions go, the little mental compartments she shoved everything into began to dissolve.

Safe within the cascading water, she began to tremble under the rising tide of her emotions. The waves tossed her between the sharp sorrow of Zeke's death, the bitter bite of Sebastian's betrayal, and the never-ending loop of what-ifs that scraped over her anger and guilt. There was no life preserver of ready answers to save her, so she rode the emotional currents, letting them run their course. When they finally calmed, she found herself adrift in a strange sort of serenity.

Her earlier come-to-Jesus moment about her relationship with Warrick had put things in perspective. If she wanted their mating to last, it was time to accept him, fleas and all, and show him she was strong enough to stand beside him, even when he tried to push her away. And he would try, much like his verbal attack tonight.

Loving him wouldn't be easy. It hadn't been a walk in the park before they bonded, and she honestly couldn't figure out why she thought the bond would make things easier. The damn thing made it nearly impossible to hide anything. At least she'd never be bored.

As for Sebastian and the mess he dragged to their door, it was time to go hunting. She couldn't bring Zeke back, but she'd make damn sure everyone involved in his death was brought down. If nothing else, it would offer his family and the pack some closure. They needed to start with Sebastian's supplier, Brant Sutler. Once Ryuu got them information on the guy, she could decide on the best approach. From there, it became a matter of working her way backwards until she found the mastermind.

Her thoughts came to a screeching halt as achingly familiar hands wrapped around her hips and drew her back. Her spine met the solid muscles of Warrick's chest and the feel of him, hot and hard pressed against her ass, sent delicate shivers over her. She let her head fall back, closing her eyes as the water sprayed over her face.

His lips nibbled a path along her exposed neck and the tantalizing hint of teeth left sparklers riding through her veins. He paused where her neck met her shoulder and drew the soft, wet skin into the heated cavern of his mouth. As he sucked on it, his wicked hands came up to cup her breasts, his clever fingers teasing her nipples.

Her body reeled under his dual assault and she forgot all about keeping her splinted wrist dry. She raised her arm around his neck, leaving her body open to his touch.

He took full advantage, his hands leaving her breasts to travel over her ribs and down her stomach until his fingers dipped into her heated core. He moved them with slow, deliberate intent, circling and teasing her clit until her hips followed his lead and her breath escaped in short, gasping pants.

Behind her, she felt him harden and lengthen, her reactions finding an echo in him. The delicious tension grew, winding tighter, taking her to the edge. Then his fingers disappeared and she reached out to grab his wrist. "Not yet," she pleaded.

He rested his chin on her shoulder. "Greedy girl." The rough edge to his voice pleased her.

"I'm hungry," she whispered, turning her head just enough to nip his jaw.

"So am I," he growled and turned her around, dragging her close until there was no space for the water between their bodies.

He plundered her mouth and, using his grip on her hips, lifted her effortlessly until she could wrap her legs around his waist. His wide shoulders blocked the majority of the water from her face, giving her a chance to blink her eyes open.

Keeping her injured arm around his neck, she used her other hand to cup his jaw, angling his face so she could feel the rasp of his stubble against her palm and indulge in his taste. She gave herself to the fury of his kiss, trusting him to lead her through the sensual storm. She could feel him poised where she needed him most, a dark temptation. She wiggled against his hold, wanting to sink down and feel him filling her aching emptiness.

He held her in place, gentling his kiss as he maneuvered their positions until his back was toward the wall. Drawing back, he leaned against the cool tile.

"Look at me," he commanded, shifting his hips and teasing her until he was certain he had her attention.

Caught in the glittery heat of his half-lidded gaze, she fought the urges of her body and relaxed into his hold, never breaking eye contact.

His smile was equal parts predatory and seduction, sending her pulse pounding.

Adjusting her good hand until her nails curled into his shoulder, she felt his muscles coil under his skin as he brought her down, one devastating increment at a time.

When he had her seated fully on him, he held her still, his fingers digging into her hips. She wanted to savor this moment, this feeling of being complete, but her body had other ideas, wiggling with small sporadic movements.

Color rushed under his tightly drawn skin, painting his cheekbones. He lifted her, the sensation of his silken-covered heat dragging over her sensitive skin made her breath catch. He brought her back down a little faster than before, this time letting her help.

Together, they set a deliciously sinful pace until she was the one moving over him while he held on for the ride. Like a wind-whipped firestorm, their shared desired began to rage out of control. Somewhere in the midst of the passion she realized their bond had been flung wide open, tangling their emotions.

It was hard to tell what belonged to whom. The urge to possess, to protect, to love, to want, to need, became a brilliant, burning tether, tying them together soul-deep.

"Warrick!" His name was a plea, a promise, as she watched the beautiful gold flare in his eyes. Unable and unwilling to look away, she hid nothing from him as the pleasure rushed through her and swept her away even as he followed, his deep groan echoing in the confines of the shower.

Xander was just starting to drift off in Warrick's arms, her body sated, her stomach comfortably digesting Warrick's delicious rare steak, when the phone rang. She ignored the imperious summons of the shrill phone, and only when Warrick reached out to pick it up, did she move off his chest to snuggle into the nest of pillows. Her wrist splint hadn't fared well in the shower and once finished eating, she hadn't bothered to replace it. Her wrist was still tender, but well on its way to mending.

"Vidis."

"I've spent some time with your wolf and we may have a problem." Even half asleep and eavesdropping, she recognized the worry in Cheveyo's voice. "We need you to come in."

Tension crowded out her fatigue. Turning over, she hitched her sore leg to rest on Warrick's thigh.

Warrick pushed himself up until his back was against the headboard, the sheet riding low on his waist. "What kind of problem?" He reached under the covers and gently pulled her leg back into place, absently rubbing it in a soothing motion.

"Whoever set that spell on Sebastian used a blood tie."

"Which means what?"

"Unless you share a bloodline with Sebastian, I think it's safe to assume he was just a Trojan wolf."

A dangerous stillness fell over Warrick. Xander's breath caught under the sudden onslaught of brittle pain running through their connection. She tried not to react, not wanting him to cut her off, as she sensed on some level that whatever was happening was important.

"You need to be completely certain of your facts, Cheveyo." Warrick's voice may have been level, but if he clenched his jaw any tighter, he'd break some teeth.

Slowly, because she knew she was dealing with a very lethal creature, she placed her palm just below his heart.

He glanced down, revealing the round amber pupils of his wolf.

The sound of Cheveyo's exhale was clear even to her. "Every source I spoke to gave me the same information, and once I knew what to look for, it was quite apparent that whoever set this spell in place is somehow related to you."

His answer sent shock rocketing through Xander, leaving her mind reeling. She tried to recall what she knew of Warrick's past and came up frighteningly empty. She heard somewhere that his parents were dead and assumed they were his entire family. In all their time together, he had been very close-lipped about anything personal. Watching the myriads of expression chase over his face, she knew there was more to his story.

The bits and pieces she cobbled together indicated he had left Russia shortly toward the end of World War II and joined the Motoki Pack. He quickly moved up to position of Second and, when the previous alpha had been mistaken for a wild wolf and shot, stepped in. Months later, he'd taken the Northwest Alpha seat as well.

"You said we." Warrick's words were soft, the threat all too clear. "Who's there with you?"

This time Cheveyo's pause was longer. "Mulcahy."

Ryan Mulcahy, head of the Northwest Fey House, CEO of Taliesin, and Captain of the Wraiths. Out of the four heads of houses that controlled the Northwest Kyn, he was the one Xander walked most softly around.

There was nothing overtly threatening about him, but you didn't make it to his position on good looks alone. A master at manipulating those around him to achieve his goals, he wore a civilized veneer that hid his ruthlessly logical mind and lethal personality. His enemies were few and far between, probably because they disappeared shortly after making themselves known. She could only guess at the depth of power a Kyn of his age and stature had garnered over his very long lifetime. It wasn't something she'd ever want to go up against.

The man in question came on the line. "Who do you share blood with, Vidis?" Mulcahy's tone retained a note of challenge.

Warrick's nostrils flared and he held her gaze, grim resolution darkening his face. "My brother," he gritted out.

"I was unaware you had any family left alive," Mulcahy replied coolly.

She bit her lip to keep from saying anything, glad this part of the conversation was on the phone. If Warrick and Mulcahy were in the same room, blood would have been shed. In the momentary silence, she heard Cheveyo ask, "You have a brother?"

"Until recently I thought he was dead." Under the tips of her fingers, his heart thundered. "He disappeared when our parents died. We—I thought he was dead."

"How recently?" Mulcahy pressed.

Warrick didn't take his gaze from Xander, and she got the impression their tenuous connection was the only thing keeping him grounded. Tremors shook his frame and, lying inches away, she held a front-row seat as signs of an impending change ran under his skin, his bones shifting slightly. "Saturday morning."

Her eyes widened. That explained the weird moment at Neil's place when Warrick had shut down so violently.

Oblivious to the damage his interrogation was creating, Mulcahy kept pushing. "What did he want?"

Warrick's free hand covered hers and held on. "The right to establish a new pack with territory and rights."

Unable to stay quiet, Xander asked, "Why now?"

"I think the better question is, what does your brother gain from your death?" Mulcahy mused.

Something wild and furious moved to the forefront of Warrick's gaze.

Xander answered for him, the pieces falling into place. "The pack and all those who fall under his authority in the Northwest."

The line hummed with a taut silence then Mulcahy asked, "Vidis, do you know where your brother is now?"

The emotional deluge crashing through their bond indicated there would be no more rational discussions with her alpha. She needed to get Mulcahy off the phone because Warrick wasn't going to be able to hold his wolf in check for much longer.

She sat up and Warrick let her take the phone. "I'm fairly certain any address his brother gave him will come up a dead end."

Mulcahy sighed. "Bring Vidis here, Xander."

She bristled at the command. The need to protect her mate overrode her common sense. "You aren't my alpha, Mulcahy."

"No, but I am your captain," he snapped, any pretense of patience gone. "Whatever game Vidis's brother is playing at is threatening more than just your pack. This latest attack has drawn too much attention from the humans. Right now, the Kyn can't afford to be seen as the monsters they are."

CHAPTER 28

WARRICK WAS BARELY ABLE TO FOLLOW THE REST OF THE conversation after Cheveyo's little bomb. Why was he so surprised by his brother's betrayal? Had he really held onto the slim hope that Dmitri had changed? Harsh memories flashed in his mind's eye, tearing apart the half-assed belief of his brother's redeeming qualities. Over half a century ago, his brother had no issue aligning himself with the humans, even if it meant the deaths of his parents and pack. All that mattered was the promise of power.

When Dmitri had fallen for a human woman who just happened to be the daughter of a very high-ranking Nazi scientist, his obsession with her had blinded him to the fact she had targeted him deliberately. Her father had identified possible shifters and sent her out to catch his attention. It didn't take long for her to sow the seeds of discontent that lay fallow in Dmitri's heart. Once they took root, the division between him and his family widened until all that was left was bitter pain and hurtful accusations.

Even as the humans ambushed the Russian pack,

leaving bloody devastation in their wake, Dmitri refused to acknowledge his role in their destruction. It was Warrick's last straw. Once the remaining pack members had been able to mount a counter attack, Warrick made it his mission to remove the woman and her father from the equation. To this day, he had no idea if Dmitri knew that the woman he claimed to love had died under Warrick's teeth.

Considering what Warrick now faced, it was a safe bet he probably did. Which meant his brother was looking for payback. His wolf howled in fury. He couldn't let Dmitri near his pack or his mate. It was too dangerous.

Small hands touched his face, bringing him out of his thoughts. "Warrick."

The sound of his name pushed his wolf back enough for him to focus. Xander's delicate face filled his vision. The heavy bruising from earlier had faded, thanks to getting her to eat and rest, but the yellows and purples still coloring her face made his heart ache.

Her lips moved but he couldn't hear the words. She must have figured it out because she repeated herself, slower this time. "Go run."

His wolf surged forward and he managed to get free of the bed before the change tore through him. The familiar ache of shifting muscle and bone was lost under the emotional storm riding him. In moments, he was on all fours, the wolf in control. He stood there, the urge to hunt competing with the equally strong desire to protect his mate.

She climbed out of bed, gloriously naked, and the man inside the wolf took pleasure in the sight. She led him out of the bedroom and down the stairs. Once they were out on the back deck, he felt her reach for her wolf. He leant strength to her change, knowing the past hours had been difficult. A flurry of magic, then she stood before him, her silver and gray fur glowing softly in the pre-dawn hours.

He nuzzled her briefly then spun and leapt over the railing, his paws absorbing the impact. He waited while Xander followed, using the stairs, still cautious of her injuries. When she stopped beside him, he nuzzled her once more, prodding her front right ankle. She nipped his ear and danced away.

Satisfied she was okay, he raced across the open yard and into the woods, Xander close behind him. Together, they ran. As the ground sped under his paws, he let the man slip away and the wolf take control. About fifteen minutes in, they flushed out a rabbit and he gave chase. Together, he and Xander ran the furry little creature down. The small hunt dulled the edge of his wolf's need. Even better was the hot blood and tangy meat against his tongue.

Xander caught her own early morning snack and when they were finished, he led them the long way around until they were back at the house. The brief respite left both wolf and man calm, while a cold determination set in.

He changed back, and Xander followed suit. Something indefinable swept through him as he stood there watching her. She had been through so much, a great deal at his hands, but she was still here. Still standing beside him. Not because she had to, but because she wanted to. And he loved her for it.

Unable to resist, he pulled her close and kissed her, trying to show her what she was to him. He ravaged her mouth, the intensity of his emotions pushing him beyond gentleness and into carnal passion.

She didn't hesitate, her response every bit as aggressive

and demanding as his. When they broke apart, she was breathing heavily and the dazed expression on her face made him smile.

He turned her toward the back door and swatted her very delectable ass. "Inside."

"What? Afraid the neighbors are going to see?" she teased.

He nuzzled her neck before answering. "No, but it's still no reason to temp them to take advantage of my private views."

A mysteriously feminine smile lit her face. She led the way into the house with an intriguing wiggle he'd gladly follow anywhere.

Inside, Xander grabbed the forgotten green blanket, wrapped it around her shoulders and settled into the couch. Drawing up her legs, she tucked her toes under the edges of the blanket as she watched Warrick, comfortable in his nudity, crouch in front of the fireplace and set the fire. Once he had a blaze going he came and joined her.

"Come here." Propped against the far corner, he pulled her back until they were lying on the soft leather.

"We have to go to Taliesin," she reminded him.

"They can wait."

There was no mistaking the anger in Warrick's voice. It was probably best that they take a few before answering Mulcahy's summons. Otherwise, she might get the benefit of seeing the head of the Fey House taking on the role of Warrick's new chew toy. The incongruous image made her lips quirk.

She wiggled around until she was comfortable, then adjusted the blanket over both of them. Together, they watched the fire, an easy silence falling between them. Under her cheek, the slight chill from their early morning run slowly faded from his skin. It its place, his subtle scent of cinnamon and cloves rose to mix with the crisp remains of forest and fur.

Their run had done him a world of good. The skin-prickling energy that had been poised on the edge of violence was gone, leaving a strange expectant calmness. He held her, running a hand almost absently over her hair.

She rubbed her nose against his chest. "Tell me about him."

There was a minute pause as his hand stilled and his chest rose and fell under her. "He was a couple of years younger." He resumed his caress, his voice carefully neutral. "My mother and father called us the Calm and the Storm."

Xander smiled at the image of painfully serious Warrick as a pup with a rambunctious brother. "You were close?"

"For a while."

She caught the encroaching tension. "Things changed."

Old anger stirred in his voice. "Dmitri changed. He met this woman, Elise, in a town where our village used to be, and fell for her, hard. He was so blinded by his emotions he couldn't see the way she manipulated him. The Germans were looking for any tool they could use to invade Russia. Rumors of beasts who could walk like men proved too tempting to ignore. A specialized group was sent to ferret out truth from fiction."

Her fingers curled against his chest as he fell silent, an ache at what she knew was coming. "She was one of them."

"Yes," he paused. "Her father, Dr. Metzger, was the head

researcher. He sent her out deliberately to seduce my brother. Their group managed to piece together the identities of a few of us. Gossip is a favorite pastime in small towns and Dmitri never had any problems generating his share."

"I'm not sure when the plan changed, but something moved the Germans' time table forward. Metzger must have been desperate because suddenly Elise became ill with some incurable human disease. It was only afterward that I found out Metzger had deliberately infected his daughter, hoping Dmitri would change her, then she'd become his living science experiment."

Horrified chills ran over Xander. How could any parent sacrifice a child like that?

Warrick continued, his voice grim. "Dmitri was frantic. He approached our father and asked to be allowed to turn her. My father refused, rightly so. Forcing a human to endure a change is never a good idea. And bringing the change on someone mortally ill—" his arms tightened around her briefly, "—the odds are even worse."

Pity and anger seeped through their bond. She gave him the only comfort she could for his old pain by continuing to listen.

"Furious, Dmitri left the pack, taking her with him. It broke my mother's heart, but my father—" he stopped and gusted out a heavy exhale. "My father was torn. Some of the wolves suggested he consider silencing Dmitri. They were worried he would betray them to the invading humans."

Stunned, Xander raised her head and looked at him. "They shouldn't have asked that of him."

Something old and weary darkened his face and he traced the edges of her tattoo with a delicate touch. "It was a dark time then, pixie girl. So many were being hunted and not just Kyn. Those wolves had families to protect. Their concerns were valid."

She frowned. "But to ask a parent to kill their child? Where was your Tracker?"

"We had none and the responsibility for dispensing justice and protecting the pack fell to the alpha."

She studied his expression. "He refused."

Warrick gave a short nod. "And he, my mother, and many others paid for it."

"Why?" Why would his brother betray his family, his pack?

He cupped her face. "He changed Elise, but lost track of her when the change started. He found her a few days later, dead." Dropping his hand, he looked over her head at the fire. "He went straight to Metzger and gave him the information. Information that was used to ambush the pack."

Watching the careful blankness of his face, she knew there was something he wasn't saying. "How did she die?"

At first, she didn't think he was going to answer, but then, "I killed her."

The three words fell like stones into the quiet, sinking down and leaving the ripples of hidden emotions in their wake. His face remained still, but what came through their bond was anything but calm. It was a tangle of anger, guilt, sorrow, resentment, and practical necessity.

"She was a threat," Xander picked her words carefully, watching. "Not just to Dmitri, but to your family, you, your pack." Maybe if he heard her say it, he'd begin to believe it.

His attention turned from the fire and focused on her. He studied her expression as if weighing her belief behind her words. Whatever he saw had him giving her a slow nod.

"Does he know you killed her?" she asked.

"If you had asked two days ago, I would have said no," he answered. "But—"

Yeah, but.

Based on what they thought Dmitri was up to, she had to agree with Warrick's assessment. No matter how much you fought with family, no matter how nasty the fights got, in the end they were still family. To be forced into a situation where your actions would forever break those ties, was unimaginable. But some betrayals were beyond forgiveness.

Her heart ached for him. "How did he survive?" There was no way Warrick would have let his brother walk away, not after that.

"There was no actual proof of his betrayal. We could never connect him to Metzger's plans. There were witnesses that put him miles away at the time of the attack, still grieving for his human. When I went to hunt him down, he had disappeared. It was thought that he had been killed."

She folded her hands on his chest and rested her chin on top of them, watching him. "Until now."

"Until now," he agreed, holding her gaze.

Studying his beloved face, taking note of the lines etched around his mouth and eyes, she wondered if he realized how much he was hurting over his brother. She knew as well as he did that if they were able to definitively link Dmitri to the spell and the drug, Warrick's only option would be to kill his brother. What would that do to him? Whether he admitted it or not, it might break something in him. She couldn't let that happen.

His eyes narrowed. "What are you thinking?"

She shook her head and pushed upright. "We need to get to Taliesin."

He leaned forward, searching her face. "That wasn't it."

She wouldn't lie to him, but she wasn't stupid enough to tell him either. "No, it wasn't, but that's the most important thing right now."

He continued to watch her and she was worried he wouldn't let it go. "Once I deal with Mulcahy, we'll call Ryuu and see what he's found out about the human who supplied the drug to Sebastian. Maybe we can use the human or Sebastian to draw Dmitri out."

She nodded and got up from the couch, bringing the blanket with her. Relief that he wouldn't press filled her and she headed for the stairs. It was time to get dressed and go hunting.

Before she reached the first stair, an arm snagged her waist as Warrick pulled her close. Her arms were trapped under the blanket, which in turn was caught against his chest. He raised her chin and took a quick kiss.

"Whatever it was, I'll figure it out," he warned her, an anticipatory light at the prospect of a different hunt in his eyes.

Since Xander's bike was still at Ryuu's, Warrick drove to Taliesin. Her pants were damp, but clean and Warrick's T-shirt hung to her knees. Even her hair was subdued, the various shades of blonde laying in a haphazard shaggy style that owed more to a towel than any styling products. At least the bruising was quickly fading. If she was lucky, it would be mostly gone by the time they made it to Taliesin.

Vicious butterflies had decided to take up residence in

her stomach and indulge in some serious partying. The constant roiling sensation was making her queasy. Instincts whispered that the upcoming meeting between Mulcahy and Warrick wasn't going to end well. There was no way. Maybe she'd ask to borrow a couple of blades from Raine just in case she had to step in between the two men.

The image of standing between Warrick and Mulcahy with a knife pointed at each man popped into her head and she frowned as it was quickly replaced by the more accurate image of her resembling a human rope in a bloody tug-of-war. When your choices were facing a pissed-off wolf or a lethal fairie king, it would probably be safer to use the blades on herself.

A rusty chuckle drew her out of her morbid thoughts. "I don't think it will be that bad."

"That's what you think," she muttered, chagrined at the reminder of their mental connection.

"Mulcahy can be an arrogant ass," Warrick said. "But his first concern is the safety and wellbeing of the Kyn. Everything else is secondary. Right now, I would bet the Council is pressuring him to get this whole thing swept under the rug as soon as possible."

"That would be enough to piss anyone off." Although she never had the misfortune to meet the Council, she knew it was composed of eleven individuals from the various Kyn populations, each one a threat in their own right. All together, they made nightmares tremble.

If Warrick was right, it meant that things were a lot more complicated than she thought. Most of the time, the Council let the territory heads of house handle any situation that cropped up. They were only pulled in when the issue was deemed a threat to the Kyn community as a whole. Granted, having a wolf go Feral in a human club was pretty damn serious, but she didn't think it was serious enough to garner their attention. "How'd they find out?"

"If I had to guess, I'd say Natasha was covering her ass." He must have caught her confusion, because he continued, "In the last six or seven months, the Northwest Houses have come under fire for their decisions."

She had a feeling she knew exactly which decisions he was talking about. "Like entering the Southwest territory and killing the alpha's crazy, nutter mate?"

His lips twitched at her disrespectful quip. "That's one. Taking out a well-known human scientist that worked under Jonah Talbot was another."

Floored, she could only gape at him. "Seriously? The twisted bitch was experimenting on Kyn. And not in a fun way either."

He acknowledged her statement with a dip of his head. "True, but her death made headlines."

"As an accidental gas explosion. There was no way for the humans to tie it back to us," she argued.

"Regardless, the Council has informed the four of us that if we are unable to maintain control in our area, they'll be forced to send a representative to evaluate the situation." Which didn't sit well with him, if the growling edge to his voice was any indication.

"Well, shit." That wasn't good. Not only would they have to smooth things over with the humans, but they'd have to get rid of Dmitri and any humans tied to him, without the Council catching wind. "Does that mean Natasha's squealing to the Council on the rest of you?"

Warrick's shoulders shrugged. "Not necessarily. The Council's very creative at utilizing moles. Still, if it is her, she's aware that her house isn't immune to the Council's verdict, so if I were to guess, I'd say she was trying to make sure that the Amanusa House comes out looking like innocent bystanders in this mess."

"Isn't that an oxymoron?" she asked. "Innocent demons?"

"Perhaps." He smiled. "But as their leader, her primary job is to keep them safe. I can't fault her for that."

"I can," she muttered. He gave her a look. "Well, I can. I understand wanting to protect your people, but not if it means throwing the rest of your community to the wolves, so to speak."

Pulling into the parking lot at Taliesin, he parked before turning to her. "Being a leader at this level requires a certain amount of ruthless practicality. The decisions you make have long-reaching effects, so what may seem to be cruel in the short term may ensure your survival in the long term." Something pained crossed his face, but in the dim interior of the car, she wasn't able to read it. "Your people may not agree with your decisions, but if they know you will do whatever it takes to protect them and theirs, they will stand behind you."

For the first time, he gave her a glimpse into what it really meant to be an alpha—the choices and the sacrifices a leader made because the ones he protected couldn't do it themselves. The weight of it took her breath away.

But this was Warrick, her mate, and she knew this was the male she wanted to stand beside. She met his gaze and stated the brutal truth. "Because you do all the dirty work."

"Yes, it's my responsibility."

Leaning forward, she brushed a soft kiss over his lips. Drawing back, she held his gaze. "The world's a messy place, and evil never plays by the rules. Sometimes to win, you have to break the rules."

Relief flared then was quickly hidden. "It's a slippery slope, and one form of dirt looks pretty much like another."

She touched his face. "I know you, Warrick, and there are lines you will not cross, regardless of the cost. If I think you're slipping too far, I'll pull your ass back in line."

As he touched his forehead to hers, she closed her eyes, hiding the rise of tears as her heart burned under the answering wave of emotion echoing through their bond.

CHAPTER 29

WHEN WARRICK AND XANDER STEPPED OUT OF THE ELEVATOR ON the top floor of Taliesin they were met by Raine and Gavin. Raine sat on top of the reception desk, swinging her booted feet. Gavin leaned next to her, his elbow beside her hip as he rested his chin against his fist. Raine didn't look happy while Gavin looked amused.

Xander frowned. "Who's with Sebastian?"

"Mulcahy and Cheveyo," Raine answered, then looked at Warrick. "Mulcahy's requesting your presence in the interview room."

Warrick stiffened at the implied command and Xander muttered, "Has anyone ever told your uncle he's a bit of a demanding ass?"

Raine gave her a fierce smile. "Every chance I get."

The interview room looked exactly as the name implied, a simple room where prospective employees could be comfortably interviewed for positions. The benign plaster hid solid metal walls etched with some of the strongest reinforced magical wards meant to contain most magic, which made it an ideal spot to conduct other kinds of interviews when necessary.

"What did they do? Kick you out?" Xander asked.

Gavin laughed and Raine growled. "They said I might mess things up."

Adopting a mock-innocent look, Xander teased, "Who? You? Why ever would they think that?"

Raine's muttered, "Smart ass," was replaced by the doors opening behind them as Ryuu joined the party.

"I have info on Brant Sutler." He didn't bother with pleasantries.

Exhaustion paled his skin to a dull sheen and the bags under his eyes held enough room for a two-week vacation. He dropped into a chair near the desk, his legs sprawled.

Warrick dragged another chair over positioning it so Raine and Gavin stood between them. "Tell me."

Xander leaned a hip against the back of Warrick's chair and settled in to listen.

"Brant Sutler, age twenty-seven, doctoral student working on his thesis entitled, The Impact of Non-Scientific Energy and Nano-Technology on DNA Sequencing, currently employed by Biovita, a biotech lab located in Hillsboro."

"Non-scientific energy?" Xander repeated.

"Magic," Warrick supplied.

"Haven't we had this discussion before?" Raine asked, a thread of anger running through her voice. "Magic never plays well with science. What the hell is so damn fascinating about combining the two that humans just can't leave well enough alone?"

Before anyone could answer, a dull boom sounded and the floor rocked under the impact. Everyone was on their feet, rushing to the hall leading to the back offices before the cloud of escaping debris reached them. Xander's heart was in her throat as she stayed on Gavin and Raine's heels, Warrick and Ryuu behind her.

The choking cloud turned everything into a dull haze of white and breathing became difficult. They were halfway down the hall when another vibration sent the floor rolling under their feet. Slipping and sliding, Xander reached out to stop herself from landing on her ass. She caught what remained of an office windowpane and the sharp sting of skin parting under a jagged piece of metal had her hissing out a breath.

Ahead of her, she could just make out Gavin and Raine jerking to a stop. The strange heavy silence that had settled over everything was shattered by a wrenching scream of anguish and anger. It wasn't until Xander stumbled closer that she realized the scream was coming from Raine. Shock and horror competed with grim determination as Gavin kept his hold on the near-feral Raine, her attention caught by something in the destruction that had once been the interview room.

Warrick moved up next to Xander and fear skittered through her as she shared a look with him. *Dear gods, Cheveyo and Mulcahy!* Together, they picked their way over the rubble. Gavin had tucked his head behind Raine's and was saying something in a voice too low for Xander to hear. Warrick reached them and touched Raine's face, his touch bringing her struggles to an abrupt halt.

Xander could feel him pull on his wolf as he caught Raine's gaze. "Enough. This is no time for hysterics."

There was compassion under the steel of his words, but it was enough. Fury replaced the sick sorrow on Raine's face and she actually growled at Warrick. He held her gaze for a few more seconds, then turned away and disappeared into the dark hole that had once been a room.

As she passed her friend, she touched Raine's shoulder in a futile attempt to comfort, trying not to think about what it would mean if either Mulcahy, Raine's uncle, or Cheveyo hadn't survived the explosion. She followed Warrick's back into the gloom.

The dust was beginning to settle, and a single light flickered above, hanging by one stubborn wire. The strobe light effect made it difficult to see. A ceiling tile lost its fight with gravity and landed on another unidentifiable pile of rubble. Warrick moved around the edges of the room, searching.

Dust and shadows curled around something sitting in the center of the room, eerily untouched by the destruction. Moving closer, her teeth clenched in recognition. Sebastian's unseeing eyes stared at the ceiling, his face oddly peaceful, which made the red ruin of his chest all the more disturbing. No sense in checking for a pulse. Whatever carved its way out of his ribcage left behind jagged bones, his viscera sprawled like worn-out tinsel. Made it easy to see his heart wasn't beating.

Looking around, she took in the broken two-by-fours and chunks of plaster littering the ground. Half a table was embedded in the back wall a few feet from the ceiling. The shelves that once covered the right wall were nothing but splinters. The chairs were reduced to so much twisted metal and part of the right wall had collapsed into a small mountain.

The metal housing the wards was exposed in great patches, some sheets curling toward the floor like old wallpaper. Yet, enough was in place to maintain the activated wards, their faint glow adding a surreal tone to the scene. The golden luminesce pulsed in a thin web around the walls, but what shocked her were the ragged gaps where the metal was savagely torn away, leaving the magical threads cut. Whatever happened, it involved some serious magic. And she had little doubt it had originated with Sebastian.

Behind her, she could hear the others make their way into the room, searching for Mulcahy and Cheveyo.

A faint groan from the back of the room was followed by Warrick's urgent, "Xander!"

She scrambled over the obstacle course of wood, wires, and plaster.

"Someone's under here." Warrick crouched next to a warped piece of metal, the wards a dull black burn on its surface. It had fallen from the ceiling, only to come to rest half-propped against the corner, creating a small hollow. He rose to his feet to get a better grip and looked at her. "Ready?"

She nodded, taking a position to the side.

He grabbed it, ignoring the jagged edges, and pulled, his muscles straining against the weight. It groaned as it began to pull away from the wall. Warrick would have to balance it until she could get whoever was trapped under it free. No tossing pieces aside until they found both men.

As Warrick maneuvered the piece back, Xander knelt in the rubble, sifting through the smaller pieces covering the form curled up against the base of the wall. Long black hair made gray by the heavy layer of dust clued her in. "It's Cheveyo," she told Warrick.

Cheveyo blinked at her, dazed. The Magi managed to protect his back and head, but as she removed a piece of plaster lying across his legs, she discovered it hadn't been enough. A jagged metal chair leg bisected his calf and embedded itself in the floor. The pool of blood was small but the minute she pulled him free, that would change.

Warrick was still struggling with the metal, so she yelled over her shoulder, "Ryuu, I need you!"

Cheveyo's lips were moving but she couldn't hear him, so she leaned closer.

"Mulcahy okay?" His question was just above a whisper but she caught it.

Drawing back, she brushed his hair off his face, noting the knot coming up on his forehead. The witch was in for a hell of a headache.

"I don't know yet. Gavin and Raine are looking for him." It was all the comfort she could give. Ryuu appeared at her shoulder. "We have to get this piece out of his leg," she told him. "But it's stuck to the floor."

"You hold him, I'll pull it out," Ryuu said.

Curled into the corner as Cheveyo was, it made it difficult to find a way to hold him down. Warrick grunted and the metal finally shifted to rest against the back wall. Xander took advantage of the newly created space and managed to get into position.

"Cheveyo." She waited until he was able to focus on her face. "This is going to hurt but we have to get the piece of chair out of your leg, okay?"

He closed his eyes, sweat popping out on his forehead, and nodded. No matter how stoic Cheveyo was, it wouldn't be enough. It was going to hurt like a bitch. Through her jeans, sharp fragments cut into her knees, but she ignored it and lay over Cheveyo's chest, her hands on his shoulders. Twisting until she could see Ryuu, she nodded and braced.

Ryuu pulled the jagged metal free and Cheveyo jerked under her hands, his hoarse scream making her wince.

Ryuu was tearing his shirt into strips to bind the wound. "We need a healer," his voice was grim as his hands worked quickly.

"Can you get him out of here?" Xander asked as Cheveyo stilled under her. Looking down, she realized he had passed out. All the better.

"Yeah," Ryuu answered. "I'll take him to the front."

"Be careful," Warrick warned. "It's early enough the explosion may not have been heard by anyone, but I can guarantee Natasha will be here shortly."

Ryuu gathered Cheveyo in his arms. "What do you want me to tell her?"

Warrick ran a hand through his dust-coated hair. "Have her run interference with anyone who comes poking around. She's good at coming up with a believable story."

Ryuu nodded. It should have looked awkward, but he managed to carry the taller man out despite his uncertain footing.

Xander looked around and found Gavin and Raine across from Sebastian's dead body. There was something in their posture that left a sick dread tightening around her. Nerves flared and her hands began to shake. She shared a worried look with Warrick before picking her way over, grateful for his reassuring presence at her back.

Her knees weakened as she got closer. They had found Mulcahy. Raine was cradling him in her lap, her head bowed while Gavin knelt in front of her, his face pale under the streaks of gray dust.

Unmindful of the debris, Xander dropped next to Gavin, reached out, but stopped as an unseen wave of magic brushed against her. It was thick, heavy, and gave her the creeps. Gavin's eyes glowed an eerie, luminescent green, his entire focus on the woman in front of him.

"Raine, enough," his voice was hoarse as if he'd inhaled a lungful of smoke. "He's gone, love. Let him go."

Xander did a quick visual scan of Mulcahy's body but couldn't see any obvious mortal wounds. Panic clawed at her throat. Mulcahy couldn't be gone. Gavin had to be wrong. But she couldn't hear a heartbeat from the man in Raine's lap, nor did his chest move.

Warrick crouched behind her, his hand curling over her shoulder. Shock and something that felt like sorrow leaked through their bond. A terrible premonition crept around the edge of her mind, leaving a soul-numbing chill behind, but she pushed it back, trying to understand the picture in front of her.

Raine lifted her head, silver eyes glowing with an uncomfortable light. Xander's heart clenched. Gone was the hard-ass warrior who could shred someone with words alone and face down any monster without flinching. In her place was a grieving child.

"No." Raine's one word answer trembled in the air with brutal fury.

Gavin's expression hardened and he grabbed her face between his hands. "You let him go right fucking now or I will tear you loose. Do you hear me?"

Vicious anger and sharp-edged grief carved Raine's features down to something inhuman and lethal.

Xander would have heeded the warning and backed off, but not Gavin. He didn't flinch and didn't let her go. "Let. Him. Go."

Xander couldn't miss the flare of energy tightening the air between them as Gavin hammered home his command.

For an endless moment, Xander was worried Raine was going to go after Gavin, something she knew her friend would never forgive herself for once she calmed down. But instead, Raine dipped her chin and the sudden release of tension was so strong, Xander actually felt it like a physical punch.

Gavin released her, his muscles uncoiling.

Raine dropped her head and curled over Mulcahy's chest. "I'm sorry. I'm sorry," she repeated, tears thickening her voice.

A painful helplessness pinched Gavin's face but he dropped a chaste kiss on Raine's bent head. "Let me take him."

Raine didn't answer but her desperate hold loosened. It was all Gavin needed.

Xander scooted back to give him room to gather Mulcahy in his arms. Warrick stepped forward and helped, giving Gavin someone to lean on as he rose to his feet, his arms full.

Watching Warrick and Gavin handle Mulcahy with such care broke through the numbing chains holding Xander's emotions in check. Her chest ached with unshed tears, her eyes burned, and it was hard to breathe around the lump in her throat. Under her grief, fury awoke and began to burn.

"It was meant for Vidis." If words could cut, Raine's would have sliced through bone.

Xander looked at her, feeling the truth of Raine's statement as it shed a ruthless light on the needling suspicions that crept into the depths of her mind. The words sang with crystal clarity and reverberated through her soul until they drowned out all other thoughts, leaving only a horrifying glimpse of what could have been.

It could have been Warrick.

With that one thought, fury changed to savage practicality. Behind Raine, Sebastian's body served as mute testimony of one man's demented need for power. Under Xander's skin, the need to hunt, to kill, rose until her human form felt too tight, as if the lightest touch would set her wolf free. She met Raine's gaze and found an answering rage as the vicious leopard that lived in her friend stared back.

CHAPTER 30

THE SCENE AT THE FRONT DESK COULD HAVE SERVED AS THE aftermath shot in some action flick. A now conscious Cheveyo was propped on the only couch, clothes torn and bloody, a thunderous expression on his dust-streaked face. "Dammit, Natasha, don't be such a bitch. We have enough problems right now!" The edge to his voice would have done any shifter proud.

"It's called being practical, Cheveyo." The picture-perfect, petite blonde was so out of place, but it didn't detract from the authority oozing like some high-priced perfume. "Mulcahy's death leaves us vulnerable on too many fronts."

Cheveyo glowered at her and when he caught sight of Xander and Raine at the edge of the hall, he hissed, "We are not discussing this now."

Oblivious to their presence, Natasha ignored him, throwing her hands up in the air. "When do you want to discuss it? When the Council decides to send in their personally chosen replacement? I don't care who steps in to take over the Fey House, but I won't allow his other responsibilities to be delegated to some puppet."

Raine brushed past Xander, and it was only due to her quick reflexes that Xander managed to snag her friend's arm before she jumped the Head of the Amanusa House in a hail of fists and fury. Even that wouldn't have stopped her, but Gavin, who just stepped out of the hall leading to Mulcahy's office, managed to get between Raine and her target.

Gavin's tall body hid Natasha's smaller form and Raine pulled up short. Her hands curled into fists and a purely feline snarl sounded as she stood before him. "Get out of my way."

He folded his arms across his chest, his face grim. "She's not the one you want."

"Trust me, she'll do."

Xander could see the fine tremors running through Raine and knew Natasha's presence was just salt on the gaping wound of Mulcahy's death. Every time the two women got in the same room, they managed to make verbal sushi out of each other.

There were three men Xander knew who could keep Raine under control right now. One was dead, one was currently staring her down, and the other was coming up behind Gavin.

Catching Warrick's attention, she sent him a wordless plea to intervene. There was enough to deal with without another head of house being murdered tonight.

Warrick grabbed Raine's arm and none too gently dragged her to a chair as far from Natasha as possible. "Sit down and be quiet, Raine."

For a second, Xander thought she'd have to beat her friend as Raine's fist swung up for a hit. Xander turned and rolled to the balls of her feet, prepared to leap into action. The only one who got to hit Warrick was her. But Raine hesitated, and common sense obviously prevailed as her fist dropped under Warrick's unwavering stare. She ripped her arm from his grasp and slammed into the chair. Only then did she switch her glare to someone behind Xander. Probably Gavin.

Satisfied his point was made, Warrick left Raine. Gavin stepped aside, giving Warrick a clear shot at Natasha, then went to stand by Raine.

One disaster down, an endless supply to go. Xander sighed and kept her position behind Warrick. Natasha might look harmless in her blonde-china-doll way, but Xander knew better. No demon-blooded Kyn was ever harmless. They thrived on chaos and strife. As a matter of fact, the more innocent and sweet an Amanusan appeared, the more dangerous they were. Natasha more than most, as evidenced by the wavering image of a looming beast hovering around her like a mirage—the only sign that tonight's events had pushed even the untouchable demon queen's control.

Warrick towered over her, ignoring the strange illusion. "Our first priority is to provide the humans with a believable story, one even Division will buy. That is why you are here, Natasha, not to indulge in your love of manipulative games. When we have hunted down the one behind this, then we'll address the rest of your concerns."

Undaunted, Natasha poked a manicured nail into Warrick's chest. "I am not one of your creatures, Vidis. I am fully aware of my responsibilities. However, unlike you and Cheveyo, I am not blinded by useless emotion. Mulcahy," her voice stuttered, then steadied, "held the reins to our most lethal hunters. I will not allow such tools to fall into the hands of a Council puppet. There's no room for Cheveyo's damn Threefold Law in that position. You have made it abundantly clear that the only ones you would be responsible for were your precious shifters. Which leaves only me."

From his position beside the couch holding Cheveyo, Ryuu shot Xander a speculative look. She refused to react, wondering when Natasha would realize that he was still in the room. Everyone else here knew who the lethal hunters were. She, Gavin, and Raine were all Wraiths. Neither Warrick nor Cheveyo betrayed any worry about Ryuu's silent presence.

"They served Mulcahy because they trusted his judgment. You may find garnering their respect more difficult," Warrick's voice was laced in ice. "Be very certain you wish to take them on, because I can guarantee if they find you lacking, it will be the last position you hold."

The warped mirage strengthened revealing something huge and monstrous wavering around Natasha's body. A hint of sulfur and something burnt teased Xander's nose. Natasha's voice was several octaves deeper when she spoke. "Do not threaten me, Warrick Vidis."

Warrick bared his teeth, amber flooding his gaze. "That's not a threat, Ms. Bertoi. It's a statement of fact."

The two stood toe-to-toe for a long moment. Then the skin-ruffling clash of their powers retreated and the lingering scent dissipated. Without a word, Natasha turned on one very slender heel and stalked out of the office. Warrick watched her leave then turned back to Ryuu and Cheveyo.

He pinned Ryuu in place with an amber-tinted glare, the power of his position vibrating in the air between them. "What's said here goes no farther, understood?"

Ryuu dipped his head in agreement.

Warrick stared down at Cheveyo. "What the hell happened in there?"

Cheveyo slumped into the couch and ran a shaky hand over his face. "A mistake."

"Mistake?" Raine hissed. "Is that what you're calling it?"

"Enough!" Warrick swung his head toward her and barked, "You aren't helping."

Since standing between the two was the last place Xander wanted to be, she moved to the reception desk and slid down until her butt hit the floor. Let Gavin run interference. Her emotional balance was shot to hell and she needed a minute. Resting her head against the hard surface, she closed her eyes and listened.

For a moment, there was nothing but a taut silence. Dollars to doughnuts, her mate was engaged in a stare down with Raine and Xander had no doubt who'd win.

Sure enough, Warrick's sharp demand sliced through the room. "Explain." Not only was he down to one-word sentences, but his wolf was sneaking out in the rough growl of his voice.

"After we hung up with you, Mulcahy said he wanted to take another look at the spell on Sebastian," Cheveyo answered. "So we went back in, taking Raine and Gavin with us. Mulcahy had Raine describe what she saw."

"What did you see?" Xander broke in, not bothering to open her eyes.

"A snarled mass of threads." Raine's answer was flat. "Mulcahy wouldn't let me untangle it. He said—" There was a pause then, "I might trip something."

Xander's heart clenched for her friend. "So he must have recognized it."

"That's what Raine and I were discussing when you came in," Gavin cut in.

"He recognized it," Cheveyo added. "He told me it looked familiar but he couldn't place it."

"If he knew what it was, what possessed him to go poking around?" This time it was Warrick.

"And what exactly was he messing around with?" Raine asked. "The whole reason you had me in there was because I'm supposedly the only one who can actually see magic. If he couldn't see anything, what did he do?"

Everyone fell silent then Ryuu offered quietly, "Mulcahy's been around for a long time, longer than either Vidis or Cheveyo. Considering his position, I think it's safe to assume he wouldn't willingly reveal every skill at his disposal."

Xander blinked her eyes open at Ryuu's very intuitive answer. She considered Cheveyo and Warrick in a new light. Maybe it was time to stop taking things for granted. Power wasn't going to be enough. Their leaders weren't invulnerable. Mulcahy's body in the other room was more than enough proof of that.

Frustration tinted Cheveyo's response. "There are more ways to deal with spells than just 'seeing' it, Raine. Mulcahy was very proficient in some very delicate magics. Unraveling a blood-tie spell shouldn't have been dangerous."

"Well, you were both wrong," Raine hissed.

Warrick stepped in before the argument could get off the ground. "Give me something to work with, something we can use."

Cheveyo's jaw tightened. "Considering the aftermath of the spell and what little Mulcahy said, all I can give you is guesswork."

"It's a starting point."

"Fine." Cheveyo straightened painfully on the couch. "I would assume that the blood spell was interfering with your pack ties and acting as a blind to another, more ancient spell. One Mulcahy recognized because, as Ryuu pointed out, he's been around awhile. If he was still here, I have a feeling he'd have a name for us."

Warrick folded his arms. "Any guesses as to who that would be?"

Cheveyo shook his head. "But if your brother is the one behind the blood spell, you have two situations to consider. One—" he held up a finger, "—he was given both spells, knowing full well what the outcome of each would be. Or —" he held up a second finger, "—he requested the blood spell and the second, older spell was hidden within it without his knowledge."

Xander saw where the Magi was going. "So we may not just have Dmitri to worry about?"

"Maybe," Cheveyo said. "I don't know. It could be that whoever Dmitri got the spell from just wanted to cause as much harm and chaos as possible, regardless of who the intended victim was. There's one very old spell that could match, but to verify I'd have to ask certain people some very specific questions." He paused. "I'm not sure that's such an intelligent thing to be doing right now."

"Why?" Xander asked.

"Because outside Vidis and Natasha, I'm not so inclined to trust anyone I get answers from once Mulcahy's death is widely known."

"Fucking politics," Raine muttered and Xander had to agree.

With Mulcahy's death, the Northwest Kyn would have to be very careful with the questions they asked. There would be no avoiding the Council's attention now. Gaping holes in an upper-level power structure didn't stay empty long.

"What kind of Kyn could cast that type of spell?" Gavin, who'd been quietly following the conversation, asked.

Cheveyo thought about it. "Wizard, of course, since they have no issues playing around with the darker aspects of magic. Numerous Fey, especially the older ones, and probably a handful of Amanusa, depending on their demonic influence."

"That doesn't narrow it down much." Ryuu tapped his fingers against his leg. "Wizards are obvious and we've already had one run in. Amanusa thrive on chaos, but I can't see one of Natasha's pulling this without her approval. They're too scared of her to do that. Does anyone know if there were any Fey who had it in for Mulcahy?"

"Mulcahy was intensely private," Raine said, rubbing her forehead.

Gavin looked at Warrick. "Then we go after who we know is tied in, Dmitri."

Warrick met him look for look. "We don't know where he is."

Xander pushed to her feet. "But we know someone who might."

All eyes turned to her and she bared her teeth in a vicious grin. "Brant Sutler, the human who gave Sebastian the drug in the first place. We find him, we find Dmitri."

CHAPTER 31

It wasn't safe to leave Raine behind so Xander and Warrick took her with them. They left Gavin and Cheveyo to deal with Natasha. If nothing else, Natasha would rival Salome and her seven veils with her public relations dance. The poor human reporters didn't stand a chance. As for Sector Chief Osborn of Division, well, they'd have to wait and see how much the combined efforts of Cheveyo, Gavin, and Natasha could accomplish.

Ryuu was in charge of getting rid of Sebastian's remains before the humans came poking around. Mulcahy's death would be shared with Division, there was no way to avoid it, but his body would remain protected until Raine was ready to make arrangements. Once Ryuu was done with Sebastian, he was heading back to the office to peel more layers away from Sutler's current employer. If someone else was using Dmitri, they needed to know who they were ultimately dealing with.

Since it was Sunday, the consensus was to try Sutler's home address first. He lived alone in one of the cookie cutter neighborhoods located in Hillsboro, where technology was king and almost every business had some connection to IT. The whole Stepford vibe gave Xander the creeps. Give her a place where your closest neighbor couldn't hear you scream or, if that was out of your price range, some eclectic collection of old and new homes where being an individual wasn't considered a sickness.

Dawn was teasing the horizon as Xander navigated their way through the still quiet city. Sutler's place was nestled among a tree-lined street with family homes that backed up to an open field. When they found it, there was nothing to set the newer home apart. It came complete with a well-cared-for, economy sedan parked in the driveway. They drove past, noting the lighted porch and parked in the lot utilized by a group of small businesses around the corner. There were no fences standing guard on the backyards of the houses, so all three cut through the greenery to Sutler's.

The homes sat close together, creating narrow shadowed alleyways in-between. Sutler's house sat on a rounded corner, with a neighbor to the west and an empty space on the east side, in full view of the street. A light burned above the door on the back. Warrick and Raine stayed under the eaves, using the shadows to their advantage. After taking a minute to listen for the telltale hum of an alarm system and finding nothing but silence, Xander made quick work of the standard lock on the back door. In no time, they were standing on the tile of a small laundry room.

At first, all Xander could smell was laundry detergent and bleach, the latter making her nose itch. Until she got out of the enclosed space, she would be scent blind. Raine took point with Xander and Warrick following behind. They came out of the laundry room into a galley kitchen.

Stainless steel gleamed under the soft light left on over the sink. Raine stopped where the kitchen met the yawning space of the living room. Warrick moved up beside her then turned to let Xander join them.

It was clear Sutler spent most of his time here. Cords led from the obligatory, oversized television to familiar black, hand-held game controllers strewn on the littered top of a coffee table. Haphazard shelves were crammed with games, music, and movies. A real socialite was Sutler. The mass of electronics that created their own universe were controlled by the small herd of remotes gathered on the couch.

Raine padded forward, down the hall toward where the bedrooms had to be located. On the drive over, Raine demanded to be allowed to question Sutler. Warrick reminded her that Sutler needed to remain breathing and able to communicate. Raine had snarled, Warrick had growled, and Xander had threatened to pull the car over. In the end, Warrick agreed to let Raine be the bad cop, Xander would be the good cop and he would wait on the sidelines.

However, when Raine came to an abrupt stop in the bedroom doorway and let out a low frustrated growl, Xander knew she wouldn't get a chance to play good cop. Nudging Raine out of the way, she surveyed the disaster area that made up the bedroom. Either Sutler's closet had a sudden case of regurgitation or someone had packed in a hurry. There were a couple of drawers open in the dresser, scoured of their contents. Plastic hangers were scattered across the floor and the bed was half made.

"Son of a bitch!" Raine stomped into the room and stuck her head in the closet.

"I'm pretty sure he's not holed up with his shoe collection," Xander muttered.

She left Raine to her temper tantrum and went back to Warrick in the living room.

"Since his car is in the drive, chances are he took a taxi." Warrick leafed through a magazine as he leaned against the back of a couch, his voice oh so casual.

She took a spot next to him. This close, there was no missing the underlying tension he was keeping ruthlessly in check. "We could have Ryuu check the airport," she said.

Warrick tossed the magazine onto the couch and shook his head. "Too much time has passed."

"So we just let him go?" Raine asked as she came into the room.

"For now." Warrick folded his arms across his chest and watched the other woman. "If Sutler has left, it means whoever he's working with knows his trap has been sprung and our first stop would be here. He's their weakest link, so they removed him."

Raine rocked on her feet, her fists clenching and unclenching. "Wish they could have left him for us to remove."

"Too easy," Xander quipped. Musing out loud, she added, "If they knew their spell was triggered, do they know who it hit?"

"Probably not yet," Warrick answered. "Once they do, they'll come back around again."

"So we wait?" Raine's tone made it clear that waiting wasn't on her to-do list.

Warrick shrugged. "For now, we leave and find another direction." He straightened and made his way through the kitchen, presumably to the back door.

Something in his voice caught Xander's attention. He was up to something. She sent her curiosity down their bond. He stopped and looked back over his shoulder. He gave a small shake of his head and continued to the back door. So, he was up to something, something he didn't want to talk about here. Fine.

"What the hell?" Raine watched Warrick walk away. She turned to Xander and opened her mouth,

Xander cut her off with a sharp shake of her head. "Time to go."

Raine's mouth snapped shut and Xander swore she heard the sound of enamel being ground under molars, but Raine heeded her silent warning and spun on her heel, stalking toward the kitchen.

Watching Raine's angry back, Xander gave a small sigh. Whatever plan Warrick was concocting she hoped he had a part for Raine. Her friend's fury and grief needed an outlet damn soon or there were going to be serious repercussions. Unfortunately, whatever her alpha had planned, she had a sinking suspicion it wouldn't be leaving her with warm fuzzies.

Warrick was the type of male who refused to let others stand in front of him. Hell, he was still trying to figure out how to deal with her standing beside him, so chances were damn good there was another argument waiting to happen. One in which she would point out that letting his psycho brother anywhere near him was a bad idea, especially considering how that had turned out for Mulcahy.

Pulling the back door closed behind her, she used the time it took to get back to the car to evaluate her chances of keeping Warrick out of the way while she pulled a few strings with Raine. By the time she settled into the front seat, she still hadn't found a solution that didn't involved a sedative dart and locking him in a silver cage.

This time Warrick was in the driver's seat. He started the car then paused and turned to her. "What?"

His abrupt question had her blinking. "What, what?"

"Why are you picturing me in a silver cage?"

Dammit! "You're up to something."

He tilted his head, considering her. "And you think that would stop me?"

Was that amusement she heard? He better not be laughing at her. "It's a start."

He chuckled and put the car in gear. "It wouldn't work."

"Would you two cut the cryptic crap and explain to me why we aren't tearing that place apart," Raine snapped from the backseat.

Xander turned until she could watch both the bad-tempered cat in the back and the devious wolf behind the wheel. "Warrick has a plan and he didn't want to talk about it in the house."

Raine snorted. "What? You think it was bugged?"

Warrick shot her a look through the rearview mirror. "Maybe, maybe not. Either way I'd rather not take the chance."

"Fine. We're out now, so spill."

Xander watched Warrick's jaw tightened at Raine's challenge. "Raine," she warned.

Her friend may be hurting but Xander wasn't going to let Raine push her mate's buttons. Not now. There were too many other things to worry about.

Raine flicked her gaze to Xander, grief deep and dark in her eyes. Her shift of attention allowed Warrick to refocus on the road. Xander met Raine's gaze and didn't flinch under the storm swirling in those gray depths. When Raine curled her lip in a silent snarl, Xander answered in kind. Finally, Raine turned and looked out the window.

Xander shifted her attention back to Warrick. "So how are you planning on flushing your brother out?"

"I'm going to give him what he wants."

"Excuse me?"

The muscles in his arms flexed as he adjusted his grip on the steering wheel. "As soon as the news hits that Mulcahy is dead, he'll realize his spell failed. Dmitri doesn't like failure."

"I wouldn't consider killing the head of Taliesin and the Fey House a failure," Raine snarled.

"It is if that wasn't his intended target. Dmitri doesn't do well when he's thwarted. I'd bet that right now he's trying to figure out how much information we got from Sebastian. He's going to take comfort from the fact that he made sure to keep a middle man between him and Sebastian, so he'll convince himself there's no way we can link him to either the drug or Sebastian. The fact I'm still breathing isn't going to make him happy. So if I invite him to attend tonight's pack meeting so we can announce the decision on his petition, he'll come."

"Arrogant much?" Xander asked.

"Dmitri won't be able to resist. He'll want a ringside seat to the fallout of his plan."

"You invite him to the meeting tonight, he'll challenge you." Xander wasn't stupid. She knew it was what Warrick was hoping for. His all-teeth smile confirmed it. Her temper spiked at his obvious disregard to his safety, but she fought it back. "You want him to challenge you."

He slid her a dark look. "You expect me to wait at Taliesin while you and Raine go out and raise enough noise to put yourselves in his sights?"

"You're the Northwest alpha, Warrick," she gritted out. "I expect you to understand that we have already lost one of our leaders and the possibility of losing another is not acceptable."

A low growl rumbled through the car. "Are you implying I would lose?"

The urge to smash her head against the window rose. "No, I'm saying he won't fight fair. He's proven to be manipulative and devious. What's to stop him from bringing along one of his mangy-ass mavericks or another wizard as a contingency plan? It wouldn't take much to stash someone near the pack's meeting place with long range rifle or have another spell in place. A silver bullet to the head or heart, or tying another nasty spell to your blood-ties, Warrick, and it won't matter if he pulled the trigger or hired a wizard. You would still be dead." And all that would be left for her would be blood, revenge, a shattered heart, and a cold bed.

"We can't afford to wait for Dmitri and whoever he's working with to instigate another attempt. We need to force him to act on our terms."

Maybe she'd have more success if she bashed his head into a window. "And you don't think he'll recognize an obvious trap?"

"No. The fact I'm still breathing will compromise his logic."

"You're putting a lot of faith into the fact that your brother has a hard-on for your corpse," Raine said. "Xander's points are valid."

"I won't hide behind others," Warrick snapped.

"No one's asking you to hide," Xander shot back. "I'm asking you to think for one godsdamn minute and listen."

"You do realize that Xander and I can offer some valuable insight here, right?" Raine's question contained a sarcastic edge. "It's not like we don't understand how to plan a successful assassination. It's what we do, for gods' sake."

Tension filled the car while Xander forced her temper back so that when Warrick quit snarling she could offer cold logic to his half-assed plan. Neither she nor Raine said another word, letting him stew.

Finally, he broke. "Fine. What would you two suggest?"

Some of her tension fled. "You said it yourself. Your brother's not stupid, arrogant maybe, but not stupid. He's spent years putting this little plan of his into place. It's obvious he isn't in this alone. Sutler, the drug, the spells, all add up to big money and even bigger power. As much as we want blood for Zeke and Mulcahy, we need to eliminate the most obvious threat first, which means Dmitri and the drug have to be our primary focus. Once he's out of the picture, we'll turn our attention to the other players." She knew none of this was new information to Warrick, but maybe hearing her say it would help penetrate that thick skull of his.

"Inviting him to a pack meeting to discuss his petition is way too obvious," she continued. "You might as well just call him up and challenge him. We know he's watching. Otherwise, there's no way he could have gotten to Sutler so fast. There was, what, less than two hours between the explosion and when we arrived? Not much time to pack up and disappear."

"He may have had more time," Warrick said.

"How do you figure?"

"We're assuming Sebastian was unknowingly working for Dmitri. When Sebastian grabbed Zeke, he called in reinforcements. Where would he get non-pack wolves?"

Too much had happened in too short a time frame. She was slipping. "Dmitri already has control of the mavericks. Getting your approval to create a pack isn't really necessary, but it gives him a reason to reappear in your life. Which means, not only does he have access to his own personal pool of guinea pigs, but he feels protected."

Warrick's face was grim. "Once Sebastian called in reinforcements, Dmitri knew things were about to go south pretty quick. Chances are, after sending a couple wolves Sebastian's way, he went and hustled Sutler out of the picture."

"If he thinks we're on to him, he may rabbit," Raine said.

Warrick shook his head. "No, he's planned this for too long. There's no way he'd walk away now. Sebastian was his way into my pack. He was never meant to survive."

"Did he really think you'd believe Sebastian would do this all on his own?" Xander asked.

Warrick was quiet for a moment then said, "Dmitri has always been a patient hunter, but he does his best work behind the scenes. He's waited a long time to make me pay for the death of his woman."

"Mate," Xander corrected, the pieces falling into place. "He considered her his mate, so he waited until you found yours."

"He's not going to touch you."

There was the possessive alpha she loved so much. "He doesn't have to. He's taking you apart piece by piece. He's stripped you of your Third, he's killed one of your wolves, he's invaded your territory and, with Mulcahy's death, he's isolating you from your allies. He doesn't just want your death. He wants to destroy you."

Raine, who'd been quietly listening, commented, "Your brother is a bit psychotic."

Xander had to agree. Dmitri's plan wasn't just devious, it was downright scary in its intelligence. "He's been studying you for a while, just waiting for the right moment." And judging from Warrick's expression, Dmitri wouldn't have much longer to wait. "Your plan won't work. Besides, as much as I hate to agree with Natasha, she's right in one aspect. Right now, we can't afford any more attention. Not from the humans and especially not from the Council and—"

"As far as the Council is concerned, that's a moot point," Raine cut in.

Xander grimaced. "True. However, we can keep as much of this mess out of the human spotlight as possible."

"How do you figure?" Raine asked.

"We can serve Sebastian up as the scapegoat for the string of suddenly feral wolves," Xander replied. "I wouldn't be surprised if Natasha hasn't already done so. Which means that Dmitri's part in all this is known only to a handful of us. We need Dmitri to disappear quietly, no fuss, no muss. So we give him what he wants and lure him out of hiding."

Warrick raised an eyebrow. "How exactly do you plan on doing that?"

His question made her stomach roil. She squelched the sick feeling and tried to ignore the chittering voice in her head, screaming that she was making a huge mistake. Her heart bled under the restraints of cold logic. "You're about to become the big bad wolf."

CHAPTER 32

RETURNING TO TALIESIN, WARRICK PULLED THE CAR INTO A SCENE of controlled chaos. Getting through the police, who had cordoned off the parking lot, took a few minutes as they passed his ID up the chain of responsibility. Finally, one veteran officer handed it back and waved him through.

A large fire engine sat between two smaller versions and an ambulance. On the ground, people in various uniforms swarmed the parking lot while a gray-tinted haze lingered around the top floor of the building. There was no sign of Natasha or Cheveyo, but Osborn stood outside the glass front doors talking with two men. A younger man interrupted their discussion and, from his abbreviated gestures, Warrick was fairly certain their arrival was being shared.

Osborn looked up and zeroed in on their sedan, watching as Warrick parked. Warrick met the human's gaze, holding it until Osborn's attention was pulled away by a question from the man on his left.

Silence filled the car.

There were things he wanted to say to Xander but not in

front of Raine. He listened to their plan. It was bloody brilliant, but there were so many points where things could go horribly wrong. There was no stopping the vivid images, of just how wrong things could go, from playing like some morbid film in his head.

"I'm going to go find Gavin." Raine got out of the car, the sound of her door closing muted by the weight of unsaid things hanging between him and Xander.

"Talk to me, Warrick." The quiet steel-coated demand made something in him relax.

"It's a good plan." He consciously unwrapped his grip from the steering wheel.

"But?"

He stared out the windshield. If he looked at her, he wouldn't be able to control the need to drag her into his arms and never let go. No matter how much he and his wolf wanted to tuck her away, it would be unfair to expect her to be anything but what she was—a protector. "It puts you in danger."

"Danger isn't a stranger to either of us." Her voice was soft, but unbreakable. "It's not the first time, nor will it be the last."

He knew that, but it didn't make it easier. "I understand, but my wolf has problems letting you stand in front of us."

Warm hands wrapped around his face. The familiar feel of her left him closing his eyes and holding her touch close. She tugged and he let her pull his head around. The soft brush of her lips across his brought his eyes open. Her hazel-shot gaze met his, determination, strength, and a silent promise swirled in the depths.

She pulled back but didn't let go of him. "I will do everything I can to make sure I always come back to you, alpha mine." A teasing grin lit her face. "I've spent a long time working on you, I'm not about to let you off that easy."

Her teasing eased some of his tension, but he narrowed his eyes and gave her a mock-threatening growl. "See that you do, pixie girl." Emotions rose to a choking cloud, but he permitted himself a brief, hard taste of her before he drew back. "Let's start the show."

He opened his door, listening to her get out on the other side. He waited for her at the front of the car before they began making their way to Osborn. His step hitched as a wave of love and acceptance poured through their bond. Before her mental touch could retreat, he sent her his tangled response. His love, pride, worry, acceptance—he wrapped it all together, gave it to her, and got a quick, heart-rending smile in return.

She fell a couple steps behind him as he wove his way through the humans. Behind Osborn, Taliesin's front doors opened, releasing Raine, Gavin, and Natasha. Osborn stepped aside, allowing the three to join the conversation.

"Ms. Bertoi, the battalion chief tells me you haven't allowed any of his people upstairs." Osborn's statement whipped out.

Being faced with three very imposing authority figures would make most people think twice. Natasha would never be most people. Unruffled, she gave Osborn a small nod. "That is correct, Mr. Osborn. Taliesin has many high-level, confidential clients, who require a certain level of discretion. We will be more than happy to let Chief Faraday's investigators inside, however, we must ensure our clients privacy."

"We understand your need to keep the loss of Mr. Mulcahy quiet as long as possible, however, we need access to the scene." Osborn tucked his hands into the pockets of his slacks and studied her. "I know how important client confidentiality is to Taliesin, but it is in the best interests of your company and clients that you allow the investigators access to the scene. Otherwise, questions may arise on the legitimacy of your company and its dealings."

Warrick gave the human credit for out-maneuvering Natasha. Since Osborn had no idea of who, or what, he was really dealing with, perhaps it was time to step in. "Natasha, perhaps Raine and Gavin could lead the investigators upstairs."

Natasha's stare remained on Osborn, who was valiantly trying to remain unmoved. Unfortunately for him, his elevated pulse and the slight acrid scent of his sweat gave him away. "Chief Faraday, please send your people with mine and let us know what we can do to help." Natasha finally released Osborn from her visual hold and turned to Faraday. "We ask that your people remain discrete, as the loss of Mr. Mulcahy impacts not just our company, but our family as well."

Faraday's mouth tightened. "My people know their job, Ms. Bertoi." He spun on a heel and barked out a string of names. A small group jerked to attention and began gathering equipment from the emergency vehicles.

The faint buzz of a cellphone caught Warrick's attention. Natasha pulled out a slim phone, tucked it to her ear and took a step away from the group. "Yes?" she paused then turned to take in the parking lot. "Tell them there will be no statement until we have more information."

Warrick followed the direction of her gaze and spotted Jamie Ryder, one of Natasha's men, standing at the far end in front of a roiling mass of cameras and microphones. The swarm of the press had begun. Ryder was obviously taking point on the public relations front. Behind him, Warrick heard Natasha say, "We'll call a press conference as soon as we have more information."

He caught Ryder's nod before the man turned back to the crowd. Letting his gaze roll over the milling group, Warrick felt a sense of unease crawl up his neck. Even his wolf was antsy. If he hadn't known better, he'd think he was being hunted. He tried to shake it off. Gods knew being surrounded by this many humans was enough to ruffle any wolf's fur, but the feeling persisted.

He wasn't surprised when Xander took a position in front of him. Linked as they were, there was no way she could miss his rising anxiety. She wasn't obvious about it, but he could tell she was scanning the area around them, trying to ferret out the unseen threat.

Gavin and Raine were holding open the doors and letting the investigative team inside the building, when Xander suddenly spun and shoved him toward the doors. "Rai—" Her voice was cut off and her weight slammed into him, sending them both stumbling back, a sharp sting leaving a burning brand across his upper arm. Only then did the sharp crack of a rifle shot echo through the morning air.

For a moment, the world held its breath, then someone screamed and chaos erupted.

Warrick didn't give a damn. All he was worried about was the limp body in his arms. The coppery sting of fresh blood hit his nose and his wolf went wild, trying to claw his way out of Warrick's skin. With a ruthlessness that made him who he was, Warrick held his wolf in check. It wasn't easy and he'd pay for it later, but right now, for Xander's sake, he needed to stay human.

She wasn't dead. That thought was the only thing allowing him to function. Using the connection of their bond, he wrapped himself around her spirit and held on tight. No way in hell was he allowing anything or anyone to take her away from him. She was his, dammit!

When someone reached to take Xander, he snapped his teeth, only then realizing how close to the surface his wolf really was. The hands retreated, only to be replaced by Raine's face. "Inside, Vidis! Get your ass inside!"

Inside was good. They were too exposed here. Inside he could keep everyone away from his mate. He gathered Xander close, spun on his heels, and stalked into the wide foyer. He didn't stop until he was back by the elevators, away from the windows and the others huddled behind the long reception desk in the foyer.

Behind him, Raine reached out and slammed the up arrow key. "Take her to your office."

Unable to respond, Warrick stared at the metal doors, willing them to open. Wet warmth seeped against the arm he had curled around her back, holding her to his chest. More plastered his shirt to his ribcage.

His blood froze.

Inside, where no one could see, he wrapped his strength and will around the light that was Xander. He held her with pure determination. On the edges of his mind, raving madness loomed, one that would wreak more devastation than any blood spell or bullet if Xander was taken from him.

The metal doors parted with a soft ding and he stepped in, Raine behind him. She hit the button for the seventh floor and the doors began to close. A hand appeared, holding them open and Warrick tensed, a low growl rumbling from his chest.

Staying outside the elevator, Gavin gave him a quick

look, then turned to Raine. "We'll be coming up behind you."

Raine gave a short nod and Gavin let the doors close. In Warrick's arms, a soft moan sounded, jerking Raine's head around. Worry had carved lines around her mouth and darkened her already bruised eyes.

"Shhhh," Warrick crooned, dropping his head over Xander's blonde one. Pain rippled across his mind as Xander swam to the surface of consciousness, her pain. It was quickly followed by a moment of panicked confusion. "I've got you, pixie girl. It's okay." It was hard to sound reassuring, especially as the edge of his wolf rode his voice, but he tried.

The elevator came to a stop, the small jerk wringing a choked off whimper from Xander. The door opened and Warrick brushed past Raine as she ran interference with Cheveyo. Since Warrick's office was on the far side of the building, it remained unscathed from the earlier destruction. Once inside, he kicked a chair out of the way, clearing a space on the carpeted floor.

Kneeling, he laid Xander down, determined to find out exactly how much damage the sniper's bullet had done. He sucked in his breath at his first good look. The bullet had ripped through the back of her shoulder and exited out the front. The damage in the front was obscene. He ripped off his bloodstained shirt and bunched it up, pressing it against the wound.

Xander's face was alabaster white under the stark lines of her tattoo. Her eyes fluttered open, pain-clouded and dazed. "Warrick?" His name was a mere breath of sound.

"Stay with me," he whispered, pressing down in a useless attempt to staunch the blood flow.

She flinched but fought to stay conscious. "You okay?"

"I'm fine," he growled.

Her left arm rose and she brushed a butterfly touch along his arm. "Not fine." Her arm dropped, blood staining her fingertips.

"Stop moving, Xander." Whatever scratch he had could wait until she was stable.

For once, she obeyed him without mouthing off. She closed her eyes and went still.

His breath hitched and his heart skipped a beat. Fear rose in a great wave. Was he losing her? His remaining emotional barriers crumpled under the deluge and he gave himself to her, heart and soul. Their connection pulsed then began to burn as Xander's formidable barriers also fell.

As the lines that kept them apart faded, their every fear, every hope was revealed for each to accept or reject—the true meaning of the soul bond apparent. There was no hesitation on his part as he gladly took all that was Xander as his to protect, to cherish, and to love. When she did the same for him, he was humbled. Under the fierce light, he watched in stunned amazement as each niche and crevice was illuminated then filled as their two souls found a balance and finally connected.

The bond clicked into place, solid and strong.

CHAPTER 33

Xander rode the wave of pain, trying to stay on top of her body's complaints at having a bullet tear through her shoulder. She knew Warrick was helping her, trying to divert her pain through their bond.

Warrick. Dear gods, he finally let her in. Amazement filled her. Tears that had nothing to do with her wound, pressed against her eyes. She guessed it said something about their relationship that it took her lying in a puddle of blood for both of them to let each other in, especially when that's what they both wanted and needed all along. In the end, it didn't matter. She'd take him however he'd let her.

Right now, it hurt too much to move, so she lay still and concentrated on her body. Fire and ice surrounded where the bullet struck, tendrils of pain radiating outward. The sound of a door closing had her forcing the heavy lids of her eyes up. They were in Warrick's office.

Raine knelt across from Warrick, holding a white gauze pad. "We need to put this on the entry wound." Raine wasn't stupid. Her gaze was focused on Xander, not Warrick, who's eyes were pure wolf.

"Don't want to move," Xander protested. Moving would make things go from *ow, ow, ow* to *shit, shit, shit*.

"Buck up, buttercup." Raine kept her tone light, both women well aware how close to the edge Warrick was skating. "I need to make sure there's nothing in there." She got her arm under Xander's shoulder, careful of the wound.

As Raine lifted, Xander sucked in her breath and fought not to black out. Sitting up hurt! Warrick held his shirt in place on her front, but shifted until she could lean against him so Raine could get a clear look at her back. Cool air touched her spine as her T-shirt was raised to expose her shoulder. As Raine pressed around the wound, Xander's vision wavered in bands of color. "It's a through and through," she gasped. "Stop poking around."

Raine's voice was level. "You lucked out. I'm not seeing any signs of silver."

Sweat beaded her forehead and her skin felt clammy. "If it had been silver, I wouldn't be talking to you." Under her head, she felt Warrick stiffen. She tangled her fingers with his free hand. "Besides, I wasn't the target. Warrick was."

Raine was quiet for a moment then said, "We could use this." She taped the gauze pad in place.

Warrick snarled.

Xander raised her head and shushed him. "She's right." Undaunted, she held his furious gaze. "This attack actually helps us. We have an audience since Gavin's on his way up with Division and other emergency personnel. Plus, we know Dmitri is watching."

Something dangerous moved over Warrick's face. "If Dmitri was behind this, the bullet would have been silver."

"Maybe, maybe not," Raine said, gently cutting through Xander's T-shirt. "Time for the front. Turn around."

Warrick and Raine carefully moved Xander until she

was half-reclining in Warrick's lap. She kept her grip on his hand, squeezing when the pain rose. Raine had another pad and more tape.

"Explain," Xander gritted out, trying not to let the pain from her wound overwhelm everything else.

Raine kept her touch light but sure. "Kyn tend not to use guns as magic makes them unreliable. So let's assume the sniper wasn't Kyn, but a hired human. Dmitri tells him who he wants hit and where he can be found. Snipers are notoriously arrogant."

"If you could shoot the wings off a fly at a mile out, I think you'd be entitled," Xander muttered.

Raine raised an eyebrow, her lips giving a brief quirk. "Probably, but if you had someone hire you to take on a job, would you follow their directions to the letter or do what you think was necessary to get the job done?"

A light bulb went off in Xander's muddled brain. "You think Dmitri told him to use silver and he chose not to?"

Raine nodded. "A silver bullet doesn't travel long distances accurately like normal bullets. If the sniper had no idea that who he was targeting wasn't human, there's no way he'd use silver over his proven ammunition." She paused and flicked a glance at Warrick. "That shot should have killed you."

Xander went to shrug, but stopped as her body revolted. "It didn't."

Raine put the last piece of tape in place and dropped her hands. "Still, how did you know he was there?"

"Warrick." She felt her mate stiffen behind her and squeezed his hand. "He was antsy. I was scanning the parking lot when I caught a flash in the trees." Instinct, something every Wraith relied on.

Raine sat back on her heels and directed her next

question to Warrick. "Let's say the sniper's now reporting to Dmitri that he didn't get you but Xander instead. What happens next?"

"He's going to want to see for himself." There was no hesitation in Warrick's answer.

"Let's make sure he sees what he's expecting then," Xander said. Her shoulder throbbed with a dull ache as her body fought to repair itself. Her mind began rearranging their previous plan as anticipation rose. First things first. They needed to get Gavin in here so they could start the ball rolling. She shared a look with Raine. "Where's Gavin?"

Raine gave a crooked smile. "Out front, keeping Cheveyo, Natasha, and Osborn occupied."

"We need to bring him in here."

Raine shook her head and tapped her temple. "Private communication channel, remember?" She fell quiet, her head tilted to the side as if listening to something no one else could hear. After a minute, a feral smile crossed her lips. "I'm going out front to get this show on the road. Gavin's been keeping them out. Be ready." She got to her feet and left, closing the door behind her.

"I don't like this," Warrick rumbled.

She wiggled in his lap until she could see his face. "Gavin's damn good with illusions. If Raine says he can do this then I believe her. If everyone believes I'm dead, they won't stop to question your behavior."

"If you were truly dead, I would never leave you behind."

She smiled. "I know, but if they think you're mindless with grief they'll be more concerned about getting you out of sight before you go furry than whether you leave me behind or not. A public argument with Cheveyo and

Natasha is the best way to make sure Dmitri thinks you're completely isolated. No pack, no allies, no me."

He leaned his forehead against hers. "I don't like it."

"Do you think I do?" Her voice shook. "You're going to be alone until I can get there, Warrick. Promise me you'll be standing when I do."

This time, he cradled her face and took her lips with heart-stopping gentleness. As he pulled back, he whispered, "I'll be waiting."

When the doorknob turned, Xander was cradled in Warrick's lap. She kept her breathing shallow and tried to keep her muscles lax. Her face was hidden against Warrick's chest, his steady heartbeat twining with the familiar scent of cinnamon and cloves.

"I'm telling you it's not smart to come in, Cheveyo." Raine's voice was harsh. "If Vidis goes for your throat, you're on your own."

"Cheveyo, let me go first." That was Gavin. There was some shuffling at the door then someone came closer. "Vidis," Gavin kept his voice carefully neutral as if he was talking a man off a window ledge. "Can you let me see her?"

A lethal snarl echoed through the room. Even knowing it wasn't real, it was hard not to react to that deadly sound.

"Vidis, please. Let her go." Tension sang through the room.

Warrick's arms tightened then slowly uncurled. As soon as Gavin touched her, she felt the air around her shift. Concentrating on keeping her limbs loose and boneless, she almost missed it. Carefully, she was taken from Warrick.

There was a pause then Gavin's soft "Dear gods!" had another set of footsteps hurrying over.

There was a rush of air as Warrick sprang to his feet and something slammed into a wall. "Stay away!" The command was all wolf.

"Vidis!" That was Raine. "Don't make me use this!"

Use what? The urge to open her eyes and find out what the hell Raine was doing was tough to ignore. Only the steady reassurance flowing to her from her connection with Warrick allowed her to remain in place.

"You think your knife would stop me, little girl?" Warrick's words were a menacing rumble. "I can rip his throat out before you move."

"Your anger is making you stupid, Vidis." Raine's voice was stripped of emotion, leaving nothing but cold certainty behind.

"They killed my mate!" His words strangled into an ear splitting howl that echoed through the room.

Xander's heart quivered under the agony in the haunting sound. She wasn't aware she was crying until Gavin's fingers swept under her eyes, brushing away her tears. She fought and found her control. If Warrick could put himself through this, then she could do no less.

"We'll get them," Raine offered, but even Xander could hear the lack of belief in her words as if Xander's supposed death had been one too many.

Another snarl then the sound of someone coughing. "Vi —Vidis, we need you to hold on. There are humans in the front office. If you let your wolf free now, there will be no way to hide this from them or from the Council."

Considering Warrick's recent animalistic howl, Xander gave a brief thought to how Natasha would spin that little item to those in the front office.

"Fuck the Council," Warrick snarled. "Fuck the humans. You think I give a damn about either of them? What could they do to me that hasn't been done? My mate is dead, my pack is fractured, and our presence is just a whisper away from being revealed. I'm not some dickless politician worried about keeping the stupid mortals from seeing the truth that walks beside them. Maybe it's time we remind them and those that hunt us what it means to fear."

There was another cough then Cheveyo tried again. "Vidis, think. Xander wouldn't want this."

"Xander. Is. Gone. And I want the blood of the one who took her." Warrick's wolf had truly slipped his leash.

"Enough!" The sharp word snapped through the room. Natasha had joined the party. "Vidis, you will pull yourself under control right this minute," she hissed, the words slipping through the room like razor-edged snakes. "The situation is dire enough without adding your temper tantrum to the mix. You will pull it together and assist Cheveyo and me with Division and their annoying questions. Once their attention is focused on something else, you may hunt down whoever you must. However, you will not lead the humans back to Taliesin or any other Kyn."

There was a grunt then Raine's voice squeezed out. "You can't kill her, Vidis."

"Get out of my way." Each word was bitten off in cold fury. Xander fought not to tense as real anger drifted through their connection. Her mate really didn't like Natasha.

"As much as I understand your need, I can't," Raine responded.

A tense silence stretched, only to snap with the sound of a something crashing through drywall.

"Perhaps you should step out of the doorway, Natasha."

There was an evil edge to Raine's voice. "Otherwise, I can't promise your safety."

"Vidis, you don't want to do this." That was Cheveyo, trying to be the lone voice of reason in an unreasonable storm.

"Actually, I do," Warrick snarled.

"Warrick," Cheveyo called.

"Let him go," Raine said softly. "There's no stopping him."

"As if I would chase him," Natasha snorted. "Foolish animal."

It was all Xander could do not to spring to her feet and bitch-slap the blonde into the next room. Only Warrick's touch through their connection and Gavin's restraining hand on her arm, kept her in place.

Above her, Gavin said, "Someone call Ryuu. Have him follow Vidis to make sure he doesn't do something rash."

Someone settled on her other side. "Silver?" Cheveyo's question confirmed Gavin's illusion was holding strong.

"If it wasn't, we wouldn't be in this mess." Gavin's answer was grim.

Cheveyo's heartfelt curse was soft. "Let me take her. I'll put her with Mulcahy. We may need to use Vidis's office when Division arrives. Dear gods." Exhaustion and frustrated grief lined his voice.

Xander actually held her breath. If Cheveyo took her, the illusion would shatter and there was no way she'd be able to leave. Warrick would be left to face Dmitri alone. Since his brother had the moral compass of a demon on a bender, that wasn't acceptable.

"No," Gavin said. "Osborn's going to have a lot of questions. It's best if you and Natasha field those. Leave this to Raine and me." Xander felt him slide his arms under her legs and shoulders and lift. She choked off her groan as his arm pressed against her entry wound.

"Gavin can stand guard over the bodies. Raine can go keep our rabid alpha on a leash." Cool and utterly without compassion, Natasha's voice grated over Xander's nerves like sandpaper as Gavin moved.

"You do realize you aren't my captain, Natasha," Raine snapped. "As a matter of fact, if I remember correctly, in the event the Captain of the Wraiths is incapacitated, authority transfers to the most senior member." Raine's voice came progressively closer before Gavin came to a stop. "Do you happen to know who that Wraith is, Natasha?" There was a dark thread of unholy glee in her question.

"Raine."

Gavin's one word warning was ignored.

"It's Gavin," Raine bit out, savagely. "Therefore, you can take your orders and—"

"Raine!" This time, both males in the room managed to create a unified vocal slap.

"Go see if you can track our shooter." Gavin's voice was cutting. "If you find him, I want him able to answer questions. Do you understand?"

Cradled in Gavin's arms, Xander had no choice but to lie there, caught in the middle of a very uncomfortable moment, listening to Raine's harsh breaths.

"Do you understand?" Gavin asked again, voice silky soft and oh so dangerous.

His only answer was a very feline snarl. The air next to Xander's head shifted, heralding Raine's exit.

"You better figure out how to keep your little pet in line, Cheveyo, or I'll do it for you." A hiss echoed in Natasha's voice.

Tension sang through Gavin's body, tightening the

muscles in his arms and chest. Xander wondered if he realized a low growl was vibrating through him. Probably not. Natasha was good at getting under everyone's skin until they wanted to peel her out with their fingernails.

"She just lost her uncle and her friend, Natasha. Perhaps you should back off," Cheveyo bit out. "Go placate Osborn. I'll be out in a minute."

A moment later, he broke the silence. "That woman would drive a saint to violence."

"And enjoy every minute of it," Gavin agreed.

Cheveyo sighed. "She's right, though."

"About?"

"We can't afford to let the Wraiths answer to someone whose loyalty may lie with the Council. Which means she's our best option."

"You won't even consider it?"

"No, I know myself too well and I'm not the type of person your group needs to function. Neither, unfortunately, is Vidis."

Gavin began to move again. "Raine's not the only one who's going to have problems answering to the Amanusa queen, Cheveyo."

Cheveyo's answer came from behind them. "I know, but we can only deal with one problem at a time. For now, the Wraiths are yours."

Gavin's step faltered. "That may not be wise right now."

"It's you or Raine," Cheveyo said from somewhere close by, resignation heavy in his voice. "Of the two of you, you're less likely to indulge in a full scale blood bath."

The sound of Cheveyo's footsteps faded. Above her, Gavin said softly, "You're wrong. I'll just hide it better."

CHAPTER 34

T HE DRIVE HOME WAS A BLUR AS THE MORNING'S EVENTS coalesced into savage fury. Warrick pulled his car into his driveway and fumbled for the door. The ruthless locks on his chaotic emotions broke with an almost audible snap.

Claw tipped fingers left ragged wounds in the leather panel as he scrambled for the door latch. It finally gave, spilling him out onto the cold, wet gravel. His spine arched as the change ran through him like lightning. The speed and fury of his emerging wolf left him panting. Material ripped, bones snapped and reformed, muscles convulsed. The brutal metamorphosis threw his head back and ripped a hair-raising howl from his throat.

The world shuddered under the sound. The eerie notes faded, leaving behind an unnatural silence.

Muscles coiled under the thick fur and the wolf began to run. Once inside the cover of the trees, Warrick let the slim barrier between him and his wolf slip. His emotions rose to a crushing tide and his powerful legs pumped harder, trying vainly to gain some sort of distance.

Damn his brother! Guilt choked him. Mulcahy, Zeke,

Sebastian—their deaths were on his head. If he hadn't held so tight to the memory of the brother who no longer existed, he would have hunted down and killed Dmitri all those years ago. Instead, he allowed sentiment to blind him to necessity. Now everyone else was paying for his mistakes —his pack, his friends, and Xander.

Dear gods, Xander! The memory of her warm blood drenching his hands and the lifeless slump of her weight falling against him tore through him. In that one endless moment, he caught a glimpse of a nightmarish reality where a small, blonde pixie no longer existed. His agonized howl tore through the forest.

He ran, heedless of time passing. In his veins, his blood sang as the air swept over him, filled with a myriad of familiar scents, and under his paws the earth was a solid, comforting presence.

Little by little, his pace slowed as the storm began to recede. The sting of possibilities began to fade as his anger and determination rose. Dmitri would take no more from him. The Motoki Pack was Warrick's, his to protect and defend. Just like Xander, whether she liked it or not. He could not change who he was at his core and she was more than his partner. She was his mate. It was time to remove Dmitri's threat once and for all.

Warrick stood still in the shadows, sides heaving, as he listened to the forest around him. Small creatures trembled in their hidey-holes, but he wasn't interested in hunting tiny things. No, his prey was much larger, but not much smarter. He and his wolf were in agreement. Dmitri would come for him, thinking him compromised by the deaths of his wolves, mate, and ally. And when he finally showed, Warrick and his wolf would be waiting.

"You're clear," Gavin said softly.

Xander opened her eyes and began to sit up. Leather cushions creaked as she moved, the muscles in her shoulder and back arguing the wisdom of her decision. She bit back her groan and told her aching body to shut the hell up. There would be time later to lounge around.

Finally upright, she gave the spinning in her head a moment to settle. When she was sure she wouldn't do a lovely face plant into the carpet, she looked up.

Next to the closed door, Gavin watched her with worried frown. "You sure you're up for this?"

She heaved to her feet, fighting not to sway like a drunken sailor. Her wound was still healing, but even the little time she'd had to heal had helped. "I'm not leaving him alone. I don't trust Dmitri to face him alone."

"You think he's going to bring back-up."

She took a couple of deep breaths and the world steadied. "Yeah, I do. Which means the faster I get there, the better."

Gavin's frown deepened and he opened his mouth. "Maybe I—" he shook his head. "Never mind," he muttered. He dragged a hand through his hair. "Raine said to tell you your bike is stashed in the back. I guess Ryuu dropped it off this morning."

"Good. Now I just need a way to get past everyone out front." She looked around. They were in Mulcahy's office. The floor-to-ceiling windows were framed by shelves and in front of them was an oversized desk. Her gaze caught on the blanket draped figure carefully laid on the dark wood. Her throat tightened and her pulse thudded dully.

She hadn't realized she'd moved until her fingers gingerly touched the edge of the blanket. "It doesn't seem real." She hadn't meant to say it out loud.

"It will be soon." The warm edge of fury and grief rode Gavin's voice.

"And Raine?" Her heart ached for her friend. Raine's relationship with her only living relative had never been easy, not even for those on the outside looking in, but still...

"She won't be alone," Gavin assured her.

Xander gave him a small nod, knowing Raine wouldn't make it easy for Gavin to stand beside her. Then, taking a deep breath, she turned away from her fallen captain. "So, how do I get out of here?"

Fifteen minutes later, Xander straddled the familiar frame of her Ducati, helmet in place, the road an asphalt ribbon under her tires. Gavin had shown her a hidden exit from Mulcahy's office that opened out into the basement of Taliesin, out of sight of the still converging emergency responders gathered in the front. It didn't take much to make her way unseen to her bike.

Urgency bit at her. Warrick had a thirty-minute head start and if Dmitri was watching, he would take full advantage of her alpha's isolation.

She kept a leery eye out for cops as she pushed the bike past the speed limit. Using her helmet's Bluetooth system, she called Ryuu. When he picked up, she didn't give him a chance to say a word. "Hasn't anyone called you?"

"No, but I have three missed messages." There was rustling on the line, Ryuu's muted voice barked out orders to whoever was with him. Then he asked, "What's going on?"

"Warrick's at his house, alone."

It didn't take Ryuu long to start cursing. "What the hell are you thinking, Xander? If I had known you were going to leave him alone, I would've had someone else take care of Sebastian. Do you want Dmitri to kill him?"

"Shut up!" she hissed, worry and fury carving a sharp edge to her voice. "We know Dmitri's watching, but he won't make a move until he's certain he has Warrick where he wants him. Right now, he thinks he's stripped Warrick of everyone, including me."

"What do you mean?"

"A sniper took a shot outside Taliesin and hit me instead. Warrick had a very loud, very obvious blow up with Natasha and Cheveyo regarding my death and his need for blood within earshot of Division and the other first responders. Then he stormed out of the office, alone."

"Who's half-assed plan was this?"

Her hands tightened on the bike as she imagined Ryuu's neck under them. "Warrick wanted to directly challenge him. You really think Dmitri would honor that little request? If we didn't want to spend the next few days mopping up more blood and burying more friends, we needed a way to end this now. I don't like using Warrick as bait any more than you do." She paused, weaving between a semi, hauling freshly cut trees, and a mud-splattered VW bus. "How far out are you?"

"Fifteen, maybe twenty minutes," he snapped. "You?"

"Five to ten," she answered. "Raine should be there, hopefully, so keep an eye out. I'm going through the woods. The bike's too loud to drive directly up." She paused. "Ryuu, I don't think Dmitri is going to come alone, so be careful."

"Have you called Ethan?"

Puzzled, she frowned. "My brother? No, why?"

Ryuu's sigh echoed through her helmet. "Because he's now Vidis's Third." Through her stunned silence, he added, "I'll call him."

Xander bit her tongue at the automatic refusal that rose to her lips. The thought of adding another loved one to the line of fire made her sick. But they needed the numbers and Ethan, for all his urbane sophistication, was a very lethal predator. "Fine," she bit out and hung up.

Her thoughts whirled, worry for Warrick, Ethan, Ryuu, and even Raine mixed with her simmering anger aimed at Dmitri. The damage the bastard had caused was staggering. She knew he was going ambush Warrick. All along he had played the puppet master, making others dance to his whims, leaving death and destruction in their path. Not once had Dmitri directly challenged Warrick, nor would he unless he could determine the outcome. Chances were Dmitri was already at Warrick's, but she'd bet good money he wasn't alone. There was no way he'd go in without skewering the odds in his favor.

Using their connection, Xander reached out to her mate and found him running through the forest, his wolf ascendant. She let her spirit brush against his, offering what comfort she could as his turbulent emotions rose and fell like unseen tides. Under it all was a solid core of ruthless determination to protect what was his, regardless of the cost.

Her wolf rose and stretched, padding forward. *Ours,* she thought, *ours to protect.* Anticipation sang through her, finding an echo in her mate, their bond pulsing with quiet strength. Together, they would remove the threat to their pack and family.

Like a silent shadow, Warrick stepped out of the heavier cover of the woods and came to a stop just inside the tree line. His lips lifted, exposing long, sharp canines. His ears flattened as his muscles coiled, the hair along his spine and neck rose, and his tail lifted.

"Surprise, brother," drawled Dmitri. Leaning against a wooden beam supporting the back deck, he waited, arms folded across his chest, his lips curled with derision. "Hard morning?"

Fury rose in a choking wave, adding a red tinge to Warrick's vision at the vicious taunt. His wolf surged to the forefront and had taken two slow, stiff-legged steps forward before Warrick leashed his more primal instincts. He lowered his head and let a menacing growl roll from his chest. Dark satisfaction flashed across Dmitri's face.

Wait, look, Warrick whispered to his wolf. Dmitri thought him lost to his animal.

Not taking his attention from his brother, Warrick let his other senses stretch. A small breeze curled through the trees. When it reached him, he siphoned through the scents, cataloguing those that belonged, and pinpointing those that didn't.

As expected, Dmitri had brought along a few friends. The problem was Warrick couldn't decipher what form they were currently wearing. There were three distinctive scents, all some combination of fur and skin. Such odds required two feet, not four.

Drawing fast and hard on his ability to change, he took another step forward, relishing the shock on his brother's face as between one step and the next, a man stood where a wolf had once been. Heedless of his nakedness, Warrick stopped where his backyard began, the forest behind him. No need to allow the others to circle behind him. "And do I thank you for that?"

Dmitri pushed off and sauntered closer with studied casualness, stopping just out of reach. He sketched a mocking bow. "How does it feel, Warrick, to be left with nothing?" A nasty grin appeared. "Do you hunger for blood? My blood?"

"Are you offering?"

Dmitri's grin widened. "Oh no. You see, there are a few others who have a bone to pick with you first." His voice dropped. "I did promise them first dibs."

A shape leapt out of the trees, slamming into Warrick and taking him to the ground with a canine snarl. Warrick let his wolf slip his skin, taking on his warrior form. Thick claws tipped his fingers and dug into soft tissue as he pushed his attacker up and off of him.

He rolled to his feet as muscles layered over bone, adding density and strength to his frame. Upright, he faced the twisted features of another drugged maverick. As he met the maddened gaze of his attacker, he felt his jaw stretch as his teeth to sharpen and lengthen.

They circled each other, both looking for an opening. Warrick ignored the skittering along his spine, indicating there were other threats waiting for their chance. For now, he needed to get rid of the one in front of him. The maverick was a mass of heavy muscles, but he was quick. Something he demonstrated when he stepped in and swung a feint that had Warrick jerking his head back, leaving him open to the bruising punch that landed on his ribs.

Warrick let his body double over the maverick's fist, using the movement to mask his hands. Digging his claws in, he anchored his hands on the beefy arm and spun into him. Taking advantage of his body's momentum, he pulled the maverick off balance and forward. Without hesitating, he slammed his elbow into the maverick's temple before releasing his grip.

Stunned, the maverick stumbled and fell to a knee in front of Warrick. Warrick didn't wait, but wrapped his arm around the wolf's throat and, using his other hand to lock his arm in place, settled his fists just under the maverick's ear. Fire ignited along the skin of his arm as it shredded beneath the clawing nails of the choking wolf.

Even though the maverick was heavier, Warrick used his own body weight to pull the maverick backward, elongating the spine. Then he stepped in and to the side, torquing the wolf's body. He tightened his hold, muscles flexing in response, and gave a sharp yank, ignoring the searing whip of agony radiating along his ribs.

The dull crack of the maverick's neck breaking was audible only to Warrick, who didn't loosen his grip until the body in his arms went lax. Opening his arms, he let the weight fall into a crumpled heap at his feet. Warm blood trickled down his forearms and dripped off the tips of his claws. His sides heaved as he dragged in air, ignoring the pain of his damaged ribs. He raised his head, letting his beast look through his eyes as he stared at the one who had once been his brother. Contempt and adrenaline rushed through his system, leaving him hyperaware.

Branches and leaves rustled off to his side. On the other side, a branch snapped underfoot. It was his only warning before two figures burst from their cover in a whirlwind of fangs and claws.

CHAPTER 35

Leaving her bike well off the roadway and half-hidden behind the trees, Xander ran through the forest. With her wolf so close to the surface, she wove in and out of the woods with uncanny ease. Something was wrong. Her connection with Warrick had gone eerily quiet. He hadn't shut her out, not completely, but he had done something that put distance between them. She knew he was alive, but that was all she was getting.

Branches whipped across her face and arms, leaving bloody welts behind. She leapt over fallen logs, her steps sure even as her shoulder throbbed. As she ran, she shoved her worry and apprehension for Warrick into a box and locked the damn thing shut. Right now, emotion was useless. Instead, she took comfort in the clear practicality of her wolf's impending hunt.

The trees blurred and she knew she was close when the nose-wrinkling scents of drugged wolves teased her nose. When the musky smell of a big cat hit, she slowed to a stop. She scanned the treetops, knowing Raine preferred to go up whenever possible. The rain from earlier was gone, leaving weak sunlight to dance on the leaves.

Xander pulled the blade Gavin had lent her from her boot and made sure to keep her footsteps silent as she continued forward. The wind changed direction and brought her the sound of snarls and growls. Her wolf pushed her faster, knowing her mate faced more than one enemy. But they needed to identify all the players. Otherwise, they were asking to be ambushed at the worst possible moment.

Above her, a branched rustled and Xander froze in place, waiting. A whiff of metal and oil hit her. She dropped to the ground. A sharp crack echoed through the forest and something slammed into the bark where her head had been. There was a muffled grunt and a short scream that was abruptly cut off. Off to her side, something heavy began to fall through the trees. She was on her feet before it hit the ground.

Raine dropped to the ground beside Xander as she stopped in front of the body. Deep claw marks replaced his throat and he was sporting a black handled blade in his chest.

She caught the rifle Raine tossed her, noting the bloody handprint on the wooden stock. It was heavier than it looked, and the smell of silver and gunpowder rose from the thick barrel to mix with the familiar scent of shifter. She sheathed the knife, examining the gun.

Son of a bitch. Since when did wolves start carrying hunting rifles loaded with silver? That was cheating. Disgusted, she vented her anger by bending the barrel of the gun and tossing it aside.

Raine curled her hand around the blade's hilt and pulled it free with a small sucking sound. She wiped the blood, coating the blade, off on the body's shirt. Rising to her feet, she slipped it back into one of her many hiding spots.

Knowing how well voices could carry in the forest, Xander used the hand signals known to all Wraiths. *Others?*

Raine raise an eyebrow and two fingers, a third waffling.

So two, maybe three still lurking about. Thanks to the shot, they were bound to come investigate. The need to be by Warrick's side tugged at her. She could leave the others to Raine and Ryuu when he finally showed up. Which reminded her...

A few rapid hand movements later, Raine slipped into the forest to hunt. Xander left her to it, knowing Ryuu would help with cleaning up the stragglers, then the two would join her and Warrick.

Drawing on her wolf, Xander continued toward the sounds of fighting. She wove her way through the foliage, using cover where she could. Speed was sacrificed for stealth. The trees began to thin and the occasional snarl and yip was accompanied by the meaty sound of impacted flesh. Natural wolves were silent hunters, using growls and yips only before or after a hunt. Mix human nature with a wolf's and, when things began to hurt, noises would emerge. Even without the over-powering scent of coppery blood, floating through the air, the noises alone would have told her that someone, or a couple of someones, were in some serious pain.

She cleared the heavier trees and stopped, caught by the savage beauty of the scene before her. Warrick was in warrior form, the graceful meld of man and wolf creating a mesmerizing creature. Muscles curled and bunched through his shoulders and spine as he caught the vicious swing of an attacker's arm in a bone-breaking lock. The dull crunch of bone snapping was followed by a high-pitched yelp of pain.

Warrick ignored the sound and spun, putting the injured attacker directly into the path of the second shifter who was in mid-leap, claws extended. Unable to change the trajectory of his flight, he crashed into his friend. The heavy impact forced Warrick back a step before he regained his balance. The muscles of his arms coiled and released as he shoved the two shifters back, giving him more room.

Now that he had turned, Xander had a clearer view of her mate. Blood decorated his skin in an abstract pattern, visible even through the light layer of fur covering his naked body. A wicked-looking set of claw marks seeped a rich red as they curled around his ribs and over his lower back. His lips were curled back, exposing sharp lethal-looking teeth. Heavy, malicious claws tipped long fingered hands. Silent, lethal, and pitiless, Warrick stalked the idiot who thought jumping him was a good idea while his buddy lay on the ground, groaning.

Leaper somehow managed to keep his feet under him and now stumbled back from the approaching monster. He found purchase and charged Warrick, swinging out with his arm.

It was a feint, one Warrick didn't fall for, turning his body to the side to avoid the punch as his claw-tipped hands wrapped around the leg aiming for his ribs. The claws sank deep, dragging a pained hiss from his opponent just before Warrick pulled him closer. He jerked Leaper off balance and forward, directly in line with his right fist that drove into Leaper's face with a sickening crunch. Leaper went limp.

Mesmerized by the fight, a mixture of pride and feral

satisfaction filling her, she watched Warrick beat the living crap out of the two lesser wolves. He wasn't an alpha for nothing. It was only when the one on the ground decided to stop sniveling and join in that she finally stepped clear of the surrounding trees.

Even with a mangled arm, the second wolf still managed to attach himself to Warrick's back, one arm wrapping around Warrick's neck as he tried to pull her mate off his friend. Xander whipped Gavin's blade free as wolf number two decided to make a snack out of Warrick's neck. The exquisitely balanced blade flew end-over-end and imbedded itself at the base of his skull. He jerked and half-turned to her, releasing his grip on Warrick. Feral madness looked at her through a human mask, before his body folded to his knees and collapsed face down on the ground.

Seeing her, Warrick took a step toward her. Behind him, something or someone moved and two sharp cracks sounded. In front of her, Warrick jerked in tandem to the sound, his amber eyes widening as he half-turned toward the shooter and stumbled.

"Warrick!" she screamed, moving before the sharp tang of silver and gunpowder hit her, her heart seizing.

She cleared the distance between them, fury and fear lending her speed. Leaping over the one she killed, she snagged the knife out of his neck and landed in front of Warrick, deliberately placing her body between her mate and the man who had shot him. Throwing under-handed, she let the blade fly just as another shot tore through the air. She rushed her throw and the blade embedded itself in the shooter's shoulder.

Even as the bullet's impact slammed the breath from her body, she watched the gun fall from his now-nerveless grip. For a moment, they stared at each other, her need for his blood meeting his dark hatred. Then the silver hit her bloodstream with a fireball rush.

She struggled to stay on her feet as agony spread its icy tentacles from the impact point somewhere below her ribs and began wrapping around her legs and spine. By the deck, the one she assumed was Dmitri took an abrupt seat on the ground, his back against a wooden support post.

Pressing a hand over the wound, she took a step and almost fell. Her legs shook, threatening to collapse, but she gritted her teeth and forced them to move. Warrick was behind her, injured. She wanted to turn and rush to his side but knew she couldn't afford to take her attention off Dmitri.

He was still conscious, fumbling with the hilt of the blade, trying to pull it out. His muscles boiled as he tried to rush his change.

Each step drove thick needles of pain through her, sending small white starbursts exploding on the edges of her vision. The only thing keeping her on her feet was the need to feel the spill of warm blood as she ripped out the throat of the one who threatened her mate and pack.

Soft snarls fell from her lips, her wolf adding her strength and fury to the mix coursing through Xander. Her gaze locked on Dmitri with lethal intent. She and her wolf were in agreement. It was time to eliminate their enemy.

Under her rising rage, warmth curled through her. Fur, love, strength, it wrapped around her. Warrick. It pushed back the instinctive need to kill and dulled the nerve-rending pain, allowing her to press forward. Grabbing tight, she wrapped their connection around her and her wolf, adding her own determination and love to the bindings until the two became one vibrating bond.

There were answers only Dmitri could give them, which meant she couldn't just rip his throat out and leave his body to rot. At least, not yet.

She came to a stop and stood over him, keeping out of his reach.

His mouth twisted in an ugly snarl as he stared at her with cold eyes. Even with his incomplete change, for a strangely disconcerted moment, she was caught by his resemblance to Warrick.

"Stupid bitch!" he growled.

And then it was gone.

Her lips curled with contempt, she took two steps closer and channeled all her rage into a savage backhand. Her blow knocked his hand away from the blade and sent him sprawling on the ground, stunned. "Coward!"

Bending over was out of the question, so she slowly, carefully crouched down, keeping her hand over her seeping wound. Watching him, she wrapped her hand around the hilt of the blade in his shoulder, leaned her weight on it and twisted it deeper.

He made a feeble attempt to claw her hand off the blade, but she ignored the sting of the deep scratches his nails carved into her unprotected skin. She took perverse pleasure in his wrenching groan before yanking the blade out, not caring how brutal the move was. Sweat broke out on his pale face as his body jerked once then went boneless. He passed out, either from the wound or her hit, she didn't care. For now, he was out. The blade was silver, so he wouldn't be healing his wound any time soon.

Her fingers tightened on the knife. The cold voice of practicality urged her to bury it in his unprotected stomach or slash it across his throat. Her hand actually trembled as she fought her darker urges. Information, she reminded herself. They needed information he had. Still, she needed to make sure he didn't go anywhere while she checked on Warrick.

What to do?

She sat back on her heels, taking shallow breaths to combat her rising light-headedness. Near her feet the black matte of the fallen gun caught her attention. She tucked the blade into her boot, picked up the gun and slowly rose to her feet. Upright, she swayed for a moment until the world righted itself. Then she peeled her hand away from her wound, feeling the blood trickled over her skin.

With both hands free, she considered the gun. Sig Sauer, P225 nine millimeter if she wasn't mistaken. She may not use guns, but it didn't mean she didn't know what they were or how to use them. The slide wasn't locked back, meaning there was a bullet in the chamber. Good enough. Depressing the magazine release button, she caught the magazine and counted. Four bullets left, one in the chamber. Dumping the four silver bullets to the ground, she shoved the now empty magazine back into place.

She raised the gun, aimed, and fired. Dmitri's hoarse scream echoed on the heels of the loud report. Blood seeped sluggishly from just above his knee. Satisfied he wouldn't be dashing off, she pressed the decocking lever on the left side then tossed the empty gun away.

Ignoring Dmitri's spitting snarls, she turned and began picking her way back to Warrick, who was crouched on all fours, blood pooling around him. Feral and beautiful and all hers. She smiled.

His eyes flickered, widened, and his hoarse shout had her turning as a brutal pain pierced near her spine and wrapped its vicious claws around the base of her skull. She dropped to her knees, a primal howl painting the air around her with its rage.

Her vision grayed and, through the bond, she caught the image of a knife embedded in her back. *Stupid, stupid move*, she thought, and slumped forward, her hands slamming into the earth in a desperate attempt to stay upright.

Air rushed over her, filled with the scent of cinnamon, cloves, fur, and fury.

CHAPTER 36

Warrick landed on four paws on the other side of Xander, teeth bared, muscles coiled, his ruff standing on end while a cold, calculating rage sang through his veins. The burn of injuries and silver fell under his driving need to sink his teeth into the throat of the darker wolf now shaking the change from its fur like water.

He didn't slow, didn't give Dmitri a chance to find his balance, but slammed into him. Dmitri stumbled and managed to pull his vulnerable muzzle out of the path of Warrick's snapping jaws. Warrick spun, his nails finding traction in the dirt and powered into Dmitri's side, driving him back and down.

Dmitri snarled, jaws snapping, trying to force Warrick back as he scrambled to get his hind legs under him. Finding purchase, he rose up and Warrick followed. Both wolves were on their hind legs, forelegs ripping along fur covered shoulders and necks as low growls rumbled and teeth flashed. Warm blood scented the air and decorated the churned-up ground.

Warrick felt the moment Dmitri's injured leg gave way.

Snarling, Warrick lowered his head, slamming it into Dmitri's neck and using the powerful muscles along his shoulders to ride his brother to the ground, ignoring the agony of the still bleeding bullet wounds.

Dmitri fell back, desperately trying to protect his belly. His claws caught along Warrick's damaged ribs, sending breath-stealing pain through his chest. His grip loosened, allowing Dmitri to escape.

The two wolves circled each other, one careful step at a time, bloody and focused. Warrick could feel his blood matting his fur. He wasn't alone. Dmitri's coat was equally covered. He snarled at Warrick, trying to hide the fact he was unable to put weight on his hind leg. Deep inside his wolf, Warrick smiled nastily.

With no warning, Warrick leapt at Dmitri, driving him back and over, the two wolves locked in a deadly embrace. Warrick sank his teeth deep into Dmitri's throat as his nails raked down.

Panicked, Dmitri struck out blindly and got lucky. His nails tore into the gunshot wounds on Warrick's shoulders. Flesh and fur gave way, sending a black wave of agony swimming over Warrick. His jaw went slack as his human scream rose to escape on a howl.

Suddenly the mind numbing pain pulled back, leaving clarity and newfound strength behind. Tenacious determination, love, and achingly familiar warmth rose, giving him distance from his pain. *Xander*.

Under him, Dmitri still clawed for freedom, twisting on his back, his teeth snapping close. Red had drowned out the amber until only instinctive madness remained. Desperate to get free, his brother was lost under his wolf, his moves instinctive instead of calculating. He slipped from under

Warrick and scrambled to his feet, lips peeled back from his teeth.

Warrick lowered his head, growling, watching, and waiting with a predator's patience. There was no mercy left for the one who had betrayed so many. All he needed was one mistake.

Infuriated, Dmitri lunged. Warrick sidestepped and snapped his teeth closed over Dmitri's muzzle, locking his jaws. Using the powerful muscles in his shoulders and neck, Warrick sank down and began dragging Dmitri to the ground, exploiting his grip on his brother's muzzle.

Tendrils of fire leeched along his spine as Xander began to lose the strength to block his pain. He was running out of time.

He set his hind legs and shook his head, his strength such that Dmitri's spine snapped with an audible sound as he was whipped from side to side. Warrick shook his head a couple of more times until the wolf's body was completely limp. He dropped to the ground. His teeth still locked on Dmitri's muzzle, Warrick stared into Dmitri's maddened eyes, hoping for something he couldn't name. Blood coated his mouth.

His brother's blood.

The light in Dmitri's eye dulled then went out. Warrick unlocked his jaw, letting Dmitri's head fall to the ground. He lay there, head on his paws, sides billowing, pain forging new paths in places he didn't even realize existed, until now. He watched the lifeless body of his brother and waited for the guilt of having the death on his hands.

It didn't show.

Two figures burst out of the forest, smelling of blood and wildness. He lifted his head, the movement causing a small whimper to escape as his body protested. Ryuu and Raine.

He struggled to his feet even as Raine stopped by Xander's small figure curled on the ground. Renewed panic speared him, even though he could still feel her through their bond. He had to get to Xander. Strength was seeping away, holding his ability to change out of reach. He stumbled and Ryuu was there.

"Vidis. Warrick, let me help." Ryuu kept his gaze on Warrick's shoulder, his posture submissive, even as he gave Warrick something to lean against. His Second was naked, blood and cuts marring his skin.

Warrick dipped his head and began to walk toward Raine and Xander. He ignored Ryuu's exasperated sigh. He was an alpha and alphas were not carried.

Ryuu kept pace as he moved.

"This is going to hurt," Raine was saying as she knelt next to Xander, an open emergency kit lying beside her. This close, Warrick saw Xander bite her lip, her pale face covered in sweat. She was on her side, Raine's thighs bracing her chest and stomach as the taller woman leaned over and grabbed the knife sticking out of Xander's back.

"...two, three."

Raine pulled the knife free and Xander shuddered, tears leaking from the corner of her closed eyes. One hand was curled onto Raine's jean-covered thigh. Raine pressed a gauze pad to the wound, working fast to tape it into place.

Warrick dropped next to Xander, nudging her face with his muzzle. Her eyes fluttered open, revealing pain-filled, hazel-shot green. He gave a soft whine and Xander uncurled her fingers from Raine's thigh. They were shaking as she buried them in the dense fur of his neck. "Did you get him?" she whispered.

He licked her chin and rested his head next to hers, letting his fur soak up her tears. He wanted to hold her but his strength was making a rapid exit.

Ryuu dropped down across from Raine. "Okay, Xander girl. We need to check out the hole you've acquired. I can smell silver."

Deep in his ruff, Xander's fingers tightened then relaxed. With utmost care, Raine and Ryuu shifted their positions until Xander's back was now to Ryuu, her front to Raine. Her breath escaped on a hiss as their movements jarred her. Warrick settled in behind her, giving her something to brace her shoulders against. He curled up and buried his nose under her short, silky hair and against the soft skin of her neck. He dragged in the faint tinge of vanilla and fur that belonged to her.

He watched Ryuu and Raine cut away her T-shirt to expose the gunshot wound. The entry wound was small, neat while the exit wound was an ugly mess, vomiting a wash of crimson. The bullet had sliced just under her ribs and torn its way through. A small mercy. If the bullet had lodged inside, they'd have to slice it out of her. Considering how much the lingering traces of silver were affecting her, that wouldn't have been good.

Raine was pouring something that stung his nose over the hole in front as Ryuu cleaned the larger wound in her back, trying to staunch the blood. "Vidis, I'm going to need you," he gritted out.

Raine raised her head and gave Warrick a once over. "Since I don't think red is his natural color, I'm not sure he's going to have much to give."

Ryuu didn't get a chance to respond as the sound of a low engine heralded another arrival. Gravel crunched under tires followed by the dull thud of a door closing.

Raine looked over her shoulder, eyes narrowed. "Expecting company?"

"Ethan," Ryuu answered, not looking up from his task. He let loose a sharp whistle that hurt Warrick's ears. Warrick growled and Ryuu slid him a look. "My hands are full."

Ethan came around the side of the house, racing pass the lifeless, but now fully human form of Dmitri, and skidded to a halt next to Raine. Seeing who lay between Ryuu and Raine had worry chasing across his face, before it disappeared under a determined mask. He dropped to his knees. "What do you need?"

"She was shot with silver." Ryuu met Warrick's gaze for a moment. "So was Vidis. We need to heal them both."

Ethan gave a sharp nod and wrapped a hand around Xander's leg. "Hey, sis. Looks like you forgot to duck."

Her grin switched to a grimace. "Don't tell Mom."

"Yeah, I'm thinking you may not be able to hide this from her."

"Ethan, come over here," Raine said, her hands holding Xander still as she shifted back. Ethan moved over to take Raine's place, gently settling in next to his sister, mindful of her wound.

Raine moved toward Warrick.

He lifted his head and growled.

"What? You're bleeding like a stuck pig."

"He won't let you near him until Xander's healed first," Ryuu told her.

Raine's hands went to her hips as she glared down at the Northwest alpha. Warrick's wolf didn't like her standing over him and he forced his legs to move.

"Raine, sit the hell down." That was Xander. "And stop pushing his buttons."

Raine dropped to her haunches with a huff. "Stubborn male."

"He's an alpha, you idiot," Xander muttered.

"And that's an excuse?" Raine asked.

"Yep," Ethan drawled. "Even pulling on death's whiskers, he'd still rip you apart."

Raine's lip curled. "Fine. Then you better get started because from the amount of blood he's standing in, I'd say your big, bad alpha is a about a quart and half low."

Warrick waited until Raine's butt hit the ground before resettling next to his mate. The minute he felt his Second reach through the pack ties, he gathered the healing magic available to him and funneled it, through Ryuu and Ethan, into Xander. It roared through the ties, slid into the mating bond and hit him like a tsunami. Unexpected heat and light rushed over torn muscles and bones, seeping deep.

Time passed and he floated in the sensation, never losing his mental touch on Xander. He could feel her and her wolf curled against him, trusting him to stand as her protector. Something in his chest loosened and the mating bond deepened. He could feel her ease past his ragged edges, her love and acceptance a quiet balm to wounds he hadn't been aware of carrying. She wound her way through his being, filling his empty spaces.

CHAPTER 37

XANDER WOKE TO THE SOUND OF A SOFTLY MUTTERING FIRE, wrapped in cinnamon and cloves and heated skin. Under her cheek, the reassuring thump of Warrick's heart kept a steady beat. His soft exhales ruffled her hair. He was sleeping.

She stretched slowly, waiting for her body to protest. There were twinges, but nothing like what she expected. She rubbed her nose across his chest, dragging his comforting scent deep into her lungs, and held her breath, wanting to hold this moment close.

Events from earlier began to trickle through her memory and she let her breath out. Dmitri was dead. Warrick had killed him. She shuddered. His arms tightened around her. She relaxed, letting her mind sort through things.

Dmitri's death may have resolved the immediate threat, but she had a sinking feeling that a bigger one was barreling closer. If they couldn't find his supplier, Sutler, they'd lose all leads on the drug used on the mavericks.

Having a human involved worried her. Hunting Sutler down would have to become a priority, not just for their pack, but for all the Kyn. She bet it would top the Wraiths' to-do list, right after get a new captain.

A wave of grief touched her and drifted away. She hadn't been close to Mulcahy, but she had respected him. Regardless of how callous some of his past decisions were, she had never doubted that everything he did was to protect the Northwest Kyn. That type of leader was rare.

Natasha's determination to take over the Wraiths made Xander uneasy. Holding the reins of a specialized group of hunters and killers gave a leader a very lethal edge. Natasha was nightmarish enough in her own right without being the Captain of the Wraiths. Add in the fact that Raine wasn't the only one who had serious issues with the Amanusa queen, and the future looked downright scary.

"Relax, pixie girl. Don't go borrowing trouble," Warrick rumbled.

Startled, she raised her head. "What? You can read my mind now?"

He chuckled, his eyes still closed. "No, but I can hear your mind racing like a hummingbird on crack."

She choked on a giggle at his unexpected humor. She dropped her head back to his chest and amused herself by tracing absent patterns on his skin. He rumbled in pleasure at her touch. Her face heated as she felt the echo of her touch against his skin through their bond. Now that they weren't facing down psychotic wolves or dodging silver bullets, she let herself really look at the tie connecting her to Warrick and was stunned at what she found.

Her heart raced and a closely held hope began to stretch its fragile wings. There were no more barriers, no more closed-off spaces. Tentatively, she reached out and touched a wealth of love, acceptance, need, and want. Her heart shattered into a million pieces, only to reform into something new and better with him.

"What happened?" she choked out.

"I told you before, I wouldn't let you go." His voice was husky. "I meant it." With serious intensity, he held her gaze. "I love you."

Blinking back tears, she stared at him. "I love you, too."

He smiled and the emotion behind it sang through her. "You're mine now, pixie girl. There's no escaping."

She laughed, even as tears fell down her face.

His fingers were gentle as he brushed them away. "Do me a favor? Next time, make sure you remove all weapons from our enemies before you walk away."

The aggrieved tone in his voice had her grin spreading. "Bite me, alpha mine."

"Gladly," he growled, dragging her up so he could nip her chin before capturing her mouth with his. Heat coiled low in her belly as he rolled her under him, their legs tangling. Then her big bad wolf proceeded to show her what it really meant to be an alpha's mate.

A long time later, Xander lay sprawled over a very sated male wolf as they lay before the fire, her body a boneless, happy mass. Unfortunately, reality began to intrude.

"Who's going to step into Mulcahy's place in the Fey House?" She racked her brain for a name or face and came up blank.

Warrick sighed. "I have an idea, but I'm not sure.

They've been called the Hidden People for a reason. They're very insular. Mulcahy never really talked about his people."

Xander frowned. "Is Natasha right, then? Will the Council send someone to take his place?"

"Oh, the Council will send someone all right." His voice took on the edge of a growl. "But it won't be to replace Mulcahy. If anything, they'll use his death as an excuse to send their eyes and ears into our business."

She saw his wolf staring back at her. She reached up and brushed a soft touch over his jaw. "Why does that worry you?"

He unwrapped one arm and tucked it under his head so he could meet her gaze. "The Council is a bunch of very old, very powerful creatures, who have no concept of what it means to live in the mortal world. They view humans as short-lived nuisances. Anything new and different is viewed with extreme prejudice."

"New and different?"

He raised an eyebrow. "Have you been paying attention to Raine and Gavin, love?"

Xander didn't answer.

He smiled at her silence and traced a finger over the lines of her tattoo. "The things Raine can do, the potential she's carried since she left Talbot's labs has been a well-hidden point of speculation between Mulcahy and myself."

"And Natasha and Cheveyo?"

Warrick shrugged. "I don't know if Mulcahy talked to either of them about her. If he didn't, they may have their own ideas, but it hasn't been discussed." He paused, his gaze roaming over her face as if he was memorizing her every feature. "That may have to change. Without Mulcahy, it may fall to the three of us to keep her safe."

She stilled. "Is she in danger?"

"Not yet, but Mulcahy was worried we might be running out of time. Ever since that scientist shot Gavin up with her little drug cocktail, he's been demonstrating some interesting twists to his magic. Twists that shouldn't exist. We can only keep them hidden from the Council for so long. I'm not sure how successful any of us will be in getting someone to listen before they decide to eliminate a perceived threat."

Temper spiked and she snarled, "Raine and Gavin have done nothing wrong. The Council has no right to pass judgment on them."

Warrick's expression remained grim. "They are the Council, Xander, and going against them is tantamount to declaring civil war. In this day and age of magic and science, you would think they would grasp the enormity of the modern world. Instead, it's extremely difficult to get them to understand that if the Kyn are to have any chance of survival, we're going to have to move out of the shadows and become part of the mortal world."

She folded a hand on his chest and rested her chin on it. "Sounds like an old argument."

His lips quirked. "Very old and the answer is no closer to being found now than when this all started."

"They can't have Raine or Gavin, Warrick," she said, her voice quiet but determined.

His smile was all teeth. "No, they can't, because they're ours."

Xander padded out of Warrick's bedroom clad only in one of his T-shirts and towel drying her hair. Male voices drifted up to her. She leaned over the newly repaired railing to find Warrick in sweats, handing her brother a drink. A bare-chested Ryuu was sprawled across the center section of the leather couch.

Warrick stepped over his legs to sit facing Ethan. "So there was nothing?"

Xander made her way down the stairs and curled up next to Warrick, her head on his shoulder.

"It's like he disappeared into thin air." Ryuu rubbed a hand over his shadowed face.

"No financial transactions, no paper trail," Ethan added. "It's as if Brant Sutler just fell off the face of the earth."

"That's not good," she said.

"No, it's not," Ryuu agreed.

Warrick rubbed her shoulder with a light touch. "We need to make sure there's no more of that drug floating around. Dmitri wasn't working alone, and there's no way Sutler was the only human involved." His chin brushed against her hair as he turned to Ryuu. "You need to reach out to the other packs and see what information you can gather."

Ryuu nodded. "It's going to take time. Without Zeke and Sebastian, I'm going to be a bit tight with people I can trust." His voice was locked down, yet she felt his sorrow. It took her a second to realize she was picking up his connection to Warrick through the pack ties. She bit her lip. This was going to take some getting used to.

"I think you'll have more help than you realize," Xander said, thinking of the Wraiths. Dmitri's death wasn't going to satiate the Wraiths' need for vengeance. She held Ryuu's gaze, hiding nothing.

He gave her a slow nod. "Maybe I will then."

"What now?" Ethan asked. "Dmitri's dead, we have no

leads on the drug or where it came from, Mulcahy's dead, and the humans are starting to ask questions no one wants to answer."

"We prepare," Warrick answered softly.

"For what?"

"For change."

CHAPTER 38
SOMEWHERE IN VIRGINIA...

AN OLDER GENTLEMAN RAISED HIS CRYSTAL GLASS, THE AMBER liquid inside sloshing gently against the sides. "Well done."

The younger man dipped his head in acknowledgement. "Although not our primary target, Ryan Mulcahy's death doesn't hurt our long term plans."

The older man chuckled. "No, it doesn't. If anything, it gives us an unexpected opening."

"How sure are you that this will work?" The question came from the heavyset male standing near the multi-paned windows.

"The public is starting to ask questions. Questions that are not easily hidden by the government's clever spin-doctors. Although the drug didn't work as intended, it has allowed us to begin peeling back the layers hiding the monsters. A few more incidents and we'll be able to use the public outcry to our advantage."

"We must be careful." The deep voice belonged to the fourth member of their group, currently pouring himself a drink. "If any of the Northwest Kyn catch wind of our plan, we can kiss our collective asses goodbye."

"You think those—what did the general call them—Wraiths really exist?" Worry chased across the florid face of the one by the windows.

"We have our own version of spooks," the older one chuckled.

"Better safe than sorry," the other said and took a sip of his drink. "Perhaps it's time to look deeper into the general's claim, maybe consider bringing in Jonah Talbot. If the Kyn really do have a specialized group of killers at their disposal, maybe we can use them to our advantage."

The younger man watched his little group with a dark light in his eyes. It was always so lovely when things went according to his plan. He turned his face away from the others, hiding his smile.

Join the lethal dance between two predators as Natasha locks horns with Darius in a dangerous game of secrets surrounded by whispers of treachery in SHADOW'S CURSE.
Now available at your favorite bookseller!

KYN APPENDIX

GLOSSARY

Amanusas:
One of four Kyn races, delight in chaos, half-demon and half-human or Kyn. Six bloodlines—War, Earth, Secrets, Enticement, Death and Inequity—referred to as 'Blood of'. For example: Natasha is Blood of Secrets.

Amá:
Navajo for "mother".

Ape':
Shoshonee for "father".

awéé':
Navajo for "baby".

ayóo-anííníshní:
Navajo for "I love you".

Baide':
Shoshonee for "daughter".

Between:

The second realm between the mortal and magical worlds, accessible by the Kyn.

Bitten:

Humans transformed to shifters through vicious attack. Magic needs human to be on brink of death to complete conversion. They are lower in the pack's structure as the control of wolf is tenuous at best. Tend not to live long.

Biovita:

A biotech lab in Hillsboro, OR where Brant Sutler, a human geneticist worked creating drug to turn Kyn wolves feral.

Blood ward:

A magical construct based on a castor's blood to defend or protect a place or person.

Bonded:

Rare metaphysical tie between Kyn, generally shifters, that connects two individuals at soul level. A step above mated. Partners generally don't survive the passing of the other.

Born:

Kyn Shifters who are born, some are Pure Bloods—rare few bloodlines.

Bound:

An Amanusa, caught in a casted circle by a summoner who uses all their names, to enslave—body and soul—to do the summoner's bidding. If a name is missed, they become half-Bound.

Chindis:
Vengeful spirits of the dead, raised by witches, however can be done by anyone with the ability, controlled by their summoner. Torment victims and rip them apart psychically. Generally are spirits of those who died violently or before their time. Once vengeance is taken, they'll rest.

Cinar International:
European based corporation.

The Council:
The ruling eleven members of the Kyn, chosen from around the world and headquartered in Turkey.

Division:
Preternatural Crimes Division, a group of talented and/or psychic humans who work for US Government and assist the Kyn on supernatural crimes.

Feral:
Wolves whose animal nature has taken control. Tend to attack humans and those closest to them. Nothing of the thinking man is left behind.

Fey:
One of four Kyn races, Sidhe descendants.

Kyn:
The entire preternatural community, composed of all four houses: Fey, Lycos, Amanusa, and Magi.

Lycos/Shifters:

One of four Kyn races, shape shifters, generally predator animals.

Magi:
One of four Kyn races, made of witches and wizards.

Mated:
Emotional bond created when two shifters commit.

Mavericks:
Lone wolves who have chosen to leave packs and roam on own. Can be Born or Bitten.

Mirroring:
Ability to send part of yourself into another by merging two magics, can add strength, but only as passenger. Empathic magic, deep level merger gives access to individual's mind/heart. Witches can mirror.

Pinnanku tease em puinnuhi:
Shoshonee for "See you again next time."

Sarielian Order:
The ultimate group of Wraiths, made of nine of the most dangerous Kyn of the world.

Shadowed Paths:
The walkways in Between, used when Shadow Walking.

Shadow Walking:
Ability to travel in the realm that exists between the waking world and the magical one.

Side:
A realm accessible to the Amanusa, not easily borne by other Kyn, completely unbearable by humans. A third plane of existence.

Sisna:
Sanskrit demon slur, lewd version of tailed demon or phallus-worshipper.

sitsi':
Navajo term for daughter.

Soul Stealer:
Nomâhtsé' héõo' Adanta - Eater of Souls, a psychic being created by black magic from the remains of a soul, tied to summoner. Gains strength eating the souls of others.

Taliesin Security:
The public security company housing the Northwest Kyn.

Tachair:
Gaelic word for "light", Raine uses it for light spell.

Three-fold Law:
Witches follow concept: What you do, will come back to you three-fold.

Tracker:
Shifters who are outside Pack hierarchy, their duty is to hunt/execute rogue shifters and threats (internal/external) to Pack.

Witches:

Practitioners of natural magic/white magic who follow the Three Fold law.

Wizards:

Practitioners of spells, potions, tend toward dark magic, use science and rituals.

Wraiths:

Twelve member highly skilled collection of North American Kyn who serve as the ultimate police for the Kyn and human monsters. They are not publicly acknowledged, basis of Boogieman stories for Kyn, even human not sure if they exist.

Yázhí:

Navajo equivalent of "little one".

88 Ivories:

Music/dance club in downtown Portland

CAST OF KYN

NORTHWEST KYN

Ryan Mulcahy (d.)
Former Head of Fey House,
Captain of the Wraiths,
Chief Executive Officer (CEO) of Taliesin

Natasha Bertoi
Head of Amanusa House,
Current Chief Executive Officer (CEO) of Taliesin

Warrick Vidis
Head of Lycos House,
Chief Financial Officer (CFO) of Taliesin

Cheveyo
Head of Magi House,
Chief Information Officer (CIO) of Taliesin

Carys Iver
Current Head of Fey House, Chief Legal Council for Taliesin

NORTHWEST WRAITHS

Raine McCord
Gavin Durand
Xander Cade
Jamie Ryder
Axel Kayser
Niall
Gideon
Dorian
Chayton
Fahd
Kevin Sullivan
Killian

SOUTHWEST KYN

Rio Castle
Head of Amanusa House

Tala Whiteriver
Head of Magi House

Tomás Chavez
Head of Lycos House

KYN COUNCIL SO FAR...

Leopold DiMarcco

Zayn Aimeric

Corwin Westbrooke

Malachi

Antonia

SARIELIAN ORDER SO FAR...

Darius Abazi

KYN KRONICLES

Welcome to a world where the supernatural walks alongside humans, their existence kept secret behind the thinnest of veils. Now modern man's scientific curiosity is determined to rip that curtain aside, revealing the nightmares in the shadows.

SHADOW'S EDGE

Raine's spent a lifetime hunting monsters, but can she stop her prey from exposing the supernatural community one bloody corpse at a time?

SHADOW'S SOUL

When a simple assignment turns into a nightmare, can Raine and Gavin unravel old vendettas before they both pay the ultimate price?

SHADOW'S MOON

Compromise isn't in Warrick's vocabulary and Xander won't abandon the hunt. As the line between instinct and intellect blurs, will they survive the fallout?

SHADOW'S CURSE

When the queen of chaos locks horns with death's justice, Natasha and Darius set a dangerous game in motion, leading two predators into a lethal dance of secrets.

SHADOW'S DREAM

Tala can't forget the past. Cheveyo can't change it. As the dreams they shared linger, can they escape the encroaching nightmare before it's too late?

SHADOW'S FALL

A trail of missing Kyn leads a powerful new threat into Raine's backyard. Will she and Gavin be able to hold their own or fall under the weight of secrets haunting the shadows?

About the Author

"This story is an emotional roller coaster, from betrayal, anger, fear, love..." —InD'tale Magazine

Jami Gray is the coffee addicted, music junkie, Queen Nerd of her personal Geek Squad, Alpha Mom of the Fur Minxes, who writes to soothe the voices crammed in her head. Her series combine high-stakes urban fantasy and edgy paranormal romantic suspense into books you don't want to put down. Buckle up and get ready for a wild ride through the fascinating worlds of the Arcane, the Kyn, the PSY-IV Teams, and the Collapse.

Come visit Jami's website at **https://www.jamigray.com** and stay up to date on what kind of trouble she's getting into and when you can expect to join in.